authentic, and well developed. . . . The present day isn't sugarcoated, showing readers that racial equity is still an unresolved problem. Appended author notes offer additional context, making it an excellent link to social studies or history units. A must-purchase."
—*School Library Journal*, **starred review**

★ "Johnson takes his readers on a whirlwind expedition with two exceptionally bright kids as they connect the dots of this mystery and gain insights into their own families' secrets. . . . He creates a narrative that's both a compelling mystery and a powerful commentary on identity, passing, and sacrifice. Fans of *The Westing Game*, which gets several textual shoutouts, and other puzzling mysteries such as Balliett's *Chasing Vermeer* will appreciate the twists and turns of this meaningful tale."
—*The Bulletin of the Center for Children's Books*, **starred review**

"A clever puzzle, a hidden treasure, and a couple of kids you'll wish were your friends . . . Dive in!" —**Sara Pennypacker**, *New York Times* **bestselling author of *Pax***

"Varian Johnson delivers once again with this rewarding mix of relevant history and challenging mystery!" —**Kirby Larson, Newbery Honor– winning author of *Hattie Big Sky***

"With a nod to *The Westing Game*, Varian Johnson has penned a smart mystery that deftly explores the history of racial segregation in the South, modern-day discrimination, friendship, love and bullying. . . . beautifully written, this complex story will captivate an adult audience as well."
—*BookPage*

"A dazzling and emotional read that deals with serious topics such as bullying, racism, and divorce." —*Booklist*

"*The Parker Inheritance* is a clever puzzle wrapped in an urgent and compassionate novel that will capture readers from the first chapter."
—*Shelf Awareness*

The PARKER INHERITANCE

The PARKER INHERITANCE

VARIAN JOHNSON

Scholastic Inc.

Arthur A. Levine Books hardcover edition designed by Nina Goffi, published by Arthur A. Levine Books, an imprint of Scholastic Inc., April 2018

ISBN 978-0-545-95278-1

10 9   20 21 22 23

Printed in the U.S.A.   40
This edition first printing 2019

Book design by Nina Goffi

"I, Too" by Langston Hughes from *The Collected Poems of Langston Hughes* edited by Arnold Rampersad with David Roessel, Associate Editor. Copyright © 1994 by the Estate of Langston Hughes. Used by permission of Alfred A. Knopf, an imprint of Knopf Doubleday Publishing Group, a division of Penguin Random House LLC. All rights reserved.

For Mom, Dad, and Crystal, the best parents
I have ever met.

And for Savannah and Sydney, my beautiful girls.
You'll never be too old to dance with your father.

CHAPTER 1

Abigail Caldwell

October 17, 2007

Abigail Caldwell stared at the letter.

The letter stared back.

The paper was bright. Crisp. Smooth. Like the pages of a new book that had yet to be cracked open. The letter, with its small, black, single-spaced words and sharp edges, spoke of a great injustice. It was written by a man who did not exist. And it promised an incredible fortune to the city of Lambert, South Carolina — *if* its puzzle could be solved.

Abigail refolded the letter, then placed it in her purse. Dusk was beginning to set, and apart from the handful of teens playing basketball, Vickers Park was empty. She sat on a bench outside of the Enoch Washington Memorial Tennis Courts. A small crew had already removed the rusted fence surrounding the courts and was now carrying over jackhammers. A large yellow backhoe loomed in the distance.

"Ms. Caldwell, you sure you want us to start tonight?" the chief of maintenance asked, handing her some earmuffs. "We're gonna have to pay overtime, and the noise alone will—"

"I know," she said. "I'll deal with any fallout tomorrow." She couldn't risk starting the operation during daylight hours. It would draw too much attention.

The chief adjusted his hard hat. "Which court do you want us to start with?" he asked.

"That one," she said, pointing to the one on the left. It sat directly across from her park bench. From what she hoped was the final clue.

"And it would be mighty helpful if I knew what we were looking for," he said.

"I agree, Odell." She rose from the bench. "Maybe a chest? A crate? I don't know. But I'm sure we'll recognize it when we see it."

Once the lights had been erected, the crew began jackhammering, breaking up the green tennis court into chunks. Then came the backhoe, its engine groaning through the night.

Abigail stood nearby, flashlight in hand, watching as the machine scooped out pile after pile of rubble and dirt. With each dump, she reminded herself of all the clues from the letter. The photos.

The money *had* to be here.

The chief paused the backhoe after a few hours, then waved over Abigail. "I'm sorry, Ms. Caldwell, but we're not finding anything. How much deeper do you want us to go?"

She checked her watch. Time was passing too quickly. It would be dawn soon. And with the sunrise would come a flurry of questions and accusations.

"Maybe just a little deeper." She glanced at the bench. "And can you have a few of your guys start jackhammering the base below there too?" He followed her eyes to where she was looking. "But don't tear up the bench. It's important."

He frowned. "But Ms. Caldwell, the work order said we're only supposed to—"

"Don't worry about that," she snapped. "I signed the order, and I'll handle any problems with the paperwork." Then she sighed. "I'm sorry. It's just . . . a lot's riding on this."

As he went to give new instructions to his crew, she peered into the deep, dark hole. Abigail had wagered her reputation, her job, and perhaps her overall career on a hunch. She hadn't even considered that she could be wrong.

A newbie from the *Lambert Trader* showed up around four o'clock that morning, followed by more experienced reporters an hour later. And then, as the sun rose over the park's majestic oak trees, a black sedan pulled up in front of the basketball courts. Abigail was a little surprised the mayor had arrived in person. But then again, he was up for reelection next year. It was probably time for him to make his annual trek to the Vista Heights neighborhood.

Abigail checked the small hole where the bench had been, then walked back to the larger hole. She didn't know it yet, but it didn't matter what, if anything, she discovered that morning. The mayor had already suspended her. She would be forced to resign by the end of the day.

The letter would remain a mystery, its secrets hidden for ten more years, until someone came along who was brave enough—or perhaps foolish enough—to take up the challenge again.

That someone was Abigail's granddaughter.

Her name was Candice Miller.

CHAPTER 2

Of course, twelve-year-old Candice Miller didn't know anything about a secret letter or hidden fortunes. She was just a girl trying to get through a horrible summer.

She sat at the kitchen table, finishing a book she'd read twice before. Then she closed the book, walked to her room, and flopped down on the carpeted floor.

Well, technically it wasn't *her* room. Her *real* room was in her *real* house in Atlanta.

This room, small and cramped, sat at the rear of a house unfamiliar to Candice, a house in Lambert, South Carolina, a city she had no desire to be living in. The house had belonged to her grandmother, Abigail Caldwell. Her grandmother had been dead for two years, but being surrounded by all of her things had brought a dull ache back to Candice's heart.

Candice's parents had been divorced for about six months, and separated even longer. Her mother had been trying to sell their house in Atlanta since the divorce, yet no one had shown any interest in buying their "cozy" bedrooms and "classic" kitchen. Candice's father eventually convinced her mother to let him bring in a contractor buddy to do a remodel.

Instead of staying in the house or finding a nearby apartment, Candice and her mother had moved to Lambert for the summer. Candice's grandmother had only owned her house there for a few years before she moved to Atlanta, but she kept the house as a furnished rental property. It had recently become vacant.

"It's a sign," her mom had said when she'd sprung the news on Candice. "This way, I won't be tempted to pop into the house every day to see how Daniel is destroying my kitchen. And we'll save a little money." Candice remembered how tightly her mother had hugged her. "As much as I hate that city for what it put Mama through, we could both use a change of scenery."

Candice didn't want to move—but not because of her grandmother. It was everything else happening that summer that Candice didn't want to miss. Natalie Thompson's birthday pool party. Trips to the mall with DeeDee and Courtney. Summer baseball games with her dad.

And their house was in a perfect location. Her friends lived in the same neighborhood. The library was down the street. Her father's apartment was only a couple of miles away.

Candice had thought her father would push back against the move. She saw him every other day—sometimes more. Surely he would demand that Candice remain in Atlanta. Maybe she could even live with him for the summer.

But her dad never offered to let her stay at his apartment, and she never asked. And before she knew it, she was saying her good-byes, leaving the only home she'd ever known.

Still lying on the floor, Candice ran her fingers along the thin, battered aluminum bracelet circling her wrist. The bracelet used to belong to her grandmother, but she had given it to Candice almost five years ago. The letters *MS*—for Mississippi, her grandmother's home state—were engraved on the outside of the bracelet. On the inside was the word *Love*. Candice had begun wearing it again two weeks ago, after their move to Lambert. It just felt right.

The back door opened a few moments later, and Candice left her bedroom and returned to the kitchen. Her mom stood at the sink, filling a glass with tap water.

Candice was still getting used to her mom's small afro—it had barely been a month since her mother had cut off all her hair in order to go natural. It looked good, but it was strange after the long, straight hair her mother had had all of Candice's life. Still, the big chop was about number 117 on the list of life-changing things that had happened over the past couple of years.

"Sorry I was gone for so long," her mother said. "I lost track of time talking to Juanita across the street. What have you been up to?"

Candice smirked. "Just rereading my books. *Again*."

"Walked into that one, didn't I?" Her mom sighed. "I promise, I'll take you to the library today."

She had been saying that for the past two days.

"Maybe you should check the attic," her mother continued. "I bet Mama's got a whole bunch of old books up there. Maybe even some puzzle books or board games." She finished her water then placed the glass in the sink. "I need to get up there as well and sort through all of Mama's stuff."

She had been saying that for the past two *years*.

Then her mother nodded toward Candice's wrist. "I'm glad you're wearing Mama's bracelet again. It looks good on you." Her mother paused, and Candice could almost hear the echo of sadness between them. The house even seemed to smell like her grandmother—like fresh lavender. Candice's grandmother had died suddenly after her second heart attack. They hadn't had a chance to say good-bye. "Maybe we could take it to the jewelry store. Buff out some of those scratches."

"Grandma used to say that the scratches are what made it lucky."

Her mother rolled her eyes. "Mama wasn't really blessed in the luck department, especially when it came to Lambert."

"What does that mean?" Candice asked. She had heard her mother make comments like that throughout the years, even when her grandmother was still alive. Grandma would always nod and counter with, "Just because you don't see the path doesn't mean it's not there." If Candice was nearby, she would turn to her and wink — like it was a shared secret between them. Not knowing how to respond, Candice would just smile back.

Her mother took a deep breath, then sat down at the table. "Since we're going to be living here for a while, there's a few things you need to know about your grandmother." She motioned for Candice to sit as well. "Technically, Mama resigned from her job here. But she was really fired. It was a pretty big deal. She could have gone to jail."

Candice's eyes widened. *Her grandmother? A criminal?* "What did she do?"

"She acted a fool," her mom muttered, almost to herself. "Your grandma somehow got it in her head that there was a buried treasure hidden somewhere in the city. She talked to the mayor about it. He told her to drop it. It seemed like one big con job."

"But I guess she didn't let it go."

Mom shook her head. "She spent months doing all this research about God knows what. Then she decided to dig up one of the old tennis courts. Forged city paperwork to pay a crew and rent a backhoe. Dug all night."

Candice leaned forward. She pictured her grandmother with a shovel, digging up a pirate's chest full of gold. "Did she find anything?"

"Nothing but dirt," she replied. "Mama was lucky. The city didn't want a scandal. They agreed not to press charges if she signed a confidentiality agreement and destroyed all her research."

Candice had to sit on her hands to stop from bouncing. Lambert suddenly seemed a lot more interesting. A mystery like this was more exciting than any of the logic and strategy games on her old iPod touch. "What if Grandma was right? What if there really was a hidden fortune?"

"I can already see the gears turning in your head," her mother said. "Let me stop you now. This isn't one of your computer games. There is no buried treasure." She crossed her arms. "That was what, almost ten years ago? If there really was a pile of money hidden around the city, I'm sure someone would have found it by now."

"But—"

"I don't think you understand. Your grandma was the first woman, and the first African American, to serve as city manager for Lambert. This was supposed to be a stepping-stone to other things. Columbia. Greenville. Savannah. Who knows—maybe she could have ended up running a big-time department for the City of Atlanta. But because she refused to let that one thing go, she torpedoed her career. And she made herself the laughingstock of the city. Of the entire state. It was all over the Internet—Crazy Lady Caldwell. Alzheimer Abigail. The Mole Lady. And of course, she never got another shot at being a city manager."

The excitement that had been bubbling up inside Candice began to simmer down. "I never knew that."

"No one likes to talk about their failures. Especially your grandmother." She tapped the table. "I know you love a good mystery, but the last thing I need is you drumming up all this old stuff about a buried treasure. The past is the past. Mama's legacy is tarnished enough. I don't want you making it worse."

"Just because Grandma made a mistake doesn't mean she's a failure," Candice said.

"Trust me, you don't know all the facts."

Candice stared at her knees. Slivers of brown skin showed through the shredded fabric. Her father had been begging her to toss the jeans for almost a year, but they were more comfortable than anything else Candice owned.

"A mistake isn't a failure," Candice said, pulling at a loose thread. "It's just an opportunity to try again." That was another of her grandmother's sayings. Candice could recite by memory the story about how her grandmother had put herself through college while raising two kids. She had to repeat a few classes, but she eventually graduated with a master's degree.

"Good lord, what it is with you and your grandmother? She thought you walked on water, and would correct anyone who said anything different. Now here you go, doing the same for a woman who's not even here anymore."

Candice tugged on another thread. It was true—her grandmother has always been protective of Candice, but not overprotective like her dad. More like, she took up for Candice when people—usually adults—said she couldn't do something. When adults said she wasn't old enough. Or when they said she shouldn't do something because she was a girl. And even when Candice made a mistake, her grandmother would tell her it was just a learning experience, and to keep trying.

After a few moments, her mother reached across the table and took Candice's hand. "Your grandmother was many things. Strong. Dynamic. And stubborn too." She sighed. "But she also made a big mistake. Maybe that doesn't make her a failure in our eyes, but the world doesn't always see people in the way we want."

CHAPTER 3

A few minutes later, Candice returned to her room to change clothes. Her mother had suggested they grab lunch at a "Lambert landmark" and then she'd finally take Candice to the library. ("But not in those holey jeans," her mother had said.) As happy as Candice was about finding new books and spending some time with her mom, she was also worried about her. Specifically, about her mom's looming writing deadlines.

Her mother was a romance novelist. Jane Harris. Roberta Caldwell. Amanda Sandstone. She had written books under those names and plenty of others. She always said she wanted to take a break from romance assignments to write her "Anne C. Miller" novel, but with the house sale dragging on she'd signed up for three more projects—all with deadlines that would have been hard to meet even if she'd been writing nonstop. But she wasn't writing, seemingly at all. Instead she watched a lot of reality television, visited Ms. Jones across the street, and took long walks around the neighborhood.

As Candice searched her dresser for a more suitable pair of jeans, she heard her mother in the kitchen, speaking on the phone in hushed tones. It was another reminder of how much smaller Grandma's house was compared to their place in Atlanta. Candice had always wondered if her parents had moved into their five-bedroom house thinking they'd have a lot of kids, and if they were disappointed when it ended up being only her.

"Well, well . . . look who's outside," her mother said breezily as they stepped out of the house ten minutes later. "We should say hello."

Across the street, Ms. Jones and her son sat on the porch, reading. Candice's mother had been encouraging her to walk over and introduce herself to the boy, but Candice hadn't seen the point. She would be back in Atlanta in two months. Why make friends when she was just going to leave? Plus, he was only eleven years old. She didn't like hanging out with boys her own age, much less boys who were a year younger.

"Hey Juanita, Brandon," her mother said. "We're off to grab a bite of lunch at PJ's and pop into the library. Care to join us?"

"I just ate," Ms. Jones said, before turning to her son. "But Brandon hasn't had lunch. What do you say? Want to tag along with Candice and Ms. Miller?"

"No, thank you," he replied. He didn't look up from his magazine.

"Maybe you didn't hear her," Ms. Jones said. "She's going to the library too."

Brandon glanced up. "How long will you be there?"

"Brandon, don't be rude," his mother snapped.

"No, he's fine," Candice's mother said. "We'll be there for a while, I imagine. I've been promising to take Candice since we moved here. Today seems like as good a day as any."

Brandon and his mother stared at each other. It was clear that their eyes were having a private, silent conversation. He closed his magazine. "Let me grab my wallet," he said, sounding defeated.

Ms. Jones smiled and motioned for him to stay. "How about I treat?" She rose from her chair. "Let me grab my purse. I'll be back in a second."

She entered the house. No one spoke for a few seconds.

"I heard you were an author," Brandon finally said to Candice's mother, breaking the silence. He had a short body and skinny legs; his high-tops kept brushing against the porch as he rocked in his chair. "Are you writing anything now?" His voice was softer than it had been a moment before.

Her mom fiddled with the clasp on her watch. "Just a few projects. Nothing serious."

"Are they like, scary?" Brandon asked. "Or is it a romance like your other—"

"They're secret," Candice said, crossing her arms. Her mother didn't like talking about her books with people—at least, not when she was in the middle of writing them. It was one of her many superstitions when it came to her work.

"Brandon, your mom told me you're a pretty hard-core reader," her mother said. "What type of books do you like?"

"A little bit of everything," Brandon said. "I guess I like boy books."

What does that even mean? Candice wanted to ask. *Books about guns and war? Books that only contain boys?*

"Who are your favorite authors?" her mother continued.

Brandon stopped rocking. "I don't know. Maybe . . . Stephen King? James Patterson?" He glanced at Candice and hesitated. Then he looked at his lap. "You know . . . authors like that."

Candice realized she was giving him a "look."

"I like Stephen King and James Patterson as well," her mother said. "Candice reads a little bit of everything too," she said. "Have you read anything new this summer, Candice?"

Candice shook her head. Her mother knew she hadn't read anything new—that was why they were going to the library.

"Look at us, a big group of word nerds," her mother said. Her grin was much too wide.

Candice frowned at her mother. Why was she trying to force a conversation when it was clear neither she nor Brandon wanted to talk?

After thinking about it for a bit, Candice realized what was going on. This had all been a setup to get her and Brandon to spend more time together. Candice was sure his mom was in on it too. Was Brandon?

It didn't matter. She already had DeeDee and Courtney back in Atlanta. She didn't need any other friends—especially not eleven-year-old book snobs.

CHAPTER 4

Candice's father used to always complain about their house in Atlanta—the uneven garage, the creaky stairs, and the backyard that flooded every time there was a downpour. As they neared PJ's, Candice realized their house could have been much, much worse. Some of the buildings in this neighborhood—her mother had called it Vista Heights—looked like they'd topple over with one good gust of wind. Every other window had bars across its frame.

She checked to make sure her and her mother's doors were locked. She didn't know where she and her mom would live when they moved back to Atlanta, but it wouldn't be in their old neighborhood. All the houses there were too big for two people, and way too expensive.

There was no way their new neighborhood could be as rough as this, could it?

Brandon remained quiet during the trip. When they pulled into the parking lot, Candice unfastened her seat belt and snuck a peek behind her. Brandon's door was unlocked.

They entered PJ's and walked to the counter. Old black-and-white pictures hung on the walls, and a weathered wooden shoeshine stand sat in a corner, collecting dust. The few people inside the restaurant stared at them. It was like the regulars could tell they didn't belong.

"The daily special for me," Candice's mother said after staring at the menu for a few seconds. "Candice?"

"Chicken fingers and fries." She had ruled out the special as soon as she'd read the menu. She hated fish with bones, and there was no way she was eating jalapeño and green onion hushpuppies.

Brandon ordered a hamburger and began to slide some money across the counter. Candice's mother stopped him. "Boy, quit and put that up," she said as she handed over a credit card.

"My mom said—"

"It's fine," her mother said. "We're neighbors."

Despite her mother trying her best to facilitate a real conversation, they ate their food (surprisingly good, Candice noted) as quickly as they could, then headed to the library. While Candice and her mother filled out forms for their library cards, Brandon bolted up the stairs to the children's section, not bothering to wait for them. It ticked Candice off, but only for a second, because with him out of the way, she could pick out the books she wanted without him judging her. The boys at her old school were silly that way—always making fun of whatever she and her friends read.

Once upstairs, Candice walked up and down the aisles, pausing every few steps to pick up a book and inspect its cover. After making her way through the children's section, she moved to the teen books. She spotted Brandon sitting against a shelf with his knees pressed up to his chest. His face was literally buried in his book.

She took a step closer to see what he was reading. Maybe he heard her, because he snapped the book shut and stuffed it behind his back.

"Were you looking for me? Is it time to go?"

Candice shook her head. "We'll probably be here for a while. Mom hasn't been to the library since we got to Lambert. It's like she stepped back into Narnia."

"You read *The Lion, the Witch and the Wardrobe*?"

Candice felt herself smirking. "I read all seven books in the series." She almost added *even though I'm a girl*, but decided against it.

"I've never finished them. They're always checked out. I want to read them in order."

She wondered if he was talking about publication order or chronological order, but asking seemed a bit *too* hoity-toity. "What you should really read is The Dark Is Rising sequence. Or *The Hero and the Crown* or *The Blue Sword*." She shrugged. "I mean, maybe *you* won't like those last two because the main characters are girls, but—"

"I love those books!" He sat up taller. "And Aerin is one of my favorite characters."

Neither one spoke for a few seconds. He reached behind him and placed his fingers on the spine of his book, but he didn't pull it out.

"What are you reading?" Candice asked. "Is it another fantasy?"

"It's . . . nothing." His hand slid away from the book.

Obviously it wasn't *nothing*. Candice wondered if he was hiding the book because he didn't want *her* making fun of *him*. She hadn't realized that was a possibility until right then.

"Do you come here a lot?" Candice asked. She used to always talk about books with her mom, but that seemed to be happening less and less with everything else going on in their lives.

"Tori used to bring me during the school year, but the timing hasn't worked out so well this summer."

It took her a moment to remember that Tori was his older sister. Her mom had mentioned her a while back. "Can you ride your bike here?" She readjusted her shoulder bag. "It's not that far from your house."

"Mom doesn't want me riding by myself."

Candice thought about this. Once she was sure of her answer, she said, "I'm sure Mom and I will be spending a lot of time here. I bet we could give you a ride the next time we come."

He blinked at her. "At home, when I said that I liked Stephen King and James Patterson, you looked like you wanted to reach out and knock me upside the head."

Now *she* was the one who sounded like a snob. "It's just . . . I don't think there's such a thing as boy books or girl books. I think there are *people* books. At least, that's what Mom always said when Dad complained about what I was reading. I'm surprised she didn't say anything at your house."

"She was probably being polite," he said. "Anyway, sorry about the way I was acting on our porch. I was kind of mad that our moms were forcing us to meet. I didn't know what they were planning until right before you walked over."

Candice smiled. At least she wasn't the only one being manipulated.

"So how many books do you have in your bag?" he continued. "You're only allowed to check out ten at a time."

"I don't know. I stopped counting at fifteen." She pulled some books out of her bag. "I'd better return these."

"Wait. Maybe we could share. You check out ten and I'll check out ten?" He pulled the book from behind his back. "Have you read *Are You There God? It's Me, Margaret?*"

After an hour, Candice headed to the computer lab downstairs. Her desktop computer had crashed right before they moved, but Candice's mom wanted to wait until the fall before buying her a new one. Which was easy for her mom, since she had her own laptop. Candice was the one forced to check her email on her mom's phone all summer.

A man sat at a desk in front of the room. "Sign up here," he said, nodding toward a notebook. "Since we're so busy, we're limiting Internet usage to twenty minutes per person."

Once she was called up, she quickly made her way to her computer. After logging in, she checked her email. No new messages.

She was about to go to her favorite puzzle website next, but she paused. She rubbed her grandmother's bracelet, then typed, *"Abigail Caldwell"* + *"Lambert"* + *"fired."*

The screen filled with links. The first articles were all about how her grandmother had been fired after digging up a tennis court at Vickers Park. The residents were really mad—especially since it seemed like the city didn't have the funds to quickly repair the court. Further down the page was a link to an editorial written in the *Lambert Trader* by a black city council member, who talked about how much of a disappointment her grandmother was to the African American community. "Instead of positively showing what a black woman could do as city manager," the politician wrote, "Abigail Caldwell's inept and incompetent actions have set back racial progress at least thirty years."

Candice quickly closed the webpage without finishing the article. So maybe her grandmother *had* made a mistake. A *huge* mistake. But that still didn't give that man the right to talk about her like that. She was sure her grandmother had done good things as city manager too.

Candice's time ran out before she could summon the courage to read any more articles. The man at the desk told her she could sign up again and get back in the waiting line, but she decided against it.

Candice found her mother, hoping she was ready to go. But her mom was furiously scribbling in a yellow notepad, with piles of books surrounding her at the table. "Thirty more minutes," her mom said, not looking up. "Can't break the flow."

She didn't know what her mother had found in the stacks, but it looked like something had kick-started her writing. Candice started back up the stairs, but stopped halfway when she saw Brandon heading toward her. "Hey, I was coming down to find you," he said. "Already finished?"

"Yeah, I'm done with the Internet for today," she said. Then she rubbed her arms. "It's kind of cold in here. I'm going to sit outside."

"Cool. I'll come with you," he said. "I mean, if it's okay . . ."

She shrugged. "Fine by me."

They checked out their books and walked outside. An ice cream truck played "Pop Goes the Weasel" in the distance. They sat down on a bench.

Candice slowly popped her knuckles. She could still see that stupid editorial in her head.

"Did you know my grandmother?" she finally blurted out.

Brandon looked up from his book. "I only moved to Lambert three years ago, but Granddad knew her pretty well. He's lived here for, like, twenty years. He moved here after he retired."

Candice wondered what Brandon's grandfather thought of her grandma. Did he see her as a disgrace? A failure?

"Do you know where Vickers Park is?" she asked. "Are there, um, tennis courts there?"

Brandon stuck a finger in his book to save his place. "Is this about your grandmother getting fired from her job with the city?"

Candice's shoulders sank. "How do you know about that? I thought you just moved here."

19

"As my granddad says, word travels fast and lingers long in the South. He said she got a raw deal." He shifted on the bench. "Vickers Park is in Vista Heights. It's not too far from PJ's."

Candice riffled through her bag, trying to decide what to read, then glanced at Brandon. He had returned to his book, his mouth moving a little as he read line by line. She couldn't tell what book he had opened, but it wasn't the Judy Blume one. At his suggestion, she had checked out all the books with girl main characters, and he had checked out the books featuring boys. She had kept her mouth shut—this time.

"Hey, I'm sorry—can I ask you another question?" she asked. He looked up again. "Do you know *why* she was fired?"

He wrinkled his nose. "The rumor is that she thought something was hidden underneath the court."

So much for confidentiality. She decided to press further. "And, um, do you know *what* she was looking for?"

"No, but maybe Mom or Granddad knows. When I get home, I can ask—"

"That's okay," Candice quickly said. Her mom was right. She didn't want to talk to anyone else about her grandmother's hunt for buried treasure. Especially other adults. She didn't want to make her grandma's reputation worse.

"Really," he said, "it's no—"

"Just forget it." It all sounded too silly, especially now that she was talking about it with someone other than her mother. She could see why her grandma lost her job. "I feel totally stupid even bringing it up."

"Sure thing," he said.

Then, almost five minutes later, while still looking at his book, he said, "For what it's worth, I don't think you're stupid. I mean, stupid people don't read all five books in the Dark Is Rising sequence, right?"

He paused, then added, "I bet stupid people don't even call it a *sequence*."

Candice waited for him to continue, but he just flipped the page and went back to reading.

She smiled. Brandon *was* a book snob, but maybe that wasn't such a bad thing after all.

CHAPTER 5

Candice stretched out on the couch with her eyes glued to her dad's old iPod touch and her feet tucked underneath a frayed throw pillow. A couple of unread library books sat on the coffee table beside her. She considered herself a die-hard book nerd, but she realized even *she* needed a break after doing nothing but reading for the past four days. So instead, Candice jammed her earbuds in her ears, cranked up one of her dad's playlists, and opened up her *Mental Twister* app. It was pretty crappy as far as logic and puzzle games were concerned, and nowhere near as good as the games on her old desktop, but it was better than not playing anything at all.

She had just started a new round when she felt her earbuds being yanked away.

"Way. Too. Loud." Her mother loomed over her. "I've called you three times."

Candice jolted up, kicking the throw pillow to the floor. She could still hear Stevie Wonder's "My Cherie Amour" coming through the buds in her mother's hand. "Sorry, I—"

The doorbell rang. Her mom dropped the earbuds and crossed the room to open the door. "Hey, Brandon," she said, her voice still loud. "Come on in." She turned back around. "New rule: The next time you play your iPod that loud, I'm taking it." She frowned at Candice one last time, then marched out.

Candice could feel the heat spreading on her neck. Her father would have never yelled at her like that in front of other kids.

"Are you busy?" Brandon was considerate enough to look at the floor instead of her. "I can come back—"

"No. It's fine." She crossed her arms and pinched her sides. It helped her to forget about her mom's hard words. Her mom hated being interrupted when she was on a roll with her writing, and she'd been pulling eighteen-hour days since they'd come back from the library. She only stopped for bathroom breaks and to scarf down canned vegetable soup and peanut-butter sandwiches. Candice was regretting not ever learning how to cook on her own.

"I was thinking we could trade books," Brandon said.

"You already finished all ten of yours?"

"I'm a quick reader." He looked at the iPod sitting on the couch. "How can you read and listen to music at the same time?"

"I wasn't reading. I was playing a game." She turned off the iPod. "I use the music as background noise."

"It's super quiet in here."

Exactly, Candice thought. "Give me a second. I'll grab the books from my room."

By the time she returned, Brandon had stacked his *boy* books on the coffee table. She wondered if he'd actually finished all ten of them, or if he had only pretended to read them.

Brandon began stuffing her books in his bag. "I've already read some of these, but I don't mind reading them again," he said. "Did you have a chance to finish *Are You There God? It's Me, Margaret*? I've read it, like, ten times, but I still love it."

"Yeah, I know," Candice said. "It's a really good book."

"Have you read any other books by Judy Blume?"

Candice nodded, which Brandon took as permission to talk about seemingly every other book the author had written. Candice stood there as he went on and on. It was obvious he wanted to talk, but she wasn't in the mood right then.

"Um, okay," he finally said. "I guess I'll go now?"

He paused, like he was waiting for her to respond. Candice just replied, "See you later."

He nodded, then smiled. "Remember, don't play that music too loud."

Candice didn't know if he was teasing her or being serious. Either way, she didn't like it. "See you," she said. She began to rearrange the stack of books on the coffee table.

Brandon must have gotten the hint, because he spun around and went out the door. She switched the iPod back on and turned down the volume. The Temptations came on next. That was another bad thing about not having a computer or Wi-Fi—not only was she cut off from her video games and email, she also didn't have any way to listen to new music. She was stuck with whatever was on her dad's iPod, which shuffled between slightly dated and extremely ancient.

She started a new round of her game. Then the doorbell chimed again.

"Candice, will you—"

"I've got it, Mom," she yelled. She removed the earbuds and crossed the room, the iPod still in her hand. It was probably Brandon again. She pulled the door open. "What do y—what happened to you?"

Brandon's shirt was covered with leaves and grass, and two red scratches lined his face. He quickly nodded behind him. Three boys sat on bikes at the edge of the yard, right beside the holly bush. One boy pointed at them, and all three laughed.

"Can I come in?" Brandon whispered. "Please?"

Candice opened the door a little wider to let him in. The boy closest to them said something loud and nasty. She pretended not to hear it.

"I knew I should have waited before coming over." Brandon leaned against the wall, looking smaller than he had seemed moments before. "I saw them riding their bikes, but I thought they were going to the Y. They must have just been circling the block."

"Who are they?"

"Kids from school. They started picking on me a month ago. Then school ended."

Candice understood exactly what he meant. Being bullied on the final day of school was like being the last one holding the ball in hot potato, except the ball was really a big *X* on your back and the game wouldn't start again until all the kids came back in August.

She looked out the window. The boys had pedaled down the street. "They're leaving."

He peered out as well. "Okay. Hopefully they're not just circling the block again." He placed his hand on the doorknob. "How bad do I look?"

"You're bleeding a little," Candice said, studying his face. "Want a Band-Aid?"

"I'll be okay." He shrugged. "A few scratches for a bag full of books. Sounds like a fair trade."

She laughed but quickly stopped. She still couldn't tell if Brandon was joking or not. He was hard to read, like all those dry British comedians her father liked. Then Brandon smiled, so she figured it was okay to smile too. "You risked life and death for books that you've already read? You must be really bored."

"It was either that or spend another night watching the Braves with Granddad, and I hate baseball."

25

The mention of the Atlanta Braves tugged something inside Candice. She and her father usually went to a few games during the summer. It could be crazy hot, and the hot dogs were often hit or miss, but it was something they always did—just him and her. She'd given up hope of it happening this year.

"What's wrong?" he asked.

How had she looked right then? "Nothing. It's—" She shook her head. "Hey, you want to check the attic? Mom thinks my grandma might have some old books up there. I'm sure we could find *something* you haven't read yet."

He nodded as he slipped off his backpack. "That would be great."

CHAPTER 6

Candice poked her head into her mother's office to tell her what they were up to.

"Be careful up there," her mother said. Any trace of anger toward Candice from before had disappeared. "This house has been boarded up for months. There's no telling what you could find."

The entrance to the attic was in the garage. Candice was already sweating by the time she pulled down the ceiling door.

Brandon flipped on the light, and they headed up the rickety stairs. The wooden slats groaned beneath them.

The attic was even hotter than the garage. There looked to be nothing but junk up there—old Christmas decorations, a sewing machine, and spools of dated cloth.

"Yuck," Brandon said, wiping at his face. "I just got some spiderweb in my mouth."

Laughing, Candice walked to the far corner of the room. Then she smiled. "Over here," she said to Brandon. There, against the wall, was a box labeled FOR CANDICE.

She had slid the box top off by the time Brandon reached her. At first, all they found inside were textbooks, dictionaries, and old encyclopedias.

27

"Not quite the new reading I was hoping for," Brandon said.

They continued pulling book after book out of the box, but nothing seemed remotely interesting to Candice. Brandon had stopped to page through a book on Greek mythology. "This isn't that bad," he said. "Can I borrow it?"

"Fine by me," Candice said as she removed the last textbook.

And that's when she saw the puzzle book.

Candice recognized it immediately. It was a thick paperback, full of logic games and brain teasers that she'd solved years ago. She brought the book to her nose—maybe it was her imagination, but she thought she smelled traces of lavender. She cracked the book open, and an envelope slipped out and floated to the ground.

Candice picked up the letter, thinking it was an old piece of mail that had been used as a bookmark long ago. She flipped it over, looking for an address. Instead, she found a small note.

Find the path. Solve the puzzle.

It was her grandmother's handwriting—swirling loops in dark blue ink. The words reminded Candice of what her grandmother used to always say: *Just because you don't see the path doesn't mean it's not there.*

Candice wiped her hands. They were sweaty. And shaking. The note felt like a message from beyond the grave.

She stole a peek at Brandon. He was still looking at the mythology book. She quickly returned the letter to the puzzle book. "We should head downstairs," she said. "We're going to melt if we stay up here much longer."

He nodded. "Sure thing. But what about these other books?"

"Don't worry about them," she said, already standing. "I'll come back later and box them up."

28

He shrugged, but followed her downstairs.

Once they reached the living room, Brandon peeked out the window. "Shoot. They're back." He smiled timidly at her. "Do you mind if I hang out here for a few minutes? I promise I won't bother you."

"Sure. Um, no problem," she said, walking toward the kitchen, the puzzle book tight in her hands. "I'll, um, I'll be back in a second."

She sat down at the table and cracked open the book. Then she read the note on the envelope again. Yep, she was sure of it. It was her grandmother's handwriting.

Since the envelope wasn't sealed, Candice decided there was no harm in seeing what was inside. It was only after she unfolded the sheet of paper that she hesitated. The letter was addressed *to* her grandmother; it seemed intrusive to read it. She almost returned it to the envelope.

Almost.

But she was a reader, she reminded herself. Readers read.

And so, Candice read the letter.

```
August 10, 2007
Dear Ms. Caldwell,


I write to you on behalf of the Washington family.
I'm sure you've never met them. How could you? The Allen
boys ran them out of Lambert long before you arrived
in the city. And when the Washingtons appealed for jus-
tice, city officials denied them at every turn. Enoch,
Leanne, and Siobhan Washington became the newest vic-
tims of the city's long-standing discrimination against
black people.
I loved Siobhan, and that is why I spent thirty
years destroying the Allens, step by step. My first
strike was physical, and then I wrecked them
```

financially. I was the majority owner of the corpora-
tion that bought out Allen Textiles. I purchased
Solara Industries simply so I could move their plant
out of Lambert, ruining the Allens' land lease. My
goal was to wreak havoc not only on the Allens, but
the entire city. It seemed fitting.

But Siobhan Washington still cared for Lambert. She
asked me to show compassion. Unlike her father, unlike
me, she believed in the balance of justice and forgiveness. And even now, seven years after her death, I
cannot deny her.

Thus I have created an opportunity for Lambert to
earn back everything I took from the city—a fortune
totaling $40 million at my last reckoning. I've created
a puzzle mystery that will take you deep into the
city's past. The person who finds this "inheritance"
will receive a tenth of the money; the remainder will
be allocated to the city. In return, the winner must
share what he or she learns through the puzzle with the
world.

Your first clue:

1. Siobhan's father loved tennis, but he grew up
idolizing a team in another sport.

I wish you'd had a chance to meet Siobhan and her
parents. Siobhan was amazing, but her mother was, too.
Leanne Washington's days as a volunteer at her church
did more for Lambert's children than most people will
ever know.

Like her mother, Siobhan believed in giving people
second chances (or in my case, three). She was truly
greater than the sum of her parts. Beautiful. Smart.
Educated. Compassionate. She loved laughter and lit-
erature and math. And she was beauty personified on the
tennis courts. Easily talented enough to thrive on the

collegiate and national levels. But because she loved me more, she chose to give it up.

She was everything a poor, simple boy like me could hope for. She loved all. Black. White. Rich. Poor. She loved Lambert, despite what it did to her and her father. She loved me, even after I became a ghost of my former self.

Here lies your challenge. Siobhan is the key; the one who will lead you to my fortune. She is the only reason you are getting this opportunity. Do not squander it.

I have sent similar versions of this letter to the mayor, the school district superintendent, the chair of the school board, and the editor of the <u>Lambert Trader</u>. Your predecessors failed to protect the Washington family, at great cost. This is your chance to make right what once went so utterly wrong. This is your chance to create a better world for your grandchild. But do not delay. These clues, like Siobhan, will not be of this world forever.

Hoping to find another page, Candice looked in the envelope, but it was empty. That was all there was to the letter. Who had written it? Why had he left it unsigned?

And what was it still doing in her grandmother's attic?

Candice placed the letter on the table, then wiped her still clammy, sweaty hands on her jeans. She had never heard of Enoch or Leanne Washington. Nor had she heard of Siobhan, whose name she pronounced in her head as SEE-OH-BON. All she knew was that Enoch Washington and his family were black. And the Allens were rich and powerful and white.

When she had told her friends she was moving to Lambert for the summer—a city in the Deep South barely a fifth the size of Atlanta—DeeDee had genuinely worried that Candice and her mom would be attacked by men in white robes on horseback. Candice's father, who was supposed to be chauffeuring the girls to the mall and not listening in on them, quickly jumped into the conversation, telling them they didn't need to worry about the Ku Klux Klan, especially in a progressive city like Lambert. Candice didn't exactly believe her father, but she also didn't know enough about the city to disagree with him. Even if Lambert was "progressive" now, though, could her father say the same about the city when the Washingtons lived there, whoever they were?

She ran her thumb over her grandmother's handwritten words.

Find the path. Solve the puzzle.

What if her grandmother hadn't made a mistake? What if there *was* a treasure?

What if her grandmother had put the letter there, on purpose?

For her?

CHAPTER 7

For the next thirty minutes, Candice Miller stared at the letter.

The letter stared back.

The paper was stiff. Stale. Brittle. Like peanut butter cookies that had been left out for too long. The letter, with its small, black, single-spaced words and yellow edges, spoke of a mystery.

She knew she couldn't tell her mother about it. Not yet, not if it had anything to do with her grandmother getting fired. But then again, how could she *not* talk to her mom about it? Candice thought about all the puzzle books and logic games her grandmother used to buy for her, including the one she had just found in the attic. Had Grandma been preparing her all this time?

The letter also spoke of an opportunity. An inheritance. A fortune. Enough for them to keep their house. Enough to stop them from moving.

She looked up when she heard footsteps approaching. Brandon cautiously crept into the kitchen, his huge backpack on his shoulders.

"Hey, Candice? I, um, I didn't know what happened to you. I wanted to let you know that I was about to leave." He held up the mythology book. "I'll bring this back in a few days."

"Oh, yeah, sure . . ." She looked down at the letter, then glanced back at Brandon. "Okay, this is going to sound a little strange, but have you ever heard of Enoch, Leanne, or Siobhan Washington? Or maybe the Allen family?"

Brandon tilted his head at her pronunciation. "See-oh-bon? Can you spell that?"

She looked down at the letter. "S-I-O-B-H-A-N."

"Oh," he said after a second. "I think it's pronounced Shi-vaun."

Candice scowled at herself. Brandon was right. A character in one of her mom's books had the same name.

"The only reason I know is because a girl named Siobhan used to babysit us," he continued. "But no, I haven't heard of her. Who were the other people again?"

She repeated the names. "The Washingtons lived here a long time ago," she said, tracing the edge of the paper. "And the Allens used to be really rich."

Brandon sat down beside her at the table, his backpack still on his shoulders. "Did you see that empty lot across from the library? The one filled with masonry bricks?"

She shook her head. "I don't remember it."

"Well, that was supposed to be the new library," Brandon said. "They were going to name it after Russell Allen. I think he was a big-time businessman around here. Then, according to one of the librarians, some rich guy paid the county *not* to open the Allen Library. He gave them a bunch of money to rehab and expand the existing building instead."

Candice glanced at the letter again. Whoever had written it had wanted to destroy the Allens. Could he have been behind the donations to the library?

"Do you know the name of the guy who gave the money for the renovations?" she asked.

"No, but maybe we could ask one of the librarians. Or maybe my granddad knows."

Candice didn't reply for a few minutes. She was thinking through the letter, trying to make the connections among the library, the Allens, the Washingtons, and her grandmother. It was all too murky.

"You seem a little busy," Brandon said, glancing at the letter. "Do you want me to come back—"

"Here," she said, thrusting the paper at him. "Can you read this?"

He frowned, but took the letter. Candice tried not to cringe as he read to himself, his lips moving silently as he made his way down the page.

She was a little surprised that she actually handed the letter to Brandon. He was nice, but she'd only known him for a few days. He was just a boy from across the street. But there was something about the way he sat there, with the welts beading up on his face, wearing a backpack way too big for his frame. A backpack full of books that, for some reason, he couldn't check out on his own because they were too *girly*. She didn't know if she could trust him, but she wanted to. Plus, she really wanted to talk with someone about the letter.

"In-ter-est-ing," he said after finishing the letter. "And what does that say?" He pointed to the envelope and her grandmother's note.

"Just scribbles," Candice quickly said, sliding it away from her. She wasn't ready to share everything yet.

"Any idea who wrote the letter?"

"No. I assume that whoever he is, he likes being mysterious. I bet he's the same guy who made the donation to the library."

"Well, there's a lot of stuff in the letter that's kind of superfluous," he said. "That means—"

"I know what it means, dictionary boy." She jutted her thumb toward herself. "Daughter of a professional writer, remember?"

He laughed. "Yeah, of course. Anyway, he wrote about a lot of things that don't even have to do with the Washingtons." Brandon scanned the letter again. "Do you know when they were forced to leave the city?"

Candice shook her head. "My guess is that it must have been in the fifties or sixties."

"You know he mentioned you in here as well," Brandon said.

"Huh?"

"Last paragraph," he said. "Where he's talking about making 'a better world for your grandchild.' He didn't say *grandchildren*. He was speaking directly to your grandmother about you." Brandon shrugged. "Granddad told me you were Ms. Caldwell's only grandchild."

"I didn't even see that. I totally read it as *grandchildren*," she said.

He handed the letter back to Candice. "I think we should talk to my granddad about it."

She was already shaking her head. "I don't know. . . ."

"We've got cookies. Mom baked them yesterday."

Candice's stomach chose that moment to grumble. Cookies sounded so much better than sandwiches.

She took a deep breath. "So . . . you actually believe this is real? My mom thinks it's a hoax."

"Well, it *could* be . . . but what if it's not? I mean, if there really is a fortune out there waiting to be found—"

"Don't you think someone would have found it by now?" Candice didn't like how much she sounded like her mom.

"Do *you* think it's real?" he asked.

Candice thought for a moment, then nodded. "Yeah, I do." It was so much easier to think it was real when two people believed it.

She looked at the note on the envelope, rubbing her grandmother's bracelet.

Make that three people.

CHAPTER 8

Candice had just bitten into her second oatmeal chocolate chip cookie when Brandon's sister entered the kitchen. She was too busy typing on her phone to notice them. Tori wore all black, except for a pair of purple boots and a small silver pendant around her neck. Her hair was natural like Candice's mother's, but longer, with twists reaching down to her shoulders.

She looked amazing.

"I'm heading to work," she said, her thumbs flying across the screen. "One of the girls is sick, so I have to go in early."

"Tori works at a clothing store at one of the strip malls," Brandon said to Candice. He was munching on a snickerdoodle. "I can't remember the name. They're all the same."

Tori looked up. "Oh. Hello there."

Candice waved meekly. "Hi," she mumbled. A piece of cookie fell out of her mouth. She could have died.

"We have company," Brandon said.

"Yeah, thanks for the heads-up on that," Tori said, pocketing her phone. "You could have told me—" She stopped, marched across the kitchen, took Brandon's chin, and tilted his face up. The scratches weren't bleeding, but they were still red. "What happened?"

He shook free of her grip. "I fell in a bush."

"You're such a horrible liar." Tori turned to Candice. "Was it that little brat, Milo?"

"You don't have to answer that," Brandon said.

"What does this look like, a courtroom?" Tori asked.

Candice set down her cookie. "I don't know their names."

"Milo's the ringleader. About as big as my pinkie, but really mean. Just like his older sister." Tori walked to the cabinet and pulled out a bottle of hydrogen peroxide. "You should have put something on those welts as soon as you got home." She doused a napkin, then began patting Brandon's face. "Mom and Granddad are going to have a fit."

"Not if you don't tell them."

"I don't have to tell them. They'll know once they see your face." Tori brushed a piece of grass out of his hair. "Let me talk to his sister. She's home from college this summer. I can probably convince her to get Milo to lay off."

"Me getting my big sister to stop a bully. That'll really go over well with the guys at school."

Tori kissed her brother on the cheek. "Will you look after him?" she asked Candice. "My brother's the brainiest kid I've ever met, but that clearly doesn't translate to street smarts."

"Sure," Candice said. Then she clamped her mouth shut. What was she agreeing to? She had enough problems—she didn't want to add getting beat up to her list.

"Thanks." Tori reached out her hand. "By the way, who are you?"

"Candice Miller." She shook Tori's hand. "From across the street."

Tori sized her up. "Let me know if you ever want to go shopping. I get a great discount. Though those shredded jeans are really cool. Kind of retro."

Candice wanted to reach down and cover her knees. She wasn't used to getting compliments about her clothes. "They're comfortable."

Brandon tapped the table. "Weren't you leaving?"

Tori rolled her eyes. *Spoilsport*, she mouthed. She tugged on her brother's ear before swiping a cookie from his pile.

"Hey, wait a second," he said as she reached the door. "Do you know when Granddad will be home?"

"He's on his way now," Tori said. "I was just texting him."

"Since when did Granddad learn how to text?"

"Since Ms. Kathy made him get a smartphone." She slung a bag over her shoulder. "Our granddad's got a new girlfriend," she told Candice.

Brandon shuddered. "That sounds strange. Old people aren't supposed to have girlfriends."

"Okay," Tori said as she went out the door. "Next time, I'll call her his *lover*."

Even with the closed door between them, Candice could hear Tori's laugh, loud and clear.

Brandon's grandfather was nowhere near as cool as his granddaughter. He entered the house wearing a grungy white T-shirt and gray slacks with red-and-blue suspenders, though his pants didn't seem to be at any risk of sliding off. He caught sight of Candice and Brandon at the table, and a large grin spread across his face. Then his eyes narrowed.

"Boy, what in the world happened to your face?"

Brandon tensed up. His mouth flapped open, but no words came out.

"I tripped Brandon by accident," Candice said. "He fell into our holly bush." She guessed this was part of her duties in "looking after" Brandon.

His grandfather grunted. "That's Brandon for you. Always stumbling over his own two left feet." He went to the sink and washed his hands. "And you are . . ."

"Granddad, this is my friend Candice," Brandon said. "From across the street."

"Ah, Abigail Caldwell's granddaughter. Should have known that. You look just like her." He toweled off as he walked to the table. "Rudolph Gibbs," he said, tipping his head toward Candice. "Nice to meet you."

Mr. Gibbs reached over Candice and grabbed a cookie. He and his grandson favored each other in a lot of ways. Both carried slight builds, with heads shaped more like ovals than circles. Mr. Gibbs's hair was short like Brandon's, but way more white than black. A few large moles covered his dark skin. He smelled like cigarettes and gasoline.

"Well, welcome to the neighborhood," he said, sitting down at the table. "There are plenty of kids around here to play with. Maybe you can get Brandon out there with you."

"I go outside all the time," Brandon said.

"Shooting hoops by yourself in the backyard don't count," Mr. Gibbs said. "In my day, me and my buddies would be all over the neighborhood. Wouldn't come home till dark. You kids, nowadays . . ." He nudged Candice. "Ain't that right?"

"Um, sure," Candice said. "Mr. Gibbs, Brandon said you knew my grandmother pretty well."

"Yep, she was good people." He broke his cookie in two. "It's a shame what happened to her."

Candice didn't know if he was talking about her being fired or the heart attack that killed her. "If you don't mind me asking, did she ever tell you why she was let go from the city?" She and Brandon had decided earlier on a plan to approach his grandfather without revealing anything about the letter.

"All I know is that it had to do with her tearing up Vickers Park," he said. "She claimed it was a mistake, but them good old boys in the city office was probably waiting for any chance to fire her. Lot of them didn't like a black woman telling them what to do."

Candice reached for the hole at her knee and pulled at one of the strands. "Do people think she was . . . I don't know. Incompetent? Crazy?"

He took a long time chewing the rest of his cookie before responding. "I won't lie, most of us were right perplexed. People couldn't understand how the city manager could screw up so much that she'd tear up a perfectly good tennis court. But when they followed the paper trail, the work order led right back to her." He reached for another cookie. "It was good that she left town. A lot of folks in Vista Heights weren't too pleased. Vickers Park has been around for a long time. During the time of Jim Crow, it was the only public place where blacks could peacefully meet. There's no way we would have been allowed to step foot in those other parks. Those were for whites only."

Candice thought about some of the books she'd read about the civil rights era. She wondered if black kids had ever tried to use the white-only parks, and if so, what had happened to them. Did police use water cannons and dogs to attack them like they had in other places in the South?

"Okay, thanks for letting us know," she said. She looked at Brandon, and he gave a quick nod. *On to Plan B.*

"Hey Granddad, do you have a few more minutes?" Brandon asked. "I wanted to talk to you about some of the old families that used to live here."

"Really? What for?"

"Just a . . . research project," he said, not looking at his grandfather. "A trace-your-roots sort of thing."

Tori was right. Brandon was a horrible liar.

"A research project? For school? In the summer?" His grandfather leaned back in his chair. "You should give Cousin Lucretia a ring. She's already completed our family tree all the way back to the 1800s. Shoot . . . most of our family ain't even from here."

"Well, it's not really focused on *our* family history . . . more like researching some of the other families from Lambert. I figured since Candice didn't have anything else going on this summer, maybe she could help me with the investigating."

"Okay. *Now* I get it." He grinned. "How about this? I've been at Chuck's all morning, helping him replace the transmission in his old Plymouth Barracuda. Let me spruce up a bit, and I'll be back down." He winked at Brandon. "That'll give y'all a chance to have a little more, you know, privacy. And then I'll answer any questions you got for me."

The two of them nodded. Once Mr. Gibbs left the kitchen, Brandon picked up a cookie and stuffed it into his mouth, and then another after that.

Candice stopped him before he could eat a third. "Okay, what just happened?"

"Wait," he whispered.

A minute later, the house shook a little, and the pipes inside the walls groaned.

"Okay. Granddad's in the shower," he said. "Sorry about that. Granddad always acts funny when I bring girl friends over." He paused, then said, "Not girlfriends. I meant girl—BIG SPACE—friends. Girls that happen to be friends. I mean, friends that happen to be girls."

Candice recalled how he had winked at Brandon. "My dad's the opposite," she said. "There's no way he would let me and a boy sit in the same room without adult supervision."

They became quiet, and Candice wondered if they had both spoken too much. She was pretty sure Brandon didn't like her *like that*. She surely didn't like him that way. But before she could say anything to fill the awkward void, Brandon opened his backpack, pulled out a book, and flipped to the first page.

Rudolph Gibbs reentered the kitchen wearing a clean white T-shirt and another pair of slacks and suspenders. As he walked to the refrigerator, Brandon placed his book facedown and pushed it closer to Candice. She put her hand on top of it and pulled the book the rest of the way to her.

Mr. Gibbs poured iced tea into a mason jar. "All right, what do you want to know?" he asked.

"Did you know the Allens?" Brandon asked.

Mr. Gibbs whistled. "Ah, the Allens. Russell Allen passed away a few years after we moved here. He was an important man." He settled at the table. "Of course, I didn't really know him. The Allens were a whole different type of white people. A little too blue-blood for us regular folks. From what I understand, Russell's daughter ran the family business after he died. She was the only halfway decent one. Most black folks steered clear of Russell Allen's sons."

"Do they still live in town?" Candice asked.

"Maybe a few cousins. But the ones with all the money, Russell Allen and his kids, have died or have moved away." He paused to drink his tea. "Not that they were really that rich in the end."

"Because they lost some contracts?" Candice asked.

"As a matter of fact, that's right." Mr. Gibbs placed his glass on the table. "Who told you that?"

"I . . . um . . . found some documents in Grandma's attic that mentioned it," Candice said. "That's, um, how I got roped into Brandon's project. What about a man named Enoch Washington? Have you ever heard of him or his wife, Leanne?" Candice wasn't even going to try to say Siobhan's name.

Rudolph Gibbs's forehead furrowed so his eyebrows bunched together. He wiped some condensation from the glass. "I didn't know him. We moved here long after he'd been . . ."

"We know," Candice said. "He was forced to leave town."

"Things were different back then," Mr. Gibbs said. "I know y'all have seen the TV specials and read all the books, but there's a big difference between reading about life in the fifties and sixties and living it. We were supposed to mind our place, with our heads bowed and mouths closed. When we didn't, bad things happened." He finished his tea, then rattled the ice in the jar. "Since you're asking so many questions, I assume you know Marion Allen, Russell's oldest—the one missing an eye—ran him out of the city."

Missing an eye? Candice hadn't expected to hear that. "We knew it was the Allens but we didn't have a name," she said.

"Do you know when it happened?" Brandon asked.

"Late fifties, I think," Mr. Gibbs said. "Not really sure. Folks didn't like to talk about stuff like that when I got here. Even without a bunch of money, the Allens were still plenty powerful. Plus, no one had proof. Or if they did, no one brought it forward." He shrugged. "Big Dub and his family were gone, and they weren't coming back. What was the point in dredging up the past?"

"Big Who?" Brandon asked.

"Big Dub. That's what they used to call him. With a name like Enoch, I'd go by Big Dub too." Mr. Gibbs let out a soft, sad chuckle. "If you really want to know more about him, you should check out the memorial at Lambert High." He turned to Candice. "Dub was a teacher and coach at Perkins High. When they finally shut down Perkins and Wallace to create a new high school, someone kicked in a bunch of money to upgrade the building and create a special memorial for Perkins."

Candice and Brandon looked at each other. She could tell he was wondering the same thing she was—was this tied to the mysterious benefactor from the library?

"Why did they create a special memorial?" she asked.

"Perkins was one of the first schools for black children in the region. Maybe even the state," he said. "Those colored schools are a big part of our history."

"Granddad," Brandon said with a sigh, "you should say 'African American.'"

Mr. Gibbs gave his grandson a long, hard look. "Son, if the worst thing you've ever been called is *colored*, then you should consider yourself very, very lucky."

CHAPTER 9

Enoch Washington

March 16, 1914

Brandon Jones was eleven years old. He had only referred to his race in two ways — as African American and black — terms that had become popular after the civil rights movement of the 1950s and 1960s.

Enoch Washington was born almost one hundred years before Brandon, in a small wooden shack outside of Luling, Texas. He lived during the Jim Crow era — when black men were considered free, but were barred from voting in elections, living where they wanted, or getting the same education or services as whites.

Enoch was colored.

Colored was not a derogatory term — certainly not at the turn of the twentieth century. However, there were many other offensive, racist names hurled at Enoch. And he was only six when he first heard them.

Enoch and his family had been at breakfast when they'd heard the stamp of hooves approaching the house. It was barely light outside, but the spring humidity had already seeped into their shack, weighting down their clothes.

"Y'all stay here," Enoch's father said, standing from the table. He walked to the door, but didn't open it.

The horse came to a stop, and a few moments later, Enoch heard the crunch of footsteps against the ground.

Someone banged on the door, making Enoch jump. "Raymond? Come on out here, boy."

His father cast a look back at the table, then opened the door. "Morning, Cordell," he said, stepping outside.

No one at the table made a sound. Enoch's mother stared at her plate, mouthing a prayer to herself. Enoch's siblings shared silent glances with one another. They were all older. Enoch didn't understand what was happening, but they did.

After a couple of minutes, Enoch's father came back inside. "It's Cordell Rackley. He's come to collect me and the boys. We're working Mr. Tidwell's fields for a few weeks."

Enoch began to stand, but his father shook his head. "You stay here. Help your mama and Winnie while we're gone."

His mother finally looked up. "What about our crop? If we don't start planting soon, the cotton won't have time to grow."

"Hush, Mary," his father said, his voice low.

"And what about the Logans?" she continued. "The Rosenwalds? Or is Mr. Tidwell only forcing colored folks to work his land? That man's gonna make us his slaves, one way or another."

"Enough," his father snapped. "We got a debt to pay. Mr. Tidwell chose now to collect. That's that." He clapped his hands. "Boys, let's go."

Enoch watched as his brothers quickly finished their breakfast. They kissed their mother on the cheek, then headed out the door.

"You're missing one," the man outside said, his voice booming. He must have been standing by the window. "Where's the tar baby?"

Enoch froze. He was darker than all of his siblings. His skin was like moist soil that had just been turned. Like swirling ash rising from a fire.

"Go on," his mother said, squeezing his hand. "Best not to keep Cordell Rackley waiting."

Nodding, Enoch rose from the table. He reminded himself to stand tall, just like his father had done a few minutes before.

He walked outside, then paused upon seeing the man standing in front of his father and brothers. Cordell Rackley was small and wiry, with skin the color of biscuits that had been cooked for just a minute too long.

Cordell Rackley was colored too.

"Ah, there he is," Mr. Rackley said, a shotgun resting on his shoulder. He motioned for Enoch to approach him. Cordell circled the boy, sizing him up like he was an animal, or a cut of meat. Still holding his gun, he squeezed both of Enoch's arms with his free, golden-brown hand, then slapped the boy on the back, so hard that Enoch stumbled forward. "What you doing, keeping a big buck like that inside?" Cordell finally asked his father. "With him, you'll work off your debt even faster."

"He's only six," his father said. He had balled his hands into fists, and he was looking at the ground, not at Enoch.

"Don't matter," the man replied. He spit into the ground, then wiped his mouth. "He's gonna end up in the field. Might as well get started now."

CHAPTER 10

It took two days, but Brandon was finally able to reach Ms. Patrice McMillan, his sister's AP History teacher and the unofficial curator of the Perkins Memorial Room. She was heading out of town, but was available to meet with them that Friday morning.

The only problem: No adults were around to drive them. Candice even tried texting her dad, who was coming into town for a visit, but he wouldn't arrive until that afternoon. So with the help of a bike Candice found in her shed—and some extra cajoling of Brandon—they had ridden over to Lambert High School.

Brandon pulled out his sister's phone once they locked up their bikes. "Hi, Ms. McMillan? We're outside." He paused and nodded. "Okay. See you in a second." He opened the door. "She says to follow the signs and they'll lead us right to her."

They entered a large atrium at least two stories high. The ceiling was painted like the sky—light blue, with clouds and birds and even a hot air balloon.

"Tori says they paint it over each year to keep it looking new," Brandon said. "The sky makes the room seem bigger than it really is."

They walked down a series of intersecting hallways. As they proceeded, the lights automatically flicked on ahead of them. Finally, they stopped at an open door. "Hello?" he called into the room.

"Come on in," a voice replied.

They stepped inside. Candice had been expecting a room with a few statues, or maybe a bookcase with a handful of photos and trophies. But the Perkins Memorial Room was a *museum*. Photos, paintings, and artwork lined each of the walls. Books and other artifacts sat behind glass, with special lights illuminating them. The wall directly ahead of them displayed rows of black-and-white and color portraits.

"Wow," Candice said.

"You sound like I did when I first saw the room." A thin woman emerged from behind a large box. "I'm Patrice McMillan. Welcome to the Perkins Memorial Room." She was younger than Candice's mother, with dark skin and a short, stylish bob, and she wore a pair of stretchy jeans and a Carolina Panthers jersey. She waved toward the wall that Candice was staring at. "Those were all of the school's principals."

Candice checked out the first photo in the row. "White men were principals at the school?" she asked. "I assumed, since it was a school for black kids . . ."

"Don't forget, hon, back in 1868 there weren't a lot of educated African Americans in South Carolina. It's hard to teach unless you've been taught yourself first."

"The high school is that old?" Candice asked.

"It started as a one-room grade school for freed slaves, founded by Methodists from the North." Ms. McMillan pointed to another portrait farther along the wall. "It didn't become a high school until the early 1900s. Ada Marie Perkins was the first black teacher, then principal. When she passed, they renamed the school after her."

Brandon squinted at the photo of Perkins. "She doesn't look black."

"Technically she was mixed. Based on the little we could find, we think she was of French descent on her mother's side. Not that it mattered. Back then, if you had one drop of black blood, you were considered colored." She rubbed her hands together. "As interesting as this may be, we have limited time, and you came here to do specific research. What can I help you with?"

"We're looking for information about Enoch Washington," Candice said. "He was a teacher at Perkins a long time ago."

"That name doesn't sound familiar," she said. "Do you know when he taught here?"

"The fifties, we think," Brandon said. "His wife was named Leanne and they had a daughter named Siobhan. He was . . . *forced* out of town."

Ms. McMillan cocked her head to the side. "Tell me his name again."

"Enoch Washington," Candice said. "They used to call him—"

"Big Dub. I've heard a few locals talk about him, but they never used his given name." She sighed. "Just to be clear, the memorial doesn't have any information about the game."

Candice and Brandon looked at each other. Brandon shrugged. So did Candice.

"You *have* heard about the big tennis exhibition?" Ms. McMillan asked.

"We have no idea what you're talking about," Candice said.

Ms. McMillan hesitated for a moment. "According to secondhand sources, in 1957 the tennis teams from Perkins and Wallace—the school for white kids—held a private match. The Perkins boys beat the Wallace team pretty badly. The next day, Big Dub and his family

51

left town. Some say he was run out. Others say he left of his own accord."

"Was Marion Allen on the Wallace team?" Candice asked.

"No, he was in his late twenties then," she said. "Plus he wore an eye patch, which I'm assuming would have made playing tennis difficult. But his younger brother, Glenn, was a member of the team."

"Isn't there anything written about the game?" Brandon asked. "It had to be a big deal—a black and a white school playing against each other back then."

"I'm sure it would have been a very big deal if it had been a real, sanctioned game. But they supposedly played in the middle of the night at one of the high school courts." She began walking. "I want to show you something."

She led them to the sports area. A large shelf took up most of the wall, with various trophies, championship plates, and photos enshrined behind glass. Above the shelf hung a number of paintings. One series of five paintings showed a tennis game between black and white players, where each painting displayed a different score, from 0–0 to 40–15. Other artwork showcased additional sports—a football player scoring a touchdown, a baseball player swinging a bat, and a sprinter handing off a baton to a teammate.

"That art is worth more than every laptop in the computer lab. It was commissioned specifically for us. Personally, I think our donor wasted his money." She pointed to the shelf. "See that trophy down there?"

Brandon knelt in front of the glass. "It says . . ." He jerked back. "It's the trophy from the game!"

"*Perkins-Wallace Tennis Exhibition. August 10, 1957. Champions.*" Ms. McMillan tapped the glass. "My predecessor came in one morning to find that trophy sitting on her desk. It seemed like someone had gone to a lot of effort to have it made, so she added it to the display. We included a photo of the tennis team from the 1957 yearbook, though we have no idea who played that night."

Candice thought back to the first clue in the letter. This was all interesting, but it wasn't giving them the information they needed. "Did Coach Washington have any hobbies? Any other sports besides tennis that he liked just as much?"

Ms. McMillan frowned, and for a moment, Candice worried she'd said too much—that somehow Ms. McMillan knew all about her grandmother's letter and the hidden treasure. Then her eyes lit up. "You know, when I was looking through some old files a few years ago, I saw a case of DVDs with his name on them. Give me a second. Maybe those have some additional information about him."

As Ms. McMillan walked away, Candice looked at the trophy again. She took off her backpack and pulled out the letter. "August 10, 2007," she said. "The letter was dated exactly fifty years after the tennis game."

"No way that can be a coincidence." Brandon pulled out his notepad. "Can you read off the inscription?"

Candice knelt to get closer to the trophy. She read the inscription for Brandon, then slid over to get a better look at the photo of the tennis team. It didn't take much for her to figure out who Big Dub was, since he towered over everyone else. A tall girl stood in the photo as well. Candice wondered if she was Siobhan.

Ms. McMillan returned with a DVD case. "I took a quick peek. It looks like someone made tribute videos for a number of past coaches. The videos are short—only ten or fifteen minutes long each."

Candice rose and took the DVD from Ms. McMillan. "Is that Siobhan Washington in the photo?" She said the name slowly to be certain she was pronouncing it correctly.

"I'm not sure," Ms. McMillan said. "But the players' names are listed in the yearbook. I'll grab one for you."

Brandon made another note on his pad. "How much do you want to bet that our mysterious benefactor is behind the trophy as well?" he said to Candice.

Ms. McMillan had begun to walk away, but stopped. "A mysterious what?" she asked.

He smiled sheepishly. "Oh, nothing. It's what we've been calling the guy who made all these anonymous donations to the city. You know, for the library and memorial."

Candice glared at Brandon. *Shut up*, she tried to say with her eyes.

"Our benefactor isn't anonymous. His name was James Parker."

Candice's head whipped toward Ms. McMillan. "I thought . . . We thought—"

"As I understand it, he was never trying to hide who he was. He just didn't want to draw attention to himself. He made most of his contributions through his charitable foundation. There's even a plaque with his name on it," Ms. McMillan said, pointing toward a far wall.

"Was he at the game that night?" Candice asked.

"I doubt it. Mr. Parker was from Colorado." She glanced at her watch. "I'm sure this was just some big tax write-off to him."

"What was his name again?" Brandon asked, flipping to a fresh page in his notepad.

"James Parker," she said. "Kids, I hate to run you out, but I've got to get moving. I'm supposed to be on my way to Atlanta right now. I'll be back on Monday if y'all want to swing by. Just give me a call ahead of time."

Candice barely heard the rest of what Ms. McMillan said. Her head was stuck on one word. *Atlanta*.

"If you don't mind, can we still borrow a yearbook?" Brandon asked.

"Sure thing. Just bring it back in good condition." She started to walk away again.

Candice stepped forward. "Where are you going?" she asked quietly.

"To get a yearbook."

"No, I mean in Atlanta. Where are you going in Atlanta? I live there." Her stomach flip-flopped as she talked.

"My sorority sister invited me to visit. We'll probably go to a cook-out, maybe a movie. She's a die-hard Braves fan, but I'm not about to let her drag me to a game."

"Oh. Okay," Candice said. Then she forced a smile and added, "Sounds like fun."

As Ms. McMillan disappeared through a door at the rear of the room, Candice wondered what had happened to her throwback Hank Aaron jersey she always wore to baseball games. She had outgrown it last summer, but her father had promised to buy her a new one this year. She considered reminding him about the jersey when she saw him that afternoon, then decided against it. It wasn't like she needed it anyway, especially not here in Lambert.

Ms. McMillan returned a few moments later with the yearbook. She handed it to Brandon. "Anything else I can help y'all with?"

"One more question," Candice said, her stomach safely back in place. "Do you have any contact info for James Parker?"

"Afraid not, hon," Ms. McMillan said. "James Parker has been missing for more than ten years."

CHAPTER 11

"Do you have a computer and Internet at home?" Candice asked Brandon as they entered the atrium. "Please tell me you do. Now that we know his name, this could be our big break."

"It's super slow, but it works," Brandon said. "Do you really think it's that simple? We do a web search on this Parker guy, and that leads us to the money? That seems . . . I don't know. Convenient. Easy."

"Maybe. It's just that I can't help but wonder—what if this was the one clue my grandma missed—just like we almost did. What if . . ."

She let her words float up to the top of the school's fake blue sky. She didn't want to talk about the rest of what she was thinking. Like, how finding Parker—or rather, *not* finding Parker—could have been the thing that sent her grandmother off track. The thing that led to her digging up Vickers Park when she should have been searching somewhere else.

"But the letter talks about Siobhan's parents, not James Parker." Brandon pushed the door open, allowing sunlight to spill into the school. "I wish we'd had more time in there. We probably should have asked more questions about Leanne Washington."

"Maybe there's something about her on the DVD." Candice tugged on her backpack straps. "Um, do you have a DVD player as well?" A desktop computer and Internet service weren't the only luxuries Candice and her mother were living without this summer.

"Our computer *should* be able to play it," he said. "I'd suggest we go to the library to be on the safe side, but it's closed on Fridays. So home it is." He gave her a nervous smile. "Unless I can convince you to stop for lunch. We're not too far from Sam's Superette. They have the best chili-cheese dogs in town."

"Hot dogs from a gas station?" Candice stuck out her tongue. "No thanks."

"A *service* station," Brandon corrected. "Or maybe we can get some ice cream."

Candice couldn't tell where Brandon was going with his comments. She was hungry, but she also wanted to see the video and look up James Parker before her dad arrived.

"Hold on," she said, pulling out her mom's phone. "Let me see where my dad is."

She quickly opened a message to her father, then typed: *ETA?*

Still a few hours away. Had to check a construction site. How is Candi?

Candice quickly typed back: *This is Candi. I'm good. Can't wait to see you. And no texting and driving, safety man!*

She stared at the screen for a few seconds, then went back and corrected the text: *This is Candice. I'm good. Can't wait to see you. And no texting and driving, safety man!*

She sent the text, then pocketed the phone. "My dad will be here soon," she said. "We should go to your house and do more research. I'm fine with a sandwich from home."

They started back toward their neighborhood on their bikes. As they entered their subdivision, Brandon slammed on his brakes. "Crap," he muttered. "I knew this would happen."

Three kids rode toward them. They were too far away for Candice to really see them, but with one glance at Brandon, she knew it had to be Milo and his buddies.

Now Candice understood why Brandon had wanted to delay coming back home. Why he'd been hesitant to bike in the first place.

He had been trying to avoid Milo.

"They'll chase me down if I try to take off," Brandon said. "You can go ahead if you want."

Candice shook her head. "I'll stay," she said quietly. It was the least she could do.

He relaxed a little. "Don't worry. Milo would never hit a girl. Probably." He started pedaling. "We should meet them in front of Mrs. Palmer's house. She's always spying out her window. She'll break things up if . . . well, you know."

Candice and Brandon came to a stop and waited for Milo and his friends to reach them. Each wore baggy basketball shorts, old T-shirts, and blue high-tops.

"What's going on, Braaaaann-don?" Milo said. He spoke the name in a singsong manner, drawing out the syllables.

"Just riding around," Brandon said. Candice had to give him credit—his voice didn't waver.

"Who's your friend?" Milo asked.

"My name is Candice," she answered. Surprisingly, her voice was solid as well.

"You're living in Ms. Caldwell's old house?" one of the boys asked. He took his T-shirt and wiped his forehead. "Your mom's the writer?"

She nodded.

"So how'd you end up hanging out with Braaaaann-don?" Milo

asked, dragging out the name again. "Is he the closest thing to a girl you can find to be friends with?"

"He's more of a girl than his freak of a sister," one of the other boys said.

"Leave her alone," Brandon warned, his voice wavering now. "Leave them both alone."

"Calm down, man," Milo said. "It's not like she's your girlfriend."

"Of course she's not my—"

"Brandon doesn't like girls," Milo said, turning to Candice. "But I'm guessing you already figured that out. It ain't hard to tell."

Candice put her hand on her pocket, over her mom's phone. Would it be okay for her to call home? Or would they try to grab the phone as soon as she pulled it out?

"Leave her alone," Brandon repeated.

"Or what? No teacher to tattle to this summer."

"There a problem here, boys?"

They turned. An older woman stood on her porch, her hands on her hips.

"No problem, Mrs. Palmer," Milo said. His voice dripped with honey.

"Then go on home, Milo," she said. "All y'all should go home. It's too hot to be standing in the middle of the sidewalk."

"Yes, ma'am," they murmured.

"And Milo, tell your momma to call me. I need a ride to church on Sunday."

Milo nodded. As soon as the door closed, he turned to one of his friends. "I hate when old people ride in our car. They always smell like medicine and Lysol."

Milo kicked his leg over his bike and took off. He steered toward Brandon, almost like he was trying to clip him. At the last moment,

Brandon leaned away, barely avoiding Milo's handlebars. But he lost his balance, and he and his bike fell to the sidewalk. Milo and his friends laughed and rode away.

Candice jumped off her bike. "You okay?"

"I'm fine," Brandon said, brushing grit from his hands.

"Brandon, I'm sorry—"

"It's fine." He didn't look at her as he got back on his bike.

"But it's my fault. If I hadn't made you ride to the memorial—"

"Drop it, okay?" He took off, his legs pumping hard in the wind.

As fast as she pedaled, Candice couldn't keep up.

CHAPTER 12

Enoch Washington

1914–1940

As fast as Enoch, his father and his brother worked, it still took them a month to finish seeding Mr. Tidwell's farm during that spring of 1914. Which meant they lost a month planting their own cotton . . . which meant their crop didn't have enough time to mature before it was time to harvest. Come the end of the season, their haul was light again, placing them further in debt to Mr. Tidwell.

This continued for the next five years, Enoch and his family planting their landowner's crops before tending to their own. Enoch grew taller and broader with each season. By the time he turned eleven, he towered over the other kids his age. He could hit a baseball farther and round the bases faster than anyone else at his school, and he could haul more cotton than two of his older brothers.

It was also at eleven that he got into his first fistfight.

His father noticed the large welt on Enoch's face, but didn't speak of the bruise at first. Five days after the fight, he took his son to the edge of their plot to repair a fence. They started at dawn, pulling up the old, rotten wood and digging new, deeper holes to anchor the posts. It wasn't until the afternoon that his father asked, "So when you gonna tell me what that fight was about? And don't lie to me. I already talked to Cordell Rackley and your teacher about it."

Enoch had gotten into a fight with a boy named Sammy. The boy, with his slim build and golden-brown skin, was the spitting image of his father, Cordell Rackley, the man who oversaw all the colored workers on Mr. Tidwell's land. Mr. Rackley may have had more money, power, and status than any other colored man in Luling, but his children were only allowed to attend the one-room Negro school, like every other colored child in the county.

Enoch shook the dirt from his shovel. "I bet Sammy to a race. First one to the flagpole and back. If I won, I'd get the slice of cake in his bag. If he won, he'd get my ham sandwich."

"You wagered a ham sandwich against a piece of cake? Boy, you know how much that meat is worth?"

"I knew I could beat him. And I did." Enoch started digging another hole. "But Sammy said I cheated. Then he swung at me. So I hit him back."

"Your teacher said you started it."

"I didn't! She's just saying that because of who Sammy's daddy is. She always treats him better than everybody else."

His father sighed. "Yeah, you're probably right. That's why you got to be smarter than the Sammy Rackleys of the world. Work harder."

"He called me names too," Enoch leaned against his shovel. "Said I was named after a slave." Enoch didn't want to admit that the comment would have bothered him less if it had come from anyone else other than Sammy.

"I named you after your granddaddy. The *last* slave in this family. Which means he was also the first *free* man in this family." His father wiped the sweat from his brow with a threadbare rag. "And if you ever learn to keep your mouth shut and ears open, you might be the first college-educated man in this family."

Enoch frowned. "Pa?"

"You're hardheaded, but you're smart. You can read better than any of us. And the way you do those numbers, all in your head . . ." Enoch's father looked down at his son. Enoch was still shorter than him — at least for another couple of years. "Your aunt Dorothy lives in Birmingham. There's a school for coloreds there. It's good too, according to your aunt." He nodded, as if he was convincing himself. "I've already talked to your mama about it. You'll leave at the end of the school year."

"What about the crop?" Enoch asked. "You need my help picking the cotton. And what about Mama? And Jasper and Simon and —"

"We'll manage. We always do." Enoch's father returned his rag to his back pocket. "Not a word of this to your brothers and sister. Understand? I'll tell them myself. In time."

"But . . . why me?"

"Because you got a chance — a real chance — of being something other than a sharecropper. Your brothers and sister are strong. Good workers. But they don't got what you got." He tapped his son's forehead. "Just don't waste it. And don't go off trying to challenge everybody that looks at you the wrong way. You're a colored man in the South. You don't have to go searching for a fight. It'll come to you all on its own."

Enoch left for Birmingham a few months later. His aunt Dorothy — his grandfather's youngest half sister — was a secretary at one of the churches. She helped Enoch acclimate to living in the big city, since the noise, the buildings, the vehicles, and the people were all new to him. She also worked with him so he could catch up with his classmates, as this new school was much more challenging than the grade school he'd left behind. She taught him how to wash his own clothes and cook his own food. She protected him as he grew from a boy to a man.

One thing that didn't change was Enoch's dislike for his name, especially as other kids continued to tease him about it. So when he tried out for the baseball team at his new school, and one of the kids asked him what his name was, he said, "Call me Washington."

Enoch shared his last name with another boy on the team, so the baseball players called him "Big" Washington to differentiate the two. Eventually, that shortened to Big W. By the time he started college at Tuskegee Institute, Enoch had become Big Dub.

While he excelled at baseball, football, and track, the sport he enjoyed the most was tennis. It was an elegant sport, far removed from the cotton fields and outhouses of his youth. He liked that he didn't need to depend on anyone else to win a match. It was just him against his opponent, one man fighting against another for dominance. He quickly mastered the game, eventually giving up baseball for it.

After graduating with a degree in mathematics, Big Dub moved North, where he spent the next few years teaching at small colored schools in Virginia and Maryland. Returning to Luling or Birmingham was never a consideration, as both his parents and aunt passed away while he was in college. He tried to maintain contact with his siblings, but as they migrated to Chicago and New York, and he moved from place to place, their letters became less frequent. Before he knew it, three years had passed without word from any of his family.

Big Dub eventually met a young schoolteacher named Leanne Diggs. She was smart and beautiful, with eyes that could captivate a room, and sweet potato pies that were the best in the county. He liked that Leanne came from a cultured family. Her father, an educated man, was the publisher of a small Negro newspaper. Her family had been free since the early 1800s, and even owned land.

But he also courted Leanne for another, more strategic reason—her smooth, light brown skin.

As Enoch had come to learn, the "brown paper bag" test was a way of life for a Negro—the fairer you were, the better you were treated and the more power you were allowed to have. With his dark skin and thick, kinky hair, Enoch knew he'd never be seen the same as his peers. But that didn't have to be the case for his sons.

A year after they married, a former classmate contacted Enoch about a job at Perkins High School in Lambert, South Carolina. Enoch didn't want to move back to the Deep South, but the school promised to let him both teach and coach. He would serve as an assistant football coach, and he would be allowed to form his own tennis team.

Five years after that, Leanne at last became pregnant with what would be the couple's only child—though they didn't know that yet. Big Dub spent every night with his ear pressed to his wife's stomach, listening to the movements in her belly. A group of his fellow teachers wagered on how large the child would be, and even took to calling the baby "Lil' Dub."

In May of 1940, Enoch and Leanne Washington welcomed an eight-pound, twenty-two-inch infant into the world. Big Dub had been hoping for a son, but it only took a second for him to fall in love with his baby girl. She hadn't inherited her mother's fair skin or fine hair, but Dub didn't care. She was perfect.

"What should we name her?" Leanne asked as she rocked the child to sleep. "And don't you dare say Lil' Dub."

Enoch knelt beside his wife and took the baby's small, brown, wrinkled hand in his. "You should name her."

Leanne thought for a few moments. "What about Siobhan? After my Irish grandmother."

"And I reckon you want to keep that silly spelling."

"Of course," she said. "Strange names run in our family, *Enoch*."

"Siobhan it is," he said. He kissed his daughter's forehead. "But she'll always be Lil' Dub to me."

CHAPTER 13

By the time Candice got home, Brandon had already disappeared into his house.

Her head knew that what happened with Milo wasn't her fault, but her heart didn't quite agree. She wanted to walk over and see him. She wanted to apologize. She wanted to see if he had hurt himself when he fell, even though she was pretty sure he hadn't. And if she was being totally honest with herself (which she wasn't), she wanted to use Brandon's computer to watch the DVD on Enoch Washington and look up James Parker.

At the same time, she felt a little unsure about what Milo had said about Brandon. Did he really like boys instead of girls? It wasn't a big deal—a few of the kids in her neighborhood had gay parents, and there were two gay teachers at her school. But she didn't really *know* anyone who was gay.

Inside her own house, she stared at the clock, wondering when it would be appropriate for her to knock on Brandon's door. Then a red extended-cab pickup truck pulled into her driveway, and she rushed outside.

"Candi!" Her father scooped Candice up into a bear hug as soon as he stepped out of the truck. His graying stubble tickled her cheek.

Candice took a deep breath. He smelled like he always did—like laundry detergent—but she could also make out the traces of a new cologne. It was strong and citrusy, like a carton of Valencia oranges. The scent was familiar, but she couldn't quite place it.

After he put her down, he opened the back door and pulled a small bag from the cab. "So what do you think of Lambert?" he asked.

"Ugh."

"That bad, huh. Any other kids around?"

"A few." Candice looked across the street. Brandon's mother and grandfather sat on the porch and waved. Candice and her father waved back.

"Who lives over there?" he asked.

"My friend Brandon and his family. He's nice. A big-time reader."

"You two hang out a lot?"

Candice had already decided not to tell her father about the letter. She didn't want a lecture from him too. "We went to a memorial today. Actually, it was more like a museum. It was really cool."

He scratched his beard. "That sounds like a date."

She wrinkled her nose. "Dad, he's eleven. That's like . . . *no.*"

"Oh, okay. Good." He patted her shoulder. "I guess we should head inside."

Her mother opened the door for them. "Hello, Joe."

"Hey, Anne." He gave her a light hug. "Sure you don't want me to get a room somewhere?"

"It's fine," her mother said. They moved inside. "How's the house?"

"Going well. Dan's crew is almost finished in the bathrooms. He's got some other guys coming out next week to work on the grading in the backyard. And then he—"

"Are they on schedule or not?" her mother asked.

Her father nodded. "They'll be finished in four weeks."

"At least he's cheap and fast." She took a step backward into the kitchen. "I'm going to start dinner. Y'all stay here. Catch up."

Four weeks, Candice told herself. She had four weeks.

Her father sat down on the couch, then frowned.

"You might be more comfortable in a hotel," Candice said, sitting beside him. "The couch doesn't fold out, and it's pretty lumpy."

"I'll make do. I want to be here in the morning when you wake up. Gonna make my special pancakes." He looked around the living room and took a deep breath. "My goodness, it still smells like her, doesn't it? Your grandma. How is that possible after all these years?"

"Me and Mom were thinking the same thing."

"Is she okay being here? It took her a long time to get over your grandma's death."

For a few months after the funeral, when Candice woke up in the middle of the night for a drink of water, she would see her mother sitting in the guest bedroom—the room her grandma always slept in when she visited. Grandma lived and worked on the outskirts of Atlanta, but she would stay with them at least one weekend every month. Candice could still smell the lavender in that room too.

(*Not* coincidentally, her father would always find a construction site outside the city to inspect whenever her grandmother came to visit.)

"So the house," she said. "Four weeks?"

He ran his hand along the cushions. "Yeah. Maybe a little longer. But don't tell your mom." He looked toward the kitchen. "Is she really okay?"

Candice sighed. She wanted to talk about the house, not her mom. "Her writing was going kind of slow at first, but she's making better progress now."

"Good." He fiddled with his thumbnail. "Is she . . . dating?"

Her father's fingers were plain now, like her mother's. Candice didn't know what they had done with their rings.

"To be clear, I'm not asking because I want to get back with your mother," he added.

"I know, Dad. It's just, I don't know if I should be sharing this with you." She shifted in her seat. "But no, I don't think she's seeing anyone."

"I want her to be happy. I want you both to be happy. To be cared for." He nudged his daughter. "You *are* happy, aren't you?"

"I'm . . . not sad. There are worse places than Lambert."

She waited for her father to offer to let her stay with him, but he just said, "I'll talk to the guys. See if I can get them to speed up. Try to get you home before the end of the month."

Candice would have liked nothing better than that—but that meant she was running out of time to solve the mystery. "Did you bring your work laptop? The one with the data plan?"

"Let me guess—your mom's gone without Wi-Fi again." He stood to get his bag. "What do you need it for?"

"Want to get online." Not a lie, technically.

He handed her the laptop. "You know the password. Don't go downloading anything suspicious."

"Do you have your phone cable as well?" After he nodded, Candice pulled the iPod from her pocket. "I want to download some new games. And maybe even some more music." She smiled. "You know, something from this decade."

"Ouch," he said, placing his hand over his heart. "At least now I know where my iPod went."

Technically, it hadn't "went" anywhere, Candice wanted to say. He'd just abandoned it when he moved out.

He handed her the cable, then watched as the iPod synced with his laptop. He pointed at the screen. "Why don't you play our song?"

Candice clicked on "September" by Earth, Wind & Fire. It was one of his favorites.

Her dad nodded to the beat as music filled the room. He kind of reminded Candice of a bobblehead doll. "Don't give me that look," he said. "You used to love this song too. Probably knew the words before you learned your ABC's." He rose and began to dance, shuffling across the carpet and waving his arms.

Candice grinned. "Your dancing hasn't improved."

"Wait until you hear my singing—"

"Dad! Don't!"

He winked as he stretched out his arms to her and began singing: "*Do you remember . . .*"

Candice, now full-out laughing, leapt from the couch. As cheesy as all this was, she loved it. She *missed* it. Her father scooped her up and dipped her, then spun her around.

"You know you're not going to be able to dance with me forever," Candice said as she tried to match her father's moves. "Eventually I'll be too big."

He took her hands and twirled her again. "Candi, don't you know? You'll never be too big to dance with your father."

CHAPTER 14

Candice woke up on Saturday morning to the most wonderful smell: frying bacon. Her dad was probably fixing his famous blueberry pancakes as well. Even now, he liked to make the pancakes into shapes. Hearts for Candice, and stars for her mom.

Candice wasn't naïve. She had studied the statistics and done the research; she knew her parents weren't getting back together. Still, she liked having both of them around (that is, when they weren't fighting). If one was busy, the other was there to listen as she rambled about her day, or help her with her homework, or whatever. And unlike her mother, her dad could *throw down* in the kitchen.

She glanced at her father's laptop sitting on the nightstand. She had brought it to her room with the intention of searching for James Parker, but it hadn't felt right to take the next step without Brandon. She decided she'd give him until the afternoon to talk to her, and then she'd start back on the hunt, with or without him.

She kicked off her sheets and headed to the bathroom, but the murmur of her parents' voices pulled her down the hallway toward the kitchen. She crept to the edge of the hallway and pressed herself against the wall. It sounded like they were standing by the stove, but she didn't dare peek around the corner to find out.

"I'm just saying, Candice doesn't need to be biking around a new city with a boy she barely knows," her father said. "She's twelve."

"Exactly. She needs to be around other kids."

"Other *girls*."

"Seriously, Joe? *That's* the stance you're taking?"

The frying sound increased. Her father must have added more bacon to the pan. "She's a baby, Anne. And she's not happy. I've been thinking . . . Maybe she should come back to Atlanta with me."

Candice's heart welled up inside her. *Finally*. He wanted her there after all.

"I can cut down on my travel for the next month," her father continued. "And if I convert the spare—"

"God, won't you ever stop lying to yourself?"

"Language . . ." her father said. He didn't like it when her mother used the Lord's name in vain.

"We both know your schedule isn't the reason she's not staying with you. Or is Danielle no longer living at your apartment?"

Candice sucked in her breath. *Danielle?* Is that what she said? It was hard to hear over the frying.

Her father said something, but he was talking too low. And honestly, Candice didn't want to hear it.

She crept away from the kitchen, then made a big production of entering the bathroom and slamming the door shut. She turned on the water to drown out all the noise in her head. Danielle? Who was Danielle? Had her dad asked if her mom was dating because he was seeing someone as well? And since when did he think it was okay to live with someone before getting married?

When Candice entered the kitchen, her parents were sitting at the table, all smiles. Bacon and pancakes sat on the table between them.

"Hope you're hungry," her father said. "We've got a long day ahead of us."

Candice sat down and stared at the platter. She counted six heart-shaped pancakes.

There were no stars.

During breakfast, her dad brought up buying a new laptop for Candice. Her mother reiterated that she wanted to wait until the end of the summer to get one, but her father wasn't having it. He and Candice then spent the rest of the morning and early afternoon driving to every electronics store in Lambert before finally purchasing a new, top-of-the-line laptop.

After grabbing a bite to eat, Candice's dad offered to take her clothes shopping, but she quickly declined. She still owned a closet full of hideous neon T-shirts and shorts from their last shopping trip, so she instead redirected him to a bookstore. They browsed for a few hours before picking up two new puzzle books for Candice. She also did a quick check of the local history shelf before they left, hoping to find something about the Washingtons or the Allens, but she didn't see any books related to them.

During their day out, she waited at each stop for her father to bring up Danielle. But as they turned into their neighborhood, Candice accepted that her father had no intention of discussing her.

"You're mighty quiet over there," he said. "What's on your mind?"

Now was her chance! She opened her mouth . . . and paused.

"Candi?" Her father frowned. "What is it?"

She sighed. As much as she wanted to, she couldn't bring herself to ask about Danielle. The day had gone really well, and she didn't want to say or hear anything that would mess that up. So instead, she said, "Did you know Grandma was fired from her job here?"

"That was a long time ago." Her father looked at her. "Why are you asking? If someone's been talking down about your grandma, tell me and I'll—"

"Dad, it's fine. I just wish I had known."

"Your mother didn't like to talk about it," he said. "Neither did your grandma. I bet that's why she never sold the house here. She probably had it in her head that she was coming back to dig up the rest of the city." He slowed as he turned on their street. "It would really be something if they ever found that treasure of hers."

She sat up, pushing against her seat belt. "So you believe she was right?"

"No, it's too outlandish to be true. But as she liked to say, just because you don't see the path doesn't mean it's not there."

Find the path. Solve the puzzle. Candice touched the bracelet.

"You still have that old thing?" He laughed. "There was a while there that you'd never take it off, even when you were sleeping or taking a bath." He let go of the steering wheel long enough to pull Candice's ponytail. "Your grandmother and I didn't always see eye-to-eye, but I still loved her, flaws, claws, and all. And she loved you more than anyone else in the world."

Candice thought back to the night her grandmother had given her the bracelet. It was right before Candice was to perform in a big Christmas play at church. "For luck," her grandmother had whispered, slipping it onto her wrist. Her father had tried to stop her, saying that shepherds didn't wear jewelry. Grandma had rolled her eyes and replied,

"And when's the last time you met a shepherd, Joe?" Candice had tried to return the bracelet after the play, but her grandmother had refused, saying it looked better on Candice.

Candice smiled and ran her fingers along the metal, just as she had during the play. Its touch calmed her now as much as it had back then.

As they pulled into the driveway, Candice saw Brandon on his porch, reading a book. By the time they got out of the truck, he was walking across the street.

"Brandon, I presume?" her father whispered.

Candice nodded. Brandon offered a small wave as he reached their driveway. "Hey," he said. "I looked for you earlier."

"We went shopping," she said. "Laptop and books."

"I'm Joe Miller, Candi's father." Her dad stepped forward and shook Brandon's hand.

Brandon flexed his fingers as he turned to Candice. "I can come back if you're busy."

"No, what's up?" Candice asked. *Please don't say anything about the letter*, she thought.

"Tori went through her things and found some clothes she thought might fit you," he said. "She said to come over anytime to pick them up."

"Can I run over?" she asked her father. Now would be the perfect time to take a quick look at the DVD.

Her father scratched his beard. "Um . . . I don't know—"

"Go ahead," her mother said from behind her. Candice hadn't realized her mom had stepped outside. "But not too long. Maybe an hour?"

"It won't take that long," Candice said.

"No, an hour is fine. Your father and I need to finish our talk from this morning."

"Um. Okay." The air suddenly seemed too thick. Everything felt wrong. She wondered if Brandon could sense it as well. "Let me run these inside," she said, holding up her bags.

Her father reached for them. "I can take these in for—"

"No. It's okay." Candice was already heading to the door. "Be back in a sec."

CHAPTER 15

Candice followed Brandon through his house, then up a flight of creaky stairs. She clutched the DVD and the letter she had just snuck out of her bedroom.

"Thanks for not saying anything to my dad," she said.

"No problem." A long, narrow hallway greeted them on the second floor. Brandon banged on a door painted black. "Candice is here!" he yelled. He turned to her. "Or do you prefer Candi?"

She shook her head. "I hate that name."

"Then why—" Brandon stopped as the door swung open.

Tori brought her phone down from her ear and pressed it against her chest. "Sorry. Got a mini emergency going on here. Stop by on your way out. I've got some vintage T's that'll probably fit you."

"Okay, thanks," Candice said. Tori waved her pinkie at them as she brought the phone back to her ear and closed the door.

"Mom's been asking her to clean out her closet for months. You're lucky—there's some really good stuff in there. I guess." He walked to an open door at the end of the hallway. The room smelled like mothballs. "Like I said, the computer's really old."

"It's okay." Candice sat on the edge of the small bed. As she patted the purple comforter, she considered the question Brandon hadn't finished asking in the hallway. Why *did* she let her father call her by a name she didn't like? Maybe it was for the same reasons Brandon hid his "girl" books. It was just easier that way.

Candice looked up to see Brandon staring at her. "Ready to get started? I already booted it up."

"Oh, okay." She handed him the DVD. "Did you try a search for James Parker yet? Or did you flip through the yearbook to see if you could find him?"

A confused look came across his face. "Of course not," he said. "I was waiting for you."

The video tribute to Coach Washington was a little less than ten minutes long, mostly consisting of interviews with past teachers and students and narration over old photos. There was no mention of the secret tennis game, and nothing at all that seemed related to the first clue—not until the last thirty seconds of the video.

"Freeze it," Candice said. "That's the answer!"

Brandon stopped the video. "What? Baseball?"

"Well, it's at least part of the answer." Candice pulled out the letter. "The clue says Coach Washington idolized a team in a sport *other* than tennis."

Brandon rewound the video, then played it back. "Coach Enoch Washington loved many things," the narrator said. "First baseball as a youth, then track and tennis in college and beyond. But truly, it was his family he loved more than anything else in the world. They were his everything." Images of the Washingtons floated across the screen. Seeing the pictures, Candice was positive that the girl in the tennis-team photo was Siobhan.

Brandon paused the video again. A black-and-white picture of the Washingtons remained on the screen. They stood in front of a brick building. Coach Washington wore a dark suit and skinny tie. Siobhan and her mother wore long dresses and lace gloves.

"They look so much realer now," Brandon said after a few moments. "I mean, I always thought they were real, but it's different now that we can see them. They were an actual family. Real people. And they were run out of the city just because of the color of their skin."

Candice nodded. She wondered what would have happened if they hadn't left Lambert. Maybe Siobhan would have become the first black city manager, not her grandmother. Maybe the new high school would be named after Coach Washington.

Brandon let the rest of the video play out. "Okay, so he loved baseball," he said once it ended. "Now we need to figure out which team, right?"

"The video said he lived in Texas until he moved to Alabama. What city was he from again?" Candice asked.

Brandon looked as his notes. "Luling, I think." He opened a browser and typed in the name of the city. "It's pretty small." He ran another search, this time with *Luling* and *baseball*. "Looks like the high school has a baseball team."

"Yeah, but he didn't go to high school there, remember?"

"Maybe the city had a Negro League team." Brandon was already typing another search. He paused. "Ever heard of a guy named Biz Mackey?" He clicked the link.

"Any connection?"

Brandon scrolled down the page. "Mackey played on a team called the Luling Oilers in 1916. He played there for two years, then moved on to a different team. He was a Hall of Famer . . . he must have been really good."

"Coach Washington would have been, what—eight years old in 1916?" Candice slid to the edge of the bed so she could see the screen better. "The Luling Oilers. That *must* be the answer!" Candice bounced on the mattress, the smile wide on her face. This felt even better than solving one of her strategy games. At the rate she was going, she'd have this puzzle solved before the end of the weekend.

After doing a little more digging on Biz Mackey and the Luling Oilers, they shifted their attention to James Parker. According to his Wikipedia page, Parker grew up in Mississippi. After leaving the military, he went into the engineering and construction business in Colorado before branching into other industries, and eventually became a multimillionaire. He was a shrewd businessman, but he also gave a lot of money to charities and supported scholarships through his foundation.

Then, one day, without warning, he sold off all his stock and disappeared. He was eventually declared dead. He didn't have any relatives or a will, so the government absorbed all the assets they could find. Parker was estimated to be worth over $120 million, but the government could only locate half of that amount.

Candice pointed at the screen. "They couldn't find everything." She began to pace the room. "That must mean the rest of the money is hidden somewhere."

"Or maybe they just couldn't find it."

"Stop being so skeptical. We're onto something here."

"But this doesn't have anything to do with the clue," Brandon said. "Don't you think we should get back to reading about Biz Mackey or the Luling Oilers?"

Candice shook her head. "I know it's not a clue, but it feels too important to ignore. Strategy games are like that all the time—intentionally misleading the reader. Maybe James Parker is the real mystery." She plopped back down on the bed. "Plus, understanding the mind of the guy behind a mystery puts you that much closer to solving it." She'd read that in a detective book once.

They kept searching the web for James Parker. Some websites added a few small details, but nothing substantial.

Brandon sighed as he stood from the desk. "I'll say this—he doesn't look like I expected. I thought he'd look, well . . . crazy." He paused. "Not that there's anything funny about mental illness. It's just—"

"Don't worry, I know what you mean," Candice said. *Crazy* was one of the words her father absolutely hated, but Candice hadn't yet been able to get it out of her vocabulary.

Plus, she agreed with Brandon. She had expected the letter writer to be a guy with a wild beard and unruly hair, like those men who lived in the woods and didn't use technology. But James Parker looked normal, for the most part. His black-and-white photo on the Wikipedia page reminded her of Professor Xavier from the old X-Men movies. In other photos, where he had hair, it was short and white. He seemed to be more tan than pale, with freckles or faint sun spots on the bridge of his nose. He never smiled in any of his pictures.

But it was his eyes that were the most striking. They were big and gray. Round. Angry. Like he was daring someone to start a fight.

There was a knock on the door. They looked up to see Tori holding a bag of clothes. "Your mom called. She said it's time for you to come back home."

"It's been an hour already?" Candice asked.

"More like an hour and a half." She peeked at the computer. "Do I even want to know what you guys are up to?"

"Thanks for the clothes." Brandon took the bag and softly nudged his sister out the room. "We'll be finished in a second."

"Okay. I'm heading to Claudia's," Tori said. "And leave the door open. Mom's downstairs."

"Nothing's happening," Brandon said.

"I know, dummy, but the rules are the rules."

Candice repeated Tori's words in her head. What did she know—that nothing was happening between them, or that Brandon was gay?

Candice was thinking so much, she almost dropped the bag of clothes when Brandon tossed it to her. "I guess you'd better go."

"In a second." She put the bag on the bed and picked up the letter. "Do a search for *James Parker, Colorado,* and *Solara plant.*"

Brandon typed in the words and began the search. "We've got a hit." He scrolled through the article. "Something called the Economic Development Commission was responsible for getting the plant to Denver, Colorado. Parker was the president of the board." He looked at Candice. "They moved the plant from Lambert, South Carolina."

"See!"

"Okay. I admit it. James Parker probably sent the letter." He leaned back and closed his eyes. "We should go through the yearbook tonight. Maybe there's another clue there."

"I'll take the yearbook. Why don't you watch the video again and see if you can find anything. Call me as soon as you figure something out."

He nodded. "What about the Washingtons? We should probably do another web search for them too."

"I already tried at home," Candice said. She had borrowed her mother's phone a few days before to try to find them on the Internet. "Nothing popped up. Which is crazy, given their names."

Brandon snapped his fingers. "Where's the yearbook?"

She handed it to him. "What are you thinking? That we misspelled her name?"

"No. Looking for Siobhan's middle name." He found her name in the book. "Siobhan *Mildred* Washington." He quickly ran the search online using her full name. "I think I have something. It's . . . a memorial page." He looked at the yearbook, then back at the screen. "I'm pretty sure it's her."

Candice studied the photo on the screen. This older version of Siobhan Washington was grayer, with more wrinkles. Her mouth was twisted into a half smile, like she was hiding something. But not in a smarmy way, Candice thought. More like the woman in the *Mona Lisa*.

"She worked at an elementary school." Brandon scrolled down. "She was a librarian. But she got a degree in math first. She—"

"Slow down," Candice said. She was trying to read quickly, but Brandon was always a few sentences ahead of her.

"Sorry, I was just trying to skim ahead. I . . ."

She frowned. "What is it?"

"Just keep reading." His voice trembled.

Candice leaned over Brandon's shoulder. Siobhan Washington had died from cancer. She had worked at an elementary school in Maryland for over thirty years, first as a math teacher, then as a librarian. Her favorite book was *The Westing Game*.

"So she didn't coach sports?" Candice asked.

"I don't think so," Brandon said.

Candice read even faster. Not married. No kids. Loved puzzles and movies. She was buried in—

"Have you gotten to the part about her favorite book yet?" he asked. "*The Westing Game*?"

Candice stood upright. "Yeah, I saw it."

"And?"

She shrugged. "What's so special about that book?"

His eyes widened and his mouth dropped open a little. "You like puzzle books, and you haven't read *The Westing Game*?!" he yelled.

Candice crossed her arms. "I'm standing right here. You don't have to shout."

"Sorry," he said, softer. "But still, you have to read it. It's awesome. There are so many twists in the book. And it's really funny . . . for a book written in the seventies. I think I have a copy if you want to borrow it."

"Okay. Fine. I'll read it after I finish my puzzle books." A small part of Candice hated that Brandon was so enthusiastic about a book she'd never heard of before.

"I wonder if it's a clue," Brandon continued. "Maybe something in the book links back to the letter. Or to Parker."

"Can you go to the bottom of the page?" Candice spun her bracelet around her wrist. "Maybe we can see who created the website. That way, we'll know if it was Parker or not."

Brandon scrolled to the end of the webpage. Both Candice and Brandon sucked in their breath.

The website didn't name who had created it, but it did list the date it was last updated.

August 10, 2007. The same date as the letter.

Candice slowly sank to the bed. "On second thought, maybe I'll take that book now."

CHAPTER 16

Siobhan Washington

March 29, 1956

It wasn't surprising that Siobhan Washington became a librarian. She grew up surrounded by books, spending just as much time in her school libraries as she did on the tennis courts. When she reached high school, her father created an after-school tutoring program for the students at Perkins and put Siobhan in charge of it. Big Dub saw it as a way to keep his players' grades up and Siobhan occupied after school. She was destined for greatness, and no one—or rather, no *boy*—was going to stop that from happening. He had forbidden her from dating.

Siobhan didn't like how overprotective her father was, but they did agree on one thing—she had no time for boys.

Of course, the boys did not agree.

She had just finished helping a student with his math homework one afternoon when her best friend, Ellie McElveen, nudged her. "Here comes your *boyfriend*," she mumbled.

Chip Douglas strolled toward them, a huge, toothy grin on his face. With his blond crew cut and clear blue eyes, he easily stood out from all the colored kids in the Perkins school library. Siobhan wasn't sure what would have happened if he had been a "regular" white boy walking through their school, but he was Coach Douglas's son, and he seemed to have a pass to go wherever he wanted.

Coach Douglas had been at the school since 1951, though it was only recently that her mother explained why he was a teacher there. A group in Summerton, South Carolina, had sued their school board in order to get better buses and facilities for the colored students — something equal to the white students. In an attempt to head off a similar fight, the Lambert school board sprung for a new bus for the Perkins students and promised to hire better teachers in order to meet the "separate but equal" law.

And just like that, Adam Douglas, an assistant football coach at Wallace High, became the Perkins High School athletic director. Everyone was upset at first, but Coach Douglas worked hard to build trust with the staff — especially her father. Coach Douglas went out of his way to get her father any support he needed, even finding the money to send the tennis team to a week-long camp in North Carolina a few years ago. He mostly stayed behind the scenes, preferring not to draw attention to himself.

The same could not be said for his son.

"Hey, SEE-OH-BON," Chip said once he reached the table.

She sighed. That had been cute when she was a kid, but she had outgrown Chip's constant mispronunciation of her name. At least he didn't call her Lil' Dub anymore. That was much worse.

He sat down across from her and nodded at the others. "Afternoon, y'all."

Reggie, a boy working on a math assignment, kept his head down and slid farther away from them, almost like he didn't hear Chip's greeting. Ellie reacted to Chip with a nod, but didn't speak.

"What are you doing here?" Siobhan asked. "Your daddy's probably out back at the track if you're looking for him."

"Was just there," he said. "Came here looking for you. Wanted to show you this." He unfolded a letter and placed it on the table.

Siobhan read the first lines. "You got into Georgetown!"

"Yep. Just found out today." He beamed at her. Even if she had wanted to hug him, she wouldn't have. Not because he was a white boy and she was a colored girl, and not because he was a teacher's son. Siobhan knew how Chip felt about her, and she didn't want to do anything to encourage him. He really was kindhearted (when he wasn't hitting on her), and smart, but she wasn't interested in him — not like that. Even if she was, there was no way a romance could happen between a black girl and a white boy. Some things just weren't allowed in Lambert, South Carolina.

"I'm really happy for you," she said.

"Not sure how we're gonna pay for it yet. Daddy and Mama have been saving up, which'll help. I figure I'll get a summer job. Glenn's daddy thinks he can pull some strings and find me something at the pool that pays pretty decent."

Siobhan noticed Ellie shifting in her seat. Glenn Allen and his brothers were one of the reasons Ellie didn't trust any white people in Lambert. They were especially mean to kids like Ellie and Siobhan — kids with the darkest of skin.

"Again, congratulations." Siobhan pushed the letter toward him. "Now, I need to get back to tutoring."

Chip peeked at Ellie's homework. "Geometry? Maybe I could help—"

"No thank you," Ellie said, pulling her paper toward her. She rose from her seat. "Siobhan, I should go. Mama will be expecting me home soon."

Siobhan watched Ellie walk away. "Chip, you can't keep running off my friends. Ellie needs all the help she can get if she's going to pass."

"I was just trying to help," Chip said.

"You made her nervous."

"I'm sorry." He looked around the library. Siobhan wondered if Chip could tell how on edge everyone was. "Maybe we should step outside. Got a few minutes?" he asked.

"I don't think that's a good idea," she replied. "You shouldn't even be in here now. If your friends from Wallace High—"

"They ain't my friends," Chip said. "I would come here if I could. You know I would."

Siobhan believed him, but that didn't matter. The rules were the rules.

"Georgetown is in DC," he continued as he rubbed his hands along the edge of the table. His skin seemed so pale against the dark, knotty wood. "That Negro university—Howard—is there as well. It's one of the best colored schools in the country. They've even got a medical and a law school."

"You sound like my daddy," she said. Her father had already plotted out Siobhan's life. First she'd be a tennis star, then she'd become a big-time doctor or lawyer. But Siobhan had other plans. She enjoyed playing tennis, but for her it was just a sport—not a battle. And while she liked the idea of becoming a doctor, she'd started to consider other careers—like teaching. She enjoyed seeing the students in her tutoring sessions succeed.

"Anyway, I'm only a sophomore," she added. "I've got plenty of time before I have to worry about college."

"I know. But still, if you went to Howard, you wouldn't be up there by yourself. I'd be nearby. And you'd be out of the South."

"Virginia is still the South."

"Yeah, maybe. But I guarantee it's better than Lambert. I know you could—"

Chip stopped talking as one of the students approached. "I need to sign out," the boy said, his eyes on Siobhan.

Siobhan flipped open the attendance notebook. Around her, other students packed up their belongings. She was responsible for making sure all the athletes logged in and out. Each athlete was required to attend tutoring twice a week. Other students, like Ellie, came for the extra help.

"Thanks for the advice," she said to Chip. "Now, really, you should go."

"I'm not leaving without one of your puzzle questions."

A small line had formed at the table. "Chip . . ."

"I win, and I get to ask you anything I want. You win, you get to ask me anything." Both of their fathers loved making bets. This seemed to have rubbed off on Chip. "Do we have a deal?"

Siobhan didn't have time for this. "Okay, if you're so good at math, this should be easy. Listen closely: As I was going to St. Ives, I passed a man with seven wives. Each wife had seven sacks, each sack had seven cats, each cat had seven kits. Kits, cats, sacks, and wives, how many were traveling to St. Ives?"

Chip furiously wrote on his palm as students began to sign out. A few glanced at Chip, but no one spoke to him. Siobhan didn't think he even noticed what was happening around him. He was too busy scribbling on his hand.

"Can you say it again?" he asked a few moments later.

She repeated the riddle twice, just to make sure he heard it all.

"I got it," he finally said. He showed his hand to Siobhan. "Two thousand eight hundred and one."

Siobhan smiled. "Sorry."

"I'm wrong?" Chip started writing on his palm again. "Wait, let me try—"

"Too late," she said. "Here's my question: Will you please stop bothering me during tutoring?"

Alton Massey, one of the football players that had just signed out, stifled a grin.

"To be fair, I only said you could *ask* me anything you want. I didn't say my answer had to be one you liked." Chip winked and stood from the table. "See you around, Siobhan."

Siobhan waited until everyone had left, then locked up the library. It was track season; she'd find her father in the back of the school with Coach Douglas. But she didn't want to run into Chip again. She decided to wait in her father's classroom. She had a big science exam in a few days; she figured she might as well get some studying done. (Plus, she'd already finished her latest book of crossword puzzles.)

She walked to her locker to get her chemistry textbook. A small note was stuck in the vent. Probably something from Ellie.

She unfolded the paper.

Only one person was going to St. Ives.

Will you meet me at the big oak tree in Vickers Park at 5:00?

Siobhan spun around. The hallway was empty.

The handwriting was small and rushed. Definitely not Ellie's or anyone else's she recognized.

Had Chip figured out the answer? Maybe. But even then, would he have asked her to meet him at the park? Vickers Park was in the middle of Vista Heights, the oldest colored neighborhood of town. Chip was bold, but not that bold.

Siobhan refolded the note, then glanced at the clock on the wall.

If she ran, she could make it to the park with five minutes to spare.

CHAPTER 17

Candice was halfway across the street when her mother came out of their house. "Sorry," Candice yelled as she sped up. "I lost track of time."

"It's okay." Her mother carried a bottle of red wine.

Candice stopped at the edge of their driveway. "You're going out?"

"Brandon's mom invited me over for dinner. I wanted you and your father to have a little more alone time." She paused in front of her daughter. "He's driving back home first thing in the morning."

"I thought he was staying until Monday afternoon. Work stuff again?"

"No. I asked him to leave early. It's just . . . I'm not ready." She twisted the bottle in her hands. "Your father loves you very, very much. He's far from perfect, but he's still about the best dad you could ask for." She kissed Candice, then continued across the street.

Candice entered the house to find her father sitting on the couch. Her laptop was open in front of him. "Hey, Candi! Figured I'd go ahead and set up your computer while you were gone."

Candice sat down in the chair across from him and dropped her bag at her feet. "What happened?"

He flashed the same silly, clownish grin he always sported right after he and her mother had been fighting. "It's nothing. I—"

"Dad, I'm not a kid. You don't have to lie to protect me."

He laughed. "You'll always be *my* kid."

"Will you please tell me what happened? Were you two fighting again?"

"No. Well, a little." He closed the laptop. "It's hard. For both of us. I'm . . . blurring the lines too much. It's hard to be a good dad to you and an ex-husband to her at the same time."

"She told me she asked you to leave early."

"I was two seconds away from offering the same." He patted the couch, and Candice moved to sit beside him. "Don't worry. Everything's okay. Really."

"Mom said she wanted us to have some alone time." She took a breath. "Is there something you need to tell me?"

Another clown smile. "Just wanted to spend time with my baby girl before I left."

Still no talk of Danielle. Not that she was surprised.

"I wish I'd gotten a chance to know Brandon a little better," he continued. "I heard you two are working on some type of summer project."

"That's why we were at the memorial."

Her father popped his knuckles. "Are you sure he's not interested in you? In my experience—"

"Dad . . ."

"Boys sometimes show that they like girls in strange ways. When I was your age, boys showed interest in girls by ignoring them or treating them badly."

"That doesn't make sense."

"Boys rarely do, I'm afraid."

Candice pulled at the fraying threads of one of the couch cushions. She couldn't get what Milo had said about Brandon out of her head. "Brandon's not interested in me," she said. "I don't think he likes girls, period."

"Oh?" Her father's voice changed tone. "Are you sure?"

She shrugged. She was a bit surprised she was even talking about this with him. She usually saved talks like this for her mom. Or at least she used to.

"I don't know if he's gay or not, but some boys were teasing him about it yesterday."

"Kids are cruel. Adults too, for that matter," he said. "Are they physically hurting him?"

She shook her head. "They're just some stupid kids from the neighborhood who like to call him names."

"Candi, no one is stupid." *Stupid* was another word he didn't like.

"You'd change your mind if you met those boys."

He squeezed her hand, then released it. "One day people will look back and be amazed—and horrified—at the way gay people were treated. But that doesn't help Brandon today. If it gets worse—"

"I'll tell Mom. I promise."

"Good." He rose from the couch. "We should eat. I cooked pork chops and asparagus for dinner. It's getting cold."

Candice followed her father into the kitchen. The food smelled delicious. Plus, she could still smell the bacon from earlier that morning.

Her mom was right. Her dad was far from perfect, but he was still pretty great.

CHAPTER 18

Candice stood on the front steps and watched as her father backed out of the driveway. The sun sat just above the houses across the street. The sky was bright and hazy at the same time. Her dad waved one last time, then drove away.

Pressure built behind her eyes, but Candice willed it away. She kept having to remind everyone that she wasn't a baby. Now wasn't the time to prove the world right by crying.

Across the street, the Joneses' front door opened. Brandon stepped out, then jogged over to her. He held a piece of paper in his hand. "Got a second?" he asked.

He was in his church clothes. Shiny oxfords. A button-down shirt without a single wrinkle and black pants with a sharp crease. He even wore a black bow tie, crooked around his neck.

"How did you know I was out here?"

"Your mom said that your dad was leaving this morning." Then he grinned. "The good thing about getting up this early is that I can cross the street without getting jumped."

Candice knew he was joking, and she knew she was supposed to laugh. But her head—and her heart—were sitting in the passenger seat beside her father, on the way back to Atlanta.

"Candice? Are you . . ." Maybe he saw something in her face—something that Candice didn't even know was there—because he paused. "I can come back later if—"

"I'm fine," she snapped. "What's up?"

"I think you should come to church with us." He handed her the paper. It was a printout from the video—the photo of the Washingtons all dressed up. Brandon pointed to the steps and door behind the Washingtons. "I knew something in that photo looked familiar. I think they're standing in front of my old church building. The church moved to a new location a few years ago, before we moved here."

Candice lowered the photo. "You think someone at your church might remember them?"

Brandon nodded, a big grin on his face. "Sure do. Some of the older members would have been around back then. It can't hurt to—"

The door opened behind them. "Candice, why are you still—oh, hello, Brandon." Her mother quickly pulled her robe tighter around herself. "I didn't know you were out here. Do you want to come in? I can whip up a quick breakfast."

"No ma'am," he said. "I should be heading back."

Candice handed the paper back to Brandon. "I'll ask Mom and let you know, okay?"

"Sure thing. Service starts at ten."

Her mother held the door open for Candice as Brandon loped away. "So he invited you to church?"

Candice nodded. "Can I go?"

"Of course. I hope you don't mind if I pass, though."

Her mom had never put up any pretenses about being overly religious. Before the divorce, she went to church along with Candice and her dad, but she didn't sing in the choir or volunteer for the usher board, unlike her father. He mom admitted once that she did just

97

enough so people wouldn't talk too badly about her. When her parents separated, her mom stopped attending, though Candice still went with her father sometimes.

Candice had plenty of time before church, so instead of getting dressed, she opened the Perkins yearbook. Last night, after studying the tennis photo, she had paged through the *P*s in the student sections, searching for James Parker. But it had been late, so she figured she'd try to look again now that she'd had a good night's sleep.

It took a few pages, but she finally realized that *of course* she wouldn't find James Parker in the student section of the yearbook. He couldn't be there.

He was white, and Perkins was an all-black school.

A few hours later, an usher led Candice and Brandon's family down the main aisle of Mount Carmel Baptist Church. Light flowed in from all the stained glass windows, making the room sunny and warm. A huge wooden cross hung on the wall behind the pulpit, right above the choir members. They wore traditional black robes with gold accents. She couldn't remember the last time her church choir had worn robes.

The usher led them to a pew in the middle of the sanctuary.

"This is the best place to sit," Brandon whispered. "Not too close, not too far." He tugged at his collar. "Oh, and you look nice."

"Thanks." Candice had dressed up a little, though not as fancy as she would have back at home. She'd found a sundress at the bottom of her drawer and chose a pair of wedge sandals to match. Her father hated them, saying they looked too much like high heels, but Candice liked how they made her taller. She had even let her mom do her hair, turning her ponytail into curled tresses.

Candice frowned as a few other families entered the church. "That's Milo," she whispered. "He goes to church here?"

"His dad's a deacon."

The usher guided Milo's family toward an empty pew, but his mother shook her head and pointed toward the front. The usher whispered something to her, then motioned with his hand about the amount of space. Milo's mother pointed again, then passed the usher and continued up the aisle. The family followed her and was able to squeeze into a pew all the way in the front, but it was crowded. Eventually, the man at the end of the row slipped out and took another seat.

A few minutes later, the organ began. The church was having a special service in honor of Juneteenth. The choir started with an old hymn — "Swing Low, Sweet Chariot." They sang in the classic way first. Everyone in the congregation smiled and nodded, all nice and polite-like. Halfway through, the drums came in. Then came the bass guitar. And then the woman leading the song sped up, with the choir right behind her. Brandon's mother, sister, and half of the church stood up and started clapping. Candice stood as well, bobbing and singing along to the music. Even though Brandon remained in his seat, he swayed to the beat as well.

Candice wondered if Siobhan sang in the choir. Or did her mother? And maybe her father was a deacon.

The choir sang two more songs, each better than the one before. Candice hoped they would sing all day, but eventually they stopped, and the pastor came to the pulpit.

Candice braced herself. She figured this would be the boring part.

The pastor started off talking about the importance of Juneteenth, equating the plight of black slaves to the Israelites in ancient Egypt.

The pastor talked about hope. About faith. About staying on the right path, even when you can't see the Promised Land.

Something tingled in Candice's body. She could feel it in her fingers and toes and heart. It was like the pastor had picked a sermon especially for her.

Candice thought back to her grandmother's note on the back of the envelope. The path to the inheritance was there. She had already solved the first clue. She knew she'd figure out the rest of the mystery. She just had to keep the faith.

"Mom, we're going to talk to Deacon Draper," Brandon said once church service ended. "We'll find you outside."

"Who's Deacon Draper?" Candice asked, stepping out of the pew.

"He's one of the older members." Brandon pointed to a short, round man standing near the front of the church. He was dressed like he was stuck in the seventies, with a three-piece chocolate-brown suit and a wide yellow tie.

"He's really nice," Brandon said. "But he also has breath like a dragon, so be forewarned."

By the time they made it to the front of the church, a woman and her family were already talking with the deacon. "Is there anyone else we can talk to about the Washingtons?" Candice whispered. She nodded toward another older man. "What about him? He looks important."

"Not Deacon Hawke. He's kind of slimy. Mom says he talks like he's trying to sell you something."

The woman in front of them didn't look like she'd stop talking anytime soon. How long did they have before Brandon's mother came searching for them? Candice spun around, hoping to find a clock, and saw Milo and his mother walking toward them. Brandon immediately stiffened.

"Hello, you must be Abigail Caldwell's granddaughter," Milo's mother said, extending her hand to Candice. "I'm Millicent Stanford. My friends call me Millie." She motioned to her son. "I believe you've already met Milo, yes?"

"We've seen each other around the neighborhood," Candice said. She tried to keep her voice flat. She didn't want Milo's mother thinking that she and her son were friends.

"I'm sorry that I haven't been able to drop by your house to properly introduce myself to you and your mother," she continued. "Milo here keeps me quite busy. Boy Scouts and choir practice at the church, swimming lessons, basketball. You name it, he does it."

Milo smiled.

Candice crossed her arms.

"I noticed a large truck with Georgia license plates in your driveway the other day," Millie said. "Did your mother have friends in town? Not that I'm trying to pry. We've just had a few break-ins around the neighborhood, and I wanted to make sure—"

"It was my dad," Candice said. "He came to visit."

"Ohhhh. I was under the assumption that your parents were divorced," Mrs. Stanford said. "Is everything okay with him and her . . . ?"

"They are just fine." Candice plastered a big, fake smile on her face, like her mother did when someone was being nosy about her marriage. "But thank you so much for asking."

The woman winked, like she didn't understand at all that Candice was seething on the inside. "Just trying to be a good neighbor." She set her sights on Brandon. "I was sad not to see you on Milo's team this summer. Are you playing in another league?"

Brandon shook his head. "I wanted to take a break."

"That's too bad. The team is doing really well. We could use a few

101

other good players." She looked around, then leaned closer to Brandon. "And where is your friend Quincy?"

"In Seattle for the summer with his grandparents," he said, his face to the ground.

"Oh. Good. That's very good." She touched the gold cross hanging from her neck. "It will probably serve the young man well to get out of the city for a while. Perhaps his grandparents can talk some sense into him. We'll be sure to keep him in our prayers."

Brandon shrugged, his gaze still on his feet.

Candice didn't know what was going on. She knew Brandon played basketball, but she didn't know he used to play on a team—with Milo, no less. And who was Quincy? Milo stood there, still grinning, which made her even more upset. He saw what was happening with Brandon, how uncomfortable he was, and he *liked* it?

She didn't blame Brandon for trying so hard to avoid Milo. She would have done the same.

Which gave her an idea.

Candice cleared her throat. "Milo, when are your games? It would be cool to come out and watch you play."

Brandon shot Candice a look so harsh, she might as well have been literally stabbing him in the back. *Trust me*, she wanted to say.

"Saturday mornings at ten," Milo said.

"You're more than welcome to come," his mother added. She cupped her hand around her mouth like she was sharing a secret with Candice. "I'll be honest—the competition around here is dreadful. We'll be off to camp next month, where he'll be able to play against some boys who at least challenge him."

Milo grinned even wider.

"What about practices?" Candice asked. "Are those open as well?"

"Um, I suppose," his mother said. "They practice three times a week. . . ."

"I'm sorry for asking so many questions." Candice added a little twang to her voice, like her grandmother used to do when she wanted to sound especially Southern. "It's just that Mom's been looking for activities for me to do this summer. You said Milo does swimming too? At the Y?"

"At the city pool," Mrs. Stanford said. "Your mother is welcome to call me if she wants any other suggestions. Brandon's mom has my number."

"I'll let Mom know," Candice said.

Millie and Milo walked off to visit with Deacon Hawke. "What was that all about?" Brandon asked.

"Later. We're up." The woman ahead of them had finally finished talking with Deacon Draper.

The deacon grabbed Brandon's hand for a firm shake. "What can I do for you, son?"

Whoa, Candice thought. His breath smelled like spicy sausage and onions.

"This is my friend Candice," Brandon said. "Do you have a few minutes? We'd like to ask you a couple questions about some past members of the church."

"Sure thing. But do you mind if we walk to my car?"

They nodded, then followed the deacon down a hallway and out of the church. He nodded to a few people as he passed, but thankfully, no one tried to stop him to talk.

"Have you ever heard of a man named Enoch Washington? Or his wife, Leanne?" Brandon asked once they were out in the sunshine.

Deacon Draper nodded. "I knew Coach Dub. He was my position coach in football. Played linebacker for him for three years in high school."

Candice walked up a little so she could see around Brandon. "When did you graduate? 1957?"

"1950," he boasted. "Went into the army right after. Korea." The deacon pulled his keys from his pocket as he neared his car—a cream-colored Cadillac sedan. "You mentioned 1957. Are you asking about the tennis game? I was back overseas when everything went down. It's a shame what happened to him. He was a good man. Tough as a box of nails, but good. Fair. Competitive."

"Do you know anyone who was there that night?" Candice asked. "At the game?"

"Afraid not. That was what—fifty, sixty years ago? Most of us ain't here anymore." He jingled his keys. "Though Lord willing, I plan to hang around for a lot longer."

Candice smiled. His breath aside, she liked Deacon Draper.

"We were also hoping to find some information about his wife," Brandon said. "We have this photo." He pulled the picture from his pocket and unfolded it. "I think this is the old church building."

Deacon Draper squinted as he brought the paper close to his face. "Yep, that's the Washingtons. Coach Dub, Mrs. Leanne, and Lil' Dub."

"That was her nickname?" Candice asked.

"Yeah, when she was a kid." He tapped his finger on the building behind the Washingtons. "That's the old church, all right. Just a couple of miles down the street. It was a good building. We just got too big for it."

"Are there any records about the Washingtons in the church?" Brandon asked. "Anything we could look at?"

The deacon shook his head. "I don't think so. There might be something in storage, but I doubt it. Maybe other members of the congregation might remember something about them." He looked at the photo again. "Where'd you get this from?"

Brandon and Candice shared a look. They shrugged at each other.

"From the Perkins Memorial Room," Brandon said. "This was a photo in the video tribute to Coach Washington."

"Ah, I knew it looked familiar," Deacon Draper said. "The church used to have a copy of that same photo."

"Do you still have it?" Candice asked. Maybe there was a clue hidden on the back of the photo.

"Perhaps. We actually had a lot of photos. Had them all touched up and hung in the old sanctuary right after we converted it to a community center." He closed his eyes and looked up. "Let's see. . . . Gretha was still alive. . . . Nathan, our great-grand, had just been born." He sighed. "Maybe that was somewhere around 2006? 2007?"

2007! Maybe they'd find something on the photos related to the date on the letter and Siobhan's memorial website. "We'd really love to see those photos," Candice said.

"I don't think they're hanging there anymore," he said. "But I suppose they could be in a closet or storage room somewhere."

"Deacon Draper," Brandon began, "if you don't mind me asking, how did the church pay for the community center?" His voice was all squeaky.

"Donations and offerings," he said. "You know Pastor Richburg—he didn't want to hold no chicken bogs or fish fries to raise money." He nodded as he braced himself against his car. "Yeah, some of it's coming back to me. We were promised a huge donation that would totally cover the renovation if we could open the building by the beginning of 2007. Can't remember who gave the money—I think it was anonymous—but I know it was plenty big."

Another anonymous donation, Candice thought. Another instance of James Parker working behind the scenes.

"Did you make the deadline?" Brandon asked.

Deacon Draper nodded. "We had to scramble, but we made it. The city manager was able to pull some strings for us."

Candice froze.

"You okay?" Deacon Draper asked her. "Look like you just saw a three-headed mule."

"It's just . . ." She let out a long breath. "Was Abigail Caldwell the city manager then?"

"Sure was. Couldn't have gotten it done without her."

"She was my grandma," Candice said softly.

"I see," he mumbled. "Well, just so you know, Ms. Caldwell was remarkable. A true friend to this church and the black community, though we didn't realize it until her successor came along. I heard she moved back to Georgia. How's she doing?"

Candice touched her bracelet. "She died two years ago."

"Oh, I hadn't heard that." He pushed himself off his car and straightened his stance. "I'm so sorry for your loss."

Candice nodded. She'd heard that phrase a lot when her grandmother first passed away, but she never knew the right way to respond.

"Can we go to the building today?" Brandon asked. "We'd really like to see if we could find those photos."

"I don't have the keys, but it'll be open tomorrow. I'll see if I can get someone to find those photos." He looked back at Candice. "It's the least I can do for Abigail Caldwell's granddaughter."

CHAPTER 19

"Hey, Candice," Brandon's mother said as she opened the door on Monday morning. She held a cup of steaming coffee. "Brandon's in the backyard with that basketball—why don't you go on out there? And feel free to stick around for dinner tonight. No point in y'all cooking when we have plenty of food here. We're having spaghetti."

Candice slipped off her backpack and walked through the kitchen to the back door. Brandon stood a few feet away from a basketball goal, the ball spinning in his hand. He squared himself up, raised his arms, and took a shot. The ball arched toward the hoop, rotating in space, before swooshing through the rim. All net.

"Nice shot!" Candice said.

Brandon's head whipped around. "Oh, hey." He looked at his watch. "Sorry, lost track of time."

"It's okay," Candice said. "You can keep practicing if you want."

"I'll just take a few more shots," he said as he chased down the ball. It had come to a stop in the tall grass. "It's kind of hard to dribble back here, so I mainly work on my shooting. Trying to up my three-point percentage." He picked up the ball, then moved even farther away from the rim. He banked the basketball off the backboard and into the net.

It wasn't until fives shots later that Brandon missed his first bucket. Brandon was good—way better than she expected him to be, even after learning he used to play on a team with Milo. She felt a little guilty about this new revelation. Brandon was so small and so bookish, she had just assumed he wasn't very athletic.

Brandon took a final shot, then lobbed the ball toward Candice. "Want to try?"

Candice straightened her stance, like she'd learned in gym class, then launched the basketball at the goal.

Air ball!

"I'm better with puzzles," she told Brandon as she chased the rolling ball.

They returned to the computer room a few minutes later. "Tori found a few more things she thought you'd like," Brandon said, nodding toward the small plastic bag on the bed.

The bag was tied tight, but Candice was able to pull it open enough to peek inside. "Some of the clothes still have tags on them."

"Tori never met a sale she didn't like." He sat down at the desk. "So what's the next step? The old church building? We need to call Deacon Draper to set up a time—"

"In a second." Candice riffled through her backpack until she found her hand-drawn calendar. "This is for you," she said. "It's Milo's weekly schedule."

Brandon took the paper. "What? How?"

"That's why I was asking his mom so many questions yesterday. I was trying to figure out his schedule."

It had reminded Candice of sudoku, a puzzle game her grandmother had first introduced her to. But instead of completing a number grid, she was trying to fill in dates, times, and locations. It wasn't easy, especially with her mom's phone as the only way to get on the Internet, but she was eventually able to piece together not only when Milo had practices, games, and meetings, but also where they were.

"Based on the city website, Milo probably has swim lessons twice a week. The closest pool is still pretty far away, so I bet someone drives him and brings him back. That's why that's colored in green. Basketball practices are in red. The Y is a lot closer, so he probably bikes there—I bet that's where he was coming from the other day." She shrugged. "I had to take a guess on Boy Scouts and choir practice based on an old church calendar I found online. It's not perfect but . . . I figured it was my way for making up for last Friday."

"What are you talking about?"

"You know, how you didn't want to bike to the school. And how you wanted to get something to eat afterward. It was obvious you didn't want to be riding around," she said. "I guess I just wasn't paying attention."

"I could have been more honest," Brandon said. "And to be fair, avoiding Milo wasn't the only reason I wanted to go to Sam's."

"Then why?"

Candice waited, but Brandon didn't speak. She nudged his chair with her foot, causing it to swivel. "Why?" she asked again.

"I just wanted to treat you to lunch."

She glanced at the bag of clothes Tori had left for her. Then she thought about his mom's dinner invitation. "Are you being nice to me because you think we're poor? You guys don't think we can afford a meal?"

"Not exactly."

"And these clothes? Did you make Tori get them for me?"

"I can't make Tori do anything."

"I don't want your charity, Brandon."

"It's not—that's not why I'm being nice." He made a face. "Okay, that's not the *only* reason I'm being nice. I also wanted to hang out more. This summer kind of sucked before you got here."

She flexed her knee, watching the hole in her jeans expand. "We're not poor."

"I know."

"But we're not rich either. Writers don't make a lot of money. And Dad is doing really well at his job but things only go so far." She took a peek at Brandon. His face was blank. Not inviting, but not condemning either. "You know we're selling our house in Atlanta."

He nodded. "My mom told me. Are you selling the house here?"

"I don't think so," Candice said. "Mom's already got another renter lined up for the fall. That'll bring in more money, but not enough to stop her from selling my house back home."

"So that's why you want to find Parker's money?" Brandon asked. "To save the house?"

Candice nodded. "I'd share whatever I found with you, of course. Fifty-fifty."

"It's okay," Brandon said. "The first priority is to buy the house. We'll figure out how to split the rest afterward."

Candice crossed her arms and pinched her sides. She hated saying all this stuff out loud. It made it more real.

"At least now I know why you want to find the money so badly," he said. "I would hate to move after living in a place for so long."

She almost corrected him. It wasn't only about the money. It was about her grandmother as well, about fixing her legacy. But there was no way Candice could say that out loud right then.

"How long have you lived here again?" she asked.

"About three years. We would visit during the summer, but we moved for good when Mom got a job at the tech college. I'm still trying to get used to this place." He smiled. "Though those chili-cheese dogs from Sam's really are the best."

"Okay, okay. We'll get your fancy hot dogs after we do some more investigating. But I'll pay for my own."

"Deal. And I'll talk to Tori about the clothes. I think my mom believes y'all are worse off than you really are."

Candice chewed on the inside of her mouth. Maybe their finances were *worse* than she realized.

"So . . . Deacon Draper?" Brandon asked.

"I already called him this morning, before I came over. He said he found some old boxes of photos that he could bring over." Candice pulled the yearbook from her bag, then handed Brandon another sheet of paper. "And that's a list of all the players and coaches from the tennis team photo in the yearbook. The same photo that was in the glass case at the memorial. None of the guys are named James Parker, but maybe there's a connection."

Brandon stared at the paper, but didn't move.

"What is it?" Candice finally asked.

"It's just . . . what does all this have to do with Siobhan?" Brandon asked. "The letter says *she's* the key, not James Parker. He's probably keeping himself anonymous because he doesn't want the focus to be on him."

"Trust me, Brandon. This is important. The more information we have about him, the better. Plus, some of these guys might lead to more information about Siobhan too."

Brandon took a deep breath, then nodded. They began their Internet search, moving down the list name by name. They were able to find information on most of them. About half had passed away. And as far as they could tell, none of them still lived in Lambert.

"Back to the athletic director, Adam Douglas. Is there any way he could be James Parker?" She had checked—he was the only white teacher at the school that year.

"I don't think they're the same person. The chin, nose, and eyes are all wrong." He glanced at his notes. "Plus, according to his obituary, he was still teaching at Perkins when James Parker was running all those companies in Colorado. There's no way he could do both."

Candice twirled a strand of hair around her finger. Her fancy hairdo for church had lasted less than a day. "Do you have the link to the obituary? Maybe he had a son."

Brandon reopened the website. "Looks like he had a son named Charles Douglas."

"Okay, so maybe *he's* James Parker."

"I guess that's possible. But we don't know if he even knew Siobhan. He could have been ten years older. Or younger."

Candice reached for the Perkins yearbook, then stopped herself. Charles Douglas wouldn't be listed there either. "We should go back to the high school to see if we can find some old Wallace High yearbooks. And maybe we could have Deacon Draper bring the photos there now. If my schedule is right, Milo should be heading to the pool soon."

Brandon nodded. "I'll call Ms. McMillan."

After he left the room, Candice opened the yearbook and flipped to the photo of the tennis team. Adam Douglas and Enoch Washington stood in the back, behind their players. A black man and a white man, side by side.

She wondered if they were friends.

CHAPTER 20

Enoch Washington

July 24, 1957

Big Dub rattled the ice in his almost-empty glass as Robert Hicks, the Perkins football coach, pulled up to his house. It was just past nine o'clock at night. The mulberry tree in his front yard swayed in the warm breeze. Dub stood up from his rocking chair, folded his well-worn copy of the *New York Times* under his arm, then finished off his scotch. It tingled as it slid down his throat.

"Already getting started, Dub?" Robert asked as he walked across the grass. Dub had mowed the yard that morning, and clippings still littered the concrete carport.

"I'm celebrating!"

"That's what you been saying for the past two weeks." Robert laughed. "You'd think you were the one playing in Wimbledon."

"I saw her play once," he said. "In high school."

Big Dub picked up the bottle of scotch for a refill, but Robert stopped him from uncapping it. "Slow down there. Save some drinking for the game."

"I saw Althea Gibson play once," Big Dub began again. "She was better than every other Negro on the court." He pushed the newspaper into Robert's hands. "And now she's better than all the whites."

Robert looked at the newspaper. It was folded to an article about Althea Gibson's ticker-tape parade in New York City, a celebration of her victory at Wimbledon. She was the first Negro to win a singles tennis championship there. "Your cousin from up North sent this to you?"

"Came in yesterday." He tipped his glass again, letting the last drops of scotch and melted ice hit his tongue. "That could be Lil' Dub in a couple of years. She could win Wimbledon. She could win them all."

"And when's the last time she picked up a racket?"

"Silly girl. So stubborn."

"Wonder where she got that from?"

Big Dub let out a sigh. Lil' Dub had even stopped accepting the crossword puzzles he used to buy for her. "I ain't gonna fight about Siobhan with you. I get enough of that from Leanne. But that girl is gonna play tennis whether she likes it or not. She will if she wants me to pay for college."

"Good luck with that," Robert said.

"You don't have kids. You don't understand," Big Dub said. "A parent's job is to protect their children, even from themselves. *Especially* from themselves."

"I think Lil' Dub might have other ideas about that." He pulled his keys from his pocket. "Come on. The sooner we get to Smitty's, the quicker I can win his money." Their friend and fellow teacher, Dwayne Smith, lived on farmland on the county line. They played cards at his house once a month, though they usually did more bragging than actual playing.

Robert pulled out of the yard and started down the street. "Turn left here," Big Dub said. "Take Loyola."

"Why?"

"Just do it. I want to see something."

Robert did as Big Dub instructed. He typically took Darling Avenue to the highway, as it avoided most of the white areas of town. But today, Dub was directing them right into a run-down white neighborhood.

"Slow down," Big Dub said. They neared a bar called The Watering Hole.

"Dub . . ."

"He's there," he said, slapping his hands on the Oldsmobile dashboard. "Turn in."

"You crazy?"

"I ain't going inside," he said. "Just want to leave something on Coach Turner's car." Coach Thomas Turner was the science teacher and tennis coach at Wallace High School. His boys' team had won the state championship that year. Dub often said that his boys would have won a championship as well—if there were enough colored high school teams in the state to *have* an actual tournament.

Robert turned on his signal but didn't enter the dirt parking lot. "Why you wanna start something with Coach Turner? What'd he ever do to you?"

"Nothing. And that's the problem." Dub folded the paper, making sure the photo from the ticker-tape parade was front and center. "Come on. I want Coach to know that tennis ain't a white-boys-only sport anymore."

Robert tightened his grip on the wheel as he steered into the parking lot. He stopped the car and scooted down. "Now hurry up. I'm not trying to get lynched because of you."

Dub opened the car door and stepped into the dark night. He slipped the paper underneath the windshield wiper, then ran back to the car, an alligator-shaped grin plastered across his face.

It was almost midnight when a car sped into Dwayne Smith's driveway.

"Who in the world is that?" Smitty asked, stumbling from the table. He'd lost all of his poker chips long ago, but since it was his house, Robert and Dub let him continue playing. He glanced out the window. "It's Coach Douglas."

"What's Adam doing here?" Dub asked. "One of y'all invite him to the game?"

Smitty opened the door for Adam Douglas. He surveyed the men in the room, then leveled his gaze on Dub. "Tell me the truth. Did you leave that newspaper on Tommy Turner's car?"

Dub smiled. "Maybe."

"Dammit, Dub!" Adam slammed his fist into his palm. "They're on their way over here now. Should be here any second."

Dub took a sip from his glass. "Fine, let them come."

Just then, a car horn pierced the night. Everyone in the room jumped.

Adam ran to the window. "Shoot. It's them."

The horn sounded again. Three long bursts. Big Dub and Robert joined Adam at the window while Smitty ran to the kitchen. "I guess they didn't like that article," Dub said, chuckling.

"This ain't funny," Adam said. "Robert, hit the light on the front porch."

Smitty returned carrying a shotgun and a case of shells. "What do you think you're doing?" Adam asked him.

He loaded the gun barrel. "I got a right to defend myself. They're trespassing."

"And you're drunk. And they're white. You'd be arrested, convicted, and hooked up to the chair before you could blink." Adam glanced outside again. "They ain't carrying. Let me go out and talk to them. Find out what they want."

Big Dub moved toward the door. "I'll come with you."

"Absolutely not," Adam said. "Wait here. I'll be back in a second."

The others crowded around the window as Adam stepped on the porch. "Turn off your brights," he called. "I can't see you."

The car headlights went dead. Dub let his eyes adjust to the dark. He could make out four men as they walked toward the house. Three he recognized as teachers from Wallace. The other was Marion Allen, the son of one of the most powerful men in the city — something Marion made sure everyone knew.

"Your coaches are paperboys now?" Coach Turner asked, holding up the newspaper. "And don't lie and say it wasn't Dub. Rich saw him in the parking lot."

"It was a joke, Tommy," Adam said.

"You see anybody laughing?" Marion Allen slurred, his two eyes narrowing into blue pinpricks. Big Dub didn't think he was armed, but he couldn't be sure. And if he was, Dub wasn't about to let Adam get hurt over something he started. He didn't always like the man, but Adam Douglas had always done right by him.

Big Dub blinked and shook his head, hoping to clear the static from his brain. All that scotch didn't seem so smart now. But he felt calm.

In control. He wasn't going to let those good old boys bully him around.

"Smitty, have that shotgun ready," he said. Then he stepped outside, his feet heavy against the creaking porch.

"Hey, Dub," Coach Turner said.

"Hello, Coach," Dub acknowledged, tipping his head. "Is there a problem out here?"

"I sure as hell think there is," Marion Allen said. He charged ahead, then stopped at the base of the porch steps.

Dub didn't slouch. Didn't show any cowardice. He wanted Marion Allen to see just how big and bad he could be.

"We're sorry about the newspaper," Adam said, stepping between Dub and Marion. "Now y'all go on home. Tommy, we can sort this out tomorrow, once we've all sobered up."

"You think coloreds are better than whites, boy?" Marion Allen asked.

"I never said that." Big Dub had to work hard to keep his body still. To keep from going down those steps and grabbing Marion Allen by the throat.

"Nobody cares about some colored girl winning a tennis match in England," Marion said.

"The people of New York City cared. They threw her a parade."

"I don't care what they do up North," Marion said. "I bet my little brother could whip that black—"

"Marion!" Coach Turner snapped. "Enough!"

Marion smirked. "All I was gonna say was that I bet my brother could beat any of the boys on Dub's team."

That was most definitely *not* what Marion Allen was about to say. Big Dub almost said as much, until he got a better idea. He crossed his arms and stared at Marion Allen. "Prove it."

"What?"

"Prove it. Have him come out and play against one of my boys."

Marion didn't seem to know how to respond. He gave off a weaselly chuckle as he looked at the men behind him.

"As good an idea as that may be, we both know that ain't gonna happen," Coach Turner said. "Now come on, Marion. Let's go."

"Why can't it happen?" Big Dub asked. He moved so he could look directly at Coach Turner. "Why not?"

Coach Turner rolled his eyes. "Adam, will you tell your tennis coach to shut up?"

Adam Douglas didn't speak for a few moments. He slowly rubbed his face, then let out a long sigh. "You know, Tommy, I think Dub might be onto something."

"You serious?" Coach Turner frowned. "Well, just because you're a fool to support this doesn't mean my athletic director and principal will let—"

"Then don't tell them," Dub said. "Y'all just built new courts at your school, right? Behind the gym, hidden from the highway?" He leaned against the porch railing. A splinter dug into his hand, but he wasn't about to wince. "Just a friendly little tournament. An exhibition. Nothing official. That is, unless y'all are too scared—"

"Enoch," Adam said. "I think he gets the point."

Big Dub's grin widened. "What do you say, Coach Turner?" He reached out his hand. "Instead of all this talk, let's settle it on the court. Your boys against mine."

Coach Turner scratched his chin. "No tricks. No publicity. Just us and the boys?"

"Just us and the boys," Big Dub repeated. "Do we have a deal?"

Coach Turner walked to the porch and shook his hand. "I'll call Adam tomorrow to sort out all the details."

Marion Allen pointed at Big Dub, then spat on the ground. "Boy, you gonna regret this day for a long time."

Robert and Smitty exited the house as Coach Turner's car pulled onto the street. Adam's face was twisted into a tight frown. "Dub, I just put my neck way out there for you. I hope you know what you're doing."

"What, you think we're gonna lose?" Big Dub asked.

"No," Adam replied. "I'm worried we're gonna win."

CHAPTER 21

Candice's schedule held up as they biked through the neighborhood—not a single Milo sighting. They reached the high school to find the door was propped open, so they walked in and headed straight to the memorial.

"I'm so glad y'all came back," Ms. McMillan said to them. "Sorry I had to rush off on Friday, but I can stay for longer today. What can I help you with?"

"Thank you for the yearbook," Candice said. "Can we look through some other yearbooks? Both Perkins and Wallace?"

"Sure thing. What years?"

"Maybe 1954 to 1960?"

"Give me a few minutes to find them—they're all boxed up I think. Oh, and Deacon Draper dropped off something for you two over there." She pointed at a pair of boxes stacked on top of a dolly.

They rushed over to the dolly as soon as Ms. McMillan left. Both boxes seemed to be filled with dusty photo frames. "Nobody's touched these things for a long time," Brandon said.

They slipped off their backpacks and began to look through the top box. The first few photos were pictures of former pastors.

"Here it is!" Brandon said once he reached the fourth frame. He picked up the picture of the Washingtons and leaned it on his stomach to get a better look at it.

"You're getting covered in dust."

"Good thing Mom makes me wash my own clothes," he said. "It's them, all right. And look at the date."

Candice stepped closer and read the caption.

Enoch, Leanne, and Siobhan Washington
August 10, 1955

"August tenth, the same date as the letter, the website, and the tennis game," Brandon said. "Way too many coincidences."

Candice searched the photo, looking for a clue. "According to the letter, Leanne Washington volunteered with the church. Whatever she did, it was important." She glanced at the remaining photos in the box. "Maybe there's more there. You study that picture while I keep looking."

The remaining photos in the top box were pictures of other families and church groups. She read each caption, but nothing seemed like it was tied to the Washingtons. The second box contained more of the same. It wasn't until the last photo that she saw Leanne Washington again.

"Take a look at this," she said to Brandon as she wiped the glass with the edge of her shirt.

"Who's covered in dust now?" he asked, smirking.

"Funny. I think that's Mrs. Washington." Leanne stood in the center of a group of women who were all holding different types of dessert. Leanne Washington was holding a pie. The caption read: *Mount*

Carmel Missionary Circle prepares a bake sale to raise funds for Briggs v. Elliott. March 14, 1951.

Brandon leaned over and studied the photo. "Missionary Circle? My grandma used to be a member. I thought all they did was visit sick people and gossip."

"My mom was asked to join one at our church, and politely declined," Candice said. "Any idea what *Briggs v. Elliott* is? Sounds like a law case."

"We can look it up. The Wi-Fi password is on Ms. McMillan's desk."

Candice placed the photo on top of a table. "Okay, so Leanne Washington was involved with the Missionary Circle. And Enoch Washington loved baseball. The letter, the photo of the Washingtons, Siobhan's memorial website, and the trophy were all dated August tenth. But this photo of the Women's Missionary Circle has a different date."

"These clues make no sense. How do they lead to the hidden money?"

"James Parker. He's the key to tying this together," she said. "Think about it. He funded this memorial room and the church building renovation—"

"Technically, we don't know if he was the anonymous donor for the church. . . ." Brandon sighed. "But he probably was. It's just—"

"I'm back! Hope I'm not interrupting anything," Ms. McMillan said, stepping into the room. "I found the books, but they're pretty heavy." She sized up Brandon. "Why don't you come with me? I could use some help carrying them."

"I'll take some notes and put these back up," Candice said, nodding toward the photos.

Brandon handed her Tori's phone. "You should probably take pictures as well," he said as he and Ms. McMillan headed out.

Candice quickly snapped pictures of all the photos, then placed the frames back in the boxes.

Had her grandmother gotten this far? And if so, how did she get from here to digging up Vickers Park? She reminded herself to talk to Brandon about going to the park that week. Hopefully there would be another clue there.

Parker. It all came back to him. She pictured him in a tuxedo and top hat, pulling at their marionette strings. Laughing with every wrong move they made.

Candice walked toward a wall filled with awards and plaques. She quickly found the plaque with James Parker's name on it. It was simple: brown wood and a black engraved plate with gold trim. She had to stand close to read the text.

> *In memory of the fine students*
> *of Ada Marie Perkins High School*
> *—James Parker, Chairman*
> *New Air Foundation*
>
> *I, too, sing America.*
>
> *I am the darker brother.*
> *They send me to eat in the kitchen*
> *When company comes,*
> *But I laugh,*
> *And eat well,*
> *And grow strong.*

Tomorrow,
I'll be at the table
When company comes.
Nobody'll dare
Say to me,
"Eat in the kitchen,"
Then.

Besides,
They'll see how beautiful I am
And be ashamed—

I, too, am America.
—Langston Hughes

Candice ran her hand along the words of the poem, then traced her finger across James Parker's name. The lettering was rough against her fingertips. Who was this man? What would make him go to so much trouble to honor a school he never attended? To reward a church he had never been a member of? And what happened to make him disappear all those years ago?

Did he really love Siobhan Washington, and did she love him back?

CHAPTER 22

Candice had just sat down at a table and logged onto the Wi-Fi when Brandon and Ms. McMillan returned.

Brandon dropped the books on the table. "They're heavier than they look."

She reached for one of the Wallace High School yearbooks while Ms. McMillan went to the storage room for the Perkins yearbooks.

Brandon eyed the laptop. "Did you have a chance to look up the court case?"

She shook her head. "I wanted to find the plaque with James Parker's name on it."

"Anything of interest?"

"No, I don't think so." She handed him Tori's phone, then opened the yearbook. "Maybe we'll learn something about him in here."

"Okay, why don't you pass me your laptop and hand me your notes. I'll look up Briggs v. whatever it was while you go through the yearbooks."

Candice decided to start by searching for Adam Douglas's son. She began with 1960 and worked her way backward, eventually finding him in the 1956 yearbook. He was a senior then. His nickname was Chip.

"Hey, can I use the laptop?" she asked. "I want to look up a picture of James Parker to compare him to Charles Douglas."

"In a second," Brandon said as he quickly scribbled something down.

"What? You found something?"

"Maybe." He turned the laptop so she could see it. "*Briggs v. Elliott* was a court case in Summerton, South Carolina, in the fifties. It challenged school segregation."

"I heard about a case like that. I thought it was called—"

"*Brown v. Board of Education*. That was the one that went before the Supreme Court. *Briggs v. Elliott* was actually one of five cases that made up the complete *Brown v. Board* case." He scrolled down the page. "It's really interesting. They won the Supreme Court case in 1954, but the states still fought desegregation. For years in some places."

"Did it take a long time here?" she asked.

"I don't know," Brandon said. "I'm pretty sure Perkins was always known as the black school, up to when it was closed."

"So . . . Leanne Washington was raising money to fight segregation," she said. "That makes sense, according to the letter. Integration helped Lambert's children—at least the black ones."

"The white ones too," Brandon said. "Who wants to go to a school where everyone looks the same?"

"Yeah, but . . ." Candice shrugged. "My mom graduated from an HBCU—Clark Atlanta. I heard her give a talk about it once. She said she loved it—she felt challenged, and she felt safe. I think she'll die a little inside if I decide to go somewhere else."

"Tori was talking about that school. Or maybe it was Spelman," Brandon said. "Though I think only because she wants to live in Atlanta."

"It's a great city," Candice said. She shook her head—she didn't want to talk about home right then. "Can you pull up a picture of James Parker?"

Brandon did as she asked. Candice squinted at the screen, then back at the photo of Chip Douglas. His father was a closer match than him. "Okay, so it's probably not him. Maybe James Parker was a student at Wallace. It's worth a look."

They divvied up the yearbooks and quickly flipped through the pages. No students were named James Parker.

They then spent the next two hours slowly paging through the Wallace yearbooks again, writing down the name of anyone that remotely resembled James Parker. One by one, Internet searches dropped each person from consideration.

Candice crossed the last name off the list. "What are we missing? There's got to be a connection between Parker and this city."

"I know you don't want to hear this," Brandon began, "but maybe we're going about this wrong. I keep thinking about *The Westing Game*. Have you started it yet?"

She shook her head. "Sorry, I was too busy coming up with Milo's schedule."

Brandon rolled his eyes. "Okay, so I'll give you a pass. But you still need to read it. And soon." He tapped the table. "Anyway, I'm starting to wonder if we're missing a clue somewhere. I need to read that letter again."

"I've read it a thousand times," Candice said as she pulled the stack of Perkins High School yearbooks toward her. "I'll take my chances with these." Maybe Parker had been a teacher there earlier in the fifties. She opened the 1956. A few seconds later, she slammed it shut.

"What is it?" Brandon asked.

She shook her head, then blinked hard. The jagged purple words that had been scrawled across the page remained seared in her brain.

"Candice . . . ?"

"Someone wrote something in the yearbook. Something stupid and ugly and racist." She pressed down hard on the book, like she was trying to stop the words from escaping.

"Well, those were different times back then. I'm sure—"

"It's not old. They dated it."

Brandon gently moved Candice's hands from the book, then opened it. Candice could see his gaze floating across every disgusting word. "It's amazing how someone could insult black people, gay people, and women all at the same time," Brandon said. "And they didn't even spell the word right. Niger—with one *g*—is a country in Africa."

For some reason, that made Candice crack up. Then Brandon laughed. And once they started, they couldn't stop.

"What's got you two laughing so hard?" Ms. McMillan asked as she walked up to them.

Brandon wiped the tears away from his face. "Racists don't know how to spell."

"Come again?"

Candice picked up the yearbook and handed it to her. "Someone vandalized this." Now that she had been laughing, the words didn't feel so powerful anymore.

Ms. McMillan read the page. "Oh, I see." Then she smiled. "And yes, if they're going to go through all the hassle to vandalize one of my books, you'd think they'd check their spelling."

"Do you know who did it?" Candice asked.

"Probably some knucklehead who was forced to work in here during in-school suspension." She tucked the book under her arm. "I'll grab another for you. You can take it with you. I should probably be locking up soon."

"What about those photos?" Candice asked, nodding at the dolly.

"Don't worry about them," she said. "Deacon Draper said he'd send someone later this week to pick them up. But if y'all could help me push them in the corner, I'd appreciate it."

Candice and Brandon helped Ms. McMillan move the photos. Once they finished, Candice took the Wallace and Perkins yearbooks from 1956 and 1957 and slipped them into Brandon's backpack. "I promise, we won't mess them up."

"I trust you," Ms. McMillan said. "I hope you find what you're looking for."

The sun seemed way too bright when Candice and Brandon pushed the door open and stepped onto the sidewalk. He glanced at his watch. "According to your schedule, we've got about two hours to kill before Milo's tied up in another activity."

"Chili-cheese dog time?" Candice asked.

"Yep!" Then he snapped his fingers and patted his pockets. "I think I left Tori's phone in the memorial room." He went to open the door. It didn't budge. He banged on it a few times. "Hello? Anyone in there?"

Candice pulled out her mother's phone. "Any chance you remember Ms. McMillan's number?"

"No, but if I call my sister's phone, maybe Ms. McMillan will hear it." He took the phone and dialed the number. "Went to voice mail," he said after a few seconds.

"You can try again in a—"

A door directly to the left of them swung open. It would have smacked Candice in the head if she had been standing any closer.

"What in the world is going on out here?" A thin man in khakis and a polo glared at them as he stepped outside. His gray hair was slicked back on his head, and his skin was red, like he'd spent too much time in the sun.

"Hello, Mr. Rittenhauer." Brandon turned to Candice. "He's one of the assistant principals."

Mr. Rittenhauer let the door bang shut behind him, then crossed his arms. "You didn't answer my question. What are you two up to?"

"We're here for research," Brandon said. "We were in the memorial room—"

"Son, the only thing I hate more than a thief is a liar. Want to try that again?"

Brandon frowned. "Sir, I don't understand—"

"I've been here all afternoon. There aren't any teachers here to let you into the school, much less the memorial room." He pointed to the parking lot. "There's only one car out there. Mine."

Candice willed her mouth open. "Ms. McMillan is in there right now. I promise. Just check. We'll wait here."

"Like you would be here when I got back. You don't even look old enough to be high school students. Let me see your IDs," he said, snapping his fingers.

"I . . . I don't have an ID card," Candice said.

"Me either," Brandon said.

"Isn't that convenient," he said. "What are your names and your phone numbers? I'll need to call your parents—"

"But we weren't doing anything wrong!" Brandon said.

"Watch your tone, young man." He stepped forward. "And what's in those backpacks?"

Everything was happening too fast, and all wrong. Candice had seen her mother answer enough questions about her father to know how to handle people who were being rude or nosy. This was something else. Something darker.

The main door opened as she and Brandon unzipped their backpacks. Ms. McMillan stepped outside. "Brandon, you forgot your — oh, hello, Mr. Rittenhauer."

The assistant principal's mouth sagged open. "Ms. McMillan! What are you doing here? Where's your car?"

"My cousin's car is in the shop, so I let her use mine for the day." Ms. McMillan handed the phone to Brandon. "Here you go, hon. Good thing I caught you before you left."

Brandon kept his gaze on the ground as he stuffed the phone into his backpack. "Thank you," he mumbled.

Ms. McMillan frowned. "Brandon? Candice? Everything okay?"

"Everything's fine now," Mr. Rittenhauer said. "Just a little misunderstanding." He patted Brandon's shoulder, making him flinch. "You two go on home."

Candice's hands had already turned into fists and her eyes stung. It *wasn't* a misunderstanding. She knew that. So did Brandon. But that probably didn't matter.

"Thanks again for the books," Brandon said, finally looking up at Ms. McMillan. His eyes were watering, but no tears spilled out.

They grabbed their bikes and walked them away from the building. She didn't turn around to see if Mr. Rittenhauer was looking at them. She didn't want to know.

"I guess we'd better bring our IDs next time," Brandon said. He sputtered out a bit of a laugh.

"I don't even have a real ID card. Just one from school."

"Yeah. Me too."

They paused at the edge of the street. "Can we take a rain check on those chili-cheese dogs?" he asked. "I'm not really hungry anymore."

"Me neither," Candice said. "But what about Milo?"

"I'll take my chances," Brandon said. "I just really want to go home."

Candice nodded, then climbed on her bike and followed her friend.

CHAPTER 23

Leanne Washington

July 25, 1957

Leanne Washington walked into her bedroom and pulled back the curtain. Light flooded the room. Her husband groaned in bed.

"Get up, Dub," she said. "It's almost ten."

She returned to the kitchen and poured two cups of coffee. It would be her third cup of the morning. She'd been up early, calling the ladies to organize another fund-raiser. It seemed like there was always another battle to fight, and they all cost money.

A few minutes later, Enoch Washington shuffled into the room.

"Thanks for letting me sleep in," he said, grinning. "Game got a little crazy last night." He gave her a small kiss before picking up his mug. His scruff tickled her cheek, but not in a good way. Not like it used to.

"Coach Douglas called." She tried to keep her voice level and quiet. Dub called Coach Douglas by his first name, but he was the only Negro bold enough—or crazy enough—to do that.

"Let me guess." Dub settled into his chair. "He told you about the bet with Tommy Turner."

"He did." She picked up her mug, then set it back down, splashing coffee on the table. "What in the world were you thinking?"

"Don't yell," he said. "Lil' Dub—"

"I sent her out," she said.

"Where? You know she ain't allowed outside of this house without supervision."

"That's your rule, not mine." She grabbed a napkin and wiped up her coffee. "Siobhan's at the store, running some errands. Don't worry, she ain't off to see that boy, though that's the least of your problems right now."

Dub poured sugar into his cup. "It's just a friendly game, babe."

"Don't give me that. This is about you and your pride." She shook her head. "You just can't pass up a fight, can you?"

"Those white boys brag too much. I want a little justice."

"You want retribution against any white man that ever looked at you the wrong way." She tried drinking her coffee again. "Don't you know how hard we worked? How much we sacrificed? But now we're finally making some real headway. One day, colored children will go to integrated schools—"

"The NAACP won the *Brown* case three years ago," he said. "Last I checked, our kids were still at Perkins, dealing with secondhand books and busted-up equipment."

"Just because you don't see the path doesn't mean it's not there," Leanne said. "Progress takes time. We will succeed. But not if you keep trying to show up the other school. That's not going to help our cause."

He sighed, then took a sip of coffee. And then another.

Finally, he said, "What if . . . what if you're wrong about integration?" He put his hands up. "Hear me out. I've been thinking about

135

this for a little while. Take Althea Gibson. She graduated from Williston. A Negro school up in Wilmington. Then she attended Florida A&M. A Negro college. Then she won Wimbledon." He snorted. "She didn't need anything from them white folks."

"You mean, except for those white folks who fought so she could even play?" Leanne asked. "They ain't all our enemy."

"And what happens if the schools do integrate?" Dub continued. Leanne didn't think he was even listening to her. "Do you really believe white folks are gonna send their children to our school? They're gonna shut us down, fire all our teachers, and bus our kids off to the other high school. And I guarantee, those teachers don't give a damn about our kids."

"Coach Douglas does."

Dub crossed his arms. "If Adam really cared, he'd give up all that extra money he's making as athletic director and donate it back to the school. Or he'd step down so some of us could have a real shot at the position."

"Like you want to be AD," she said. "With your temper, you probably would have been fired a long time ago if not for Coach Douglas."

He picked up his mug. "Well, as long as he's in charge, I guess we'll never know."

Leanne took a sip of coffee. Siobhan would be back soon, and she didn't want to argue in front of her. Things in the house were already strained enough with Siobhan refusing to play tennis just to prove a point to her father. Leanne didn't agree with her daughter's choice, but she understood.

"Enoch, I followed you here to Lambert, even though I didn't want to come. I quit teaching and stayed home to raise our daughter because you asked me. Now I finally got something I'm good at. Something

I'm passionate about. And everything you're doing is putting that at risk."

"Like I said, it's just a friendly game. An exhibition. That's all, babe. I promise."

A small part of Leanne Washington wanted to believe her husband. But she had known Enoch for over twenty years. She knew when he was lying, even if he didn't know it himself.

CHAPTER 24

After leaving the high school, Candice spent the next few hours in her room looking through the Wallace yearbooks again, hoping to find anyone who could have been James Parker. She thought about calling Brandon to see what progress he'd made, but she didn't want to talk to him right then. It would have just reminded her of their run-in with the assistant principal.

Candice finally gave up when her mother poked her head in her room. "I'm about to start dinner? Want to help?"

Nodding, Candice crawled out of bed and followed her mom down the hallway.

"Got a taste for anything?" her mom asked. "There's plenty to choose from." Candice's dad had gone shopping while he was in town, and had stocked up on enough food to last for two weeks.

"You pick," Candice said. "I'm not really hungry."

Her mom grabbed a package of king salmon from the fridge and held it up to her. "Your father and his fancy foods," she muttered. "Grab a bowl. Why don't you start with the salad?"

Candice searched the cabinets for a large salad bowl while her mom pulled food from the refrigerator. They worked side by side for a while, cleaning all the food, neither speaking.

Finally, her mother asked, "Did something happen between you and Brandon?"

Candice began to pull the lettuce apart. "No. What makes you think that?"

"Juanita called about an hour ago. She said Brandon was pretty upset when she got home, but he wouldn't say why." She washed her hands, then patted them dry. "You sure everything's okay?"

Candice ripped the lettuce into even smaller pieces. It felt good to be doing something with her hands. "It's nothing. Something stupid — I mean, silly."

"*Stupid, silly* — I don't care what words you use." Her mother pulled the salad bowl away from her. "What happened?"

Candice could feel the sting behind her eyes again. "Someone vandalized one of the yearbooks we were looking at," she said. "And then the assistant principal accused us of trying to break into the school. Or something like that." She looked at the floor. "Probably because we didn't look like high school kids."

Her mom tilted Candice's face up. "Are you sure that's why?"

"Or maybe it's because we're black?" She said it like a question, like she was doubting what she knew was true.

Her mother opened her arms, welcoming Candice in.

"Why are people so mean?" Candice asked once she had explained what had happened. Her face was smashed into her mother's shirt. It was hard to breathe, but she didn't want to move. "We weren't doing anything wrong."

"Old habits — old opinions — die hard. He probably thinks all black kids are hoodlums."

"It's not fair."

"I know," her mom said, rocking and squeezing her tighter.

"Mom, you're smooshing me."

"Sorry." She loosened her grip. "It's taking everything inside of me not to jump in the car and hunt down this assistant principal right now." She leaned back so she could see Candice. "I'll call Juanita tonight. She and I will figure something out. What's his name?"

"Mr. Rittenhauer. But Mom—"

"No buts," she said. "I'm your mom. It's my job to deal with things like this. I want to make sure this doesn't happen again—to you or any other kid."

"What about your writing?" Candice asked. "Your schedule?"

"You're more important than that." She tapped Candice's nose. "You do know that, right? Whenever you need me, I'll always be there."

Candice nodded. "I know, Mom."

"Good." She let her daughter go. "Anything else you want to tell me?"

Candice returned to the bowl of lettuce. There were a million things they should be talking about: the letter, Milo, Brandon, her dad, Danielle. She pushed those things out of her head. Those weren't important. At least, not right then.

"Are we poor?" she asked.

"I'm a writer." Her mother smiled. "Of course we are."

"I'm serious, Mom. Are we really selling the house in Atlanta because it's too big? Or is it too expensive?"

Her mother took a deep breath. "Maybe a little of both. We don't need all that extra room. And it costs a lot of money to heat and cool that house. But yes, the mortgage is really expensive too. Even with your father's alimony, it's a lot for us to cover."

"Are we going to be okay once we sell the house?"

"Yeah, I think. There will be an adjustment. I may take on a few more writing projects."

"You've already got three."

"Maybe I'll teach," she said. "The community college is always looking for instructors."

"You always said you couldn't teach and write at the same time."

"So maybe I won't write." Candice opened her mouth to argue, but her mother cut her off. "Don't worry. Things aren't that bad. And your father and I always have a backup plan. Just in case." She looked at the fancy salmon. "Though I'll have to work on your father's spending habits."

Candice crossed her arms and pinched her sides. Since her mother was talking about money, maybe she'd be honest about a few other things too. "Maybe when Dad's at home, he's not buying groceries just for him," Candice said. "When I hugged him the other day he smelled like he was wearing a new cologne. It was citrusy."

Her mother began pulling spices from the cabinet — salt, pepper, paprika, thyme, and oregano. Then she grabbed the cooking wine. It wasn't very strong at all, not like real wine, but Candice still felt a little sophisticated whenever her mother used it.

"He *does* have a girlfriend, doesn't he?" She moved to block her mother from the fish. "I heard you guys talking in the kitchen the other day. You mentioned someone named Danielle."

"I didn't say . . ." Her mother rearranged the spices on the counter. "You shouldn't eavesdrop. You can't always be sure you're hearing the right thing."

"So Dad's not seeing someone?"

"I didn't say that."

"So he is seeing someone!"

"I didn't say that either." She sighed. "This, my dear, is something you should take up with your father. All I'll say is—I just want him to be happy. I know I'm not the right person for him."

"You guys sound a lot alike, you know."

"That's what happens when you're married for a long time." She leaned in and kissed Candice's forehead. "Enough talk about your father and his love life. The big Juneteenth Festival is on Saturday. Do you want to go?"

"Um, sure," Candice said, grabbing a cucumber. "But shouldn't you be writing?"

"I'll get the writing done. I promise." Her mother rubbed some spice into the fish. "Your grandma started the festival when she was city manager. She always saw it as one of her best achievements." Her mother paused, and Candice thought she would say more, but she just flipped over the fish to season the other side.

Candice began to cut up the cucumber. "Can I invite Brandon to the festival too?"

"I already did. I talked with his mom about it this afternoon. I figured it would be good to have some friends there for moral support."

"Oh? Why?"

"Because it's at Vickers Park," her mother said. "The scene of the crime."

CHAPTER 25

On Tuesday, after a little needling from Brandon, Candice put the Wallace yearbooks aside to help him run web searches for anything related to the Luling Oilers baseball team or school desegregation in Lambert—since both related to Siobhan's parents. But after a few hours, it was clear they weren't making any real progress. Every once in a while, when Brandon stepped out of the room, Candice went to the Atlanta real estate webpages to see if her house was on the market. It wasn't there. Yet.

Later that afternoon, after running more web searches that didn't yield anything, Brandon said, "I've been thinking . . . your grandma wasn't the only person who got a letter. Parker contacted four other people." He reached for the letter and opened it. "*The mayor, the school district superintendent, the chair of the school board, and the editor of the* Lambert Trader," he read. "Maybe we should look for those people."

Candice was already shaking her head. "No way!"

"Why not? They may know something."

"Well, if they did have information, they should have used it to help my grandma. Maybe they would have found the money. Maybe she wouldn't have gotten fired."

Candice rubbed her grandmother's bracelet. *Maybe she wouldn't be known as the crazy lady*, she thought.

"For all we know, they'll want to split the money with us," Candice continued. "Or worse, they'll tell my mom and she'll shut us down." She reopened the Wallace yearbook. "How about this—if we're still stuck tomorrow, then we'll call them and ask about the letter."

Brandon scratched his head. "We have to tell an adult about the letter eventually."

"I know," she said. "But not yet, okay?"

The following day, instead of heading over to Brandon's first thing in the morning, Candice began *The Westing Game*. It was good. Really good, though she didn't plan on admitting that to Brandon.

Candice had just reached the part where a second bomb went off when the phone rang.

"It's me," Brandon said. "Can you come over?"

"Um, yeah. I think."

"Bring the 1957 Perkins yearbook," he said. "I want to show it to someone."

"Brandon . . ."

"We're not going to talk about the letter," he said. "Just hurry up and get over here."

She peeked in her mother's office and told her that she was heading to Brandon's house. Her mother responded with a half-hearted wave, which Candice took as permission.

"It's open," Brandon called after she rang the bell.

She followed Brandon's voice to the kitchen. He sat at the table with his grandfather and a woman she'd never seen before.

"This is Ms. Kathy," Brandon said. "My granddad's . . ."

Candice rolled her eyes. The boy couldn't even say the word.

"*Girlfriend* ain't a bad word," Ms. Kathy said as she stood up from the table. Candice went to shake her hand, but the woman wrapped her in a hug. Ms. Kathy was fairly heavy-set—her mother would have used the term *big-boned*—and she squeezed Candice hard enough to make her lose her breath.

"So you're Ms. Caldwell's granddaughter," she said after letting her go. "She was a good woman. Passed away too soon."

Candice nodded. It seemed like *everyone* in the city knew her grandmother. Mr. Gibbs held the chair for Ms. Kathy as she sat back down. Candice put the yearbook on the table, then sat between him and Brandon.

"Thanks," Brandon said. "I was telling Granddad and Ms. Kathy about our research—"

"Yeah, *research*," Mr. Gibbs said, grinning. "Back in my day, we called it courting."

"Granddad," Brandon groaned as the adults laughed. "You promised."

Candice could feel her face burning.

"Granddad suggested we interview some people who may have attended Perkins back then," Brandon said. "And then Ms. Kathy offered to help us find them."

"I'm a Perkins alum as well," she said. "Class of seventy-four. A lot of older alums moved away. Lambert lost a lot of jobs when I-26 was built to the north and then again when the textile plant and auto factory shut down."

Candice assumed the textile plant she mentioned was the one owned by the Allen family. And the auto factory must have been the Solara plant that Parker relocated to Colorado.

Ms. Kathy adjusted her glasses. "I don't know many of the alums from the fifties, but I figured it wouldn't hurt to see if any names rung a bell." She took the yearbook from Candice. "1957. I was a baby back then. Still in diapers." Ms. Kathy opened the book and began flipping through the pages. She would mumble a name to herself every so often before shaking her head. It seemed like most of the people she knew had died, or moved for work, or moved to be close to their kids.

Then she paused. "Hmm. Maybe . . ." She positioned the book so Mr. Gibbs could see it. "Is that Ellie Farmer?"

"Yeah. Could be," he said. "I'm pretty sure her maiden name is McElveen."

"She married Gene Farmer right out of high school, I think," she said. "Didn't they move to Columbia a few years ago?"

Candice scooted closer to Ms. Kathy so she could get a better look at the yearbook. Ellie McElveen was thin and dark-skinned, with black bangs straight against her forehead.

"I'll see if I can get her number," Ms. Kathy said.

Candice continued to stare at the photo. Something was tugging at her memory. "Do you mind . . . ?" she began as she flipped to the back of the book. Sure enough, she had seen Ellie McElveen in a photo with Siobhan. They were both members of the newspaper staff.

She slid the book to Brandon. As soon as he saw it, he grinned. "Do you recognize anyone else from this photo, Ms. Kathy?" he asked.

She glanced at it for a few seconds, then shook her head. "Afraid not."

"That's okay. Just finding this woman is a big help," Candice said. "Thank you."

"That's my sweetums. Always ready to pitch in." Mr. Gibbs leaned over and gave Ms. Kathy a peck on the lips.

"Kissing is the number one way to pass germs," Brandon said.

"I'm not spreading germs," Mr. Gibbs said. "I'm spreading *love*." Then he kissed Ms. Kathy again, this time longer.

Brandon pretended to gag.

"Don't frown, boy," Mr. Gibbs said when he pulled away. "You should try it sometime. Women like their men a little sweet."

"Granddad!"

Ms. Kathy laughed. "Let him be, Rudolph."

"Not too sweet, of course," Mr. Gibbs continued. "Can't be all sissified. Can't have your nose in those books all the time. But a kiss every now and then don't hurt nobody."

Candice saw the exact moment when Brandon stiffened during their exchange. It had only lasted for a second, but it had happened. Brandon didn't like the word *sissified*.

"Enough, Rudolph." Ms. Kathy handed the yearbook to Candice. "Glad I could be of some use. Makes me want to pull out my own yearbook. I was lucky. My son never got a chance to attend Perkins. They combined the schools the year before he reached high school."

"Isn't that a good thing?" Brandon asked. "Lambert High is much better than both Perkins and Wallace used to be, right?"

"Newer isn't always better." Ms. Kathy removed her glasses. "There's something special about being a Perkins graduate. Sure, our building was falling apart, and we didn't have the newest equipment. But we loved that school. The *community* loved that school. It didn't matter if you had kids there or not—if you were black, Perkins was *your* school. The same teachers that taught us history and math sang in the church choirs with our parents. Shopped in the same grocery stores. And a lot of them were alums as well. They were more than teachers. They were . . ." She shook her head. "I wish there was a better way to explain it."

"It's hard for you young'uns to understand," Mr. Gibbs said. "Nowadays, we expect you kids to go off to college. High school is just a stepping-stone to something else. But back then, especially for black folks, high school *was* our college. It meant something to wear your high school colors. It meant something to be a graduate. The entire community rallied around the school."

"Is that why you and Grandma used to always go back to Tennessee for your high school reunions?" Brandon asked.

Mr. Gibbs nodded. "It wasn't like we were going back to see classmates. They were our family. Our blood."

Ms. Kathy snuggled against him. "Maybe I'll get you to take me one day," she said. She was playing, but there was an air of seriousness to her voice.

"I'd like that," he said. He started to lean toward her. "Brandon, you might want to close your eyes."

CHAPTER 26

The next day, Candice sat in the front passenger seat of Tori's red Honda Civic as it crept up Highway 176 toward Columbia. They had lucked out. After Ms. Kathy found Ellie Farmer's number, they spoke to Mrs. Farmer on the phone, and she suggested they visit in person. Even better, Tori had the day off. It took a bit of coaxing (and Brandon promising to wash her car) but she eventually agreed to drive them.

Candice shifted the dashboard vent so the air conditioning wouldn't blow directly on her. She had offered to sit in the back, but Brandon claimed it for himself. Now he was slumped over in his seat, an open book cradled in his hands. He'd fallen asleep about twenty minutes ago.

"Should I wake him up?" Candice asked, turning around to look at him. "He's going to hurt his neck."

"He'll be fine. You should see how he sleeps at night. Can't even count the number of times he's fallen out of bed. So anyway, when will you guys tell me what's really going on with all this research?"

It took Candice a moment to process what Tori was asking. She tried to make her face blank. "I have no idea what you're talking about."

"I know Brandon's not working on a school project." She peeked at him in the rearview mirror. "Either y'all are up to something, or y'all are dating."

Candice's skin went supernova. "We're not dating!" Somehow she yelled and hissed it at the same time.

"I'm kidding. Brandon doesn't even know what 'dating' means. But if you're not dating, that means . . ."

Just as she had felt with Brandon, Candice *wanted* to trust Tori. It would be good to talk to someone else. Someone older—but not an adult. Someone who might actually believe them instead of calling them kids. Someone who wouldn't say anything too bad about her grandmother.

"Don't laugh, okay?" Candice readjusted the dashboard vent again. "I think—*we* think—there's a fortune hidden somewhere in town."

Tori didn't laugh, so Candice continued. She told her about the letter addressed to her grandmother, and how they believed James Parker wrote it. She even told her about the secret tennis game, and how the Washingtons had been forced the leave the city. Tori nodded with each revelation.

"What do you think?" Candice finally asked. "Are we crazy?"

"You're . . . imaginative," Tori replied. The navigation app on her phone directed her to turn onto the interstate. "I'm guessing you haven't told your mom yet."

"Mom was pretty mad at Grandma over this mystery. I don't think she'd like me picking up where she left off."

"You're probably right." Tori slowed as she passed a highway patrol car. Candice leaned over to peek at the speedometer. They were already going well below the posted limit. "Anyway, at least it gives Brandon something to do," she continued. "This has been a tough summer for him with Quincy gone. Quincy is his best friend. He's in Seattle with his grandparents."

"Milo's mom mentioned something about that."

"Yeah, I bet she did." Tori shook her head. "Some people don't know when to mind their own business."

Candice knew Tori was talking about Mrs. Stanford and not her, but she still took that as a sign not to ask any questions. "I don't think you have to slow down so much," she said, looking at the speedometer again.

"Sorry." She sped up a little. "Just don't trust the police. I don't want to give them any reason to stop me. You know about all the black people getting killed or hurt by the cops, right? Even when they're unarmed?"

Candice nodded. She didn't follow the reports too much—her dad didn't like her looking at violence, even if it was on the news. Still, there was no way to avoid hearing about it.

"It's not like I think all police officers are bad," Tori said. "But I also have a lot less to worry about if I don't get pulled over. Plus, Mom would yank my driver's license if I got a ticket. The last thing I need—"

The phone spoke up again, cutting Tori off. She turned on her signal and moved to the right lane.

"Thanks again for agreeing to take us," Candice said.

"No problem. If not for this, I'm pretty sure Mom would have us doing something else to stay out of the house." She checked the dashboard clock. "Any second now, the school district superintendent should be showing up there."

"Really?"

"Yep. Our moms talked to Mr. Rittenhauer and the principal yesterday about what happened to you and Brandon at the school. I guess

151

they didn't like what they heard, so they called the superintendent. He thought it would be better to come to our house instead of our moms making an appointment in the office. Probably wanted to avoid a paper trail." She laughed. "Your mom is a real firecracker, by the way. I overheard her talking to my mom last night. She's very . . . colorful when she's mad."

"I can't believe they're going through all this trouble because of us."

"It's not the first time Mr. Rittenhauer has mistreated black kids."

"Will he be fired?"

"Probably not. But that doesn't mean our moms shouldn't speak up." She jerked her head behind her. "We're almost there. Better wake up Brandon."

Twenty minutes later, they turned into a gated subdivision. It reminded Candice of her neighborhood in Atlanta. Every yard was perfectly manicured with lush green grass. They passed a large playground and pool, both filled with laughing kids.

"I think this is it," Tori said as she parked in front of a large, two-story, redbrick house. A huge SUV sat in the driveway. It must have been new; it didn't even have a real license plate.

Candice didn't notice the older man in the yard until he stood up from behind a hedge of red tips. His knees were covered with rich black dirt, and he wore a pair of green gardening gloves.

"Can I help you?" he asked as they stepped out of the car.

"We're here to meet Ellie Farmer," Candice said.

"Oh, you're the kids she was talking about." He peeled off his gloves and hurried over to them. "I'm her husband, Gene."

Before they had finished shaking hands, a woman with a pink blouse and capris opened the door. Her gray-and-black hair was pulled into a short ponytail. "Daddy, what are you doing? The lawn guy will be here next week."

"Why pay for something I can do for free?"

"Are you at least wearing sunscreen?"

"This skin ain't getting no darker."

"Cancer, Daddy? You've heard of it, right?"

"I'm fine, Rosalie. Can you take these kids in to see Ellie?"

"I'm coming right back with the sunscreen." She turned to Tori. "I'm sorry for that. Momma's inside. She's been looking forward to meeting you all."

Rosalie led them through the house. Pictures lined the walls. Gene and Ellie Farmer had a big family.

"You have a beautiful home," Tori said.

"Thank you, but it's not mine. Momma and Daddy moved here a few years ago and insisted on getting a house large enough for all their great-grandkids to visit at the same time." Rosalie stepped into a large den. "Momma, your guests are here."

A small woman sat on a recliner, her stocking-covered feet up in the air. She clutched a soda can, with another within arm's reach on a small end table. A cane lay on the floor beside her.

"Where did that soda come from?" Rosalie asked. "Did Daddy get it for you while I was upstairs?"

"No," the woman replied. "I walked into the kitchen and got it myself."

Rosalie picked up the can from the table. "Please have a seat," she said to the others. "I'll bring cookies and lemonade. But none for you, Momma."

Candice, Brandon, and Tori huddled together on the couch. Now that they were there, Candice wasn't sure how they were supposed to start.

Ellie Farmer pushed a switch, lowering the footrest on her recliner. "I've got diabetes, high blood pressure, a hyperactive thyroid, and poor circulation in my legs. And she's worried about a little caffeine."

"Two cans is not a little," her daughter called from the kitchen. "And it's the sugar I'm worried about, not the caffeine."

"That girl hears like a hawk," Ellie said, quieter. She scooted forward in her chair. "What can I help you with? You had questions about Perkins High?" she asked, looking at Tori.

"I'm the chauffeur." Tori thumbed at Brandon and Candice. "These two are the junior detectives."

"We're interested in Siobhan Washington," Candice began. "We were looking through yearbooks and saw that you and Siobhan were members of the same club. Did you know her well?"

A small smile came to Ellie's lips. "That is a name I haven't heard for a very long time," she said. "Yes, I knew Siobhan. She was one of my best friends."

Candice felt Brandon sit up beside her. "What was she like?" he asked.

"Siobhan was one of the smartest girls I ever knew, though she never rubbed it in your face like other people. She loved puzzles, especially ones involving math."

Now Candice sat up.

"She was a whiz with numbers," Mrs. Farmer continued. "She could do math in her head, multiplying and dividing numbers that would take most people five minutes to figure out with pencil and paper. She got that from her daddy."

"What about tennis?" Candice asked. "Did she like that as much as her father?"

"Oh, she loved it. She was a great player. Her daddy wanted her to be the next Althea Gibson. Of course, back then we didn't have a girls'

154

tennis team. It was hard enough to have a boys' team. Not enough colored schools around to play against."

Rosalie returned, carrying a tray of cookies and lemonade. She placed it on the coffee table, then lightly touched her mother's shoulder. "I'll be outside."

Ellie nodded as Brandon picked up a cookie. "Can you tell us about the tennis game against the boys from Wallace?" he asked.

She adjusted the blanket covering her thighs. "I wasn't there. Siobhan was, though. The way she explained it, our boys beat those other kids in tennis fair and square. Whupped 'em like they stole something. But it was just a game. Once it was over, that was supposed to be the end of it."

"But it wasn't?" Tori asked. She was leaning in, just like Brandon and Candice.

Ellie Farmer shook her head. "Word started to spread that night. How could it not? The Perkins boys had just beat the best tennis team in the state. The best *white* tennis team in the state. Most of us couldn't care less about tennis, but that didn't matter. Our boys won. That meant something."

Candice was reminded of how Mr. Gibbs and Ms. Kathy talked about black high schools. Ellie Farmer sounded just as proud.

"Anyway, Marion Allen didn't like that a whole bunch of us knew about the game. He gathered up some of his buddies and attacked Coach Dub. Beat him and one of his players up real bad. Coach was never the same after that. But neither was Marion Allen. He lost his left eye that night." Her hands shook as she clutched her blanket. "What's worse—the cowards didn't just threaten Coach Dub and the boys. They threatened—" Her voice caught. "They threatened to do horrible things to Siobhan."

Candice had to turn away. She couldn't take the look on

Mrs. Farmer's face. It was like she was pained and sad and furious all at the same time.

"Of course, the police didn't do anything about it. Wouldn't even consider arresting Marion. If anything, they would have found a way to arrest Coach Dub." She sighed. "Siobhan and her family moved to Maryland. She came back a handful of times to visit, but never stayed too long. Think it brought up too many bad memories."

"What happened to Mr. Washington?" Brandon asked.

"He passed away a few years after they left Lambert," Mrs. Farmer said. "They built and dedicated the tennis courts at Vickers Park to him. He's buried in Maryland with—"

"Wait." Candice lurched forward. "I'm sorry—those tennis courts . . . they were dedicated to Coach Washington?"

Ellie nodded. "Sure were. I was there for the ceremony."

"Do you know when they were built?" Candice continued. "2006 or 2007?"

"Long before that," Ellie said. "It was back in the eighties. Siobhan was still alive. Came to the dedication and everything."

"Did they reconstruct them, or something like that, a few years later?" Candice asked. "Maybe with a private donation?"

The older woman shook her head. "Those tennis courts were perfectly fine until that crazy fool from the city went and had them dug up. I mean, come on. What was she thinking?"

Candice's stomach twisted into a knot as Ellie railed on her grandmother. Candice balled her fists up, and then shoved them underneath her thighs. As much as she wanted to argue, Candice could tell it would do no good. Ellie Farmer had long ago made up her mind, and there was nothing Candice could say to make her reconsider. She had to *show* her.

"Going back to Siobhan," Brandon said softly. "Did she ever date anyone when she was in high school? Or even after she left town?"

Ellie picked up a cookie. "She was married once, but very briefly. Otherwise, she never mentioned anyone serious. She never dated anyone in high school either. Of course, Coach Dub would have killed her and the boy if she had. No one was good enough for his Lil' Dub."

Candice wiped her hands on her jeans. "Mrs. Farmer, have you ever heard of James Parker?"

"Hmmm . . ." Ellie Farmer tilted her head and blinked a few times. "Can't say that I have. Why do you ask?"

"We think he knew Siobhan," Candice went on. "He donated a bunch of money to create the memorial room at Perkins. He spent most of his life in Colorado, but we thought maybe he grew up in Lambert."

"I know almost everyone who graduated from Perkins while I was there," she said. "Sure you got the name right?"

Candice shrugged. To be honest, she wasn't sure about anything.

"Well, I wish I could be more help with that," she said. "Anything else you want to know about Siobhan?"

Candice and Brandon looked at each other. "I think that's it," she said. "Can we call you if we have more questions?"

"Sure thing," she said. "Now I have a question for you. Did you bring any of those yearbooks?"

"We brought one," Brandon said. "It's in the car. I'll get it."

The door chimed as Brandon exited the house. Rosalie was with him when he returned.

"It's about time for your medicine," Rosalie said to her mother. "And then you need to lie down."

"I'm fine," she said. But Mrs. Farmer had begun to slump in her seat, and had yawned more and more as the conversation went on. "Where's that yearbook?"

"It's from your senior year," Brandon said, handing it to her.

She held the yearbook like it was fragile glass. "Want to see your mother when she was young and sexy?" she asked her daughter.

"Momma . . ." But Rosalie sat down on the armrest and watched as her mother opened the yearbook. Mrs. Farmer murmured to herself as she flipped through each page, pausing every once in a while to talk about someone from long ago. Candice couldn't tell if she was talking to her daughter or to herself. Or maybe she was talking to the people in the pictures.

Mrs. Farmer stopped on the page with Siobhan and ran her fingers across the photograph. "She was so kind. And generous," she said. "I wouldn't have graduated without her. And if I hadn't graduated, I would have never gotten that job at the telephone company, and I would have never met Gene, and . . ." Ellie's eyes were wet as she looked up at her daughter. "You have no idea how much we owe her."

Rosalie leaned over and kissed her mother on the forehead. Her eyes were wet too.

"Well, I really appreciate this," Mrs. Farmer said once she'd finished paging through the yearbook. She closed it and held it out to Candice. "It's nice to go back and—*where did you get that?!*"

Candice froze, her arms stretched forward, reaching for the yearbook. "Ma'am?"

"The bracelet." Ellie put the yearbook down in her lap, then grabbed Candice's arm, almost causing her to fall over.

Rosalie placed her hand on her mother's back. "Momma, you should calm down—"

"The bracelet," she repeated, cutting her daughter off. "Where did you get it?"

"It's . . . it's my grandma's," Candice said after a moment. She didn't want to admit who her grandmother really was, especially with the way Mrs. Farmer had talked about her.

"That used to belong to Siobhan. I'd recognize it anywhere." Mrs. Farmer traced a dark, wrinkled finger across the letters stamped into the aluminum. "See, right here. *SW*. For Siobhan Washington."

Candice's eyes widened. She had always thought the letters were *MS*. For Mississippi. She'd been sure of it.

Rosalie pried her mother's hand away from Candice. "It's getting late," she said. "Perhaps y'all should leave."

"Mrs. Farmer, do you know if Siobhan had anything engraved on the inside of her bracelet?" Candice asked, rubbing her wrist.

The woman pursed her lips together, then shook her head. "No, I never saw the inside. But I'm sure it's hers." Ellie Farmer frowned. "Or who knows. My memory isn't what it used to be." She picked up the yearbook and handed it to Candice. "When you get home, you be sure to ask your grandma where she got that from."

Candice took the yearbook. "Sure thing."

———————————————————————————

"Okay, what just happened back there?" Brandon asked as soon as they reached the car. "Is that really Siobhan's bracelet?"

"I don't know," Candice said. "Grandma never mentioned that it used to belong to someone else. But then again, Grandma didn't talk about a lot of things."

"And what was that about another engraving?" he asked.

"The word *Love* is stamped on the inside." She slipped the bracelet off her wrist and inspected it. "All this time, I thought the letters were *MS*. For Mississippi, where my grandmother was born." She knocked her fist against her forehead. "I'm such an idiot. I didn't realize I was looking at it upside down."

"But how could your grandmother have Siobhan's bracelet?" Tori asked as they pulled away from the house. "They never met, right?"

"No, I don't think so." The aluminum was cool in Candice's hands. "But who knows."

Brandon didn't speak for a long time. Finally, once they reached the interstate, he said, "You said your grandmother didn't find anything underneath the tennis courts, right? But what if that's not true?"

"You think she found the bracelet there?" Tori asked.

"It's the only way," he replied. "What do you think, Candice?"

But Candice was too busy staring at the bracelet to answer. If Brandon was right—if her grandmother *had* found the bracelet there, then her grandma might not have been off track. Maybe she was *supposed* to dig up those courts. Maybe this was another clue.

Maybe she hadn't made a mistake after all.

CHAPTER 27

Chip Douglas

July 31, 1957

Chip slung his duffel bag over his shoulder and rushed out of the pool locker room—the same locker room that Milo Stanford would use sixty years later. Chip's hair was wet, and his shirt clung to his damp skin. He paused to reach under his pant leg and scratch at the red splotches on his calf. He hadn't put on enough sunscreen during his shift. He'd pay for it come tomorrow, but he wasn't going to worry about it now.

He hesitated once he passed the pool's wrought-iron fence. Glenn Allen and some of the other lifeguards—his old teammates—remained in the parking lot, with Glenn's truck idling beside Chip's Chevy.

"Looking good, Chip," Billy Maynard said as Chip neared them. "Got a hot date? Me and Penelope can double."

"Get a real car and some real money, and I'll *consider* letting you date my sister," Glenn said through his open window.

Billy had had a crush on Penelope Allen for years, though she never gave him the time of day. Chip could empathize.

"Aren't y'all late for practice?" Chip asked. "Coach Turner's gonna have a fit."

"It's the middle of the summer," Glenn said. He revved his engine. "What's he gonna do?"

In the year that Chip had been away at college, Glenn had started to sound a lot like his older brother. "It's your funeral," Chip said.

Glenn stepped out of his truck. "You off to help the coloreds?"

Chip's fingers tightened around the strap of his bag. "I'm off to help my father."

"Who is helping the colored kids."

"It's his job," Chip said. "It's what he's supposed to do."

"Yeah, but it ain't your job," Harold Buckner said. If Chip had to, he figured he could take Glenn in a one-on-one fight. He wasn't so sure about Harold. "Know what I think?" Harold continued. "I think you like it."

"What if I do?"

Harold fished his tin of snuff from his back pocket and pinched off a piece. "How about that—you went off to that fancy college and came back a darkie lover." He tucked the tobacco in his mouth, between his cheek and jaw. "That's what happens when they let them use the same water as civilized people. You start to become contaminated. Good thing they can't swim here."

Yet, Chip wanted to add. *They can't swim here yet.*

Billy cleared his throat. He had moved to the bed of Glenn's truck, his racket in hand. His affection for Penelope Allen aside, Billy was clearly the most levelheaded of the three boys. "We could use your help, Chip."

162

"I can't play," Chip said. "You know the rules." Coach Turner and Big Dub had agreed to let this year's graduates participate, but no one older.

"But you've seen them in action," Glenn said, now leaning against Chip's Chevy. "You know their weaknesses."

"Y'all sound nervous," Chip said. "Think you gonna lose?"

"We ain't gonna lose," Glenn said. "But we want to beat them bad. Teach them a lesson."

Chip shook his head. "You guys will be fine. And don't forget, this is supposed to be a friendly game."

"I guess that's a no," Glenn said as he stepped away from Chip's truck. "And Chip, there ain't nothing friendly about this game."

Chip looked at himself in his rearview mirror, then patted down a tuft of hair at the top of his head. He had been to tennis practice at Perkins twice that week—mostly to give pointers to his dad about the players. He was also hoping Siobhan would stop by. He hadn't seen her all summer. He wanted to show her how much he'd grown, how much he'd changed during his year away at college.

He was so focused on getting to the school that he almost didn't see her walking along the street. But when she stopped to talk to a passing woman, she turned her head ever so slightly, just enough for him to catch a view of her beautiful brown face.

Siobhan!

Chip hastily pulled over. He was on Darling Avenue, the heart of Vista Heights. Barbershops, shoe stores, and other businesses lined the street. He could count the number of white people on two fingers. He'd been here before—meals at PJ's, a shoeshine at the stand outside—but only with his father. He didn't belong here, but he didn't care. He wanted to be anywhere she was.

She was still talking to the woman as he neared her. He didn't know how to explain it—she looked the same, but different. Her hair was pulled into its usual ponytail, and her checkered dress looked like the same type of clothes she'd wear any other day. She carried a small bag.

She turned and saw him. She seemed to falter for a second, then continued forward, toward him. He realized it was her stance and walk that were different. She stood taller; moved with confidence. She was no longer Lil' Dub.

"Hey, Siobhan," Chip said. "It's good to see you." He hoped she would hug him, but she kept her distance. "For a while, I thought I wouldn't run into you at all this summer."

She smiled and offered him a small nod. "Well, here I am." She repositioned the bag. Now that she was closer, he could see that she was carrying shoes. "What brings you out here?" she asked.

All of Chip's bravado melted away. "I, um, I was headed to the school but stopped when I saw you." He nodded toward her bag. "Can I carry that for you?"

"Oh, it's—"

He was already taking the bag from her. As he grabbed it, he noticed the thin metal bracelet around her wrist. "Since when did you start wearing jewelry?"

She quickly brought her arm up and covered her wrist. "Maybe the same time you started shaving every day?"

He grinned. Did that mean she noticed that he'd shaved? Did she think he'd cleaned himself up just for her? (He had, of course—he just didn't want her to know that.)

"You taking these shoes to the store to get fixed?"

"Just shined," she said.

"I'll walk with you." The shoeshine stand seemed to only be busy during the lunch hour at PJ's, as people — mainly white people — would get their shoes shined while they waited for their food. Today, two older Negro men sat in the chairs above, though neither was getting a shine. Two teenage boys sat on the platform beneath them.

"I heard you were helping to get the boys ready for the game," she said. "How do they look?"

"Good. Real good. You should come and see them."

"Daddy and I aren't really on speaking terms right now."

Chip hoped she didn't see the surprise on his face.

"And if you don't mind, I would appreciate you not telling him that you saw me," she said.

"Sure. But why? Big Dub got you under lock and key?"

"He would if he could." They stopped at the shoeshine stand. The older men stood, but Chip shook his head. "Y'all can stay there." He handed the bag to one of the boys sitting down. "We need these shined."

"Thank you," Siobhan said. "But shouldn't you get out to the school? Haven't they started practice already?"

"They're just warming up. I've got plenty of time." He looked at the other boy, who was tall, lanky, and light-skinned. "Can you run into PJ's and grab us a couple of Cokes?"

"Chip, really. I'm fine," she said.

Chip fished some change from his pocket. He bypassed all the nickels and dimes before finally picking up a quarter and dropping it in the boy's hand. "Appreciate it." It was a whole fifteen cents more than the Cokes cost. He hoped Siobhan would notice his generosity.

The boy stared at the quarter as if he'd never seen one before.

"Go ahead, boy," one of the men sitting in the chairs said. "Get the young sir a drink."

The boy curled his fist around the money, then headed into PJ's.

"You decided about college yet?" Chip asked Siobhan after a moment. "Still leaning toward Howard or Hampton?"

"I'm not leaning toward anything. I've still got a year left." She wrapped her arms around her body. "Chip, really, you should go. Why don't you ask me for one of those puzzles you could never solve?"

"In a second. This is important." He wanted her to know he was too old for games. "Some of the students from Georgetown have been meeting with the Howard kids," he said. "They're excited about what Dr. King did in Montgomery. Change is coming, but much too slowly. I want to do something to make things happen quicker."

"Like what?"

Chip hadn't figured out that part yet. He had been reading books and had gone to some lectures, but that didn't seem like enough. "Maybe I'll go down and help protest."

"That seems dangerous," Siobhan said.

Before she could say anything more, the boy returned with their two uncapped Cokes. He offered the change to Chip, but he waved it off and took a long pull of his soda. "Try it," he said to Siobhan. "It's ice cold."

Siobhan took a quick drink. "Thank you." Then she let out a breath. "Chip. *Charles.* You should head on to the school."

She looked around the street, and after a second, he did the same. A few Negroes shot uneasy glances at them. A white man glared as his car rolled by.

"I'll drop by the courts for a practice. Or at least for the game," she said. "You can tell me more about school then."

He nodded. "Sounds good." He left, hopeful he'd have another chance to prove his worth.

Practice was in full swing by the time Chip reached Perkins High School. Four boys played against one another on two of the courts. Big Dub and Jackie Harris, one of the school's best players, occupied the third court. Jackie looked pretty fatigued, but Big Dub didn't seem tired at all. He'd wait for Jackie to take a sip of water and get back into position, then Dub would fire another tennis ball across the net at him.

Chip joined his father in the bleachers.

"What took you so long?" his father asked.

"Had to make a quick stop." He nodded toward the court. "How long they been out there?"

"Just a few minutes," Adam Douglas replied after checking his watch. "Except for Jackie. Dub's had him out there for an hour already."

"His legs'll be rubber by next week if they keep that up."

"From your mouth to Dub's ears. But ignore them for now. Watch the others."

Chip studied the boys for the next two games, taking mental notes of what he saw. A year ago, he would have gone down there himself and tried to give pointers. But like he tried to tell Siobhan, he had learned a few things about race relations in his time away.

"Mordecai needs to open up when he's doing his backhand," Chip finally said. He watched a few more volleys. "Pratt looks good, but he gets too nervous. He's trying to hit an ace with every serve. Those courts at Wallace are too new. He's not gonna be able to control the ball like that."

His father jotted it down. "Me or Dub will talk to them about it."

Chip glanced at Jackie. The boy sat on the court, a towel draped over his head, while Big Dub squatted beside him. Chip couldn't tell what Dub was saying, but whatever it was, it didn't seem pleasant.

"Will they be ready?" Chip asked.

"Hard to tell. They're good. But so are Tommy's boys, and we're playing on their home court." He took off his glasses. "But that might be for the best. These boys don't need to win that game."

"It would mean so much to them," Chip said.

"In the short term, yeah. It would be great for our boys. Give them some confidence. In the long run . . . confidence is a very dangerous thing for a Negro boy to have 'round here."

Chip scratched the three blotches on his leg. "I've been thinking more about what we talked about the other day. Maybe joining the NAACP, or going South to help next summer."

"You keep thinking about that while you work at the pool next year."

"But—"

"I didn't save up all that money just to have you—" His father shook his head. "You're not about to throw your life away just to impress a girl."

"This doesn't have anything to do with Siobhan," Chip said.

His father glared at him. "This has *everything* to do with her. You've been hot for her since you were thirteen."

Chip didn't bother trying to tell his father otherwise. "It doesn't matter how I feel about her. It's still the right thing to do."

"Leave Siobhan alone," his father said. "Leave all these Negro girls alone. Focus on your books. Get your degree."

"There's nothing wrong with dating a Negro girl."

"No."

Chip stood up. His father was just as bad as the boys from the pool. "They don't have diseases! My skin won't suddenly turn dark if—"

"Boy, sit down!" Chip must not have moved fast enough, because a second later, his father had grabbed his arm and forced him back to sitting. "I don't know if it's the heat or if you got water on the brain or what, but you must have forgotten who you're talking to."

Chip rubbed his arm. "They aren't monsters."

"Don't you think I know that? I wouldn't teach here if I believed otherwise." He looked out at the court. Big Dub was showing Jackie how he wanted him to attack the net. "Enough of this. Focus on the game. If you want to help somebody, help them."

"You know, you were just a little older than me when you married—"

"Oh, what? So now you've gone from dating to marriage?" his father asked, throwing up his hands.

"I'm just—"

"First, we're both white. Second, I was in the army, not some dumb college freshman. And third, your mama didn't have a daddy like Big Dub. He would kill you if he knew you were trying to court his daughter."

"He wouldn't have to know. Not if she went to Howard."

"Forget about Dub for a second. You think those good old boys are gonna let you two date each other? It ain't even legal for a white person to marry a colored person in Virginia, much less anywhere else in the South."

"We could move up North."

"There are racists there too. How you gonna protect her? What you gonna do when people spit at you? Throw bottles at you? Attack you? Shoot, you don't even know how she feels about you. For all you know, she could be in love with another fella."

"I should at least try, right? You always said to go after what I wanted."

"I was talking about sports. Education. Not dating Negroes." His father rubbed his eyes. "Tell me this: How many times have you gone to a Negro church? Once? Twice? Better yet, how does it make you feel? Do you sway with the music? Do you want to jump up and clap your hands? Or do you just sit there, hoping that nobody's staring at you?"

Chip looked at his lap. That was answer enough.

"I don't care how many courses you take or how many books you read. You'll never understand what it means to be a Negro. You'll never face the discrimination they see every day. You'll never struggle the way they do. Now, enough talking. Here comes Dub."

Chip shielded his eyes as Big Dub walked over to them, his racket perched on his shoulder. Siobhan had definitely inherited her height from him.

"Hey, Dub," Chip said, stretching out his hand. "You're really working them today."

Big Dub shook his hand. "Got some pointers for the team?"

"Yep. Already gave them to Daddy."

"We can go over them tomorrow," Adam Douglas said as he stood. "So what do you think, Dub?"

Big Dub frowned at the court. "If we had two more weeks—"

"We don't."

Big Dub switched his racket to his other shoulder. "They're good . . ."

"But not good enough." Chip's father glanced at his son for a second, sighed, then turned back to Dub. "What you do think about bringing in your star player?"

"No."

"I thought you wanted to win." Adam Douglas shrugged. "But I get it. Winning ain't everything."

Chip looked at both men. "Who are y'all talking about?"

"Your daddy wants me to let Reggie Bradley back on the team," Big Dub said.

"Reggie?" Chip vaguely remembered hearing about the boy, but he couldn't place his face. "I didn't think he was that good."

"He got a lot better last year," Adam said. He hesitated, then said, "Turns out he was getting a lot of extra practice."

Big Dub narrowed his eyes. "We don't need Reggie."

"You want to punish the boy or do you want to win?" Adam Douglas placed his hand on Dub's shoulder. "Let me go talk to him."

Dub flexed his fingers. His face had twisted into a scowl. "I'll let him on if he wants to play," he finally said. "But that doesn't mean I approve of him and Lil' Dub's . . . *whatever*. And I'm still not gonna allow them to see each other."

Chip tried to keep his face steady. Siobhan had been seeing this Reggie Bradley boy while he was gone? And his father knew about it? Clearly Dub was mad about their relationship . . . was that why Siobhan and her father weren't on speaking terms?

Chip shook his head. He had just assumed . . . he just *knew* Siobhan liked him as much as he liked her.

"You know Reggie won't apologize," Adam Douglas said.

Big Dub started back down the bleachers. "Good. Neither will I."

Chip waited until Big Dub had returned to the court. "Why didn't you tell me?" he whispered to his father.

"Well, I'm telling you now. Not that Reggie had any better chance than you. Dub's not about to let his daughter date some high-yellow poor kid from Vista Heights. Boy doesn't even know who his daddy is." He checked his watch. "I'll be home late. It might take a while to convince Reggie to come back."

"Why can't you just call him?" Chip asked as they exited the stands. He didn't want his father talking to this boy. His . . . *rival*.

"Everybody don't have a phone, son. Plus, he ain't even home right now." He took a few steps, then stopped. "I know you think you're better than most whites, but you're not. You mean well, but you're not. To be honest, it's as much my fault as yours—I allowed it."

"What?" Chip said.

"That man is twice your age—older than me," his father said. "He's the father of the girl you supposedly love. And you can't address him as *Mister*? You can't call him *Sir*? Or even *Coach*?"

Chip replayed the conversation he'd just had with Big Dub. He tried to replay *every* conversation he'd had with the man.

"Tell your momma I'll be down on Darling Avenue," he said. "I'll pick up some PJ's for dinner."

Chip frowned. "I thought you were going to see Reggie."

"I am. He works at the shoeshine stand," his father said. "Want some fish too? The daily special?"

As much as he loved food from PJ's, Chip wasn't thinking about fried croaker and jalapeño hush puppies. He was thinking about the boy at the stand. The tall, lanky, light-skinned boy he had asked to buy two Cokes.

That boy.

That was Reggie.

CHAPTER 28

On Friday morning, Candice walked over to Brandon's house so they could go to Vickers Park. Even though they were planning to attend the Juneteenth Festival there the following day, Candice figured they'd have better luck looking around when it was quieter. Her mom might ask too many questions if she saw them hanging out around the tennis courts.

Tori opened the front door, said that she needed about ten more minutes, then told Candice that Brandon was shooting hoops. Candice stepped into the backyard to see Brandon carrying bricks across the lawn.

"Is this some old-school workout routine you're doing?" she asked as he dropped the bricks in the grass beside the basketball goal.

He wiped his face, leaving a streak of dirt across his forehead. Then he picked up a broom. "I'm hoping to use the bricks to prop up this broom. I need to practice shooting over a defender."

Candice walked across the lawn and took the broom from him. "Next time, you could just ask me to help." She held up the broom, the bristles at the top. "Is this high enough?"

"A little lower." Brandon asked her to take a step forward, then he grabbed the ball. He squared himself up and shot. The basketball hit the rim, but rolled in.

"I usually start here and work my way around the hoop," he said. "Just follow me around."

They began to move around the yard. "By the way, I really, really appreciate this," he said.

"No problem," Candice replied. She didn't want to admit it, but her arms were starting to burn from holding the broom. "Where'd you learn this from?"

"My friend Quincy. I used to practice with him and his dad. We're both small, so his dad had us working on getting more air under our arc." He smiled as he spun the ball in his hands. "Whenever Quincy held the broom, he would always try to yell to break my concentration." He shot the ball again. "But it never worked."

Candice lowered her arms and shook them out as Brandon chased the ball. "Did you ever try yelling at him?"

"All the time. And it worked too." Brandon chose a spot even farther away from the goal. Candice dragged the broom over to him and hoisted it up again.

"Quincy was never good with tuning out all the noise on the court—all the trash talk," Brandon said. He licked his lips as he readied himself to shoot. "Quincy would jump at every little—"

"AAAGH!" Candice yelled.

Brandon jerked his hands just as he released the ball. The basketball flew to the left, missing the hoop entirely. It crashed into the pile of bricks he had just been carrying.

Candice grinned. "Score one for me."

It took Tori more like twenty minutes to get ready, but eventually they were all on their way to Vista Heights. As they neared the park,

Candice found herself stewing over Mrs. Farmer's words about her grandmother.

Crazy.

Fool.

What was she thinking?

If their search in the park led them to Parker's fortune, and if the bracelet really was Siobhan's, then everyone would have to take back every mean thing they'd said about her grandmother. Candice ran her hands over her grandmother's bracelet. Or should she think of it as Siobhan's bracelet now, she wondered. It was hard to rewire her brain to see it differently.

Tori parallel-parked along Darling Avenue. "Y'all keep an eye out for each other, okay? I'll be right here." She thumped her brother on the head. "And don't do anything stupid."

Candice and Brandon exited the car. Vickers Park was definitely different than her community park back home. The playground was almost empty, with rust collecting on the swing chains and monkey bars. Most of the activity was at the basketball court, where a group of boys shot hoops and talked trash. Workers from the city were unloading tables underneath a pavilion — probably for the festival tomorrow. There was supposed to be live music, face painting, games, and even a rock-climbing wall. Candice just hoped Milo and his friends wouldn't be there to ruin it.

Candice started toward the tennis courts, but stopped when she realized Brandon wasn't following. He stared at the basketball game, his head going back and forth as the boys went up and down the court.

"You want to play?" Candice asked.

"No, I'm too young to play with them."

"Um, don't you remember how I just held up that broom for you?" she asked. "You could totally shoot over them."

Brandon shook his head. "Those guys talk a lot of smack."

"You could just ignore them," Candice said. "Or talk back."

But Brandon was already walking away. "Maybe another day. And anyway, that's not why we're here, right?"

Candice followed Brandon to the tennis courts. The fence surrounding the two green courts was as rusty as the playground equipment.

"You'd think with all the money he was throwing around, James Parker would have made a donation to this place too," Brandon said. A small wooden sign hung on the outside of the fence: *The Enoch Washington Memorial Tennis Courts.*

The asphalt on one court was old and deteriorating, with multiple potholes and fissures. The other was in much better shape, with smaller, hairline cracks and a newer net.

Candice walked to the center of the new court. "This must be the one." She took a deep breath. What had led her grandmother to dig up this court? Had she really found the bracelet there? And if so, why hadn't she said anything to anyone about it?

Brandon stood on the white boundary line, away from her. She didn't know if he was intentionally giving her space or not, but she appreciated that he kept his distance.

Her grandmother was not crazy.

She was not a fool.

"I know these courts weren't here when they held the secret tennis game, but maybe they found a way to play here anyway." She pointed to the basketball court. "Maybe they put up a net there."

He joined her on the tennis court. "I don't see how. It's so close to the street — too many people would have noticed it." Brandon tugged on the net. "I'll be honest — I'm not really sure what we're looking for. There's nothing in the letter about this tennis court."

Candice looked around. "Something led my grandma to these courts," she said. "There's got to be a clue here. Something with a date." She pointed to a bench along the sidewalk in front of the court. "Does that bench have a plaque on it?"

"Yeah, I think so."

"You check that out," she said. "I'll look at the benches over on the other end."

Candice had barely made it to the other side of the court when Brandon yelled her name. She turned to see him jumping up and down and waving his arms by the first bench he'd checked.

She ran to him. "Found something?"

"Oh yeah," he said, beaming.

The bench was old, and the plaque was scratched and tarnished, but Candice could still read the inscription.

In Loving Memory
Siobhan Mildred Washington
"She Loved All"

"She loved all," Candice repeated. "That's in the letter!" She fished it out of her pocket, then nodded once she opened it. "Yeah, right there." She looked back at the bench. "But the plaque's not dated."

"Can I hold the letter?" Brandon asked. After taking it, he sank to the bench and read over it. He looked up, blinked, then read the letter again, counting as he moved down the page.

"It's a clue," he finally said.

"Um, yeah, but what does it—"

"No. I mean, it's all clues. It's *full* of clues." He was talking too fast. "It's just like in *The Westing Game*, when—"

"Wait. I haven't finished it yet."

Brandon actually scowled at her. "You haven't?"

"If you haven't noticed, I've been a little busy."

"How far along are you?"

"I'm almost done."

"Good." He stood up. "Come on. You have to finish that book."

"You mean now?" Candice asked. "We should look around here more."

"We can come back if we need to." He started toward his sister's car. "Just finish the book. I'll ruin it if I say more."

CHAPTER 29

Siobhan Washington

August 9, 1957

At seventeen years old, Siobhan Washington did indeed love all.

But she loved Reggie Bradley the most.

Siobhan hadn't taken Reggie very seriously at first. He was a boy. A distraction. A small bit of defiance toward her father.

But as she got to know Reggie, she learned that he was more than just a boy. More than one of her father's tennis players. He was smart. He loved math. And he loved to read too. They would sit at the park, in the back, hidden from view, and would spend hours talking about books. *Black Boy. Native Son. Invisible Man.* They didn't always agree, but that was what made the conversation so interesting.

She especially loved when Reggie got to the park before her, like today. The sun had almost set, but the park was still full of kids. She stood behind a tree and watched as Reggie ran back and forth between four kids on the swings, pushing each one as they yelled, "Higher!

Higher!" Then he helped another child across the monkey bars, his hands lightly around her waist, ready to catch her if she fell.

Siobhan had asked him once why he played with the kids. His reply: *Because I didn't have anyone to do it for me.*

Reggie checked his watch after the girl made it safely across the monkey bars, and that was when Siobhan stepped out from behind the tree. She made sure that Reggie noticed her, then she continued on farther into the park, beyond the playground and basketball courts, underneath a canopy of oak trees.

She heard his footsteps a few minutes later. Even now, she still became giddy whenever he approached. He was tall and lanky, but he walked with a purpose. Like he had somewhere to be, like he was trying to do something with his life.

She rose from her spot underneath their oak tree. "I'm glad you got my note," she said. She had left word for him at the shoeshine stand, but sometimes the other boy forgot to deliver the messages. He took her hand then, and they sat down in the grass. "Your turn or mine?" he asked.

"Yours." Ever since their first meeting, they began their dates with a puzzle. Siobhan liked puzzles based on math. Reggie was more of a trickster—his riddles always had a twist.

She leaned in as he began: "One night, a king and a queen boarded an empty ship," he told her. "They set sail for France, sailing all day and night. When they landed, everyone on the boat went ashore. How many people got off the boat?"

Siobhan repeated the riddle in her head, trying to find the twist. Finally, she sighed. "I give up. Two?"

He grinned. "Want a hint?" After she nodded, he said, "Think about the pieces on a chess board."

Siobhan closed her eyes and tried to picture the board. There was the king, queen, rook, bishop, knight . . .

"Three!" she yelled. "The king, the queen, and the knight—spelled K-N-I-G-H-T."

He pulled her closer to him. "Technically, you know I'm still winning, right? Twenty to eighteen."

Reggie had been keeping track of who had solved each puzzle over the past year. In some ways he was just as competitive as her father.

"Don't you know it's in your best interest to let your girlfriend win?"

He was already leaning into her. "Well, maybe I can give you some bonus points. . . ."

They kissed, but he pulled away after a few moments. "Where does Coach think you are this time?" he asked as he ran his fingertips across the bracelet circling her wrist. He had made it for her in his shop class, for her birthday. He had been trembling so much when he handed her the small box he'd wrapped it in. And then, as soon as she opened it, he started complaining about how cheap and small it was, and how she deserved better. She finally had to kiss him so he'd shut up. She loved her bracelet, and had worn it every day since he'd given it to her.

"He thinks I'm at Ellie's," Siobhan replied. "She's on a date with a boy from the telephone company. She likes him. We'll see what happens."

"Where are they going?" he asked.

"She made him a picnic. They're going to watch the stars out by Murray Creek."

"A girl that brings food to her boyfriend?" His eyes crinkled as he grinned. "Doesn't Ellie have a sister? Maybe I should see what she's doing next weekend."

"Boy, hush." Siobhan slapped his arm. "You want me to make a picnic for you next time? A turkey sandwich, a plate of potato salad, a couple of Cokes, and a big slice of apple pie? Wouldn't be too hard . . ." She paused as Reggie's face turned to a frown. "What's wrong?" she asked.

He sat back and shook his head. "Nothing."

"Reggie . . ."

"Really, it's nothing. . . ." He scratched a mosquito bite on his arm. "I just don't like Coca-Cola. That's all."

She crossed her arms. "Reggie, is this about the other day at the shoeshine stand? That was over a week ago."

"You didn't have to drink it."

"What was I supposed to do, give it back?" she asked. "And why are you worried? I'm here with you, not him."

He smiled and reached out to her again. He kissed the back of her hand. "I'm sorry. It's just . . . the way he dismissed me. I should have thrown that money right back in his face. But . . ."

"I know." She traced the fine freckles on his skin with her thumb. For Reggie, every little bit of money helped. Even dimes and nickels. That why he worked so many odd jobs — shoe shiner during the day, busboy at one of the local bars at night, and even a janitor at Mount Carmel. Ironically, her father helped Reggie land some of those jobs — before he knew they were a couple, of course. It was all good work, but she knew Reggie felt it was beneath him. He was capable of so much more. He just needed a chance. Just like every other Negro in Lambert.

"You ready for tomorrow?" she asked him.

He nodded. "I'm gonna cram that ball right down their throats. Especially the Allen kid. He's the worst." Then he shrugged. "Actually, they're all bad."

Siobhan recalled the conversation she had overheard a few weeks ago between her parents — the day after her father challenged the Wallace team to the game. She had stood outside, at the window, and listened as her mother talked about the difference between vengeance and justice. Talking with Reggie was like reliving it all over. She almost told him so, but she knew that would cause another argument.

Then he kissed her again, and they both forgot about tennis and soda pop and everything else in the world.

At least, for a little while.

"I have to go soon," Siobhan eventually said.

"I know." He took a breath. "I had a dream last night. We were living in Chicago. I was working, and you were in school. We had a small apartment. Shabby furniture. A leaky sink. But it was ours. And we were together."

Siobhan pressed her hand against his cheek. "Reggie . . ."

"I know. But a fella's allowed to dream, ain't he?"

"I still think you should reconsider college—"

"How can I afford to spend four more years in school when we need food on the table today?" he asked. "I can't do that to Grandma."

"But you could make so much more money—"

"Says who? The only place paying decent money to Negroes around here is the city. And the last I checked, I didn't need a college degree to collect trash or dig ditches."

"What about the military? I don't want you to go away, but if you really need the money—"

"Remember Vic Draper? Big as an ox. Breath like a sewer. Best linebacker on the 1950 championship team. Anyway, he went into the army. And you know what he's doing for them? Scrambling eggs and baking biscuits." Reggie rested his head in his hands. "You deserve better than a cook. Better than a ditch digger."

"Reggie, I'd love you no matter what you did." She hugged him hard. "Things will be different once I graduate. Daddy won't be this way forever."

She didn't know how, but she had faith that everything would work out. She believed in them, even when Reggie didn't. But she couldn't carry the burden for both of them. She needed Reggie to believe it too.

But instead of saying any of this, she kissed him again, because sometimes that was easier than trying to come up with the words.

"Before you go, tell me that poem again that you like so much," he said, still holding on to her. "The Langston Hughes one."

She squeezed him tighter, wishing she could make this moment last forever. Then she began to recite: *I, Too, Sing America*.

CHAPTER 30

"Finally!" Brandon yelled as Candice entered his kitchen late Friday afternoon. "You finished the book?" He and Tori sat at the table with a platter of cookies in front of them.

"It's so good," Candice said. Then she frowned. "Except for the Hoo family. They were a little stereotypical."

"Yeah, good point." He rubbed his hands together. "So are you ready to talk about how it applies to the letter?"

"I was thinking about that," Candice said. "Were you talking about the part of the book where—"

"No spoiling it!" Tori said.

"Tori, you're not going to read it," Brandon said.

"How do you know?" She elbowed him. "What? Are you going to say I'm too old for it?" She looked at Candice. "Brandon's been telling me and Mom how there aren't any boy books or girl books. If that's true, there aren't any old people or young people books either."

Candice glanced at Brandon. Did this have to do with the conversation they'd had at the library about boy books and girl books?

Brandon flashed Candice a quick smile, then turned to his sister. "Are you really going to read it?"

"Maybe. If it interests me."

Candice pulled the letter from the book, then slid *The Westing Game* to Tori.

He popped the last of his cookie into his mouth. "Fine, let's go upstairs so we don't *spoil* it," he said, standing up from the table.

"So what was your big revelation about the letter?" Candice asked as they climbed the stairs.

"In *The Westing Game*, most of the information you need to solve the puzzle is provided right at the beginning of the story, in the will," he said. "I bet the letter is doing the same."

"Makes sense, I guess," Candice said, thinking it through. Siobhan's memorial page stated that she loved *The Westing Game*. Maybe Parker wanted to make sure someone linked his puzzle to that book.

They entered the computer room and sat down beside each other on the edge of the bed. "Like I said at the park, the entire letter is filled with clues." His grin widened. "Read the letter again."

"I've read it a thousand—"

"Just read it again," he said.

Candice huffed, but quickly scanned the letter.

"Okay, so how many numbered clues do you see?" he asked.

"One."

He clapped his hands together. "That's what I thought at first too. Then we saw the bench at the park. *She loved all.*" He slid closer to her and traced his finger along the page until he found what he was looking for. "What's the word directly preceding that sentence here?"

Candice sighed. "*For.*"

"Exactly! That had me thinking about *The Westing Game*. And I thought, what if he didn't mean *for* like F-O-R. What if he meant F-O-U-R?"

Candice opened her mouth to argue.

Then she closed her mouth.

"Do you see what I'm talking about?" he asked, his pitch rising.

Candice was too busy reading the letter. She went line by line, and tried to reorganize the words in her head.

```
(1.) Siobhan's father loved tennis, but he grew up
idolizing a team in another sport.
Too (2.) Leanne Washington's days as a volunteer at
her church did more for Lambert's children than most
people will ever know.
Three (3.) She was truly greater than the sum of her
parts.
For (4.) She loved all.
```

She snapped her fingers. "Can I borrow a sheet of paper to jot this down?"

"Already did it," Brandon said. He walked to the computer and opened a file. "So that got me thinking . . . we've found three of the four clues. The Luling Oilers is the first clue, Leanne Washington's work with the Women's Missionary Circle is the second, and the park bench is the fourth."

"*Maybe* it's the fourth," she said. "It's not dated."

He nodded. "True. But for sure we haven't found the third clue: *She was truly greater than the sum of her parts*," he said. "But maybe it's not something we're supposed to find. Maybe it's not a physical thing."

Candice repeated the clue in her head. *She was truly greater than the sum of her parts.* "We need to be adding something up!" She looked at the photo of the Washingtons on Brandon's desk. "The sum of her parts. Her parents. We need to somehow add up her parents!"

"Yep, and that's where I'm stuck," he said. "You're the puzzle master. What do we do next?"

Candice was sure Brandon was saying that to soothe her bruised ego. The funny thing was, it actually worked.

"So we have to add up something about . . . what? Baseball and the church?" She wrapped her ponytail around her finger. "Tennis was a big part of who she was. Do you remember if there was a score on the trophy at school?"

"I'm pretty sure there wasn't. Let me see what I can find about tennis scoring online." Brandon opened the web browser. He ran a search, clicked a few links, and eventually landed on a page on how the game was played.

Candice read over his shoulder. In tennis, both players started at zero, except they called it love. Every time you hit the ball and your opponent couldn't return it, you gained fifteen points. That is, until you scored three times — that was forty, not forty-five. But if you were tied at forty, it was called deuce. And the first person to reach sixty won the game — except they didn't call it sixty. And you had to win by two points. Or was that thirty points? You had to win at least six games to win a set, and two out of three sets to win a match.

All in all, they read ten web pages about tennis over the next hour.

"Maybe we're looking for the wrong numbers," Candice finally said. "We should go back to the memorial room."

"And do what?"

"I don't know. I just feel like we're missing something there. Not only is that the first clue, it's the only one that's *written* to look like a clue," Candice said. "He wanted us to start there."

"Well, while you think about that, I'm going to get more cookies."

Once Brandon left, Candice opened up the file with the photos from the community center. She clicked through until she found the photo of Leanne Washington and the Women's Missionary Circle.

Mount Carmel Missionary Circle prepares a bake sale to raise funds for Briggs v. Elliott. *March 14, 1951.*

Then she reread the second clue. *Leanne Washington's days as a volunteer at her church did more for Lambert's children than most people will ever know.*

Days as a volunteer.

Days.

Date.

As in, March 14, 1951.

Was that why the date on the photo of the Women's Missionary Group was different than all the other dates? Was that what Parker was trying to get them to notice?

She leaned back in the chair and spun in place. *Maybe we're reading this too literally. Maybe it's more figurative. Like, if it's a sum, maybe we should convert the clues to numbers. The dates to numbers. But if so, what is the right date for the first clue?*

She grabbed a sheet of paper and started by adding the date on the photo, March 14, 1951 and the date on the trophy, August 10, 1957.

3/14/1951 + 8/10/1957 = 3141951 + 8101957 = 11243908

She spun around in the chair again. *11243908 = 11/24/3908 = November 24, 3908? Maybe November 24, 1939?*

She looked through the pictures she took at the memorial room, hoping this new date was listed on one of the other photos. After discovering that none of them matched the date, she restarted the tribute video of Coach Washington. Perhaps they had overlooked something there.

She had just fast-forwarded to the part where the video talked about Coach Washington's love for the Luling Oilers when Brandon returned, a plate of cookies in his hand.

"Shoot, nothing there either," she mumbled, stopping the video. He sat down on the bed, and Candice filled him in on what she'd been working on.

"That's amazing," Brandon said once she finished explaining her new theory. "I would have never thought about turning the date into a number."

"Yeah, well, I'm still stuck," she said. "I added up the dates, but the solution doesn't make sense. I don't know what it's supposed to mean."

Brandon handed her a cookie, then motioned for Candice to move out of the way. "Let me do a web search for those dates. Maybe there's a clue there."

Candice munched on her cookie as Brandon typed in *November 24, 1939*. Nothing of interest popped up, at least not anything that jumped out at them. Brandon then typed in *August 10, 1957*, followed by *March 14, 1951*. Then *November 24. August 10. March 14.*

And that's when Candice dropped her cookie.

"Pi Day," she said.

"Um, okay," Brandon said.

"Like the number." She stood. "Open up that picture of Leanne Washington."

He quickly opened the file.

"See!" She punched his shoulder. "She's holding a pie!"

"Ouch! That's my shooting arm, Candice."

"Sorry," she said. "But look at the date! March 14. What if the clue here is P-I, not P-I-E? You know, 3.14. The number you use to calculate the circumference of a circle." She spun her bracelet around her wrist. "And maybe it connects with Big Dub's clue . . . with the Oilers or that guy Mackey!"

He slowly nodded, looking at the computer screen.

"Well?" she asked after a few seconds. "What do you think?"

Finally, he grinned at her. "Like I said. You're the puzzle master."

CHAPTER 31

Siobhan Washington

August 10, 1957

Siobhan readjusted the red scarf around her neck as she and Coach Robert Hicks parked outside the Wallace High School tennis courts. She was glad she'd worn a blouse and poodle skirt—it was almost eighty degrees outside, much too hot for the jeans she'd originally planned to wear. Plus, she liked how she looked in her current outfit—everything from the high heels to the deep red lipstick that matched her scarf. She had wanted to look nice for herself, and for Reggie. She didn't know when she'd see him again.

A full moon hung high in the sky, illuminating the parking lot. Ahead of them, ten vehicles sat just outside the chain-link fence surrounding the court, including Coach Douglas's Buick and Chip's truck, all of them with their engines running and their headlights on. They must have been using them to provide additional light for the game.

Siobhan paused as the door to Chip's truck opened. He stepped out of the cab, then began walking toward them.

"Hello, Coach," Chip said, shaking Robert Hicks's hand. Then he nodded toward her. "Hey, Siobhan. Glad to see you made it."

"There was no way I was missing tonight," she said. She turned as another car entered the parking lot. Her body tensed as the vehicle rolled past them and parked alongside the fence.

"That's just Reverend Hollister," Robert Hicks said, placing his bear of a hand on Siobhan's shoulder. "Let me catch up with him. I'll see you in the stands in a bit." His gaze bounced from her to Chip. "Don't stand out here talking for too long. Siobhan—I'll be sitting with Smitty."

They both nodded as Coach Hicks walked over to greet the thin white man exiting the car. Her father and Coach Turner could only agree on one person to serve as an umpire—Reverend Stephen Hollister. He was a pastor of a small Methodist church just outside the city, and he was known to be sympathetic to Negro causes. Given the secrecy of the exhibition, he was as close to impartial as the Perkins team was going to get.

But with only one umpire, it would have taken all night for each of the boys to play, so the coaches decided to modify the scoring. The exhibition would consist of three sets—Wallace's top three players against Perkins's best three. Each pair would play a shortened set, where the first boy to win four games with a two-game advantage would win the set. The team with the best two out of three sets would be the victor.

"Is the team ready?" she asked.

Chip picked at some grit underneath his fingernail. "As ready as they're going to be." He paused for a moment, staring at the ground, then added, "Your boyfriend plays in the second set. Coach Dub wanted to put his best two players first."

So Chip knew about Reggie too. But she was glad. She was tired of all the secrets. All the silence. "Who's Reggie playing against?"

"Glenn Allen," Chip said. "But Reggie can beat him. I think. As long as he stays focused." Chip finally smiled. "How is it that I go off to college, and you fall head over heels in love with another fella?"

"It was a surprise to me too." She touched her bracelet. The metal felt cool, even in this hot weather. "But I really do love him. He's kind, and smart, and so good . . . most of the time."

She smiled at the thought of Reggie. It felt strange to be saying all of this out loud. But it was also empowering. She'd wanted to talk about Reggie to someone—anyone—ever since they'd started seeing each other. "I guess you know my daddy doesn't really approve of him."

Chip nodded. She tried to read his expression, but it was a clean slate. "Maybe in college, if you and he—"

"Reggie's not going to college. His grandma barely has enough money to keep the lights on, much less send him off to school."

"What about scholarships?"

"They don't grow on trees. Plus, his grades weren't good enough. He was always working too much to finish his assignments." She took a step forward. "For a second, I thought about running away with him."

"What?!" Anger flashed across Chip's face. "Please don't tell me you're running off with that boy!"

"Don't yell," she said. "And Reggie isn't a *boy*. He's only a year younger than you."

Chip seemed to consider this. "You're right," he said quietly. "I'm sorry. I didn't mean it like that."

She nodded at him, letting him know it was okay. "And of course I'm not going to leave with Reggie. Not because I don't want to. It's just . . . if I ran away, I'd never be able to come back home. I'd never see Mama and Daddy, or any of my friends."

"Your daddy would eventually forgive you."

"Are we talking about the same Big Dub?" She looked toward the court. The cars were blocking her view, but she could hear the sound of tennis balls bouncing against the ground. "We should head on in."

Chip rubbed the back of his head. "Want to sit with us?"

"Better not," she said. "Don't want to cause a scene."

"Yeah, you're probably right. Marion Allen is already riled up. It would just make things worse if he saw you with us." He shook his head. "People aren't even forcing us to sit apart, and we're still segregating ourselves."

"I wasn't talking about that," she said. "I don't want Reggie to see us together. He doesn't really like you."

As Chip smirked, Siobhan rolled her eyes. "Don't let that get to your head, *Charles*." She started toward the gate. "Wait here for a few minutes, then you can follow me in."

Siobhan caught sight of Reggie as she entered the fence. He and the other boys stood with her father in the court nearest the stands, softly lobbing tennis balls to one another. They all wore white shorts and white collared shirts. Her mama has spent the last few nights sewing the school logo onto the pockets.

She walked up the bleachers and took a seat beside Coach Hicks. He sat about halfway up, with Mr. Smith and a few other Negroes. Siobhan quickly counted the number of white people in the stands. There were at least twenty, and many of them seemed to be friends with Marion Allen. She wondered how many people Marion had told about the "secret" game.

Siobhan glanced back toward the court. Reggie had finally caught sight of her. He smiled, giving her a small wave with his racket.

Of course, her father noticed this as well. He tapped Reggie on the head, breaking the boy's eye contact with Siobhan. Then he ordered the boys to sit back down. The first set was about to begin.

Jackie Harris took his place on one side of the court, and a large Wallace player lined up on the opposite baseline. Coach Hicks told her his name — Harold Buckner. Siobhan didn't know him — the only player on the Wallace team she recognized was Glenn Allen.

Harold lofted the ball high into the air, then delivered his serve. Siobhan felt herself leaning forward as Jackie returned the ball.

Tennis matches were always quiet. There was never any of the hooping and hollering you got at football or basketball games. But the silence at the beginning of this game was unlike anything Siobhan had ever experienced. It was like everyone was holding their breaths, waiting for the first point. Waiting while the ball bounced between Jackie and Harold — between black and white. One, two, three, four, five times. Eventually, Harold scored the first point against Jackie. Everyone let out a breath, and Marion Allen stood up and cheered.

The game continued, with Marion letting out a little whoop every time Harold scored, and her father nodding in approval when Jackie returned the favor.

Harold was good enough to easily win the first two games. But Siobhan noticed how hard he was breathing. He was out of shape, and was clearly tired by the middle of the third game. Her father must have noticed as well, because after a time-out, Jackie moved to the baseline and played a more defensive strategy. Instead of trying to hit winning shots like before, Jackie focused on just keeping the ball in play, forcing Harold to expend more energy chasing the ball around the court . . . which led to Harold becoming more tired and making more errors. Harold was barely even trying to move by the last game.

Set one went to Jackie, 5–3.

The boys met at the net. Jackie held out his hand, and after an eternity, Harold gave it a half-hearted shake.

Siobhan rubbed her bracelet for luck as Reggie warmed up with his teammate, Mordecai. A few feet away, Glenn Allen knocked around balls with another Wallace player. Glenn was wound up pretty tightly, Siobhan thought — he was pounding the ball when he only needed to gently return it. His Wallace teammate had to duck once to avoid the tennis ball smashing against his jaw.

Reggie looked loose, but his face was stern. He kept stealing glances at everyone — Glenn Allen, Siobhan, and even Chip. Siobhan saw Chip flash Reggie a thumbs-up the next time he glanced in the stands, but Reggie just snorted and went back to trading serves.

She shook her head. Chip really didn't have a clue.

"Keep your eyes open," Coach Hicks said to Mr. Smith as the boys returned to their seats. "It's about to get real interesting with Glenn Allen taking the court."

After a quick discussion with the coaches, Reverend Hollister motioned for Reggie and Glenn to greet each other before the game started. Neither one moved. Likewise, neither coach made any attempt to tell his player to shake hands. Finally, the Reverend shook his head and pointed them to their positions. He threw the ball to Reggie for the first serve.

Reggie bounced the ball a few times, called out the score, and fired the ball at Glenn so hard that the boy couldn't return it.

15–0.

30–0.

40–0.

Game.

Reggie looked at the stands, toward Marion Allen, and smirked.

After switching sides, Glenn served for the next game, and started off just as strongly as Reggie, with two aces. But Reggie figured out how to return his serve on the next point, eventually bringing the score to 30-all. Then when Reggie earned the lead on the next score, a devastating cross-court shot, he smirked again, this time at Chip.

"He's way too cocky for his own good," Siobhan whispered.

"Yeah, but look where he learned it from," Coach Hicks said, nodding toward her father. He had a grin on his face even larger than Reggie's. Dub jumped up and fist-pumped after Reggie won the final point, giving him the second game.

The boys switched sides again, but instead of crossing on opposite ends of the net like before, they crossed on the same side. Reggie whispered something as he passed Glenn. Glenn responded by ramming him with his elbow.

Siobhan tensed up, ready to move. Reggie just laughed.

Siobhan closed her eyes and offered up a prayer. She wanted Reggie to hurry and win these last two games, and then it would be over. The Perkins team would have proved they could beat the best tennis team in the state, and everyone would go home safely.

When she opened her eyes, she saw her father talking with Reggie. Reggie pulled back, with a look of shock on his face. Then he smiled and nodded.

On Reggie's first serve, he mistakenly double-faulted, giving Glenn a 15–0 lead for the game. Siobhan didn't understand it. Reggie was the best server on the team. He never faulted, much less double-faulted. On the next point, Reggie was slow to respond to a drop shot that barely crossed the net, giving Glenn another score. This went on a few more times, and suddenly, Glenn Allen had won his first game.

Siobhan looked at her father, assuming that steam was about to shoot from the man's head. But Big Dub just sat there, slowly nodding, his hand on his chin.

Siobhan realized what was going on. They were toying with Glenn. Stretching the match out. They wanted to humiliate him.

Glenn began game four with a weak serve. Reggie responded with an even weaker return that bounced into the net. But after letting Glenn run up the score to 40–0 in Glenn's favor, Reggie came storming back, showing off the ferocious returns he'd put aside for the past two games. He surged ahead, easily winning every remaining point.

Siobhan took a deep breath. Reggie needed one more game.

She watched as Reggie glanced at her father. Big Dub pressed his hands together, then slowly pulled them apart.

And Reggie lost the next game through a mix of unforced errors and weak backhands.

Siobhan was sure everyone could see the farce this exhibition had become. That is, everyone except Marion Allen. He kept cheering, getting louder and louder as his brother pulled ahead, only to fall silent and sulk whenever Glenn began to lose.

Finally, as Glenn prepared to serve for the sixth game, Siobhan saw her father run his hand across his neck in a slicing motion. Reggie grinned. Then his eyes narrowed, and he turned his attention to his opponent.

Glenn served the ball. Reggie knocked it back so fast that Glenn could only watch as the ball bounced pass him.

As it became clear that Reggie planned to win this game, Coach Turner tried to argue a couple of the umpire's calls. But even he eventually stopped once the score became out of reach.

Glenn glanced nervously at his brother. Then, right before what was sure to be his final serve, Glenn made a grand gesture of pulling a tennis ball from his pocket and placing it on the ground. He went to kick it out of the way, but instead, he somehow stepped on it. Yelping, he dropped his racket and fell to the ground. "My ankle! I think I sprained it!"

Siobhan rolled her eyes. Sure, it wasn't nice the way that Reggie had toyed with him, but this was just delaying the inevitable. Was it so insulting for Glenn to lose to a colored player that he would rather fake an injury?

Coach Turner knelt in front of Glenn as Marion rushed over. They helped Glenn to his feet and led him to the bleachers. She was sure Glenn favored the wrong foot.

"We need to reschedule the exhibition," Marion yelled. "He can't play on a bum ankle."

"Yeah," another white man yelled. "Don't let the game end like this. This ain't fair."

Siobhan watched her father and Adam Douglas saunter over to Reverend Hollister and Coach Turner in the center of the court. "Come on," Robert Hicks said, standing. "It's time for us to leave."

Siobhan frowned. "But—"

"I promised Big Dub I'd get you out of here the minute things went bad," Coach Hicks said. "And that's exactly what's about to happen."

"I'll follow you down," Mr. Smith said. "See if I can talk some sense into Dub."

"Look, I didn't make up the rules here," Reverend Hollister was saying to Coach Turner once Siobhan, Coach Hicks, and Mr. Smith reached the bottom of the bleachers. "No substitutions."

Coach Hicks kept walking past the court toward the exit, but Siobhan paused. Then she slowly inched along the bottom row, trailing behind Mr. Smith. She wanted to get closer so she could hear better.

"Siobhan?" Coach Hicks hissed. "What are you doing?"

Ignoring him, she took a seat. Reggie stood a few feet away, but he was too caught up in the conversation to notice her.

"Either your player forfeits the set, or he gets back out there and finishes the game," Reverend Hollister continued. "That's final."

"No, we need to reschedule," Coach Turner said.

"And what? We forget the current score and start all over again?" Big Dub shook his head. "Come on, Coach. You're a man of integrity."

"You're a fine one to be talking about integrity, with the stunt you just pulled." Coach Turner crossed his arms. "And I don't care what the rules are. I am not about to let word get out that we lost to a bunch of colored boys."

"Who exactly are you worried about?" Dub asked, his grin widening. "Marion Allen? Fine, I'll tell him."

Adam Douglas grabbed Dub's arm. "Reverend Hollister is the one in charge here. Let's have him make the announcement." He turned to the Reverend. "Don't tell them we won. Say they lost because of forfeit due to injury."

"But that's a lie," Big Dub said.

"A win's a win," Adam said.

Siobhan looked up as Robert Hicks wrapped his hand around her arm. "You've heard enough." He pulled her to her feet. "Or do you want me to talk to your daddy about this?"

Shaking her head, she glanced back at her father. He was talking with the team, the grin on his face wide and bright. She wanted to call out to Reggie, to tell him good-bye, but decided against it.

As Siobhan followed Coach Hicks from the court, she heard Reverend Hollister addressing the small crowd. A few people booed, and others cursed. Someone yelled, "Them colored boys cheated, didn't they?" Then she heard glass smashing against the ground.

She whipped back around. Adam Douglas and Chip had corralled the Perkins teams and was leading them away from the bleachers. A glass bottle had shattered a few feet away from them, but none of the boys seemed to be injured. Her father remained on the court, but Mr. Smith was doing his best to pull him away as well.

"Let's go," Robert Hicks said, grabbing her arm again. This time, he didn't release her until he'd placed her in the car. As she rubbed her arm, she searched the crowd, looking for Reggie.

All she saw was a sea of white faces. And they were all angry.

CHAPTER 32

On Saturday morning, after a quick game of basketball, Candice and Brandon biked to the library to search as many books as they could about sports. It turned out there were a whole bunch of teams called the Oilers, so Brandon picked books about the Negro Leagues, hockey, and football. They made a list of all the famous players from each of the teams, then added pi to each famous player's jersey number, but didn't know what to look for after that.

In addition to Brandon's books, Candice chose a book about tennis and a biography of Althea Gibson, the African American woman who won Wimbledon in 1957. Ellie had mentioned how Coach Washington had wanted Siobhan to be "the next Althea Gibson." Maybe there was more to the connection.

They returned home to see their mothers on Brandon's porch, drinking coffee. They dropped their bikes in the yard and walked up the steps.

"About time," Brandon's mother said. "We've got to get a move on. Don't want to miss the African dance performance. It's the best part of the festival."

"Sorry we're late," Brandon said. "Research."

"I can't wait to see your project," his mother continued as she kissed him on the cheek. "Y'all sure are spending enough time on it."

Brandon shrugged. "Yeah. Um, Candice has been a big help."

"And what about you, Mom? How was your morning?" Candice asked, trying to change the subject.

"Pretty good," she said between sips of coffee. "I revised one chapter and added a new scene. Slow and steady wins the race. But enough about me. Tell me about this project."

"Not yet," Candice said. "You know, *slow and steady wins the race*. We'll tell you all about it once we're finished." Then she smiled. "So, do we need to grab lunch before we head to the park?"

"There'll be plenty of food there from local restaurants," her mom said.

"I hope Sam's has a booth," Tori said as she stepped onto the porch from the house. *The Westing Game* was tucked underneath her arm. "I'm craving a chili-cheese dog."

"That sounds . . . nice," Candice's mother said. She smiled as she noticed the book. "Hey, I know that book," she said, reaching for it. "My mother loved it."

Candice could feel her eyes bugging out of her head. "She did?"

Her mother nodded as she flipped it open. "Yeah. We have a copy at home, somewhere. She even tried to get you to read it when you were younger, but you didn't seem interested, and she didn't want to force it."

Candice turned to Brandon. His mouth was hanging open.

"So, about those chili-cheese dogs," her mother continued, handing the book back to Tori. "Do you know if they have a low-fat option? Or maybe a vegetarian . . ."

She trailed off as a large SUV pulled up in front of the Joneses' house. The windows were too tinted for them to see who was inside.

"Trouble," Tori mumbled.

"Hush," her mother said. She waved as Millie Stanford stepped out of the vehicle. Milo was dressed in a black basketball jersey.

"We saw y'all and figured we'd stop to say hello," Mrs. Stanford said.

"Okay, you've said it," Tori whispered. "Now you can leave."

Ms. Jones smiled at Millie as she pinched her daughter's arm. "Enough," she whispered through her teeth.

"I was hoping to see you at the game," Mrs. Stanford said to Candice as she reached the bottom step. "Milo scored fifteen points."

"And seven rebounds," Milo added. "Almost a double-double."

Candice shrugged. "Oh. Sorry. I guess I got the dates wrong."

"It's so nice to finally meet you," Mrs. Stanford said to Candice's mother. "I'm Millie, and this is Milo. I met your daughter at church last week." She batted her eyelashes. "Maybe we'll see you there this Sunday."

"Perhaps," her mother replied, shaking the woman's hand.

Mrs. Stanford looked at their house across the street. "I was so sorry to hear about your mother's death. If you don't mind me asking, how did she pass away?"

"Heart disease," her mother said.

"Ah, yes. It's one of those silent killers." She readjusted her sunglasses. "I thought that—and please don't take this the wrong way—perhaps she had been suffering from dementia," she said. "You know, given everything that happened before, with the park and the tennis courts and—"

"Trust me." Her mother crossed her arms and stood taller. "It was a heart attack."

Mrs. Stanford clearly wasn't getting the hint. "There are a lot of factors that could lead to someone passing away," she said. "My best friend's father has Alzheimer's. It's such a dreadful disease, and it causes him to act so strangely." She smiled wide enough to eclipse the sun. "I'm sorry for prying. It's just, the more we know about our loved one's health, the more we know about *our* health."

"Yes, well. Thank you so much for your concern." Candice's mother looked at her watch. "We were about to head to the Juneteenth Festival. Perhaps we'll see *you* there."

"I heard it was boring," Milo said, frowning. "Nothing but a bunch of stories about how we used to be slaves."

Mrs. Stanford quickly patted Milo's shoulder. "Oh, you know these boys. They don't appreciate cultural education. We've hoped to attend every year, but we've always had a conflict." She leaned closer. "Although out of all the places to hold it, why would they choose Vickers Park? It's just not safe."

"I hadn't heard about any crime at the park," Brandon's mother said. "Has something happened there recently?"

"Perhaps not at the park itself," Mrs. Stanford clarified. "But, you know, that neighborhood—"

"Isn't Vista Heights the oldest African American neighborhood in Lambert?" Candice's mom asked. "It seems like the perfect place to hold a celebration of our freedom."

"Oh, yes. Perhaps . . . if you put it like that . . ." Mrs. Stanford looked at her own watch. "I should let you all go. Feel free to call if you need anything. Juanita has my number." She smiled at Candice. "Same for you. Maybe we should have you over for a playdate? I'm sure you're into just as many of those dreadful shoot-them-up video games as the rest of these kids."

She and Milo walked back to their SUV.

"I will never speak to you again if you go to Milo's house for a 'play-date,'" Brandon deadpanned to Candice.

"But what about all those dreadful video games?" she asked. "And how else is his mom supposed to spy on us if I don't talk to her?"

"Don't be so snarky," Candice's mother said. "We hardly know them. I'm sure Milo is quite nice."

"He's not," Candice said.

"Nope," Brandon agreed.

"They're right," Tori said, still rubbing her arm where her mother had pinched her. "We've known Milo since we moved here. He's as rotten as they come. I'm guessing pretty much everyone in the neighborhood knows that."

"Everyone except his mother," Ms. Jones said. "But what can I say—people see what they want to see. Especially about people they love." She leaned over and pecked Tori on the cheek. "It's the fallacy of mothers." She sighed. "And wives."

Candice turned to watch Mrs. Stanford drive off. It seemed rude to be looking at Brandon's mom right then, when she felt sure Ms. Jones was really talking about someone else.

"But at least you two don't have to worry about Millie for much longer," Ms. Jones continued, filling the silence.

Candice turned back around. "Why do you say that?"

Ms. Jones's mouth gaped open. She looked at Candice's mother. "Did I . . . oh dear. I ruined the surprise, didn't I?"

"It wasn't a surprise," Candice's mother said, her words measured. "I just wasn't sure until last night." She glanced at Brandon. "Maybe we can talk about it later."

"You sold the house, didn't you?" Candice asked. She crossed her arms.

"No, it's not that," her mother said. Then she sighed. "Might as well tell it. The house is still on the market. But your father's friend completed all the major renovations and brought in a new crew for the finishing touches. The realtor thinks she can sell the house even if we're living in it." She took a deep breath. "We can head back to Atlanta as early as next weekend."

Candice blinked. "That soon?"

"I know the idea of moving has been really hard on you," her mother continued. "I know how much you miss your father—and how much he misses you. Now you'll have a chance to hang out with DeeDee and Courtney a little before school starts. Isn't that great?"

Candice nodded. "Yeah. Um . . . yeah." She looked at Brandon, but she couldn't see his face. He was staring at the ground, his hands tight around his backpack straps.

Would he keep searching for Parker's fortune without her if they didn't find it before she left? Would he still share it with her?

And once she did leave, who would play basketball with him in the backyard? Who would he trade books with?

Who would *she* trade books with?

Tori wrapped her arm around her brother's neck. "Hey, I left something upstairs. Walk with me, okay?"

He nodded quickly, still looking down, and let his sister lead him inside.

Candice wanted to follow them so badly. She wanted to say something to Brandon. Anything. But she didn't know what. And then he was gone.

CHAPTER 33

Chip Douglas

August 11, 1957

For the next few hours after the tennis game, everything was calm and back to normal in Lambert, South Carolina.

Then Chip's world exploded.

The ringing phone cut through the house, jarring him awake. He switched on his lamp and glanced at his clock. One a.m.

After pulling on a T-shirt, he entered the hallway. His father leaned against the doorjamb to the living room, the phone cradled on his shoulder. His eyes were closed and his breaths were deep. A few steps away, Chip's mother stood in her nightgown, her hands fiddling with a dish towel.

Adam mumbled a few things into the phone. "How bad is he hurt? . . . Is everyone else okay? The boys? . . . What about the car?" Finally, he said, "Sit tight. We'll be there in a bit."

He hung up the phone. "That was Dwayne Smith. Dub was attacked tonight. They ambushed him as he was leaving the Green Olive Bar.

Smitty found Dub in the parking lot and got him back home." He grabbed his wife's pack of cigarettes from the table and started searching for a lighter. Chip hadn't seen his father smoke a cigarette in years. "Put on some clothes, Chip. You're coming with me."

His mother dropped the towel. "What? He's a baby."

"He'll be fine, Joyce." Adam finally found a lighter. He took a long puff of the cigarette before slowly blowing out the smoke. "Go on, Chip. And pack a bag. Enough clothes for a day or two." His father walked off to his own bedroom with Chip's mother a few steps behind, still asking questions.

Chip hurriedly got dressed, then tossed some clothes into a duffel bag. He didn't have much cash on him, but he took the few bills he had and stuffed them into his pocket.

His father knocked on his door. "Ready?"

Chip looked around his room. "Yeah, I guess." He followed his father outside and into the Buick. "Is everyone okay? Is Siobhan—"

"She's fine. They're all fine for the most part. But Dub took a real bad beating. Smitty's convinced that the men who attacked him are coming back—and that it'll be a lot worse next time."

"Why?"

His father didn't immediately speak. Finally he said, "You wanted to help the Negro race? Here's your chance."

A small crowd had gathered at the Washingtons' house by the time they arrived. Men wore bathrobes, and women stood with their hair hidden underneath scarves. A few people carried guns.

Chip recognized a few faces in the yard. The crowd parted and let him and his father pass into the house.

Chip gasped upon seeing Dub. The man was slumped over in the recliner, his left arm in a sling. A white towel, wet with blood, had been wrapped around his head. Dub's jaw was swollen, his nose was clearly broken, and his face was covered with scrapes and cuts. As Dub breathed through his mouth, Chip could see that his front two teeth were missing.

Chip had seen pictures of Negroes who had been attacked by white men, but he had never seen it up close. As he looked at Dub, Chip was afraid he was going to throw up.

"Smitty! You said he was bad, but this . . ." Adam Douglas ran his hands over his head. "We got to get him to a hospital. Now."

"Nooo," Dub wailed. He shifted in his seat just enough to look at Chip and his father. Dub's eyes were glassy and distant.

"He won't go," Smitty said. "That's why I called my friend Bettye. She patched him up as best she could, then shot him full of morphine. But she said he'll need a proper exam once he reaches Maryland."

Chip tried to keep up with the conversation. *Maryland?*

"Think it was the Allen boys?" Adam Douglas asked.

Smitty shrugged. "I can't really be sure of anything—but they'd be my first guess. All I saw was three people in masks running away while Dub lay on the ground, choking on his own blood."

Adam kneeled in front of Dub. "Look, let me take you to the hospital," he said. "I can protect you. The Allens can't get to you there."

Dub shook his head, then pointed to Smitty. "Ive im oll."

Chip had no idea what Coach Dub was saying, but clearly Smitty did. He walked to the couch and pulled something out of a small paper bag. "I found this doll on his car."

Chip stepped forward to get a better look. The baby doll's white skin had been painted the color of midnight, with thick cherry-red lipstick smeared over its small mouth. The doll was naked, with horrible words scratched into its plastic skin. A noose hung around the doll's neck.

"Why did they leave a doll?" Chip asked, his stomach twisting. "What does it mean?"

His father cleared his throat. "It's a girl. A *black* girl. Who do you think it's supposed to be?"

Suddenly Chip connected the pieces of the puzzle. Then he ran to the wastebasket and threw up.

"You okay?" his father asked.

Chip wiped his mouth on his T-shirt. He stared at the wall—he couldn't stand to look at that doll anymore. "It's supposed to be . . . to be . . ."

"It's meant to be me, isn't it?"

He turned to see Siobhan standing in the doorway. No one spoke for a few seconds. Then Dub began to sob, his tears mixing with the blood and dirt. His shoulders shook and his body crumpled in the chair.

"You should go back to your room," Adam Douglas said. "You don't want to see your daddy like this."

Siobhan didn't budge. "What about the other boys?" she asked. "What about Reggie? Is he safe?"

Smitty rubbed the back of his neck. "Now don't you worry about—"

"Mr. Smith, please," Siobhan said. "They'd be just as mad at him as they were with Daddy."

"Smitty?" Adam Douglas began.

Dwayne Smith sighed. "Just before they sped off, I heard one of them yell that they were going after the half-bred mutt next. I'm assuming they were talking about Reggie." He held up his hands. "But I already told Robert. He's on his way to his grandma's house."

"Reggie's not there," Siobhan said. "He cleans up at the High Horse Juke Joint sometimes." She started toward the door. "If we hurry, we can—"

"*We* ain't doing nothing but getting you all packed up," Smitty said. "Your daddy didn't get the life beat out of him for you to go waltzing around the city, inviting them to do the same to you."

"But Reggie—"

"I'll find him," Adam Douglas said. He stepped forward and took Siobhan's hands in his. "Trust me. I'll find him."

Siobhan stood there for a long time as water pooled in her eyes. She released Adam Douglas's hands, then slipped a small bracelet off her arm. She held it up, and for a moment Chip thought she was going to hand it to his father, but she eventually placed it back on her wrist. "Please find Reggie," she said as the first tears broke free. "Keep him safe. He's got such a temper. I'm worried he'll do something stupid."

"I will," Adam Douglas said. "Now you go on and finish helping your mama get packed up." He glanced at Dub. "And you should lay down. You've got a long trip ahead of you."

Dub nodded, then tried to right himself in the chair. Eventually, Smitty grabbed him underneath his arms and hoisted him from the seat. Siobhan rushed over and let her father lean into her.

"I've got you, Daddy," she said. Chip didn't know how she could support so much weight.

Adam waited for her and Dub to leave the room before speaking again. "Smitty, I need you to find the other boys. We got to get them out of town too. At least for a little while—maybe just until school starts."

"But what about Dub and his family?" Smitty asked. "There's no way he can drive his car up to his sister-in-law's place."

"Chip will take him," he said, turning to his son. "Now listen up, Chip. I want you to drive straight there. Don't speed. Have Dub and the others stay down in the back seat until you get to Virginia. They'll be uncomfortable, but it'll be safer for everybody that way." He patted his son's cheek. "Can you handle that?"

Chip nodded. "Yes, sir. I'll take care of them."

"As soon as you get them settled, you take the bus home," his father said. "I'll be back as soon as I can, once I get Reggie out of here." Adam Douglas took a deep breath and looked up at the ceiling. "Smitty, I need to borrow the keys to your place. And I'm also gonna need to borrow your gun."

CHAPTER 34

Candice couldn't sleep. The bed was too hot. The pillow was too flat.

She kept thinking about the way Brandon disappeared into his house the previous afternoon. Tori had come back out a few moments later, saying that Brandon wasn't feeling well and was going to skip the Juneteenth Festival. Candice hadn't seen him since.

The festival was great—she climbed the rock wall three times, and tried a bunch of different foods, including PJ's world-famous hush puppies (which were so good that she went back for seconds and thirds), and pulled pork from a local barbecue restaurant. Candice hung out with Tori and her friends, and they were all *so cool* and *so fun* . . . but she still missed Brandon. Tori kept checking her phone, hoping that Brandon would call and ask to be picked up, but he never did.

He didn't come out of his house for church that morning. He didn't drop by that afternoon. She had emailed him a few times from her mom's phone, but he never replied.

Finally, after a few more minutes of tossing and turning, Candice got out of bed. Her iPod was almost dead, but she figured it had enough battery to last through a few songs. She pressed the buds into her ears and scrolled through until she found one of her dad's playlists.

Happy Music - Volume 1.

It was filled with the late seventies and early eighties music he loved. Earth, Wind & Fire. Michael Jackson. Chaka Khan. Teena Marie. The music didn't help Candice fall asleep, but she felt better. She picked up her notes on Parker's letter. She still believed the third clue was telling them to add something up—that the sum would lead to Parker's inheritance—but the idea was beginning to seem more and more unrealistic.

Then again, *all* of this seemed unrealistic.

And if she was really leaving soon, maybe none of it mattered anymore. Maybe it was already too late.

She decided to page through the yearbooks again. That was her default when she was stuck—to look at the photos. James Parker had to be there, and she was just overlooking him. She reached down by her bed, then realized all of the Wallace yearbooks were on the kitchen table by her laptop. Instead she grabbed the 1956 Perkins yearbook. She had already checked all the teachers, but she figured she'd look again.

She flipped through, and just like before, there were no teachers who even remotely resembled James Parker. She turned to the photo of the tennis team.

Candice sat up.

She rubbed her eyes.

She looked again.

Candice had studied the tennis team photo from the 1957 yearbook. But she hadn't looked at the photo in *this* yearbook. She hadn't seen any need to.

There was a boy in the black-and-white photo. Tall. Lanky. Light-skinned. Candice would have almost said that he was white, but that was impossible. White kids weren't allowed to attend Perkins back then.

The boy had curly hair. No, not curly—frizzy. Kind of like her classmate Heather's hair when it rained.

She found his name in the caption. *Reginald Bradley.*

She flipped through the book until she found his photo. There he was, with the same fair skin and frizzy hair. He was a junior in 1956. Had he been a senior in 1957? And if so, why had he stopped playing tennis?

Candice sprinted to the kitchen table. She flipped the 1957 yearbook to the senior photos. There he was again.

It took an eternity for her laptop to boot up.

She opened the photo she had downloaded from the Internet while at the school. The man was older, with more wrinkles and less hair. His nose and cheeks looked a little different. Thinner. Sharper. But the eyes were the same. Big, gray, round, and angry.

She had found James Parker.

CHAPTER 35

Reginald Bradley

1957

When Reginald Lawrence Bradley was a child, his grandmother would threaten to pop him with one of her wooden baking spoons anytime he complained about being poor, or not having a father, or wearing the same pair of jeans day after day after day. "Boy, you're better off than most people," she would say. Later that night, she would slice him an extra-thick piece of corn bread with his dinner.

His grandmother didn't want to acknowledge it, but Reggie really did have it worse than a lot of his classmates. His mother had run away from home as a teenager, only to return three years later with a half-white baby in her arms. She never told anyone who the father was. All Reggie knew was that he lived in New York. His mother promised to take him to Brooklyn to meet his daddy, but when she left home again five years later, Reggie remained in Lambert.

It took five more years for Reggie to accept she was never returning for him.

Kids liked to tease Reggie about his mother. About his father. About his tattered clothes and golden skin and funny gray eyes.

Reggie responded with his fists. He didn't care if his opponent was bigger or smaller. If it was one boy or a group. He wasn't taking lip from anyone.

Coach Dub was the first person to take Reggie's anger and channel it into something positive. He first put Reggie on the football and basketball teams, but the boy got into too many scuffles with his teammates. Reggie tried track next, and liked it. He didn't have to work with anyone—he only had to compete against himself and the clock. From there, Coach Dub had him try out for tennis. With a racket in his hand—and when he could remember to keep his temper and his serve under control—Reggie really thrived.

Coach Dub was the best thing that had ever happened to Reggie. He gave Reggie structure and purpose, and a means to find personal success. Thanks to Coach Dub, Reggie believed he could be more than just a poor boy from the South.

Then he messed everything up by falling in love.

To be fair, most of the boys at school were at least a little in love with Siobhan. She was so smart, and so kind, and extremely easy on the eyes. She never said or did anything that made Reggie feel bad about himself, even when he was sitting at her dining room table, stuffing his face because he didn't know where his next meal would come from. She never laughed at him for wearing the same threadbare clothes.

They had only been seeing each other for a year, but it felt like so much longer. Coach Douglas's son had strode into the library like he owned the entire school. Siobhan had given him a word puzzle. Chip didn't know the answer, but Reggie did. His mother used to play word games like that with him, before she left.

Feeling bold, Reggie left a note at her locker, asking her to meet him in the park, not really expecting her to show up. But she had come, and she kept coming back. And a year later, they were in love.

But since her father wouldn't allow her to date, they had to keep their relationship a secret. Outside of group functions, they rarely talked to each other at school. They didn't send each other many notes. Whenever Reggie ate a meal at Coach Dub's house, he was sure to sit as far away from her as he could. He didn't tell any of his friends, and neither did she. But eventually Coach Dub discovered their courtship. He responded by kicking Reggie off the tennis team—in the middle of the season—and threatened to send Siobhan away for her last year of high school.

Reggie wanted to run off with her. But Siobhan had always been the smarter of the two, and she wisely turned him down. Reggie didn't believe he had anything to offer her. He was intelligent, but that wouldn't put food on the table. He was kind, especially toward children, but that wouldn't cover the rent. Reggie had no real way to support her. Provide for her. Protect her. He knew she deserved better than him.

Still, he hoped Coach Dub would come around to give Reggie a real opportunity with his daughter. When Coach Douglas approached him about playing in the exhibition game, he thought he finally had his chance.

But he didn't. On the night of the game, after they'd won, Coach Dub shook Reggie's hand, then leaned in and told him to leave his daughter alone.

"A poor, high-yellow, country-dumb Negro like you will never be good enough for Lil' Dub," he said.

When Reggie saw a car behind the High Horse later that night, he foolishly thought that maybe it was Coach Douglas, coming to check on the boy's battered ego. Instead, three men in masks jumped out of the vehicle. The largest man wielded a knife, while the other two carried baseball bats.

Reggie took off running down a maze of alleys, his feet stumbling in the darkness. He paused every few feet to check a door, hoping to find one unlocked. Finally, he hid behind a row of garbage bins and held his breath. Seconds later, two sets of footsteps rushed by. Kneeling lower, Reggie felt around on the ground, looking for anything he could use as a weapon. Taking a chance, he stood and opened one of the garbage lids. Inside the bin, sitting on top of the trash, was a broken mop handle.

As he picked it up, he heard more footsteps. "Guys, I found him," someone yelled.

Reggie took off again, this time heading back to the bar. The owner kept a gun inside. Maybe he could find it. But before he could reach the back door, someone grabbed Reggie by the arm.

It was the largest attacker—the one with the knife. He swiped at Reggie, tearing a gash in Reggie's side. The man was too big, with arms that were too long. Reggie waited for the man to swing again. But this time, instead of jumping backward to avoid contact, Reggie stepped forward, allowing the man's forearm, not knife, to make contact with Reggie's side. Clamping his arm down, Reggie pinned the man's hand to his side while stabbing at the man's face with the mop handle. The stick, with its jagged, sharp end, sank into his attacker's face. Into his eye socket.

The man screamed.

He dropped his knife and pulled away from Reggie. Flopping on the ground like a fish gasping for air, the man continued to howl as he pressed his hands against his eye.

While Reggie stood there, trying to decide what to do, the other two attackers approached him from behind. One hit him in the leg while the other went for Reggie's shoulder. The boy fell and covered his head as the men began to strike him with their bats.

Then a shotgun blast pierced the air.

Reggie's attackers stumbled away from him. They grabbed the large one, still writhing on the ground, and escaped. A few seconds later, Coach Douglas was there, helping Reggie to his feet and dragging him to his car. Reggie's eyesight was blurry, and his chest hurt every time he breathed. But he was alive.

Coach Douglas took Reggie to Mr. Smith's house in the country. An hour or so later, a nurse showed up. She cleaned his wounds and stitched the gashes on his side and forehead. He had two broken ribs, a dislocated shoulder, and a sprained wrist.

"How you feeling, son?" Coach Douglas asked Reggie the next afternoon.

Reggie winced as he sat up in the guest bed. "I've had better days. I'm sore all over, and my eyes are still a little blurry."

"At least you've got both of them. Word is, Marion Allen was rushed to the hospital last night with a right-nasty facial injury. The doctors tried but they couldn't save his eye."

"So it *was* the Allens," he said. "I figured as much. I just wish I'd gotten Marion's other eye as well." He grimaced as he rubbed his shoulder. "Did they attack the other fellas?"

"The boys are fine. We got them out of the city." Coach Douglas hesitated, then sat down beside Reggie. "But they jumped Big Dub. His injuries are a lot worse than yours. Broken jaw. Missing teeth. Not sure how many blows he took to the head from those bats."

"Is he at the hospital?"

He shook his head. "We thought it best to go ahead and get him and his family out of town. They're in Maryland, staying with Leanne's sister."

"For how long?" Reggie asked. The thought of being apart from Siobhan hurt worse than his body.

"Hard to say. Dub wants to come back, but I don't see that happening. The administration at Perkins found out about the exhibition game. I'm not sure he'll have a job waiting for him if he returns. Shoot, I might not even have a job. Wallace High has already fired Tommy Turner." Coach Douglas rubbed his eyes. "The sad thing is, I'd bet Tommy would still have his job if they'd won."

Reggie didn't care at all about the game right then. "What about Siobhan? They didn't hurt her, did they?"

"She's fine," Coach Douglas said. "But son, you need to forget about her. Like I said, they ain't coming back. It ain't safe for them here anymore. You neither. Not after what you did to Marion Allen."

"Are you going to take me to Maryland too?"

"Dammit, boy! Enough about Siobhan. I don't care how bad Dub was whipped, he ain't never gonna accept you."

Reggie didn't argue. The truth was the truth. He leaned back onto the headboard and let out a long, slow breath. He had done everything Coach Dub asked him to do, even down to intentionally losing points during the match. In Coach's eyes, all Reggie was good for was hitting a ball or running around a track. For a second, he wondered if things would be different if Coach Dub passed away from his injuries. Then he pushed that thought out of his head. He hated the man, but he didn't want him dead.

"But why can't Siobhan and Mrs. Leanne come back? The Allens are mad at me and her daddy, not them. Doesn't Siobhan want to finish up her senior year at Perkins? And Mrs. Leanne is so involved in the church. . . ."

Coach Douglas looked up at the ceiling and mumbled something to himself. Then leaned in close to Reggie and told him about the doll. Its dark skin and red lipstick. The words etched into it. The noose around its neck.

Reggie did not want Enoch Washington dead. He could not say the same about the Allens.

"So what's the plan?" Reggie asked. "How do we get them back?" He sat up taller, and winced when the pain hit his side. "I'm not afraid to fight."

"Don't you understand? It's over," Coach Douglas replied. "This isn't another tennis game. This is real life. They won."

"But we can't—"

"You're just a kid. What, you're going to take on the Allen family? You might as well dig your grave now. And dig a grave for your grandma and everyone else you love," he said. "The best you can do is move away, start over, and live your life."

"What? Move to Chicago? Detroit?"

"No, I think you should join the military. Like I did."

Reggie laughed. "No offense, Coach, but there's a big difference between the way the army treats you and how they'd treat me."

"I know," he said. "But it doesn't have to be that way."

"I don't understand."

"You will, in time." He rose from the edge of the bed. "Get dressed. We're leaving tonight."

———————

Reggie returned home long enough to grab some clothes and kiss his grandmother good-bye, then Coach Douglas instructed him to lie down in the back seat until they reached the state line. He had no idea where they were going. A few hours later, they stopped to grab some snacks and use the restroom.

"Want a Coke?" Coach Douglas asked.

Reggie frowned. "No thanks. Where are we?"

"Georgia. Hopefully, we'll make Mississippi by morning."

"What's there?"

"Patience, son. You don't have to lie down anymore, but you'd better stay in the back. People don't like to see colored kids riding up front with white folks."

Coach Douglas found a Negro gospel station outside of Tuscaloosa. He didn't have a great voice, but that didn't stop him from singing along. At one point, he caught Reggie staring at him. "What? Didn't think I knew all these hymns?"

"I didn't know white people sang songs like that."

"They don't."

Dawn was beginning to break when they pulled up to a large farmhouse. Coach Douglas instructed Reggie to remain in the car. After a few minutes, he returned with an older white woman.

"What happened to his face?" the woman asked. Her stringy brown-and-gray hair whipped in the wind. Liver spots covered her hands.

"Long story," Coach Douglas said. "So what do you think?"

She looked Reggie up and down. "Hmm. Don't know if Walter'll do it."

"Let us stay long enough for me to talk to him. We'll hide in the barn."

"I don't know, Vern. A lot of people will be right surprised if they see you driving around here. Would cause issues for all of us."

"Even better reason for me to hide out for a while," he replied. "Reggie's a good kid, Rita. He deserves a chance at a better life."

Who was this woman? Reggie wanted to ask. *And why did she call Coach Douglas Vern?*

"Go on and pull your car to the back," she said. "Walter'll be home soon."

Reggie and Coach Douglas parked farther onto the property, then walked to the barn. The silence was thick enough to slice. Finally, after sitting on a bale of hay, Reggie asked, "Now will you tell me what's going on?"

"First, let's get a few things straight," Coach said. "I'm about to tell you something that no one knows. Not Chip. Not my wife. If you even think about breathing a word of this to anyone . . ."

"A word of what?"

"I will be forty-eight in three weeks," Coach Douglas continued. "However, according to my birth certificate, I turned forty-five in April. Long before I was Adam Douglas, I was a kid named Vernon Thompson. I'm three-quarters white. The other quarter . . ."

Reggie slowly stood. "You're colored."

He nodded. "I grew up around here. Lived with my uncle—he liked to knock me around when he was drunk, which was all the time. But it wasn't like I had anywhere else to go. My mama died when I was a baby, and my daddy didn't want anything to do with me, even though he lived right down the road.

"Only thing I lived for was working this farm in the summer. This land has belonged to Rita's family for five generations. Walter was born in Philadelphia. They met in college up North, and somehow Rita convinced him to move to Mississippi. Walter never was much of a farmer, but he was a good doctor. And thanks to those Quakers, he had some pretty radical notions on how Negroes should be treated. So did Rita. They always hired colored kids to help out for the summer. Paid us and fed us too. It was better than shining shoes.

"One morning, when I was working the farm by myself, a family came looking for Walter and Rita. They were away in the city, so I kept the family company till they got back home. You know what that family told Rita about me? They said, 'You have such a fine son. He must have gotten all his charm from your side of the family.'" Adam Douglas slapped his knee. "Here's the truth about people: We make a lot of assumptions about each other. People don't think you're colored just because of your skin. They think you're colored because your grandmother is dark-skinned, and you attend a Negro school, and a Negro church, and because you're poor. But what if those same people passed you on the street when you were dressed in a sharp suit? What if they met you in the white part of town? What if you were driving a Cadillac instead of walking? What would they see then?"

Coach Douglas began to pace. "As an old country doctor, Walter dealt with a lot of births . . . and every once in a while, an infant death. It took a while, but Rita eventually convinced him to tweak one of those birth certificates so I could have a new life. And poof—Vernon Thompson died, and Adam Douglas was reborn."

"I can't pretend to be white," Reggie said.

"It ain't pretending. You *become* white. You don't fake being white in public, then turn back into a Negro when you're at home. You have to commit all the way. But if you do, think of all the opportunities. I was able to join the military. I learned a real trade, moved up in the ranks, and then I got my degree. You could do the same."

"But I could never return to Lambert."

"Maybe you ain't figured it out yet, but you can't go back to Lambert anyway. You took Marion Allen's eye. You think he's just going to forget that? And why go back in the first place? In Lambert, you'll always be a poor, pitiful Negro."

"What about my grandma?" Reggie said. His grandmother was all right now, but her health wouldn't hold up forever.

"I'll watch out for her," Couch Douglas said. "Believe me, she'd want you to take this opportunity."

Reggie picked up a stick and began drawing in the dirt. "I don't know, Coach."

Coach Douglas grabbed the stick from Reggie and broke it in half. "One of the guys from my army company is now the vice president of a bank. Another owns his own law firm. And another is a judge." He stuffed his hands in his pockets. "You go to the military and then attend a good school on the GI Bill and you can do the same. As smart as you are, you could write your own ticket. Have more money than God himself, if you wanted it."

Coach Douglas stepped out, leaving Reggie to contemplate what he would do if he were rich and powerful. It didn't take long for him to figure it out. Reggie would use his money to impress Siobhan once and for all. He'd provide her with her every want. He could already see himself—walking up to her while dressed in a crisp army uniform, a grin on his face and a bouquet of roses in his arm. He shook his head—not an army uniform, but a brand-new three-piece suit, his paycheck from his office job tucked in his coat pocket. Or instead of just working at the office, maybe he would even own the company.

But he didn't limit his daydream to Siobhan. He would also get back at the Allens. A single eye wasn't enough to make up for what they did to him and Coach Dub. What they threatened to do to Siobhan. They had to pay.

Finally, Reggie stepped out of the barn and found Coach Douglas. "I'm in," Reggie said. "How do we start?"

Although it was fairly easy to convince Reggie to go through with the plan, it was much harder to get Walter Hamilton to agree. He would lose his license if he was discovered, but that was the least of his worries. The idea of what those good-old boys might do to Rita to exact their revenge made him break into hives. But although Rita was worried, she was also determined, and finally, after a week of prodding, she convinced Walter to look through his files to find someone who might be a good fit.

Meanwhile, Coach Douglas and Reggie worked to create a credible backstory for the person Reggie was to become. Coach Douglas also schooled Reggie on how to pass as white. How to talk with the confidence of a man who could do anything he wanted in this country. How to resist making a scene when someone told a racist joke. How to sit calmly at the front of a bus, or walk into a restaurant that was for whites only. How to look white people boldly in the eye and see them as peers, not the enemy. And when necessary, how to put down and further degrade his own people in order to protect his new identity.

Two weeks later, Reggie left Mississippi for Killeen, Texas, where he would be stationed at the Fort Hood Army Base. He'd already had his hair shaved into a low buzz cut to hide his natural curls. If anyone asked, he was to say he got his tanned skin from working outside.

When he stepped onto his bus for the trip, he sat at the front like all the other white people. He looked them in the eye, trying to be kind and helpful. And when they asked him his name, he smiled as widely as he could and said, "I'm James Parker. Pleased to meet you."

CHAPTER 36

Candice didn't bother trying to go to sleep. That would have been impossible. While waiting for morning, she got her mother's phone and searched the web for any mention of Reginald Bradley. She couldn't find any information about him, which wasn't surprising. Why would anything exist, if he ceased to?

Finally, six o'clock came.

Her hand shook as she punched in the number. It was probably still too early to call, but she'd ask for forgiveness later.

"Hello?" Ms. Jones said, yawning. "Anne? Is something wrong?"

"Hi. It's actually me, Candice. Sorry to be calling at this time in the morning—is Brandon awake?—I have something really important to show him, it'll only take a—"

"Whoa, slow down there," Ms. Jones said. "Unfortunately, Brandon can't come to the phone. He's on punishment for the next two days."

"Oh. Okay." It took her a second to process this, and then another few seconds to formulate a response. "So . . . I can't talk to him at all? Not even for a quick minute?"

"I'll tell him that you called, sweetie. You can see him on Wednesday."

Candice hung up. She wondered what Brandon had done to get grounded for so long.

She returned to her room and stared at the picture of Reginald Bradley. Her confidence didn't waver. She was sure he and James Parker were the same person.

But why had he become someone else?

She assumed life was easier back then if you were white. You could go to any school, or live in any neighborhood. She thought about how Tori slowed down when she drove, and how Mr. Rittenhauer had accused them of breaking into the school, all because of their skin tone. Life would have been like that for Reginald Bradley too. And probably much worse in the fifties.

But not for James Parker.

Candice cracked open one of the tennis books she'd checked out from the library. She kept thinking about Reginald Bradley at that secret tennis game that night. How had they played in the dark? Did they keep score—and use all that confusing tennis terminology? And how did a simple tennis game lead to all those people being attacked and run out of Lambert?

The house phone rang about two hours later. Candice ran back to the kitchen, hoping it was Brandon.

"Hey, Candice," Tori said. "Want to come over?"

"I thought Brandon—"

"He's upstairs and Mom just left. See you in a bit."

As usual, the door was unlocked. "I'm in the kitchen," Tori yelled.

Candice held her notebook and the yearbook tightly in her hands as she entered the room. Tori sat the table with a bowl of lumpy oatmeal in front of her. She was reading *The Westing Game*.

"Pretty good so far," she said, shutting the book. "Here's the deal. I don't know what you have to tell my brother, but it has to be really important to call here at six in the morning. So in exchange for an additional month of car washing, I've agreed to serve as an intermediary between you two."

Candice sat down and opened the yearbook. "I think I found James Parker." She flipped to the page and pointed to Reginald Bradley. "That's him."

Tori turned the book to get a better look at it. "I thought Parker was white."

"I think he was only pretending to be white."

"Hmm. Just like *Imitation of Life*. That's an old movie Mom likes about a girl that passes for white." Tori tapped the photo. "Let's say you're right. Now what?"

"We should call Ellie Farmer. I think she knows more than she's letting on."

"I agree," Tori said. She slid her cell phone across the table. "Make the call."

"What about Brandon? I don't want to do it without him."

"I think he'd understand. This is a big deal, and you don't exactly have time to waste."

Candice paged through her notebook until she found Mrs. Farmer's phone number. She picked up the phone and started to dial, then ended the call before completing the number.

"I want to wait for him," Candice said, giving the phone back to Tori. "He would do the same for me."

Tori rolled her eyes as she rose from the table. "Hold on. I'll be back in a second."

Candice heard the familiar sound of creaking wood as Tori ran upstairs. She returned with Brandon in tow. He smiled at Candice and offered her a slight wave, but didn't speak.

Tori handed the phone to Candice again. "Brandon's only down here to listen to the conversation. He's not supposed to talk at all. And the second we hear Granddad's car turning into the yard, he hightails it back to his room."

Candice searched Brandon's face, hoping to see a hint of . . . she didn't know. Maybe she was looking for a clue as to why he had been grounded, or how he felt about her returning to Atlanta, or how he felt, period.

Brandon held her gaze for a few seconds, giving off no information, then sat down.

Candice quickly dialed the number. She turned on the speakerphone so they could all hear.

Mr. Farmer answered, then passed the phone to his wife.

"Hey, Candice," Ellie Farmer said. "How are you doing, dear?"

"I'm good. We're all good." Candice took a shaky breath. "I was hoping to ask a few questions about one of the students at Perkins. Reginald Bradley."

"Oh? Reggie Bradley, you say?" Candice could hear the change in the woman's voice. She was certainly more guarded. "What do you want to know about him?"

"Did he . . . did he disappear? But not die . . . like . . . maybe he became someone else?"

There was a long pause. "What makes you ask that?" Ellie said.

Candice looked at Brandon. Both his eyebrows were raised. "I . . . we think that maybe . . . well, we aren't for sure . . ."

"I ain't getting any younger," she said. "If you figured it out, then say it."

Brandon lurched forward. "He *is* James Parker, isn't he?"

Tori snapped her fingers and shushed her brother.

"Oh, hey, Brandon. Didn't know you were there." Ellie sighed. "Yes, you're right. Reggie Bradley is James Parker. I'm sorry I lied, but there are some secrets that aren't mine to share. But since you figured it out anyway . . . Reggie was the player who got beat up along with Coach Dub."

Candice stared at the phone. She wished she were in front of Mrs. Farmer so she could see her face.

"Couch Douglas told us that Reggie had found a job in Georgia," she continued. "And then, a few months later, we heard he died in an accident. We didn't think too much about Reggie after that. Life went on, you know? Can't spend forever grieving for folks that are already gone."

"And he never came back home?" Candice asked. "Never saw his family again? Or his friends?"

"Not as far as I can tell," Ellie said. "Coach Douglas would check in on Reggie's grandmother—we were all worried about her, an old woman living by herself. He'd cover a few of her bills on months she was short. But Lizzy Bradley was a tough old bird. She outlived just about everybody else her age. She didn't have any family, so I started dropping by Mount Carmel to visit her. This was years ago—back in the early eighties, when they didn't have a dedicated building for the seniors."

Ellie coughed, then paused to take a sip of something. Candice hoped it was water, but was pretty sure it was something sugary and caffeinated. "Okay, where was I?" Ellie asked. "Oh, yeah . . . when Reggie's grandmother passed, me and some others pitched in to take care of her funeral. Turned out, it had already been paid for by an anonymous donor. I didn't think much about it. Time passed . . . and then one day I received a ten-thousand-dollar check for each of my grands, specifically to help cover college. Didn't know where it came from. Whoever had written the checks had made them impossible to trace. Wasn't until even later that I pieced it all together, when all the fuss started about donations to the school and church and such. One look at a picture of James Parker and I knew it was Reggie. It was the eyes. He always had funny eyes."

"Did Siobhan ever learn who he really was?" Candice asked. "And did you know that they were a couple?"

The line was quiet for a few seconds. "I guess I might as well tell it all. Siobhan was never officially seeing anyone in high school, but she *was* sneaking around with someone, though she'd never tell me who. I had to be her alibi a few times. Always figured it was Coach Douglas's son, but it could have been Reggie. That would have made a lot more sense, now that I think about it. She had a pretty fancy funeral as well."

"Why didn't you ever say anything?" Tori asked. Candice was so busy staring at the phone and listening, she'd forgotten that Tori was beside her.

"You don't go off and start spilling secrets about somebody after they give you that much money. Plus, who was I gonna tell? Everybody he cared about was dead by then." She coughed into the phone. "I didn't blame Reggie. He had a chance at a better life. Lord knows he got dealt a bad hand. His mama was a floozy and alcoholic. He never met his daddy—didn't want anything to do with a black baby."

That made Candice think of something. "His father wasn't one of the Allens, was he?" she asked, her stomach twisting at the thought.

"Oh, Lord no. That would have been even worse. His daddy lived somewhere in New York, I think." She coughed again, this time much harder than before. "I'm sorry. My throat's not feeling so well. I need to get off this phone. But y'all call back tomorrow if you have any other questions."

They said their good-byes and hung up the phone.

"Okay, back upstairs," Tori said to her brother.

Brandon's eyes practically bugged out of his head.

"Upstairs," his sister repeated.

He huffed as he rose from the table, but before he left the room, he offered another small smile and wave to Candice.

"I'll let you know if Brandon has any worthwhile thoughts," Tori said once he'd left. She spun the phone around on the table. "That's such an amazing story. And sad. Do you think he ever talked to Siobhan or his grandmother again?"

"I hope so. I couldn't imagine not seeing my parents again. Or my other family and friends."

"Believe me, there are plenty of jerk fathers out there who are just fine not seeing their families." She cut her eyes at Candice. "Sorry for the snark. You and your dad are on much better terms than me and my biological."

"Yeah, maybe," Candice said. "But he's hiding something from me."

"All parents keep secrets from their kids." She slowly spun her phone on the table again. "What do you think he's hiding?"

"He's seeing someone," Candice said. "A woman named Danielle."

"Um . . . are you sure? I mean, how do you know?"

"I overheard him and Mom talking about it."

"You could always ask him. Give him a chance to explain everything."

Candice eyed Tori. "Do you know something that you're not telling me?"

"Just some things I've overheard as well," she said. "You should talk to your dad. Seriously. Sometimes we have to remind our parents that we understand how the world works." She checked the time. "You should go. Granddad'll be here soon, and I don't think he'd agree with my liberal interpretation of Brandon's punishment."

Candice grabbed the yearbook and rose from the table. "What did Brandon do that was so bad to get himself grounded?"

Tori shook her head. "You can ask him on Wednesday."

CHAPTER 37

Candice didn't know what had happened to change Ms. Jones's mind, but when Brandon called on Tuesday morning and said that he was off punishment, she didn't question him about it. She also didn't ask him what he had done to get grounded in the first place. He didn't ask her if she was excited about going back home. They just got together and worked on the mystery of James Parker.

By that afternoon, they had come to one major conclusion.

So what.

So what if Reggie Bradley was really James Parker? It didn't get them any closer to finding his fortune.

"Do you think he was happy?" Brandon asked. "James or Reggie or whoever he was. I wonder if he liked being someone else."

"Well, he was really rich."

"But was he happy?"

Candice considered his question, then shook her head. "If he was happy, he would have never sent that letter. If he was happy, he would have ended up with Siobhan somehow."

"Do all the people end up together in your mom's books?" he asked.

"Yeah, but she writes romances. It's one of her publisher's rules."

When this was all done, and Candice had told her mother about everything, she hoped her mom would somehow turn it into a book.

"Candice." He looked directly at her. "Face it. We're stuck. It's time to contact the other people who got a letter."

"But Brandon—"

"Last week, your mom said that y'all could be home as soon as this weekend," he said. "That still true?"

"Maybe." Candice pinched her palm. She hadn't started packing, but her mom had.

"We're running out of time," he said quietly. "Don't you want to find the money?"

Candice squeezed her palm even harder, then gave Brandon a small nod.

Brandon spun around and opened a photo of the letter. He'd taken it last Friday so they'd both have a copy. "Before Mom grounded me, I was able to piece together the names of the people who received a letter like your grandmother's. I could only find contact information for one of them." He opened another document. "William Maynard. He was chairman of the school board when your grandmother was city manager."

Candice frowned. "William Maynard . . . that sounds familiar."

"It should." He picked up a Wallace yearbook and flipped to the picture of the tennis team. "He was a member of the team in 1957," he said. "And 1956 too. Maybe he was even there that night."

Candice stared at the photo. William stood next to Glenn Allen. She flipped to his senior photo. He sported a mop of black hair. His eyeglasses looked too small for his face.

"Well, what do you think?" Brandon asked.

She closed the yearbook. "How do we know if we can trust him? If he was there, maybe he was also one of the men who beat up Coach

Washington and Reggie Bradley. Maybe he's as racist as Marion Allen."

"I know, but I think we have to take the chance." He looked out the window, and Candice followed his gaze. She wondered if he had noticed Milo riding by a few moments before. "Okay?" he asked.

Candice took a deep breath. "Okay."

Brandon had found all of William Maynard's contact information online, but instead of calling, they decided to send him an email from a newly created, anonymous email account. It took them a full hour to write and rewrite the message.

Hello. We would like to discuss a letter concerning a lost fortune, and the Allen family's role in driving Enoch Washington and his family from Lambert. Please contact us at your earliest convenience.

Candice hadn't wanted to add the part about the Allens and the Washingtons, but Brandon had been adamant. He wanted to get William Maynard's attention.

It worked.

Less than five minutes later, Brandon's computer dinged. They crowded around the screen.

Who is this? And what letter are you referring to?

While they were figuring out how to respond, another email popped into their inbox. William Maynard wanted them to call him. Now. He'd sent a phone number.

"So now what?" Brandon asked. "I don't really want him to have our phone number. Do you want to call him from your mom's cell phone?"

"No way. Maybe we can do some type of video chat?"

Brandon typed in a return message. *Are you available for video chat?* William Maynard's reply: *Yes. And bring the letter.*

The man on the screen looked well put together. His hair, now stark white, sat high on his head. He wore a plain wedding band on his ring finger (Candice always noticed this now), and his tie was pulled loosely to his neck.

"You two are not who I expected," he said. "Where did you find the letter?"

"With my grandmother's belongings," Candice said. She held up the letter to the screen. "It was in the attic."

"You're Abigail Caldwell's granddaughter, huh." He smiled, and it actually seemed real. "She sure was in love with you. Always talked about you. Said you were the smartest baby ever created."

"You knew her well?" Candice asked.

"Well enough. I was chairman of the school board for about twenty years, both before and during your grandmother's time as city manager. We worked on—" The sound of squealing kids came through the video, cutting him off. "Sorry about that. I've got my grands for the summer." He shifted in his seat. "As I'm sure you're aware, five of us received letters. The mayor asked us all to destroy them."

"Even the editor of the *Lambert Trader*?" Brandon asked.

William Maynard nodded. "The mayor was a very powerful man, with a lot of influence." He played with the end of his tie. "I'm real sorry about what happened to Abigail. If she had just thrown that letter away and forgotten all that nonsense . . ."

"It's not nonsense," Candice said.

"We can prove it," Brandon added. "We know who sent the letter."

"So do I. Reggie Bradley. Or James Parker. Or whatever he was calling himself."

Candice stared at the screen. "You knew?"

"Not at first. Your grandmother was the one who figured out Parker was tied to the donations around the city. She told us all about her research, hoping to get our support. When we refused, she dug up the courts at Vickers Park. I finally looked him up online after that. One glance at that photo and I knew it was him."

"You were there, weren't you?" Brandon said. "You were at the game."

William Maynard sighed. "Those boys beat us fair and square. Beat us like we'd never seen a tennis racket before, much less picked one up."

"What about . . . after?" Brandon asked.

From the look on his face, Candice could tell William Maynard knew what Brandon was talking about. "I had no part in those attacks," he said. "But I knew what Marion and Glenn were going to do." He held up his hands. "Look, they were just trying to make a point. They weren't really trying to hurt nobody. You have to understand, in the fifties—"

"They beat them up and drove them out of town," Brandon said. "How can you justify that?"

"They weren't the only ones hurt," William said. "Marion Allen lost an eye!"

"He only lost an eye because he attacked two innocent people!" Brandon exploded back. Candice had never heard him so upset before. It was a little scary.

"I'm not excusing it. I'm just trying to explain what happened." He reached for a glass of water. "Me and Penelope supported Marion for ten years after his father disowned him. Marion was a mess right up until he died, but what can I say. His sister loved him."

"His sister?" Candice looked back at the wedding ring on William Maynard's hand. "You married an Allen?" She was pretty sure she sneered as she asked the question.

"Don't you dare talk about the dead like that," he said. "She wasn't like the others. Neither of us were."

Brandon crossed his arms. "Tell that to Enoch Washington and Reggie Bradley."

"Look, there's not a day that goes by where I don't think about what those boys did to Dub and Reggie. What I should have done. How I should have stopped them. Said something." Maynard paused to take a drink of water. "Me and Penelope spent the rest of our lives making up for it. You know, if it wasn't for me, Perkins would have been shut down a long time ago, and all of the students would have been sent to Wallace. I was the one who convinced the rest of the board to combine both schools. It was fair that way. And I've always been a supporter of the black community. Shoot, I even became a registered Democrat." He laughed, but stopped after a few moments when they didn't join in.

"The letter says Parker's money would be used to help Lambert," Candice said. "Didn't you want to do that? Get the money for the city?"

"Penelope talked to her brother. He lived up in Seattle," he said. "Like the rest of us, they felt a scandal would further divide the city. They offered to make a sizable donation in order to preserve the peace."

"Was the donation as big as what Parker promised in the letter?" Brandon asked. "Was it forty million dollars?"

He coughed. "No, of course not. But—"

"Was it even as big as what Parker had already donated to the school, the church, and the library?" Brandon added.

Instead of replying, William Maynard finished the rest of his water.

"You were scared," Brandon continued. "You didn't want people to know what you did. Who you really were."

"Look here, son," he said. "James Parker — Reggie Bradley — he wasn't no saint. He just about drove Penelope's company to bankruptcy. He almost destroyed the economic backbone of the city. If he really wanted to help Lambert, he could have made a donation and foregone all the trickery."

"You destroyed his life!" Brandon yelled.

"From where I'm sitting, he ended up doing just fine. He was rich. Powerful. Famous. What more could he want?"

"His old life," Brandon said. "His identity. He had to give up who he was." Now his hands were trembling.

"You kids will never understand," he said. "Sorry to be curt, but this conversation is over. I only wanted to see who you were and what you knew."

"You're going to pretend none of this ever happened?" Candice asked.

"1957 was a long time ago. No one cares. And pretty soon, no one will be alive who even remembers." He reached toward the keyboard. "Some things should remain in the past."

"We'll tell someone!" Brandon said. "We'll go to the police."

"And I'm *sure* they'll believe you. How old are you? Ten? Eleven?" He waved at the screen. "Have a good afternoon. And please, do not contact me again. It's nothing personal, but I have my wife and my family's reputation to protect. At the end of the day, all you have is your name."

The screen went blank.

Neither of them spoke for a few minutes. Candice was playing catch-up with everything Maynard had said. Brandon just stared at the dark screen.

"He's a racist coward," Brandon finally said. "A bully. It's not fair. He doesn't care about the city. All he wants to do is protect his name."

Candice hesitated, then placed her hand on his back. "It's okay. We don't need him."

"Aren't you mad?" he asked.

"Of course I am," she said. "I'm still trying to sort through everything in my head. Trying to figure out what to do next."

Sniffing, Brandon wiped his nose with the back of his hand. "He's right. No one will ever believe us."

"We can prove that James Parker is Reggie Bradley."

"So what? Who'll even care?" He stood up quickly, tipping over his chair. "We should go back to the library. I need more sports books. We have to figure out the rest of the code."

"Brandon, we can wait. I saw Milo—"

"No, we can't. You're leaving, remember? Returning to your fancy life in Atlanta."

Candice slowly stood. "Don't be mad at me. I didn't ask to go back home."

"But you want to go, right?"

She didn't know how to respond, so she kept her mouth shut.

"Come on," he said, already leaving the room. "I'll meet you out front."

Candice returned home. After she used the bathroom and told her mom where she was going, she pulled her bike from the shed and wheeled it to the front of the house.

Across the street, Milo and three of his friends had surrounded Brandon. The boys were yelling at him while Brandon stood still, his arms crossed against his chest.

Candice dropped her bike and ran over. "What's going on?"

"Oh, Brandon, here comes your *girlfriend*," Milo said. "Or is she the boy and you're the girl?"

"Shut up!" Then Brandon looked at Candice. "Go home. I can handle this."

"Just leave him alone," Candice said. If she stuck around, maybe they wouldn't beat him up.

"Oh, she *is* the boy, isn't she?" Milo grinned. Then he called Brandon one of the dirty, horrible, vile names that had been scrawled in the vandalized yearbook. The other boys laughed.

Brandon narrowed his gaze on Milo. Knuckled his hands. Stood taller. "Speaking of girlfriends, is Deacon Hawke still seeing your mom? Does your dad still go to therapy because of it?"

Everyone fell silent.

"Shut up," Milo said. His voice sounded small. Shrill.

"Is that what your dad said to your mom when he caught them together?" Brandon continued. "Do you think it's possible you're actually Deacon Hawke's son?"

"At least *my* parents are still together," Milo said.

"I know," Brandon said. "Some women are too weak to live on their own."

Candice didn't know who was talking, but it wasn't *her* Brandon. It was someone too cruel and cold to be her friend.

Milo cocked back his arm like it was in slow motion. Brandon easily leaned away from the wild swing. And then, while Milo was off-balance, Brandon crushed his fist into Milo's stomach.

"Brandon! No!" Candice yelled.

Brandon turned to Candice. He stared at her like he was seeing her for the first time.

Because he was looking at her, he didn't see Milo swing until it was too late. Milo's fist exploded against Brandon's face. He fell, his arms billowing out. His back and head bounced against the sidewalk with a loud crack.

"Brandon!" Candice yelled, pushing past the boys.

He wasn't moving.

Oh God, he wasn't moving.

"Are you okay?" she asked. "Please, be okay."

Brandon's body had flayed out on the sidewalk. His eyes were closed, and his cheek was already beginning to turn puffy from where Milo had hit him.

One, two, a thousand seconds later, Brandon groaned. Candice decided this was a good thing. She looked up. Milo and one of the boys had taken off down the street, their bikes wobbling underneath them. The other two stood nervously nearby.

"Go get my mom," she said to them. When they didn't move, she screamed. "Go! Now!"

The boys dropped their bikes and ran to her house.

CHAPTER 38

Brandon was trying to sit up when the boys returned with Candice's mom. "Oh my God. Brandon!" she cried, her phone in her hands.

"I'm okay," he mumbled. Blood dripped from his nose. "Help me up."

"Are you kidding?" Candice said, pushing him back to the ground. "You were unconscious! You probably have a concussion."

Her mother knelt beside them. "Yes, I'm with him now," she said into the phone. "He looks okay." After a pause, she said, "No, he doesn't need an ambulance. We can take him." She hung up. "That was your mother," she said to Brandon. "She wants us to take you to the emergency room. She'll meet us there." She placed her hand against his forehead. Then she pointed to the boys on the other side of the street. "Do you know who these two are? Where they live? I'm sure Brandon's mom will have questions."

Candice shook her head.

"I know them," Brandon said.

"Boys, come here," her mother demanded. They quickly crossed the street. "I want you to go straight home. You need to think about what happened here today. Do not try to get together to change your story. Lying will only make things worse."

The boys nodded.

"There were two others," Candice whispered. "Milo and another boy."

"Four boys against one?" Candice's mother slowly flexed her fingers. "Go. Now," she said to Milo's friends.

They left, and her mother turned her attention back to Brandon. "Hang tight, kiddo. I'll be back in a second. Candice, you stay here while I get the car."

Brandon covered his face with his hand. Candice thought it was because he was trying to block the sun, but then she saw the tears rolling down his cheeks.

Candice didn't know what to do. So she just took his other hand.

———————————

Candice didn't cry on the way to the hospital. She even held it together as they entered the brightly lit building, with Brandon squeezing her hand so tightly she was sure she would have bruises. Then Brandon's mother rushed in, her face streaked with tears, and Candice could feel the pressure building behind her eyes. But when they put him in a wheelchair, Candice's chest heaved, and finally sob after sob began to break through.

"Oh, my dear, sweet Candice." Her mother pulled her into an embrace. "It's just a precaution."

After they had wheeled Brandon off behind the white security doors, Candice's mother led her to a quiet corner in the lobby. "What happened out there? Something tells me this has been going on for a while."

Candice told her mother how Milo and his friends bullied Brandon at school, and how it had continued during the summer. Then she started to explain what happened that day, but froze at the part between Brandon's and Milo's punches—the part where she had yelled out Brandon's name.

"It's all my fault," Candice mumbled. Her mouth had gone all coppery, and she couldn't breathe. It felt like she'd been the one hit in the stomach.

Her mother frowned. "I don't understand."

She grabbed her mom's hand. "I yelled at Brandon to stop. He looked at me, and that's when Milo hit him. And he fell, and there was the sound of his body and his head hitting the concrete, and—"

"Stop right now," her mother said. "You are most certainly not to blame for this."

Candice let her mother hug her. She knew she was acting like a baby. She didn't care.

"I'm sorry about all this," she said. "I know you're on deadline."

"Candice, you are more important than any deadline in the world." She smoothed her daughter's hair. "Let's find the cafeteria. It's a good day for a mommy-daughter lunch."

CHAPTER 39

Brandon's doctor suspected that he had a concussion, though she wasn't completely sure. If anything, Brandon received it when his head hit the sidewalk, not when Milo punched him, but Candice was sure Milo would say the opposite when school started.

She went to visit Brandon at home the following day.

"Hey, Candice," Ms. Jones said as Candice crossed the street. She sat on the porch, flipping through a magazine. "Go on up. But he needs his rest, so don't stay too long, okay?"

"Yes, ma'am. I understand." She put her hand on the door handle, then let it linger there. "Mom told me this morning that y'all aren't going to press charges."

She nodded. "Millie and I had a very long, very frank conversation yesterday. I've made it abundantly clear what steps I will take if this bullying continues." Ms. Jones closed her magazine. "But Milo wasn't the only one in the wrong here. Brandon told me what he said about Milo's mother."

Candice let her hand fall from the door handle.

"If you hadn't guessed, Brandon's outbursts of late haven't been just about Milo," his mother continued. "It's been a really hard summer for him. And it got even tougher when he found out you were leaving."

Candice looked at her, then back at the door. What was she supposed to say?

"Go on up," she said. "And Candice, thank you for being a good friend."

Candice entered the house and took the stairs to Brandon's room. His door was already cracked open, so she softly knocked and stepped into the room. The lights were off, and the curtains were drawn shut. All she could see of Brandon was a lump underneath the sheets.

"Please tell me you brought me something to read," he said. "Anything. Beggars can't be choosers."

"Sorry. Mom wouldn't let me bring any books over." She looked around, trying to find somewhere suitable to sit. She had never been in a boy's room before. She had expected it to smell . . . well, like a boy. But Brandon's room smelled like cinnamon and new books, which fit him perfectly, she had to admit. It was a way better scent than her father's citrus cologne.

"How much longer do you have to stay in bed?" she asked.

"I should be okay tomorrow. They want to make sure I don't have any lingering effects." He sat up and kicked off his sheet. Candice was glad he was wearing a T-shirt and shorts, not pajamas. That would have made things even weirder.

"You should lie back down."

"No. It's okay. I feel a lot better."

Once he was sitting up, Candice figured it was all right for her to sit on the edge of the bed. "What's this about you not wanting to press charges?" she asked.

"I can't turn Milo in to the police. He's a kid."

"And so are you. And he hit you. And you fell. And your head smashed against the concrete and . . ." She shook her head. She was not about to cry again. "Milo's going to keep being a bully unless you do something."

"Mom and I talked about it. I'm going to take self-defense classes. Not because I want to fight him, but Mom thinks it'll help with my confidence. Maybe I'll meet some new friends." He drew his right leg underneath him. "What else am I going to do once you leave?"

Candice poked at the hole in her jeans. It had grown so large over the past couple of weeks. There was no way she'd be able to wear these jeans to school come August. "I talked to my mom too. We'll be here for another week, until next Friday."

"Nine days?"

"Yeah. Nine days." It wasn't a lot, but it was better than the alternative.

He slapped his hands together. "We've got to get to work if we're going to find Parker's fortune before you leave. I've got an idea—"

"That's not why I'm staying," she said. "Well, it's not the only reason." Her eyes had finally adjusted to the dark, so she could see Brandon's face. "You're my friend. Like, a real friend. I don't want the summer to end yet."

"You're my friend too. Like, my *only* friend right now."

"Because Quincy is gone?"

He nodded.

Candice slid closer to Brandon. "Want to tell me about him?"

Brandon shrugged, then went back to staring at his bedsheets. Candice was willing to wait as long as necessary if he wanted to talk.

Then she thought, *Friendship goes both ways.* It was like one of the fancy bridges her dad sometimes inspected. Bridges over water that were so big, so long, they had to be constructed from both sides.

She decided to go first.

"I didn't find that letter in any old box," she began. "You probably didn't notice it, but the box in the attic was labeled *FOR CANDICE*. The letter was tucked in one of my old puzzle books."

Brandon looked up.

"And the scribbles on the back of the envelope — that was my grandmother's handwriting. *Find the path. Solve the puzzle.* I think it's a note addressed to me." Candice wished it was even darker in the room. That would have made things easier. "She's the reason I like puzzles and mysteries so much. Crossword puzzles, riddle books, strategy games — you name it, she bought it. Every birthday. Every Christmas."

"You think she was preparing you for this?" Brandon asked.

Candice nodded. "And now it feels as if I'm the only person left in the world to prove she was right. Like it's my destiny. And if I fail—"

"But we haven't failed. We know the fortune is out there. Whether we find it or not, we know it's there."

"But the world doesn't know," Candice said. "My grandma deserves more than being the punch line of somebody's bad jokes. Her name means something, just like everyone else's."

Candice stopped talking because she knew if she said one more word, she would lose her battle with the tears. They sat in silence for a few minutes.

"Quincy's gay," Brandon said. "Last year, he told his parents and some of the teachers. Everyone freaked out. Well, almost everyone."

"Not you?"

He shook his head. "He's been my best friend since I moved here. He officially came out last year, but a part of me has always known." Brandon kicked his legs over the edge of the bed and sat beside Candice. "It was strange. Most of the kids didn't really care. Some people were nice, but still talked to him like he was . . . I don't know . . . like he was a whole different person. But a few kids teased him a lot."

"Milo and his friends."

"They never hit him. That would have been easier. They just called him names. Bad names. Quincy was taking it pretty hard. That's why his parents sent him to stay with his grandparents for the summer."

"Are they trying to convert him to straight or something?"

"Not at all. They're cool with it," he said. "Again, if you've known him for a while, you kind of already knew."

"When my parents separated, they made me see a therapist," Candice said. "It helped a lot. Maybe Quincy should do the same. And maybe you should too."

"Granddad doesn't believe in head doctors."

"But I bet your mom would get one for you."

"Yeah, I know she would." He shifted on the bed. "I haven't talked to Granddad since Saturday."

"What happened?"

Instead of immediately responding, Brandon began playing with the hem of his T-shirt. Candice quickly added, "I mean, you don't have to tell me if you don't—"

"No, it's okay," he said, letting the fabric go. "Granddad saw me right after I found out you were leaving. I, um . . . I wasn't taking it so well." He laughed a little. "Granddad told me to toughen up. I got mad and called him ancient and a dinosaur. Then he called me . . . um, some other stuff."

Candice's stomach worked itself into a knot. She began flexing her fingers.

"Anyway, that's why I was grounded," he said.

"Did you tell your mom what he said?"

He nodded. "She's pretty mad at both of us. She agreed that Granddad was from a different generation, but she also said that I can't call people names every time I get mad at them."

"So he gets to say whatever he wants? That's not right."

"If it makes you feel better, she yelled at him more than she yelled at me. I'm sure she would have grounded him too if she could have."

"Well, once we find the money, you probably won't have to live with your granddad anymore," Candice said.

As Brandon wrinkled his nose in response, Candice realized maybe that wasn't the solution he was hoping for. Maybe Brandon *wanted* to live with his granddad—he just wished his granddad treated him better.

"Actually, I'd use the money to start a basketball summer camp," Brandon said. "For LGBTQIA kids. Where it's safe to be whoever you want to be. Where you don't have to worry about people saying nasty things to you on the basketball court."

Candice's mind began to race. "Maybe we could make it a camp for all sports. Tennis too. That would be really cool."

He cocked his head to the side. "*We?* You'd want to start a camp with me?"

"Sure. Why not? We're partners, right?" She grinned. "And who knows, maybe I'd learn how to shoot a decent three-point shot."

He laughed. "There's no camp in the world that would help with that."

They fell quiet again. Candice wanted to ask him more about this camp. Was it for gay kids like Quincy . . . or for gay kids like him?

But he was her friend. If he needed to tell her something, he would.

"I brought you something." She reached into her pocket and pulled out her iPod. "I know you can't watch TV or read, but maybe you can listen to music."

Brandon took the iPod from her. He pushed the button to turn it on, casting his face in a blue glow, then swiped through the music. "These are old songs."

"My dad likes to call them classic."

He pressed play, and "September" started. "This is my mom's favorite song by Earth, Wind & Fire, since she was born on September twenty-first."

"Oh. Um, okay."

"That's one of the lyrics."

"No it isn't," Candice said.

"Really, it is." He turned up the music, then started singing along. "*Do you remember / the twenty-first night of September?*"

"They're saying, 'When we were young in September.'"

Brandon covered his mouth as he yawned. "Check the lyrics online when you get home. If I'm right, you owe me a chili-cheese dog."

"Deal." Candice rose from the bed.

"Wait. One more thing." He let out a long, shaky breath. "I'm sorry for what I said out there to Milo. You know, the stuff about his mom. It was . . . I'm sorry."

"It's okay," she said. "I mean, I was a little surprised. But I'm not mad at you." She rubbed her arm. "If anything, I should be the one saying sorry. If I hadn't yelled your name like that, you wouldn't have been sucker-punched." Candice was afraid she'd remember the way he fell against the sidewalk for the rest of her life. The sound his body made when it slammed against the concrete. It was like a stupid infomercial that was on repeat in her head.

"See, that's exactly why *I'm* apologizing," Brandon said. "The way you looked at me . . ." He sniffed. "I just . . . I'm not like that. I don't want you thinking of me like that once you go back home. Okay?"

"Brandon, don't worry. I know who you really are."

She had just reached the door when he said, "Oh, and Candice . . ." She turned around. "You're not the only person left in the world to prove that your grandmother was right," he said. "We're partners, remember? I've always got your back."

Candice beamed at him. "And I've got yours."

CHAPTER 40

Siobhan Washington

1958–1985

"Mama, I'm home," Siobhan said as she stepped into the house and pulled off her heavy winter coat.

She let the door bang shut behind her. *Home.* When had her aunt's worn beige carpets, wood-paneled walls, and stucco ceilings come to represent home?

Was it when she enrolled in the local school? When Perkins High School fired her father? When the Lambert police finally declined to press charges against the Allens? When her parents' lawyer told them they'd taken things as far as they could legally?

"Mama?" she called again. The car was outside. And her father hardly ever left home anymore. Where were they?

She paused upon entering the kitchen. Her parents sat at the table, in the dark. Ever since his attack, her father didn't like sitting in brightly lit rooms. It made his constant headaches that much worse.

Her mother rose from the table and walked over to Siobhan. Once she was near, Siobhan could see that her mother's face was wet. "It's Reggie," she said quietly. "He passed away."

"What? How? Was it . . . ?" Siobhan had to stop, to take a breath. In the darkness, her fingers found her wrist. Her bracelet. She pressed it against her skin. "Was it Marion Allen?"

Her mother shook her head. "Reggie died in Georgia. According to Coach Douglas, he'd found work on a shrimping boat. There was an accident out in the water. He went overboard."

Siobhan's mother hugged her then, and that's when the tears truly began to fall. It had been six months since she'd last seen Reggie. She had been waiting, hoping that he would show up. She hadn't known where he was—all Coach Douglas would tell her was that he was safe.

"When is the funeral?" she asked.

"There won't be one," her mother replied. "They couldn't find his . . . the waves were too strong . . ." She patted her daughter's back. "Coach Douglas and Reggie's grandma are going to hold a small memorial at the church." She pulled away and looked at Siobhan. "But we can't go back."

Siobhan let go of her mother. "Mama. You can't be serious!"

"If the Allens knew you were back in town, there's no telling what they'd do to you. I can't let that happen." Her voice was shaking. "We already lost Reggie. We can't lose you too."

Siobhan crossed her arms. "I could sneak back on my own."

"Yes, you could," she said. "But do you think Reggie would want that? If he were here, he'd say—" She stopped as the phone rang. "That's probably your aunt. I need to answer that." She touched Siobhan's cheek, then walked toward the hallway. But before she left the kitchen, she flipped on the lights, illuminating the room.

"Leanne! The light!" Her father barked from the table, covering his eyes. Even with a reconstructed jaw, her father still slurred his words a little, but Siobhan had grown to understand his speech.

Her mother kept going down the hallway, leaving Siobhan there to stare at her father. His eyes still closed, he pointed to the wall. "Do you mind . . . ?" he began.

Siobhan remained in place.

After a few seconds of silence, he slowly rose from the chair and began limping toward the wall. He owned a cane, but was too proud to use it. A thick salt-and-pepper beard now covered his face—perhaps to hide the scars from his attack.

Big Dub made it halfway across the room before Siobhan finally marched past him. She flipped off the light. "There."

He sighed. "Mind helping me back to my seat?"

Reluctantly, she walked to him. Even before taking his arm, she could smell the alcohol on his breath.

She helped him return to his chair, then turned to leave. "Wait," he said, grabbing her arm. "Look . . . I'm sorry about what happened to the boy."

"Reggie," Siobhan said, yanking her arm away from him. "Can't you at least call him by his name?"

Her father nodded. "I know how much you cared for him. For Reggie. And while I don't think he was the right boy for you—"

"Daddy," she warned.

"Well, he wasn't. The boy was poor. With skin as bright as a light bulb. Look, I had to marry someone light-skinned. But you didn't need to."

"Did it ever occur to you that I loved Reggie for who he was, not for his money or skin tone?" She shook her head. "And how can you even say something like that, being married to Mama?"

"Leave me and your mama out of this," he snapped. "Now like I said, I didn't approve of the boy, but I didn't want anything like this to happen to him. But don't worry. As soon as I get better, I'll finish what he started."

Now she frowned. "I don't understand."

"Marion Allen," her father said. "Reggie took one eye. Maybe I can take the other. I've been talking to Smitty about it, and we think—"

"Are you serious?" She gave her father a sad, pathetic laugh. "You want to attack Marion Allen? You can barely walk."

"He destroyed my life!" he yelled. "Our life! We'd still be in Lambert—"

"If you didn't make that stupid bet!" she yelled back. "I'd still be at Perkins, and you would still have a job, and no one would be hurt, and Reggie wouldn't be dead!"

She took in a few ragged breaths. This was another thing that had happened since she moved. She had found her voice. Before, she had been passive in her rebellion—sneaking off to see Reggie, refusing to play tennis. Now whenever her father—or really, anyone—challenged her, she roared back.

"Don't you want to get back at the Allens?" her father asked. "Don't you want justice for Reggie?"

"Justice is trying to work with the police. With lawyers. Trying to change the system." she said. "You want revenge. And this has nothing to do with Reggie. This is all about you."

Siobhan left the room then. She was through talking to her father. It was easy for him to be bold when he was propped up by liquor and bravado. But when the time came to actually put in the real work—going to therapy, trying to find a new job, taking responsibility for his actions—he would shrink back into the shell of a man he had become.

Her mother had already begun to move on. She'd become involved in the local NAACP chapter. She was going to church again. She had friends outside of their home. Leanne Washington had decided not to let Big Dub's mistakes define her.

Neither would Siobhan.

Siobhan Washington wouldn't return to Lambert until 1985 — twenty-eight years after she and her family were driven away. After years of neglect, the city was finally renovating Vickers Park. In addition to new playground equipment, they planned to add tennis courts, and thanks to community input, they had decided to dedicate the courts to her father.

Siobhan wanted to be there when the plaque was unveiled. Her father had passed away in the fall of 1962, just before Siobhan graduated from college. Her mother had filled in some of the blanks about her father's childhood, including how he'd been mistreated because of his skin tone and his family's poverty. Her father had been consumed by hate for others — and perhaps even himself — but he had still been a great man, and had done much for the community. He deserved to be recognized.

By now, Siobhan had moved from the classroom and was now serving as a second-year school librarian. Being surrounded by stacks of books every day, along with the upcoming tennis court dedication, caused Siobhan to think more about Reggie than she had in years. His grandmother had passed away recently. Siobhan worried she was the only person left in the world who remembered him.

One night she pulled a small memory box from the top of her closet. Inside was the red scarf she'd worn at the tennis game. The faded note she'd found at her locker all those years ago, asking her to meet at the park. There was also a creased picture of the tennis team that she'd cut out of a Perkins yearbook. Reggie stood on one side of the photo, and she on the other, but when she folded it the right way, she was standing right beside Reggie, her arm pressed against his.

And there was the bracelet. She'd stopped wearing it when she got married, and hadn't thought to put it back on after her divorce. But now, as she was preparing to return to Lambert, it felt right to have it on her wrist again. It was a way to bring Reggie with her as well.

On a whim, she decided to slip off to Lambert a few weeks before the dedication. So much had changed about the city, yet there were things that brought her right back to 1957. PJ's on Darling Avenue, still serving their daily special. Perkins High School — now integrated, but still the pride of the African American community. Mount Carmel — her mother's home away from home.

And Vickers Park, where she once fell in love with a boy, and where he loved her back.

It was spring, and everything was beginning to turn green. The park was already under renovation. The city had dug up a lot of the old trees to make room for a pavilion and the tennis courts. But their oak tree was still there.

She placed her hand against the tree's rough bark and thought about all the secrets she'd whispered underneath its branches. All the kisses she shared underneath its canopy of leaves. If she had known what would have happened to Reggie, she would have taken more pictures of him. With him. Maybe they should have carved their initials in the bark so they could be together forever.

Maybe, maybe, maybe.

She walked over to the location of the future tennis courts. The ground had been dug up; the soil was still fresh from where deep tree roots had been. She wished she had something of Reggie's from back then. She wanted to place a memento in the dirt, underneath the green courts. He had been forgotten by so many people, but he deserved to be memorialized too. Reggie was important, and even in death, she wanted him to know that.

She slipped off her bracelet. Old and scratched, it looked more like something a child would win from a carnival than a piece of jewelry suitable for a woman her age. She had already memorized every curve of her initials, the feel of the word *Love* against her skin. Perhaps she didn't need the bracelet anymore. She had him in her head and in her heart, and that was most important.

But as she held the bracelet over that deep, dark hole, she still didn't know if she could let him go.

CHAPTER 41

"I found the lyrics to 'September' yesterday," Candice said as she entered Brandon's kitchen late Thursday morning. "What do you want on your chili-cheese dog?"

Brandon grinned. He had three sports books from the library open in front of him—one on football and two on tennis. "Don't feel bad," he said. "When I was little, I once heard our pastor talking about the Seven Seals in the Book of Revelations. I thought he was talking about real seals. You know, the cute little animals? I had a thing for Arctic mammals."

"How old were you when you figured out the truth?"

"Six, but that's beside the point," he said. "Like my mom says, sometimes we hear what we want to hear and see what we want to see." He flipped a page. "What have you been up to?"

"Playing *Mental Twister*," Candice said, not looking at him. "And packing."

"Oh. Yeah. Nine days."

She was actually down to eight, but she wasn't about to say that.

Candice and Brandon didn't make much headway that day. Partially because they were stuck, and partially because Candice came down with a huge case of indigestion. Both Brandon and Tori had warned her not to eat two chili-cheese dogs, but the smell overrode her common sense, and she ended up scarfing them down. One had extra onions.

That night, Candice got up to find something to soothe her stomach. She heard her mother's heavy breathing as she passed by her room. Both of her parents snored, but the two noises had always seemed to fit together. To her, it sounded like melody and harmony.

We hear what we want to hear. We see what we want to see.

It seemed like everything that summer had been pointing to that. It was on the tip of everyone's tongues, in the misunderstood lyrics of her favorite songs, and stamped on the jewelry she'd owned for almost half of her life.

Parker's mystery was the *perfect* example of seeing what you wanted to see and hearing what you wanted to hear. *Too* instead of *Two*. *For* instead of *four*. *Pie* instead of *pi*. And a white man from Colorado instead of a black man from South Carolina.

Candice found a box of chewable antacid tablets in the cabinet. She washed down their chalky, gritty taste with a glass of water, and returned to her room.

The letter sat unfolded on her nightstand. She had read it so many times that she almost had it memorized (though she still had to remind herself to think "Shi-vaun" instead of "See-oh-bon").

She paused.

We hear what we want to hear. We see what we want to see.

Candice scanned the letter until she found the first clue: *1. Siobhan's father loved tennis, but he grew up idolizing a team in another sport.*

His first love was baseball.

The Luling Oilers.

Oilers.

It was a funny-looking word, at least in her head. A funny-sounding word.

She crept into her mother's room and took her cell phone from her purse. Her mom stirred, but didn't wake up.

Back in her room, Candice opened the web browser, typed in *number* and *oiler*, and hit SEARCH.

Brandon had run a search like this before, but they had been looking for numbers related to sports. They had tried *"Luling Oilers"* + *"number,"* and then *"Houston Oilers"* + *"number."* Even *"Biz Mackey"* + *"number."*

But now, right at the top of the browser, was exactly what Candice and Brandon had been looking for. It had been there the entire time.

They just hadn't been able to see it.

CHAPTER 42

James Parker

1957–1986

When people looked at James Parker sitting behind his large mahogany desk in his high-rise office, they always saw what they wanted to see. What *he* wanted them to see.

A successful engineer. A shrewd businessman. A loyal army veteran. A rich white man.

The truth of the matter was, no one knew the real James Parker. Every meaningful detail about his real life remained hidden away, like the contents of a safety-deposit box that even he had lost the key to.

When he first joined the army, he kept to himself, convinced that someone would surely realize he wasn't who he claimed to be. As time passed, he became increasingly comfortable in his new skin. He stopped hesitating when people referred to him by his new name. He resisted flinching every time a police car passed. He mastered how to bury his pity every time he asked a young black man to shine his shoes.

After Parker finished his military service, he used the GI Bill to earn a degree in civil engineering from the Colorado School of Mines—as far from the South as he could get. Then he moved to Denver to work for the city engineering department. The work was good and the pay was fair. But Parker wanted more than just a paycheck. He wanted to be his own boss. He convinced two of his coworkers to quit their jobs and form a design firm with him. As the company prospered, Parker branched out into new areas. He eventually bought out his partners, making him the majority owner, president, and CEO of his company.

When he was thirty-five (in real life, not on his birth certificate), he made his first corporate acquisition when Parker Holdings Inc. purchased a small construction company. After meeting with his new employees, he turned to Beatrix Halliday, his longtime assistant, and asked, "What do you think they're saying about me?"

He expected her to say, *They're excited* or *scared* or *worried for their jobs.*

She replied, "Caleb down in accounting thinks you're the grandson of a mob boss. And Mary Alice in the secretarial pool thinks you're saving up to run for governor."

That made him chuckle. Given his history, he'd never become the governor of Colorado—too many background checks were required.

"And what do you think?" he asked.

Mrs. Halliday smiled politely, readjusted her spectacles, and said, "I'd be happy to answer that for you . . . as soon as I'm ready to retire."

Beatrix Halliday had followed him from his job with the city to become the fourth-ever employee in Parker's business empire. Her business card said *Executive Secretary*, but she was part mother, part assistant, part gofer, part confidant. She knew when to restock his office refrigerator with Dr Pepper, and the exact time he liked to eat lunch every day.

As Parker Holdings grew, James Parker became more important in the business world. Colleagues asked him to join important organizations. Donors asked him to support various charities. The mayor began to call on him for financial advice. And then the governor. And then United States senators and representatives.

He had a few friends at the beginning of his engineering career, but the more successful he became, the more fearful he grew of someone discovering his true identity and exposing him. So he slowly pulled away from anyone who ever tried to befriend him, like a starving man hoarding his last scraps of bread. Eventually, Mrs. Halliday was the closest person to a friend that Parker had. Which wasn't close at all.

But Parker didn't forget everything about his true identity as his wealth and power grew. He remembered Marion Allen—how the man had tried to destroy him; had threatened to destroy Siobhan. Marion Allen had forced him to flee the only city—the only people—he'd ever loved. He had already died at this point, but Parker didn't care. As far as he was concerned, all the Allens were to blame for what happened on that August night in 1957.

Parker ordered Mrs. Halliday to develop a file on the Allens. He wanted to know everything about their businesses. Their property. Their investments. He hired a private investigator to dig into their personal lives.

They were surprisingly easy to destroy.

He started with Allen Textiles Inc., buying up enough shares to oust the family from control. Then he ruined their land development company. Their accounting firm. Over the course of ten years, they went from wealthy to filing for bankruptcy.

Eventually, Parker purchased his eighth company, a large tech firm. And for the eighth time, he turned to Mrs. Halliday and asked, "What do you think the employees at the new company are saying about me?"

Beatrix Halliday patted her gray hair and said, "The boys in the warehouse think you fund the CIA, and the ladies at the front desk think you're a descendant of the Queen of England."

"What do *you* think?"

Instead of offering up her usual smile, Beatrix Halliday cleared her throat and said, "Ask me again in two weeks. I'm putting in my notice. I'm retiring."

James Parker didn't respond, so she kept talking. "Gary quit selling insurance three years ago. I have grandbabies to spoil." She removed her glasses and wiped her eyes. "It's time."

"If it's about the money—"

"It's not," she said. "It's about my family. Friends. It's about living life. Spending time with the people you love while you still can."

Then Mrs. Halliday rose from her desk, took a step toward her boss, and said, "Maybe it's time for you as well. You know where she lives. Talk to her."

Beatrix Halliday didn't just know about the Allens and Lambert, South Carolina. She had seen the briefings from private investigators. The newsletters from the Silver Spring School District. The clippings from the *Washington Post*. Items that even the most careful of men couldn't completely hide away.

She knew what he wanted the most. *Whom* he wanted the most.

"You know where she lives," she repeated. "So try. You owe it to her, and you owe it to yourself."

James Parker had kept tabs on Siobhan Washington throughout the years. She lived in Silver Spring, Maryland, now, the librarian at the same elementary school she had been a teacher at for many years. He knew she had attended her high school reunion three years prior, and the dedication of the Enoch Washington Tennis Courts in Vickers Park a year ago. He had known about the dedication for some time, but couldn't bring himself to make a donation. As far as he was concerned, Enoch Washington was as much to blame for what happened as Marion Allen.

Siobhan had been married, but was now single. She had returned to using Washington as her last name.

Parker had wanted to contact her so many times over the past twenty-nine years. But he was never ready. Was never powerful enough. Rich enough. He always needed one more deal, one more zero added to the end of his bank account. She deserved only the best, and he had yet to achieve it.

But he was also scared. Terrified, even. He had become a different man. What if she no longer loved him? Or what if she asked him to change—to become the man he used to be? What was he supposed to do then?

But Mrs. Halliday's words had emboldened him. They gave him the permission he'd been seeking for his entire life. He found himself booking a flight to Dulles International Airport. He couldn't sleep the night before nor on the flight. What was he supposed to do? Just walk up to her after that many years?

He rented a car and drove the thirty miles from the airport to Silver Spring. It was early afternoon when he reached her school. Black kids and white kids climbed on the monkey bars and played on the swings. Black teachers and white teachers chatted with one another. It was a different world.

Sweat poured down his back as he entered the main office. He cleared his throat once, then twice, and then asked, "Is Ms. Washington in today?"

The woman behind the counter nodded as she picked up a phone. "Do you want me to call her?"

"No. Wait." He couldn't talk to her now. He wasn't ready. It had been twenty-nine years, and he still wasn't ready.

He reached for a sheet of paper. "If I could just leave a note for her . . ." He uncapped his pen, then hesitated again. What could he say? Should he sign it as Reggie? He hadn't used that name in so long—he could barely remember how to spell it.

He glanced at the receptionist. "Is there a park nearby? Or a landmark. Or a—"

"Acorn Park," the woman said. "It's a small park, just off the highway. I can give you directions."

Parker nodded, and then wrote:

Only one person was going to St. Ives.

Will you meet me at Acorn Park at 5:00?

James Parker watched as Siobhan approached. He rose from his seat slowly. It was cool, but not cold. He already planned to give her his jacket if she were chilly. If she would take it.

She hesitated when she saw him, then continued on to the gazebo. She looked different, but also the same. Her hair was shorter. She had gained weight, but hadn't they both? The glasses were new.

It was amazing how much she looked like her mother.

She stopped a few feet away from him. "Is it really . . . ?" she began.

"Hello, Siobhan." He wanted to touch her hand. Her skin. He wanted to confirm that she was real and standing before him.

"Reggie," she said.

He was eighteen all over again.

"What happened to you?" she continued. "I thought . . . I heard you had died."

"Maybe you should sit down," he said.

"I need to walk. I need to move. It helps me think." She started off, but stopped when she noticed he wasn't following. "No. Come with me."

Parker nodded, then fell into step beside her.

Siobhan met Parker again the next day. And the day after that.

He was supposed to return to Denver for a series of meetings. He canceled them. He cleared his schedule for the next week. Then the month afterward. In the mornings, while Siobhan was at school, he sat in on conference calls with his board members and employees, existing clients and new customers. During lunch, he read all the books she raved about. *A Wrinkle in Time. M.C. Higgins, the Great.* And her favorite, *The Westing Game.*

His afternoons and evenings were reserved solely for her.

"You should let me buy you a new bracelet," he said one night as they finished dinner at an upscale restaurant in DC. "A woman of your beauty shouldn't wear something so juvenile."

"But I like it," she said, glancing at her wrist. The aluminum bracelet was scratched and weathered. He had been surprised and even happy to see it, but these feelings were soon eclipsed by shame. He had been so poor back then. So powerless. So insignificant. Now he could give Siobhan anything she wanted. She could leave that bracelet in the past, along with everything else.

"My mother noticed that I started wearing it again," she continued. "When she asked why, I told her my new friend liked how it looked on my arm. Now she's all eager to meet you."

Parker hadn't even known her mother was still alive a month ago. She stayed in an assisted living facility not far away. Siobhan saw her three times a week. Every time she visited, he felt a pang for his own grandmother. He never got a chance to see her again before she died.

He reached for her hand, and she allowed him to take it. "I could see how introducing me to your mother could be problematic," he said.

"Problematic? That's a polite way of putting it." She laughed a little. "I don't even know what to call you. You'll never be James Parker to me."

"It's only a name."

"I don't think so. A name helps to define who we are. It reminds us of our history."

"Is that why you went back to using Washington?"

She nodded. She hadn't talked much about her marriage, and he hadn't pressed her on it. He felt he didn't have the right to ask certain questions.

"You know you can't stay here forever," she said. "You eventually have to go back home."

He was in negotiations to acquire another company. He had done as much as he could from his hotel suite, but he needed to return to his office to finalize the purchase. The real world was at their doorstep, and it was dangerously close to barging in.

"What if . . . what if you came with me?" he asked.

"For the winter break?"

"No." He squeezed her hand. "Forever."

Siobhan stared at her dessert—a chocolate mousse covered in strawberries and whipped cream. Parker had already finished his. It was richer than he had anticipated.

"How could we even make that work? How—"

"We'd find a way."

"And what would life be like for me there? With you?"

"You'll be my . . ." He struggled for the words. *Girlfriend* didn't sound right. Not big enough. He should have bought her a ring! She should be his fiancée. "It will be fine."

"And would you be okay with dating someone who's black?" she asked.

Parker didn't answer. Siobhan pulled her hand away.

"What do you want me to do, Reggie? Pretend I'm someone else?" As she held up her brown hands, her bracelet slid down her arm. "All of us can't pass."

"There are creams you can take. Medicine—"

Her face twisted into a frown—or worse, a look of disgust. "I'm forty-six years old! I'm not going to change who I am now." She pushed her plate away. "I *won't* change who I am. Not after what I've been through."

"I'm sorry," he quickly replied. "Of course you don't have to change. My board . . . they will be fine. I'll deal with any fallout. I mean, there will be some financial repercussions. . . ."

"Do you seriously think you'll lose clients if you start dating a black woman?"

"Don't be so naïve. Of course I'll lose work. There are still a lot of racists out there."

"Then why do business with them in the first place?"

"It's not that simple," he said. "Sometimes, I don't even know their beliefs until they make an off-color joke about black people." Parker took a long drink of water. This was going all wrong. "Why are we arguing about this now?" he asked. "We don't have to decide anything today."

"Why don't you just quit?" she asked. "You have more than enough money. Stay here."

"I can't. I worked too hard to build what I have." He thought for a second. "Plus, it would hurt my employees."

Yes, he told himself, *that sounds better.*

Her eyes hardened. "Speaking of those employees . . . how many of them are black?"

"I . . . I don't have any idea. I don't keep count. I'm sure Human Resources could—"

"What about your board of directors?" she asked. "Your vice presidents. Any of the executives in your company. How many are black?"

"Siobhan."

"Two? One?"

He took another drink of water.

"Oh. I see."

"Change happens slowly—"

"But you're in a position to facilitate that change! Every day I tell my students that the world is getting better. But I look at you and wonder if I'm lying to them."

"It is better. I'm proof."

"Yes. By pretending to be something you aren't." She sighed. "Let's be honest. You aren't pretending anymore, are you?"

"Siobhan. That's not fair—"

"Do I have to lie about who I am if I move to Denver with you? What am I supposed to say when people ask me how we met? What if I call you the wrong name in public?" She crossed her arms. "What am I supposed to tell my mother?"

"Please," he said, looking around. "Keep your voice down." He motioned to the waiter. "Where is the bill?" he mumbled. "We shouldn't be talking about this here."

Parker paid for their meal, then ushered Siobhan outside. He handed the valet his ticket and waited for the car. "Did I do something wrong?" he whispered. "I don't understand why you're so upset."

She wrapped her shawl tightly around her. "Today is the anniversary of my daddy's death. He didn't even see me graduate from college." She looked at Parker. "He was never the same after we left Lambert. Most of that was his fault. Too much drinking. Too much pride. But I also can't help but blame the world, at least a little. He needed a second chance, but no one was willing to give it to him. Perkins wouldn't write him any letters of recommendation. And my mother — bless her heart — could only put up with him for so long." The valet pulled up with the car, but she didn't move toward it. "I guess that's why I'm so mad. He had a tenth of what you have now. A twentieth. A thousandth. And he *still* reached out to help people worse off than him. Or do you not remember all the meals he fed you when you didn't have anything to eat?"

Parker took her hand. "I can do better, Siobhan. I promise."

She nodded, then pulled away and walked to the car.

Siobhan remained silent for most of their drive back to Silver Spring. Finally, she asked, "You don't drink Coca-Cola, do you?"

He gave a half snort, half laugh. "What are you talking about?"

"Your suite. It's the biggest hotel room I've ever seen. The refrigerator is stocked full of every drink imaginable. Expensive water. Fancy juices I can't even pronounce. Every type of soda ever made. Everything except Coke."

His hands tightened on the wheel. "No. I don't prefer it."

"When's the last time you tasted it?"

He sped up, his eyes staring straight ahead.

"Oh my God. You haven't drunk it since 1957? You're still mad at Chip Douglas?"

"Aren't you?" Parker exploded. "His friends destroyed our lives!"

"They weren't his friends, Reggie. He helped get us out of town, remember?"

"Sorry, I was too busy running for my own life."

She shook her head. "I can't believe you still hate that city so much. It's all-consuming. It's . . ." Her mouth dropped open for a moment. "The Allens. I heard their company had filed for bankruptcy. They lost out on a lot of contracts. One of their businesses had been bought out." She pointed her finger at him. "It was you, wasn't it?"

"How can you have any sympathy for the Allens?" he asked. "After what they did to your father. To us?"

"A lot of people depended on those jobs. And you stole them from the city."

"People could move. There are other jobs."

"Oh, and I guess they can pretend to be white too."

"Siobhan—"

"Who else do you hate? My father?"

Parker turned on the radio. He didn't want to talk about this. He wasn't mentally equipped to talk about it. Not now. Maybe not ever.

She turned the volume down. "Reggie? Answer me."

"If he had just let us be together . . ." Parker began.

"I can't believe I'm hearing this. You're just like him." She picked up her purse from the floor. "Stop the car."

"Siobhan."

"Now."

Parker pulled into a gas station parking lot but kept the car running.

A man pumping gas glanced in their direction. Parker flipped down his visor so he wouldn't have to see him.

"I've known you've been alive for a month," she said. "Tell me the truth. You've known where I was since . . . ?"

He sighed. "I've always known."

"The way I see it, you had twenty-nine years to find me. To prove my father was wrong when he said we didn't belong together. And you have the audacity to say it's *his* fault for keeping us apart?" Siobhan reached over and touched Parker's cheek. Her hands were so soft. "Whatever happened to that boy who gave me word puzzles? Who played with kids in the park? Where is the boy I used to love?" She pulled away, then opened her door. "I'm sorry, but I can't be with a man who hates the world as much as you do."

"Wait," he said as she stepped out of the car. "Where are you going?"

"I'll call a cab."

"Siobhan."

"Good night, *James*," she said, closing her door.

He watched her walk into the convenience store. A few minutes later, a yellow taxi pulled up front. She didn't look in his direction as she stepped in and rode away.

The next morning, Parker was awakened by the phone ringing on his nightstand. An envelope was waiting for him downstairs. Inside was a letter, three pages long. And a bracelet.

He read the letter twice. Then he packed and drove himself to the airport. He paid a ransom to catch the next direct flight to Denver.

At the gate, he spun the bracelet around his finger. It was smaller than he remembered. Lighter. He had slaved over it in his shop class. He had wanted to give her something she could wear with little suspicion. That was why he put *Love* on the inside. The message was just for her.

Across from his seat stood a black trash can. He could drop the bracelet in the garbage, and that would be the last of Reggie Bradley. He would truly be dead, like everyone believed him to be. Like Siobhan now believed him to be.

He walked over to the trash can, peered in, and tried to will himself to drop the bracelet. To be rid of Reggie — of Siobhan — forever.

But after a few seconds, he slipped the bracelet into his jacket pocket, where it would be safe. Then he boarded the plane and went home.

CHAPTER 43

Candice texted Tori: *Wake Brandon up NOW. Tell him to check his email.* She had already sent him a link to a biography of Leonhard Euler, an eighteenth-century Swiss mathematician. Euler, pronounced *Oiler*. Euler, who had an important number named after him—2.71828.

Ten minutes later, her mother's phone buzzed. It was Brandon. He wanted to meet right then. After a little back and forth, they decided to meet for breakfast at six o'clock that morning.

While Candice waited, she tried to piece together the letter's secret message. She knew she had to sum up the numbers, so she added pi—3.14159—and e—2.71828—to yield 5.85987.

That meant absolutely nothing.

She read the letter again. It said: *Siobhan is the key; the one who will lead you to my fortune.*

The one, Candice thought. She added a one to the number, making it 6.85987.

That still didn't mean anything.

She finally went back to bed—and promptly overslept.

Candice woke to find her mother shaking her. She quickly sat up. "What time is it?"

"A quarter to eight," her mother said. "Brandon's in the living room. He said that y'all were supposed to meet this morning. Do you want me to ask him to come back?"

She jumped out of bed. "Tell him I'll be there in five minutes, okay?"

Her mother nodded. "You know, you still have plenty of time to spend with Brandon. And we'll be coming back—"

"Mom, I know. This isn't about that," she said as she searched through her clothes for something to wear.

"Then what's it about?" she asked. "His summer project?"

Candice was glad she had put the letter away before she'd fallen asleep. It remained safely tucked in one of the yearbooks. "I promise, everything's okay. We're not up to anything devious."

Her mother sighed. "I'll be in my office."

Candice brushed her teeth and quickly changed into a T-shirt and shorts. She grabbed the yearbooks and her calculations, then ran to the living room. Brandon sat on the couch. He had placed her iPod on top of her library books on the coffee table.

"Sorry I took so long," Candice said, out of breath.

"It's okay." He scooted over so she could sit. "You found the missing piece of the code! Hadn't we seen a link to Euler before? We skipped right over it."

"I know," she said. "But I'm still stuck. I've been trying to crack the code all night, and I can't figure out what I'm doing wrong. It's just a bunch of numbers." She showed him the sheet with her calculations. "Maybe it leads to an address. Or a safety-deposit box. Or maybe . . ." Candice eyed the grin forming on Brandon's face. "Oh my God. You figured it out, didn't you?"

He broke into a toothy smile. "Solved it right before I walked over." He took her paper and placed it face down on the coffee table. "Let's start with the obvious—we have to add something up. That's why *sum* is there."

"What are you, a math teacher? Just tell me the answer."

He shook his head. "Are you kidding? I've got to savor every chance I get like this." He paused. "*Savor* means—"

"Just get on with it!" she said, pushing him, but she was smiling as well.

"Like I said, we have to add it all up first." He took a pen from his pocket and rewrote Candice's calculation:

$$\pi + e = X$$
$$3.14159 + 2.71828 = X$$
$$5.85987 = X$$

"What about Siobhan?" Candice asked. "She's 'the one.' I think we should add a one."

"That's what I thought at first too. Until I read the letter again."

She opened the letter, and he pointed to the same line she had struggled with earlier: *Siobhan is the key; the one who will lead you to my fortune.*

"You know those games on the back of cereal boxes, where the letters stand for numbers? What does every code need in order to be cracked?"

Candice slapped her hand over her mouth. "A key," she mumbled.

He started writing again.

A B C D E F G H I J K L M

N O P Q R S T U V W X Y Z

"So if Siobhan is the one, does *S* equal one?" Candice asked.

"I already tried that. It didn't work." He did a little hand dance. Candice had never seen him so giddy. "But Siobhan was also called Lil' Dub."

"*W*," Candice said.

"Exactly." Brandon filled in the digits, starting with *W*.

A B C D E F G H I J K L M
5 6 7 8 9
N O P Q R S T U V W X Y Z
                1 2 3 4

By now, his fingers were flying. "And so . . ."

5 . 8 5 9 8
A D A E D

"It took a little while," he continued, "But I finally figured out I had some extra numbers and letters there . . ." He struck out the last two digits and letters.

5 . 8 5 ~~9 8~~
A D A ~~E D~~

"Ada," he said. "Ring a bell?"

"Ada Marie Perkins! The first principal of the school!" She grabbed his arm. "You think the fortune is in the memorial room?"

He nodded. "Or at least another clue."

The school, the church . . . Parker had hidden clues in places he could control. Places where he donated money. It was totally logical for the next clue to be hidden in the memorial room. But . . .

"The first and second clues led to *e* and pi," she said. "The third clue told us to add them up. The key for the code was Siobhan's name." She sighed. "But we still haven't figured out the fourth clue. *She loved all.*"

"Maybe it's a trick," Brandon said. "Maybe we don't need it to find the money. Parker could have just put it there to throw us off."

"I don't know. Most puzzles don't work that way." Candice spun the bracelet around her wrist. Had her grandmother gotten this far, only to fail to figure out the fourth clue too?

"Well, unless you have other options, I still think we have to go back to the memorial room," he said. "We need to check out the portrait of Ada Marie Perkins."

She nodded. "Think we could get Ms. McMillan to meet us at the school this afternoon?"

"Only one way to find out. And we'll need someone to distract her."

Brandon looked at Candice. She looked back.

"TORI!!!"

CHAPTER 44

"This is crazy. Insane. Absurd," Tori said as they drove to Lambert High School. Then she smiled. "But it's also really, really awesome. I'll keep Ms. McMillan busy as long as I can."

It wasn't until they pulled up to the school that the doubt began to creep into Candice's head. She mapped out all the ways this could go wrong. It was like a Jenga tower that would topple with one wrong move. She wondered what her mother would say when she was bailing them out of jail.

"Oh, hello, Tori," Ms. McMillan said as they entered the memorial. "You decided to tag along today?"

"Actually, Brandon and Candice have inspired me a bit," Tori said. "I was hoping to do some research as well. Not about Perkins High School—about Wallace. Do you have any more of those old year-books around?"

"Oh, well, they're in storage in another part of the building."

"Great. I'll come with you to get them," Tori said.

Ms. McMillan eyed Candice and Brandon. "Are you two okay? Do you need anything?" The questions were innocent enough, but to Candice, it felt like an inquisition.

"We're fine," Brandon said. "We know exactly what we're looking for."

"Sounds good. Be back in a few," Ms. McMillan said, pulling her keys from her back pocket.

As soon as Tori and Ms. McMillan left, Brandon dragged a chair to the Ada Perkins portrait. He stood on the seat and stared at the image.

"Anything?" Candice asked.

"If there's supposed to be some secret code here, I don't see it," he said. "I think we need to cut it open."

Brandon lifted the frame off the wall. Candice took one side of it and helped carry it to a nearby table. They placed it facedown. Just as they had hoped, the back was covered with brown kraft paper.

She ran to her bag, then returned with box cutters and masking tape. "Don't mess up the portrait," she said, handing him the box cutters.

He nodded, then began cutting. Candice's stomach sank with every slice of the blade.

Finally, he cut enough to pull the paper back.

Candice could hardly breathe. There was a small envelope taped to the inside of the wooden frame. The envelope was small—the size of a credit card. Brandon opened it and pulled out a small slip of paper.

```
The heir must find the . . .
```

Candice's insides churned. "We're wrong," she said.

"No, we're close." He stuck the note and envelope in his pocket. "Quick, let's get this back up."

After taping the paper in place, they returned the frame to the wall. It was a little crooked, but they didn't have time to level it.

"That note . . . it sounds familiar," Candice said. "But it wasn't in the letter, was it?"

Brandon snapped his fingers. "It's like the clue in *The Westing Game*! He's telling us that we have to—"

"*FIND THE FOURTH!*" they said at the same time.

Candice rubbed her eyes. "It's the fourth clue," she continued. "I *knew* we had to solve it."

"Maybe there's something in here we overlooked," Brandon said, spinning around. He took off toward the trophy case. "We should check the championship trophy."

"There's no way we're breaking that glass," she said, following him.

As he scanned the trophy case, looking for a way to open it, Candice kept repeating the fourth clue in her head.

She loved all.

She loved all.

"Every other clue is tied to a number. To math." she said, pacing in front of the trophy case. "Clue one led to Euler's number. The second clue led to pi. The third clue told us to add them up. So the fourth clue has to lead to a number as well. It has to—"

She came to a complete stop.

Brandon frowned. "Candice?"

She looked at the aluminum bracelet on her arm. Then she slipped it off. *Love.*

The answer had been there the entire time.

"Love," she said. "It means zero in tennis. It's a score."

Brandon's mouth dropped open. Then he spun around and pointed to one of the paintings above the trophy case. The painting of a tennis match between black and white players where neither had yet to score. "So if love is zero, then *love all* is zero–zero." He looked back at her. "That's what they call it, right? *Love-all?*"

She nodded. "Come on, let's grab a chair."

They pulled another chair over, then Brandon used it to climb on top of the trophy case. It wobbled underneath him.

"There's a bulge underneath the tennis court," he said. "I think there's something sewn into the painting."

Outside, Candice heard two claps. Tori's signal. They had just reached the end of the hallway. "Hurry up," she whispered.

"Here," he said as he pulled the picture off the wall and handed it to her. "Don't wait for me."

Candice placed the painting on the table. Brandon was right—there was a small bulge in the canvas underneath the green of the tennis courts. "How am I supposed to open it?" she asked.

"Break it!" He'd made it off the trophy case. "I'll try to stall Ms. McMillan."

As he rushed out of the door, Candice quickly ran to Ms. McMillan's desk to look for something to break the glass. She heard voices in the hallway! They were close.

Finally, she ran back to the table and flipped over the picture so the glass was facing down. Holding it in both hands, she raised it high above her head.

Behind her, she heard Brandon, Candice, and Ms. McMillan enter the room. "Brandon, I appreciate the offer, " Ms. McMillan was saying, "But I don't think—Candice! What are you doing with that picture frame? What's going on?"

"I'm sorry," she said. Then, with trembling hands, she brought the frame down against the corner of the table.

Ms. McMillan may have screamed—Candice wasn't sure. All she could hear was the cracking glass. She hit it again, trying her best to break the glass right above the tennis court.

By the time she'd flipped the frame back over, the others had reached the table. The glass has shattered in multiple places, including in the area by the tennis court. The canvas has ripped as well. They could make out a small glint of silver beneath the green paint.

"Girl, you'd better explain what's going on," Ms. McMillan said. "And quick."

"Look," Brandon said, pointing at the flash of silver. "Do you see it?"

Frowning, Ms. McMillan leaned closer to the painting. "What *is* that?" she asked.

"One way to find out," Tori said. She picked up the box cutters from the table and handed them to Candice. "Be careful. That glass is sharp."

Slowly, Candice began cutting away at the canvas. It wasn't lost on her that she had destroyed a tennis court, just like her grandmother.

As strips of canvas fell away, they could finally see what was underneath.

It was a key.

Candice carefully pulled the key from the picture. "Where is the First Lambert National Bank?" she asked, reading the text engraved above a long number.

"I've never heard of that bank," Tori said. "Have you?" she asked Brandon.

He shook his head.

"Enough. Let me see that." Ms. McMillan took the key out of Candice's hand. "It used to be a local bank. It was bought out a few years ago. All the accounts were transferred over to Spirit of Independence Bank."

"You mean the one on Main?" Tori asked.

Ms. McMillan nodded. "Last I heard, they kept safety-deposit boxes there—which is what I assume this key unlocks." She placed the key on the table, beside the torn painting and shattered glass. "But before we get into that, now would be an excellent time for you all to explain exactly what in the world is going on."

CHAPTER 45

James Parker

1999

A young man with short, spiky hair knocked on James Parker's office door.

"I said I didn't want to be disturbed," Parker said as he ate his lunch and read the newspaper. An unopened can of Dr Pepper sat on his desk in front of him. This was his fifth executive assistant since Mrs. Halliday had retired. They were all horrible.

"I know, sir, but—"

"No excuses."

"But Ms. Washington said—"

"Who?" James Parker dropped his fork. It bounced off his desk and fell to the floor. "Siobhan Washington?"

"Yes, sir. She's on the phone. She—"

"Put the call through immediately."

James Parker wiped his mouth and took a deep breath. His phone lit up in front of him.

"Siobhan?" he asked. His voice was so hopeful.

"Hey, Reggie," she said. But she did not sound like Siobhan from 1957, or even 1986. The voice on the other end was ragged. Raw. Tired.

"Are you sitting down?" she asked. "You should sit down. There's something I have to tell you."

Two days later, Parker pushed Siobhan Washington's wheelchair across the National Lawn in DC. She could still walk, but she tired easily. Plus, Parker liked taking care of her. He had wrapped two blankets around her legs before getting out of the car, but she still felt cold. Her old bracelet was too big for her wrist, but after being away from it for so long, she refused to remove it. She wore a warm knit cap that hid her balding head.

But Parker only saw the woman he had loved for most of his life.

They came to a stop. The Lincoln Memorial sat ahead of them. The Washington Monument stood at their backs.

"You're staring again," she finally said.

"I'm sorry." He turned away.

"No, it's okay. I like it." She smiled as their gazes met. "I've always loved your eyes. So gray. So stunning."

"Some say they're cold."

"Yes, but not when you look at me." She patted his hand. "I have a riddle for you. Ready?"

He arched his eyebrows, surprised. "Sure. Go ahead."

She cleared her throat. It was so much raspier than before. "Here goes: I am larger than three and smaller than four. To make me your food I need little more than a small simple vowel tacked on to my ending. What am I? PS, I'm still winning."

He laughed. "The last I checked, I had the lead."

"Didn't we have a conversation about you letting your girlfriend win?" She ran her thumb over his knuckles. "Plus I needed a way to make it rhyme. So do you have a guess?"

Parker repeated the riddle in his head. "A hint?" he finally asked.

"It was one of your favorite desserts. Sweet potato was your—"

"Pi!" he said. "Pi plus the letter *e*. Very good." He leaned into her and whispered, "But I'm still winning."

They sat like this for a while, their arms pressed against each other. "They're going to build a memorial for MLK over there," he said after a few moments, pointing over his shoulder. "Maybe I should make a donation."

"That sounds like a good use of your money."

"I would rather use my money to fly in a specialist. I don't care about the cost."

"Reggie, I would let you if I thought it would do any good. But I do know something you can do with your fortune. Something more than donate to the MLK memorial—though that is important. Something other than ruining the Allen family."

"I stopped fighting the Allens," he said. "I backed Penelope's new company without anyone knowing. And I helped her brother find a job when he moved to Seattle."

"I figured as much," she said. "I also read an article about how you reorganized your company, naming people of color to new senior management positions. And how you started a foundation to fund scholarships for women and people of color. Ellie also told me about those anonymous checks she received for her grandkids."

Parker took in a deep breath and let it out. The steam floated between them and up to the stars. "I was trying to change," he said. "To be better. Do better. For you and for me."

"Yes, I know." She patted his hand again, and let it rest against him. "I don't want you to think I'm a saint. I never said the Allens didn't deserve to be punished. I did want them to pay for what they did to us. But I've never blamed the city for what happened. There are good people there. Friends. Almost family. They need your help. Especially Vista Heights."

Siobhan started coughing then. James Parker stood to help her, but she waved him away. "You can save Vista Heights," she said after a few moments. "Do it for your grandmother. Do it for yourself. Do it for me."

He looked up at the sky. He didn't remember stargazing as a child. He was always too busy looking at the ground, trying to survive from one day to the next. Had the moon and stars been just as brilliant when he was a kid?

"Remember that book you liked so much?" he asked. "*The Westing Game?*"

"Of course. I reread it every year." She squinted at him. "Why do you ask? What's going on in that head of yours?"

Parker didn't know yet, exactly. All he had was a seed, newly planted by Siobhan's last riddle—pi plus *e*—and her favorite book. The beginnings of an idea that could honor Siobhan's family, force the city to face its dark past, and acknowledge what had happened so long ago.

"If I help the city—if I do this—the people will have to work for it. Puzzle over it," Parker said. "I won't make it easy for them. I want them to remember what they did to you and your family."

"That sounds fair. But don't make it too hard. You want to be alive when they figure it out, don't you?"

It was supposed to be a joke, but neither laughed.

"They need to remember you as well," Siobhan added. "You were a victim, just like Daddy. You deserve to have your story told too."

She shivered, so he took her hands and blew warm air on them. Her fingers were so fragile and so beautiful. "I should get you back to the hospice."

"In a moment." She squeezed his hand. "I'm glad you're here."

"I was stupid. I never should have left. I should have fought harder to—"

"We both made mistakes," she said. She reached up and touched his cheek. "I'm so proud of you." She glanced at the paper bag at his feet. "Did you bring the wine?"

"More like sparkling cider." He pulled a thermos from the bag, then poured cider into two paper cups. He had considered bringing Coca-Cola, but he didn't care about the past right then. He wanted to be in the present, with her.

"What are we drinking to?" she asked.

"To second chances?"

"No," she said. "To third."

CHAPTER 46

Ms. McMillan had decided to believe them. For now. There was still the matter of the damage to the artwork, but she agreed not to say anything to the principal until they saw things through.

Which meant a trip to the bank.

Candice felt like everyone was staring at them as they entered the Spirit of Independence Bank lobby. Brandon started toward the row of tellers, but Ms. McMillan directed him to a cluster of desks.

A man wearing a black suit stood up from the nearest desk. His smile seemed faker than Monopoly money. "How can I help you all today?" he asked Ms. McMillan.

She pushed Candice forward. "Go on. Tell him, hon."

Candice cleared her throat. "I would like access to this box," she said, holding up the key. It was sharp, like it had been cut yesterday.

"Sure thing, little lady." Somehow, his smile remained still even as his lips moved. "I'll just need some ID to make sure you're authorized to open it."

Candice lowered her hand. "I have to have ID?"

"Standard practice."

She shook her head. "My name won't be on the list," she said.

The man's smile faltered. "Maybe your mother—"

"I'm not her mother," Ms. McMillan said. "And my name won't be on it either. None of our names will be there."

The man finally frowned. "Whom does this key belong to?"

"That's a long story," Tori said. "Look, is there any way we can open the box? It's been here for a long time. Maybe there's a clause in the box rental paperwork that says we can access it."

"Or perhaps a statute of limitations?" Brandon added.

The man snapped his fingers. "Let me see that key."

Candice started to hand it to him, but Ms. McMillan stopped her. "Why don't you write the box number down?" Ms. McMillan said to the man. "We'll wait here."

Candice read off the number. The man jotted down the digits, then disappeared behind a large wooden door.

"Ten dollars says we'll be arrested," Tori said.

"Fifteen," Ms. McMillan replied. "I'll say one thing—this is not how I expected my Friday to go."

They turned when they heard footsteps. A woman wearing a beige pantsuit approached them, carrying a small file in her hand. "Would you all follow me?" she asked, motioning to an office.

"Yep," Tori mumbled. "We're going to jail."

"No one's in trouble," the woman said. "We just need to clear some things up." She led them to the office, then shut the door behind them. It was a small room, but they all fit.

"I'm Suzanne Sawyer, the branch manager. My associate told me that you wanted to access a safety-deposit box." She opened the file. "Most of our boxes can't be opened by anyone not previously authorized for access. Actually, *all* of our boxes are like that—except this one." She tapped a sheet of paper. "This box has specific instructions to contact a law firm in Denver if anyone ever arrives with the key." She held out her hand. "May I see it?"

Candice looked at Ms. McMillan. After she nodded, Candice handed it over. The woman checked the engraved number against her paperwork, then returned the key. "A representative from the law firm is on the phone now," she said. "If you're okay with it, she'd like to speak to you."

Candice nodded, and the woman pressed a button on the phone. "Hello, Ms. Halliday? I have you on speaker with the persons who came in with the key."

"Thank you," the woman on the other end of the line said. "My name is Tiffany Halliday, and I am one of the trustees of this account. I would suggest you be truthful in responding to all of my questions. Now, who found the key?"

No one spoke for a moment.

"Hello? Are you still there?"

Brandon nudged Candice. "I did," she said. "I mean, I found it with my friend Brandon."

"And who is speaking?"

"Candice Miller."

There was a long pause. "How old are you, Candice?"

"Twelve."

"I see. And where did you find this key?"

"In a painting at Lambert High School. In the Perkins Memorial Room."

"I'm going to ask you one more question, Ms. Candice Miller. Just to be clear, how you answer will dictate what happens next." The woman took a breath. "Whom do you think this box belongs to?"

Candice stared at the phone. The puzzle pieces twisted and turned in her head.

"Ms. Miller? Do you know? Or did you happen upon that key by accident?"

"It's not an easy question to answer," Candice finally said. "The person has two different names."

"That's . . . correct." The woman cleared her throat. "Please continue."

"Well, it could either belong to James Parker or Reginald Bradley." She thought for a second. "Maybe it could belong to Siobhan Washington as well."

"Thank you, that is enough. Mrs. Sawyer, please take me off speakerphone."

The branch manager picked up the receiver. As hard as she tried, Candice couldn't make out what the woman on the other end of the phone was saying.

The manager finally hung up. "Ms. Halliday requests that you return tomorrow afternoon with the key. She will be here around two o'clock."

"I thought the bank closed on Saturday afternoons," Ms. McMillan said.

"Yes, it usually does. But tomorrow, we'll make an exception." She winked and rose from her desk. "Until then?"

Everyone shuffled out of the room back into the lobby.

"Now what?" Brandon asked. "We just have to wait?"

"Well, you're not breaking into *this* place, that's for sure." Ms. McMillan said as she patted Brandon's shoulder. "You all have done very, very well. I'm proud of you. But I think it's time we called your parents."

CHAPTER 47

Beatrix Halliday

June 12, 2007

Beatrix Halliday was scrambling eggs and sipping her second cup of coffee when the doorbell rang.

"You'd think those salesmen would wait until nine before bothering people." Her husband took a drink of orange juice as the bell rang again. "Coming!" he yelled as he slowly rose from his chair. He had undergone hip surgery the year before. He no longer needed a cane, but Beatrix still worried whenever he was out of her sight.

A few seconds later, he returned. "Bee," he said. "It's Mr. Parker. He's outside, waiting for you."

Beatrix placed her mug on the counter. Mr. Parker. She hadn't seen him in over nineteen years. Not since he presented her granddaughter Tiffany with that scholarship to Colorado Law.

Mr. Parker smiled as she stepped on the porch. A large envelope was tucked under his arm. "Hello, Mrs. Halliday."

"Good morning, Mr. Parker. It's been a long time."

"Do you have a few minutes? Can we sit?" He motioned to her swing. It had been a gift from her son.

They sat down and slowly began to sway. "I know you keep in touch with a number of employees at my former company, Mrs. Halliday. What are they saying about me?"

She put her foot down, stopping the swing. "Former?"

"I'll get to that in a moment. What are they saying?"

A tricycle sat in the middle of her yard. It belonged to Tara, her youngest great-granddaughter. "They say you've lost your ever-loving mind. That you're giving away all your money in strange investments. And some of them still aren't happy that so many woman and minorities are in leadership positions." She raised her foot and the swing began to move again. "Now what's this about former company?"

"I liquidated my stock and turned in my resignation."

"But you built that company from the ground up."

"No, James Parker did."

"You're not making any sense."

"Twenty-one years ago, you told me to go to her. Thank you. You saved my life."

Beatrix didn't need to ask who the *her* was. "What happened?" she asked.

"She didn't like the new me. The person I had become. So I changed. And became better. But I was too late."

"Mr. Parker, you're not making any—"

"Please don't call me that," he said. "I know what I'm saying sounds strange. It's all outlined here." He patted the envelope sitting between them. "Siobhan died seven years ago."

Beatrix placed her hand on her old boss's arm. "I'm sorry."

"It was cancer. I didn't know until she'd exhausted all her treatment options. I flew to her as soon as she told me. In typical Siobhan fashion, she spent most of our time talking about *my* well-being." He turned to Beatrix. "How is your granddaughter doing at that law firm?"

"She's well on her way to making partner. And she's met someone. Don't know if she'll get married. We'll see." Beatrix frowned. "Why do you ask?"

"I need a favor."

She removed her hand from Mr. Parker's sleeve. "I don't know—"

"It's not illegal. I promise. I could hire any old lawyer to handle this, but I want someone I trust." He handed the envelope to Beatrix. "Everything she needs is in there."

"Mr. Parker—"

"Take at look at it yourself if you want."

She pulled a few papers from the envelope. "*The New Air Foundation*? But don't you already have a—"

"This is a different type of organization. I'm looking for a . . ." He laughed. "It's a search for an heir, spelled H-E-I-R." He rose from the bench. "If you think anything is illegal or even questionable, you can toss the packet and pretend you never saw it. Either way, you won't see me again."

She rose as well. "Mr. Parker, I don't like how you're talking."

He smiled. Beatrix wasn't sure, but it seemed like the first real smile she'd ever seen from the man. He stepped off the porch, then turned to look at her one last time. "Reggie, Mrs. Halliday. My name is Reggie."

CHAPTER 48

Candice's father arrived in Lambert that evening. He'd jumped on the road immediately after talking with her mother. Candice had prepared dinner for them — very little of it burnt — but they barely touched their food. She had explained everything that had happened over the summer, but they seemed to struggle with processing the information.

"From what I can tell, this James Parker guy was rich. Like millionaire rich," her father said. "You're telling me you kids found all of his money?"

"I don't know. That's why we're going back to the bank tomorrow."

"I wish you had told me what was going on," her mother said. "I could have helped. She was my mother. . . ." She rested her head in her hands. "I can't believe this is happening."

"I'm sorry, Mom," Candice said. She wanted to fast-forward through this part. "I wanted to tell you, but I thought you'd tell me to stop."

"I would have," she said. "Just like I told her ten years ago."

"Anne, don't beat yourself up," her father said. He looked like he wanted to reach out to her, but he didn't. "But you should have told someone, Candi. Me. Your mom. Brandon's mother. Any adult."

"No offense, Dad, but Brandon and I did pretty okay by ourselves. And Tori helped."

"Tori is not an adult," her father replied. "What if this turns out to be a sham?"

Candice shrugged. "There are worse ways to spend the summer."

"Don't be glib, Candi."

"I'm not." She sat up taller. "And please don't call me Candi anymore."

Her father shook his head. "What happened to our baby girl?"

"She grew up." Her mother stood from the table and picked up her plate. "If you'd been paying attention, you would have realized Candice hates it when you call her that. You never noticed how she flinches every time you call her Candi?"

Candice hadn't even realized she'd been doing that. "And Dad, did you know we've been messing up the lyrics to 'September' this whole time? I didn't know until Brandon told me."

Her father coughed. "Oh, is that right?" He kept his eyes on his plate instead of looking at her.

"Wait. You knew?"

He gave her a sheepish grin. "Candi—"

"Candice," she said.

He sighed. "I'm sorry, sweetheart. It's just . . . you were so cute. I didn't have the heart to tell you when you were younger. And it seemed harder to correct as you got older. The way I saw it, it was like our little secret. Our little joke."

"Except the joke was only on me," Candice said.

"It's not a big deal," he said. "It's only a song."

"Dad, I'm not a baby anymore! You don't have to lie to me all the time!"

"Enough," her mother said. Candice waited for her mom to chide her for talking to her father like that. Instead, she placed her arm on her dad's shoulder. "She's right, Joe. She's not a baby." Her voice was soft. Almost like a blanket. "Talk to her. It'll be okay." She leaned over and kissed her dad on the forehead. It was almost like old times.

"Okay, what was that about?" Candice asked after her mother left the room.

Her father pushed his food around on his plate. "Nothing, sweetheart. Your mother just wants everyone to be happy."

"I am happy," she said. "And I think Mom is too."

Her father cut into his chicken breast.

"Dad, is something wrong? Are *you* not happy?" she asked. "Are you sick?"

"No, I'm fine. Really."

"Is it about Danielle?"

He put down his utensils. "Who?"

"Danielle. I overheard you and Mom talking about her. And before you start, she already scolded me about eavesdropping," Candice said. "Anyway, I know you started wearing a new cologne. That citrus scent. Is it to impress her?"

He frowned. "That's not cologne. That's special cleaner for my hands. Helps to get grime off."

Candice picked up her one of her dad's hands and brought it to her nose. It still smelled citrusy, but not as strongly as before.

The scent was still familiar. She tried to remember where she'd smelled it before.

"Did you use this at home?" she asked.

He pulled his hand away. "Probably some of the crew at the house used it. It's pretty standard in home construction."

That was enough to jog her memory. She'd smelled it at the house, in the kitchen. When her mother was arguing with Daniel, the contractor.

"Okay, so it's not cologne. Does that mean you're not seeing anyone?"

Her father tried to smile, but his face seemed so tired.

"Dad. Please?"

"Lord, I am not ready for this," he said. "I planned to tell you when you were older. When you were ready. Or more like when I was ready." He paused for a moment, and the lines grew even deeper on his brow. His eyes shifted from Candice to the table. "I'm . . . I'm not seeing someone named Danielle. But I am seeing someone. I'm . . ." He shook his head. "It's funny how it's hardest to talk to the people you love the most."

She reached out her hand again. Her father took it.

Candice found herself thinking about what Ms. Jones had said. How people saw what they wanted to see, especially when it came to family.

She thought about her mother, wanting her father to be happy, even if she couldn't be the person to provide that happiness.

She thought about how she could never go over to her father's apartment without calling first, although it never seemed like another woman had been there.

She thought about the scent on his hands. Strong and citrusy. The same smell as the contractor. The contractor that her mother seemed to hate.

It was like a puzzle, with all the pieces finally in place.

"Mom didn't say Danielle, did she?" Candice said quietly.

He shook his head.

She took a breath. "Daniel."

His head moved a fraction of an inch, but it was a nod.

"You're gay?" She asked it like a question, even though she already knew the answer. "Why didn't you tell me?"

"I didn't want you to see me any differently. I wanted you to still see me as Dad."

"You'll always be my dad."

He squeezed her hand. "Just so you know, nothing happened between me and Daniel until after your mother and I separated." He scratched his beard with his free hand. "It was probably a bad idea to have him work on the house. He gave us a great discount on materials and labor, but I think I was asking too much of your mom. Part of me believed that if she met him, if she *liked* him, she would understand. . . ."

"Yeah, Dad, not smart. Not smart at all."

"Your mom reminds me every time I talk to her about how bad of an idea that was. That's why we brought in another crew to finish the house."

"At least now I understand why we had to move so far away from home. I'm glad it wasn't just because of those stupid tiles."

"Language, Candice."

She rolled her eyes. "You're kind of not in any position to criticize right now." Then she smiled, and he smiled back.

"Are you mad at me?" he asked. "It's okay if you are."

"I mean, yeah, I'm mad that you didn't tell me. That you've been lying to me for I don't know how long. And that you forced Mom to work with Daniel."

"I didn't force her—"

"Fine. Strongly encouraged her," Candice said. "But no, I'm not mad that you're gay."

His entire body relaxed. "I'm so glad to hear that. But again, it's okay if you're mad now. Or later. It might be hard for you to picture me dating a man."

Candice's stomach flipped. "Okay, you're right. That *is* weird," she said. "But it would also be strange to see you dating another

307

woman. I guess I don't want to picture you with anyone except Mom."

"You realize that will never happen. Me and your mother."

She nodded. "I know."

But as she said it, she realized that somewhere down deep, she *had* hoped they'd somehow get back together. That they would wake up one morning and realize they wanted another chance. A second chance. But that was impossible.

Her father released her hand. "I think it would be good for you to talk with Dr. Patton again when you get back home."

"You know, two of the teachers at school are gay. And a lot of my favorite authors are gay. Like the guy who wrote the books about the raccoons."

Her father tilted his head. "I didn't know that."

"Yeah, it's not that big of a deal."

"It is at work. The construction business is light-years behind the rest of society."

So are Milo and his friends, Candice wanted to say. "Can you quit?" she asked.

"A discussion for another time." He picked at the chicken on his plate. "You're taking this a lot better than I thought you would. Any other questions?"

She shrugged, then asked, "Did you always know you were gay?"

"Maybe. I'm still trying to figure that out. But I always loved your mother—just not in the way she needed to be loved. And I always wanted a perfect daughter, and now I have one."

Candice took a deep breath. It was like the citrus from his hands and the lavender from Grandma's walls were mixing together, at least in her head. The past and present, all jumbled up.

In some ways, her father was like Reggie Bradley. He got everything he wanted, but at a horrible price. He had to hide his real self. She had been at her father's office enough to hear some of the crude jokes. How did it feel to listen to things like that every day, knowing the people you worked with thought horrible things about who you really were?

Her father stood up from the table. "What about Brandon? Do you still think he's gay?"

"I don't know for sure, but I don't think it really matters," Candice said.

Her father winked. "That's my girl."

CHAPTER 49

They had all agreed to meet at Brandon's house before heading to the bank. All the adults, including Ms. McMillan, wore work clothes—jackets and slacks and blouses. Her mom had even put on lipstick, which she hardly ever wore. Tori was dressed in all black—Candice assumed she'd just gotten home from her job at the store. Candice wore a sundress. She had wanted to wear her comfy jeans, but both her parents had vetoed that. Clearly, they were still united on some fronts.

Leaving the adults in the kitchen, Candice went to look for Brandon. She didn't have to travel far—she found him in the living room, reading one of the Dork Diaries books. His tie was crooked.

He slid over as Candice sat down next to him on the sofa. "Too much noise in there," he said.

"How can you read at a time like this?"

He shrugged. "It's a good book."

She looked up as the stairs creaked. Mr. Gibbs entered the living room. Unlike everyone else, he wore his usual getup: T-shirt, suspenders, and slacks. Candice glanced at Brandon. His gaze remained glued to the book.

After acknowledging Candice with a nod, Mr. Gibbs sat down and snatched the remote from the coffee table. With his free hand, he pulled the lever on the recliner, leaning back. He powered on the TV and turned up the volume, way louder than it needed to be.

Brandon stared at the same page in his book for another couple of minutes.

His grandfather switched to a sports channel, then turned up the volume again.

Brandon's mother popped her head into the room. "Why is that TV so—oh, hey, Daddy. Sure you don't want to come with us?"

Glancing at Brandon, he shook his head. "Don't want to go where I'm not appreciated."

Brandon's mother closed her eyes. "I'm surrounded by children," she muttered. "Brandon, Candice, we're about to go."

Candice heard her parents talking to Ms. McMillan in the driveway. They must have used the back door.

Brandon placed his book on the coffee table, then he and Candice rose from the couch. As Brandon moved toward the front door, Mr. Gibbs picked up the book. A few pages later, he huffed and tossed it back on the table. His sneer was audible all the way across the room.

Candice waited for Brandon to walk out first. "Be there in a second," she said. "Just forgot something."

Once the door clicked shut, she leveled her gaze on Mr. Gibbs.

"I want you to know, there's nothing wrong with Brandon." Her voice was shaking, but she didn't care. She needed to say this. Brandon was her partner. She had his back. "He's the best thing that happened to me this summer. One of my best friends. He is what is good and right with this city. With the world. He is perfect just the way he is."

Mr. Gibbs stared at her for a few seconds, like he wasn't quite sure what he was supposed to say. Almost like he didn't recognize her.

But that was good, Candice figured. He shouldn't recognize her. She wasn't the girl she had been when they'd first met.

"It's hard out there for kids," Mr. Gibbs finally said. "Boys. Black boys. Brandon's got to be tough. He can't—"

"He. Is. Perfect," Candice repeated. As she spoke, she wished that Milo and his mother and Mr. Rittenhauer and William Maynard and everyone else who had ever said anything mean to Brandon were sitting there. But they weren't, so his grandfather would have to do.

"Back in my day, children didn't talk back to their elders."

"Maybe not," she said. She looked directly at him. She wanted to be sure he got the message. "But I'm right about Brandon. I hope one day you can see that too."

She had calmed down a little by the time she got to her dad's truck. She opened the back door and was surprised to see Brandon sitting there. "Okay if we ride together?" he asked.

"Sure." She climbed in, and her father pulled out of the driveway. The others followed in Tori's Honda.

"What were you doing back in the house?" Brandon asked after a few minutes. "It almost sounded like you were yelling."

"It was nothing," Candice said. "Just doing my job, partner."

Brandon arched an eyebrow at her, but let it go.

As they reached downtown, they passed a police car driving in the opposite direction. Candice glanced behind her. Tori drove with both hands locked on the steering wheel, her eyes straight ahead. Candice knew Parker's money probably couldn't do anything to help with Tori's fears, but she wished it could.

Only a couple of cars sat in the parking lot when they arrived at the bank. Everything looked dark inside. Before they could knock, Mrs. Sawyer, the manager, appeared behind the glass door. She unlocked it and ushered in the group.

"You've multiplied," she said.

"These are our parents," Candice said. "We filled them in on everything."

"That was wise," a woman said, walking toward the group. Her hair sat in a bun on top of her head. "I'm Tiffany Halliday. You must be Candice."

Candice shook her hand. It was warm, which Candice liked.

After everyone else introduced themselves, Ms. Halliday turned back to Candice. "Now for the business at hand. May I see the key?" she asked, opening her purse.

Candice pulled it from her pocket and handed it to the woman. She slipped on a pair of glasses and inspected the key. "There are only two keys in existence that open Mr. Parker's safety-deposit box. One has been in my possession for ten years. I didn't know where the other was located until yesterday." She returned the key to Candice's palm. "I have to admit, I didn't think I would ever see this day. I was sure the letters had been lost, or the city had decided to treat them like a hoax."

"The city leaders knew about it," Brandon said. "The editor of the newspaper too. None of them were brave enough to act on it. No one except for Candice's grandmother."

Tiffany Halliday checked her watch. "I've already called the press. They'll be here in thirty minutes. They will want to know your story. Mr. Parker's story. This city's story."

Candice's father stepped forward. "We didn't sign up for a media circus, Ms. Halliday."

"But *she* did," she said, nodding toward Candice.

"It was in the letter," Brandon said. "The city has to admit how the Washingtons were driven out of town."

"If you want to gain Mr. Parker's inheritance, you will have to do the same," Ms. Halliday said. "You'll have to be part of telling their history."

Candice looked at Brandon. "It's an important story," she said. "It deserves to be told. Not just his story. Siobhan and Leanne and Big Dub's as well." She rubbed her bracelet. *And my grandma's too*, she thought.

Ms. Halliday smiled. "Well, it seems you *have* done your homework. I know some of Mr. Parker's true background. Perhaps we know enough between us to piece it all together." She squeezed Candice's shoulder. "He would have been proud. I think he found a worthy heir."

"Do you know if he's still alive?" Brandon asked.

"I'd like to believe he's out there somewhere. Enjoying another chance as Reginald Bradley." Tiffany Halliday opened her purse again and pulled out a small key. "Candice, are you ready?"

Candice took Brandon's hand, then nodded.

"Good." Ms. Halliday turned to the bank manager. "It's time to collect Mr. Parker's inheritance."

CHAPTER 50

The safety-deposit box contained information for ten offshore bank accounts.

But that wasn't what interested Candice, at least not immediately. It was the other items in the box that caught her eye:

A red scarf, still kinked from where it had been knotted around something.

A creased tennis photo from the 1956 yearbook. When it was folded, Siobhan and Reggie stood side by side, their arms touching.

Two faded slips of paper, both about someone traveling to a place called St. Ives.

An older, more recent picture of Parker and Siobhan. She was clearly sick. The sky was dark, and the Washington Monument stood behind them. They looked so happy.

Candice carefully ran her fingers over each item. Had Parker placed them in the box with his own hands? What did they mean? Why were they important? She and Brandon had just solved Parker's puzzle, only to be presented with a new challenge.

By the time they exited the vault, the press had converged upon the bank. The group stepped outside, and Ms. Halliday explained who she was and what had happened. Then she invited Candice and Brandon up to take questions.

The first questions were about the letter that Parker had sent. Who had received it? What had it said? How did Candice find it?

The reporter asking the questions was from the *Lambert Trader*.

Candice and Brandon grinned at each other. And then they began to tell their story.

Of course, unlike Brandon and Candice, the adults were much more interested in the bank account information. It was two days later that they discovered the combined accounts were worth more than forty-eight million dollars.

But there were strings attached. Most of the money could only be spent for the betterment of the city—specifically the Vista Heights neighborhood. With Ms. Halliday's help, they formed a foundation to decide how to best use the money. At the top of the list was a new library building to be located on Darling Avenue, across from the park. Candice and Brandon stipulated that it had to be named after Siobhan Washington. They also decided to remodel the tennis and basketball courts at Vickers Park. They would need them to be bigger for the summer camp they planned to start.

Parker also left directions to correct some of the items he had manipulated for the purposes of the letter, such as the photo of Leanne Washington. While the Missionary Circle truly held a bake sale to raise money for the court case, the correct date was June 9, 1951.

Two months later, after buying Tori a new car with unlimited car washes, Candice and Brandon split the remaining money fifty-fifty. Their parents made them put most of it away for college and "the

316

future," whatever that meant. Candice thought about buying their house, but decided against it. It didn't seem all that important anymore. Plus, she was spending more time at her dad's apartment, which was close to her old friends. She even had dinner with her father and Daniel a few times. She didn't know what to think of him yet, other than he looked way too hip to be dating her dad.

It made Candice a little sad, her father being with someone who wasn't her mother. But it also made her happy, because *he* was happy. And while her mother wasn't dating, she was happy as well. Thanks to the money from Parker's inheritance, she was able to put her other projects aside to focus on her "Anne C. Miller" novel. She was finally following her passion, writing what she needed to write, and that made her the happiest of them all.

Candice couldn't even remember how many reporters they'd met with. Everyone wanted to talk about the mysterious James Parker, his secret life as Reggie Bradley, and his money. Fewer people wanted to hear about the Allens. Even fewer wanted to know about the Washingtons.

That made Candice a little sad too.

But there were also good things that happened because of the media attention. A week after the news broke, she and Brandon received a call from Charles "Chip" Douglas. Or rather, *Dr.* Charles "Chip" Douglas. He had been a superintendent for a number of rural school districts in Mississippi, where he had spent his life forming busing systems and magnet schools to better integrate the black and white students. Chip told them more about the Washingtons, and the night of the tennis match, and even shared secrets about his father's heritage.

There were also other stories. Candice heard from many of Coach Washington's students—some as far away as California. She received letters from Siobhan's former coworkers in Maryland, who all raved about how passionate she was about her work. Candice even talked to a ninety-four-year-old woman who had served with Leanne Washington in the Women's Missionary Circle.

So many stories. So much history.

And as she saw her mother punching away at her keyboard one night, four different pens stuck in her hair, Candice thought, *If the news won't tell the right stories, I will. One day.*

CHAPTER 51

Three months after discovering Parker's safety-deposit box, Candice returned to Lambert. The city had decided to issue a formal apology to her grandmother, and were holding a ceremony to rename City Hall in her honor. It was a nice gesture, but Candice didn't care much about having her grandmother's name on a building. She'd rather just have her grandma back.

It was funny—as much as Candice hated what people had said about her grandmother, she was sometimes glad she had been fired. If she had remained in Lambert, Candice would have never grown as close to her as she did. Her grandmother's "failure" led to Candice spending so much time with her.

A small crowd had already formed in front of a podium and stage outside City Hall by the time they reached downtown. The woman organizing the event saw Candice and her mother as they walked up, and quickly rushed them over to the stage.

As Candice took her seat, she spotted Brandon and his family at the front of the crowd. She quickly waved and mouthed that she'd meet him right afterward. They had been emailing every day but she hadn't seen him in months.

The program began, with the current mayor telling a very long and very boring story about her grandmother's bravery and ingenuity. It quickly became clear to Candice that he'd never met Abigail Caldwell. The program would have been much more interesting if the former mayor—the one who had fired her—had been the one to give the speech. Likewise, she hoped that Milo and his mother were somewhere in the audience, as well as William Maynard. She didn't want vengeance, but a little justice would be nice.

She also wondered if James Parker was there. She wanted to give him Siobhan's bracelet. As much as she loved it, she felt that its rightful place was with him.

The ceremony ended with Candice and her mother unveiling a plaque that had been fastened to the red brick outside City Hall. In addition to a small biography of her grandmother, Candice and her mother had decided to include one of her grandmother's favorite quotes: *Just because you don't see the path doesn't mean it's not there.*

Afterward, Candice was swarmed by a group of people wanting to know what she'd done with her share of the money. She answered the questions as politely as she could, then slipped off to find Brandon.

"It's so great to see you!" she said, hugging him. He seemed to have grown taller.

"There's someone I want you to meet," he said after pulling back. He pointed toward a boy standing far off from the crowd. He waved when he saw them looking at him.

"Quincy?" she asked.

Brandon nodded. "Don't tell him I said this, but he's a little jealous of you. He goes off for the summer, and I have this great adventure without him."

"It wouldn't have been so great if we hadn't found the money," Candice said, laughing.

He tilted his head. "No, but it still would have been pretty awesome. Right?"

Candice nodded. "Yeah. You're right." They started walking toward Quincy. "Want to get lunch afterward? Maybe Sam's? Or—"

"Candice Miller?"

She stopped and turned. An older man approached them, a small smile on his face. But instead of golden skin, his fingers were dark. Instead of gray eyes, his irises were as brown as Candice's.

"I'm Odell Davis," he said, stretching his hand to her. "I used to work with your grandmother."

Candice quickly shook his hand. Then Brandon did. "Thank you for coming out," she said. "Grandma really loved working here."

"She sure did. She was a good boss too," Odell said. "A lot of us could have lost our jobs over excavating the park, but she protected us all. Every man out there that night kept his job thanks to her."

Candice blinked. "Wait. You were there on the night she dug up the tennis court?"

"The bench too, though no one seems to remember that." He grinned. "But to be fair, that hole was a bit small. But underneath the tennis court . . ." He whistled. "Sometimes I think Ms. Caldwell would have had us digging all the way to the other side of the world if the mayor hadn't stopped us."

Candice looked down at the bracelet on her arm. "Do you know why she never said anything about the bracelet?"

Odell frowned. "Come again?"

"The bracelet." She slipped it off and handed it to him. "Didn't you find this underneath the tennis courts that night?"

He slowly shook his head. "Candice, that hole was as empty as a pool in the desert. There was nothing there. Certainly not this."

Now Brandon was frowning. "Are you sure? Maybe she found it and didn't say anything."

Odell shrugged. "I don't know what to tell you. I was there all night, and I was chief of the crew." He returned the bracelet. "If someone had found something, I would have known." Then he nodded. "I just wanted to pay my respects. Your grandmother was a wonderful woman. You did her proud."

Candice watched the man walk off. "But . . ." She turned to Brandon. "My head is exploding right now."

"We're sure that bracelet is Siobhan's, right?"

"Yeah. I mean, I think so."

"And your grandmother never met her, did she?"

"How could she? When would she . . . ?" Candice rubbed her eyes. "None of this makes any sense."

Brandon pulled Candice's hands away from her face. "Come on. Let me introduce you to Quincy. We can talk about this later. Over chili-cheese dogs."

Candice looked at the bracelet once more, touching the scratches on its surface, wondering what secrets it held. Then she slipped it back on her wrist and followed Brandon through the crowd.

The mystery of the bracelet would remain unsolved.

CHAPTER 52

Abigail Caldwell

2007

Abigail Caldwell hated not having a job.

She had been working for as long as she could remember. Even when she was in college, raising her two kids on her own. Even when she was obtaining her master's degree. She'd had a number of jobs over the years, but had never taken a break between them. She'd never been unemployed. Until now.

Officially, she had resigned due to "mismanagement of city resources." Officially, she had "mistakenly directed" one of her maintenance crews to dig up the tennis courts at Vickers Park.

Unofficially, she was fired because of a secret letter that no one except her wanted to investigate.

At first she'd assumed the letter was a hoax. Then she asked around. She heard about the infamous tennis match of 1957. She learned who Enoch Washington was, and how he was driven from the city.

Slowly but surely, the hoax gained credibility.

It took a lot of late nights and early mornings, but she began to unravel the mysteries of the letter. She discovered that Enoch loved baseball, and she saw the photo of Leanne Washington holding a pie when it was still hanging in the church reception hall, not hidden in a dark, dusty closet. She found Siobhan's name on that plaque on the park bench—a plaque still fresh and new. She learned that James Parker, a millionaire who had just disappeared, was responsible for all these improvements within the city.

Then she became stuck.

So she dug up the tennis court. It seemed like the right move. Enoch Washington loved tennis. So did his daughter. And the courts had been dedicated to him. Sure, she hadn't found a link to Parker and the actual construction of the tennis courts at Vickers Park in 1985, but she couldn't see any other solution. So she dug up the ground, hoping to find a treasure.

And then she was fired.

She'd retreated to her daughter's house in Atlanta to lick her wounds and plan her next move. She hadn't even packed up her house in Lambert. She just disappeared, not even telling her neighbors that she'd left.

But if there was one benefit to being unemployed, it was that she had all the time in the world to spend with her favorite person. Her beautiful granddaughter, Candice.

One Saturday morning, a week or so after she resigned, Abigail babysat her granddaughter while Anne and Joe met with yet another counselor—perhaps hoping this time they would hear something different about their relationship. Abigail had set up Candice's play kitchen in the living room, and the two-year-old happily made broccoli and ice cream pizzas, and served soda and lemonade to all of her stuffed animals sitting on the couch.

Abigail stood when the doorbell buzzed about an hour later. Peeking through the peephole, she saw a tall, lanky older man standing on the doorstep. A Denver Broncos cap sat low on his head. Aviator sunglasses hid his eyes. Freckles spotted his nose. His goatee was stark white.

She opened the door. "Hello?"

"Hi, I'm looking for Abigail Caldwell." She couldn't quite catch his accent. Perhaps it was Southern, but she wasn't sure.

"This is she." She wondered how he even knew where she was.

"So what happened at Vickers Park?" he asked. "What were you doing—looking for buried treasure?"

She tensed up. "Who are you, a lawyer?" She began to shut the door. "I don't have time for—"

"Wait," he said, sticking his foot in the doorway. "I'm not a lawyer. I'm here to help."

"Well, unless you know where I can find a new job or—"

"You were on the right path, but you must have made a mistake," he said. "Or as Siobhan's mother used to say, 'Just because you don't see the path doesn't mean it's not there.'"

She pulled the door open. "You knew Siobhan Washington?"

"I did." He cleared his throat. "May I come in?"

Abigail studied him for a few moments, trying to decide. She stared at herself in the reflection in his glasses. "Who are you?"

The man removed his sunglasses, greeting her with big, round, angry gray eyes. "None of the other four even attempted to solve the puzzle, did they? The cowards."

"How do you know . . . ?" That face. Those eyes. It clicked in her head. "James Parker?"

He took off his hat. "Now may I come in?"

Abigail quickly opened the door wider. Parker looked around as he entered the house. "Your daughter has a beautiful home. Are she and her husband meeting with their new counselor?"

"How do you know—"

"I make it my business to know things." He paused at the entrance to the living room. "And this must be your granddaughter, Candice."

Abigail rushed past Parker and sped toward the couch. She helped Candice to her feet and nudged her toward her toy kitchen in the corner. "Why don't you go over there and play for a while."

"Okay," the girl said in a singsong voice as she scooped up her animals and walked away.

Abigail motioned for Parker to have a seat. "That's correct; none of the others wanted to pursue the letter," she said. "They told me it was a hoax."

"They were lying." He placed his hat over his knee. "All four of the others were born in Lambert," he said. "One was even there the night of the tennis game. But you . . . you risked *everything* for a city you owed nothing to. Why?"

Abigail fiddled with her fingers. "It was my job," she finally said. "Businesses are struggling and the economy is down. People are hurting, especially in Vista Heights. If there was even a chance, I had to try. That's why I was hired in the first place. To manage the city. To *protect* the city—and the people still living in it."

"You are a fool," he said. "But perhaps the world needs more fools." He sighed. "Next week you will receive a call from an associate of mine in College Park. She wants to interview you for a job. When I told her about your qualifications she leapt at the chance."

"I don't understand. Why are you—"

"Wanna Coke?"

Abigail turned. Candice walked toward them, her arms full of plastic toy Coca-Cola bottles. But instead of heading to her grandmother, Candice was on a beeline to James Parker.

"Candice," Abigail began, reaching out to her. "I thought I asked you to play over there."

Candice, even with wobbly legs, was deceptively fast. She ran past her grandmother, slipping around her outreached arms, and made her way to Parker. Candice dropped everything in her hands—everything except a lone plastic toy soda bottle.

"Wanna Coke?" she asked again, offering it to him. "It's fee."

Abigail shook her head. "She means *free*."

Parker stared at the girl for a long time. Candice wore a red dress that was much too long for her short legs. She also wore a matching red plastic bracelet on her arm. Her name had been embossed on the bracelet in glittery silver, making it shimmer.

Parker finally took the bottle from the girl. He brought it to his mouth, then made a gulping sound as he pretended to drink it down. Smiling, he handed it back to her. "Thank you. That was the best Coke I've had in a long time, sweetheart."

"No." She shook her head. "I'm Candice."

"Oh, I'm sorry." Parker bent down, close to Candice's ear, and whispered something to her. Then he pulled back and shook her hand. "It was a pleasure meeting you, *Candice*."

"We go swinging. Wanna come?" she asked.

"Candice, leave the man alone." Abigail stood up and pulled her granddaughter away from the couch. "Please excuse her. I promised to take her to the park after her nap."

Parker looked at Candice. "I would love to go," he said. "But I can't push kids on the swings like I used to." He winked. "Good thing you have a grandma to help you. I bet she's the best swing pusher in the world."

Then he stood. "I should be leaving," he said, placing his hat on his head. "Thank you. Thank you both."

Abigail walked him to the door. "Mr. Parker, I don't understand—"

"You and your granddaughter are very close, aren't you?" he asked. She nodded.

"What about you and your daughter? Do you two get along?"

"Well enough," Abigail said, though that was further from the truth.

"Take the job," the man said after opening the door. "Be close to the ones you love. At the end, that's all that really matters."

"Wait," she said. "Mr. Parker, I have more questions."

The man put his sunglasses back on. "Nice meeting you, Ms. Caldwell. And I'm not James Parker. Not anymore." His mouth curled into a smile. "But ask your granddaughter. She knows who I am."

Abigail watched as the man crossed the yard. He slipped into a small white car, then sped away.

She locked the door and returned to the living room. Candice was making another pizza.

"Sweetheart—"

"Candice," the girl corrected.

"Yes, of course." Abigail knelt in front of her granddaughter. "Candice, what was that man's name?"

"Who?"

"The man who was just here. He drank your soda?" She placed her hands on her granddaughter's shoulders. "What was his name?"

"Umm . . . Eggy."

"Eddie?" her grandmother asked.

Candice shook her head. "No. Eggy."

"Freddy? Teddy?"

The girl kept repeating his name, and Abigail kept guessing.

Try as she might, the man's name remained a mystery.

Two days later, there was another knock on the door. Abigail flew through the house, determined to reach the door before anyone else. But it wasn't James Parker, or whomever he was calling himself. It was a delivery man. He carried a package addressed to her.

She opened the box to find a card and a small aluminum bracelet. She quickly read the note on the card.

Because everyone deserves a second chance!

Good luck with the interview! I'm sure you'll do well.

The card, of course, was unsigned.

Abigail took a closer look at the bracelet. The letters *MS* were stamped on the outside. *Mississippi*, she thought. Of course Parker would know she'd been born there. He seemed to know everything about her. On the inside of the bracelet was the word *Love*. Perhaps as in love for her family? For her granddaughter?

Abigail had no idea what Parker had truly given her. It *was* a second chance—but not for the job. For his inheritance.

But while Abigail was a great administrator and fair leader, she was not made to solve puzzles.

The next day, Abigail turned the bracelet over and over in her hands, thinking about the letter and Parker and what she could have missed. She had been thinking about the mystery all night, but she just couldn't put it together. A laugh from the floor in front of her made her pick her head up. Candice was playing with the beach ball globe again.

Abigail had bought Candice the globe a few weeks ago; she wanted her to get a jump start on learning the countries. She knew this was unrealistic, but she was also a grandmother—and part of her hoped her only granddaughter was a genius in the making. The first time Abigail had given the globe to her, Candice turned it over so the North Pole was on the bottom and Antarctica was on top. Whenever Abigail tried to correct her, Candice would roll the ball right back over.

"But it's the wrong way," Abigail finally said after five minutes of this.

Candice looked at the ball, then at her grandmother. "Why?"

"Well, because . . . because the words are upside down."

Of course, this didn't matter to Candice. She couldn't read.

But on that day, as Abigail watched Candice turn the ball upside down again, she asked herself: Why *was* it wrong? In space, who knows what is up and down? What made the mapmaker's perspective any better than Candice's? She was sure he hadn't been to space either.

Abigail thought back to her time in Lambert. The mayor had forced her to destroy all of her research, but she'd been able to hold on to the letter. Not that *she* knew what to do with it.

She looked at Candice again as she played in her toy kitchen. She sat on the globe. North pointed down.

Maybe that was the problem. Abigail was set in her ways. Locked into a limited point of reference. Perhaps the letter had to be solved by someone with a new perspective. Someone who could see the letter—history—*the world*—from a different point of view.

Not now, of course. Later, when she was older. When she was ready. Abigail would leave Candice the letter, and offer just enough of a hint, just enough of a clue, to catch her granddaughter's attention. Abigail wouldn't force it on her. It would be Candice's choice to try to unravel the mystery.

But perhaps she could give her granddaughter a running start.

Abigail walked to Candice's room and grabbed a box from the top of the closet. It was a puzzle she'd bought for Candice for Christmas. One hundred pieces, for ages four and up. Her father had put the puzzle aside, thinking Candice was too young for it.

She returned to the living room and dumped the pieces on the coffee table. Candice abandoned her play kitchen and walked over to her grandmother.

"It's a puzzle?" she asked, still using that singsong voice toddlers use.

"Yes, it is," her grandmother said. "But it's a little hard. There are a lot of pieces."

"Can I help?" Candice asked.

Abigail pushed her lucky bracelet farther up her arm, then hoisted her granddaughter into her lap. "Yes," she said, handing her the first piece of the puzzle. "Yes you can."

AFTER WORDS™

VARIAN JOHNSON'S

The Parker Inheritance

CONTENTS

AUTHOR'S NOTE

Are the main characters based on real people?

The Parker Inheritance is a work of fiction. Candice and Brandon, Siobhan and Reggie, and even Lambert, South Carolina, are all fictional. However, real people, places, and events inspired much of the book.

The city of Lambert was partially based on my hometown of Florence, South Carolina. Although smaller than the imaginary Lambert, Florence has a similar government structure, made up of a mayor, a city council, and a city manager.

Perkins High School was largely inspired by Wilson High School in Florence, South Carolina. The school was founded in 1866 by the Bureau of Refugees, Freedmen, and Abandoned Lands, also known as the Freedmen's Bureau, which was a government agency established near the end of the Civil War to aid newly freed slaves in beginning their lives as American citizens. However, Congress eliminated financial support for the Freedman's Bureau in 1872, leaving schools such as Wilson with limited government support.

Despite this setback, Wilson survived and has thrived to the present day. Similar to the fictional Perkins High School, many of the Wilson teachers and administrators live in the same neighborhoods and attend the same churches as their students, and are former students themselves. The school remains a pillar in the African American community, with a large yearly homecoming celebration and alumni reunions.

My parents, my siblings, and I count ourselves as proud alumni of the school.

The Perkins-Wallace Tennis Exhibition was inspired by a secret basketball game held on March 12, 1944, between the North Carolina College for Negroes (now known as North Carolina Central University) and the Duke University medical school team—a team that included at least five former collegiate basketball players (and had already beat the Duke varsity team). The secret game was a danger to both teams—in the Jim Crow South, the races were meant to be separate at almost all times. Playing integrated basketball was inviting trouble, with jail time being the *least* of the players' worries.

The two teams met in a locked gym on the North Carolina College campus. Game play was sloppy at first, but eventually the Eagles took command of the game, beating the medical students by a score of 88-44. Remarkably, the teams then mixed squads and began another game—black and white students playing on the same team.

So who was real in the book?

There was a real baseball player named James Raleigh "Biz" Mackey. Born in Eagle Pass, Texas, Mackey would play for a number of teams, including a Prairie League team called the Luling Oilers, before playing in the National Negro League. Mackey played professionally until 1947 and was inducted into the National Baseball Hall of Fame in 2006.

Another pivotal sports figure highlighted in the novel is Althea Gibson. She was the first African American tennis player to compete at the U.S. National Championships (now known as the US Open) and Wimbledon. She won both the women's singles and doubles championships at Wimbledon in 1957, and was honored with a ticker-tape parade in New York City afterward. Over the course of her career, Gibson played in nineteen major tennis finals, winning eleven titles. A gifted athlete, Gibson also played professional golf for a time. She was inducted into the International Tennis Hall of Fame in 1971.

Most students have heard of the mathematical constant, π (pi), but e is a mathematical constant as well. The constant was named in honor of Leonhard Euler. Born in 1707 in Basel, Switzerland, Euler was responsible for developing many concepts still used today in mathematics, science, and engineering. In my former career as a civil engineer, I routinely used Euler's theories on beam deflection and column buckling to design bridges and other structures.

I've heard about *Brown v. Board of Education*, but I haven't heard of *Briggs v. Elliott*. What is that case about?

In 1896, the United States Supreme Court voted to uphold the legality of racial segregation in the *Plessy v. Ferguson* case. This ruling allowed state and local governments to continue to create and enforce "separate but equal" schools, facilities, public transportation, and other accommodations for blacks and whites. However, these separate accommodations were frequently inferior for blacks, such as for children in Clarendon County, South Carolina—a county directly southwest of Florence County—in the late 1940s. Black students could not even ride the bus to their school. None were available.

Black students had to walk as many as eight miles each way to attend school.

Reverend Joseph Armstrong DeLaine, a local pastor, teacher, and civil rights leader, worked with others including Levi Pearson, Harry and Eliza Briggs, and the NAACP to build a case against the school district. At first, the case was developed simply to request equal accommodations for busing and facilities. However, the lawsuit was soon reconstructed to attack segregation head-on. The case was eventually combined with four other lawsuits to become *Brown v. Board of Education of Topeka*, which in 1954 stuck down the separate but equal doctrine and made segregation illegal.

Although the lawsuit was ultimately successful, many of the key members of the *Briggs v. Elliott* case were harassed, attacked, and threatened due to their involvement. Harry and Eliza Briggs lost their jobs, eventually relocating to Florida and then New York. Reverend DeLaine also lost his job as a teacher. Both his home and his church were set on fire under mysterious circumstances. DeLaine fled South Carolina in 1955 after he was charged with assault and battery with intent to kill upon returning fire at a passing vehicle from which someone had shot at his home. He died nineteen years later in New York, having never returned to his home state. DeLaine eventually received a symbolic pardon in 2000, and in 2003, DeLaine, Harry and Eliza Briggs, and Levi Pearson were awarded the Congressional Gold Medal of Freedom.

So, segregation was ruled illegal in 1954. But in *The Parker Inheritance*, kids were still attending separate schools in 1957. Did that happen in real life? And if so, why did it take so long for schools to become integrated?

After the Supreme Court voted to end segregation with *Brown v. Board of Education*, they noted that state and local governments should end segregation "with all deliberate speed." This vague term allowed governments to drag out and even openly challenge the ruling. Eventually, the federal government had to step in and provide protection for black kids brave enough to integrate all-white schools, such as for the Little Rock Nine, a group of nine black high school students attending an all-white high school in 1957; six-year-old Ruby Bridges attending an all-white elementary school in 1960; and Vivian Malone and James A. Hood attending the University of Alabama in 1963. Even then, the courts had to enact additional rulings in cities across the country to guarantee that integration took place.

But Coach Douglas and James Parker were able to attend better universities by pretending to be white. Did people really "pass" as a different race?

Yes. The act of passing—pretending to be of a different race, usually for preferential treatment—has been fictionalized in popular works such as *Imitation of Life* by Fannie Hurst (later made into two movies) and *Passing* by Nella Larsen, but it happened in real life as well.

Jazz bandleader Ina Ray Hutton, known as "the Blond Bombshell of Rhythm," was a famous singer and dancer in the 1930s, and even headlined her own television show in the 1950s. However, Hutton was actually born as Odessa Cowan, a mixed-race girl, in Chicago. Similarly, George Herriman, the noted creator of the "Krazy Kat" comic strip, lived as a white man, yet was born as a mixed-race child. Herriman often wore a hat when posing for photos, which researchers speculate was to hide his naturally kinky hair. And Anatole Broyard, a celebrated critic and writer for the *New York Times*, was also a mixed-race man passing as white. During World War II, Broyard enlisted into the still-segregated military as a white man, eventually earned the rank of captain, and served as the officer in charge of a regiment of black stevedores (dock workers). He continued passing as white for his entire adult life, with his children only learning of their mixed-race heritage shortly before Broyard died of prostate cancer.

Of course, many other less famous people passed for white as well. There were clear negatives to passing—the risk of being discovered, the pain of cutting yourself off from family and community, the feeling of giving up a part of who you really were—but there were obvious benefits as well. Jim Crow laws made it extremely difficult, if not impossible, for people of color to thrive in the United States. Black people were American citizens—but in many ways in name only—and were stripped of basic constitutional rights such as the freedom to vote. Also, black people often had less access to education, meaningful employment, health benefits, and even proper housing. Those that could pass were often encouraged to do so—both for themselves and their future children—even if it meant never seeing their families again.

Was life really so bad for black people that they would want to pretend to be white?

Life was hard for the newly emancipated American Negro — probably worse than we could ever imagine. The Equal Justice Initiative estimates that almost 4,000 lynchings of black men, women, and children took place between 1877 and 1950 in the American South. These figures do not include the lynching of young Emmett Till, a fourteen-year-old boy killed in Mississippi in 1955 for allegedly whistling at a white woman (a claim that has since been called into question). Nor does it include Reverend George Lee, one of the first black men to register to vote in Humphreys County, Mississippi. Reverend Lee used his church and printing press to urge black people to vote. He was killed in 1955, two weeks after speaking at a rally for black voter registration. Also omitted are the murders of Addie Mae Collins, Denise McNair, Carole Robertson, and Cynthia Wesley — four girls killed by a bombing at the Sixteenth Street Baptist Church in Birmingham, Alabama, in 1963. So yes, life was very dangerous for a person of color in the 1950s and 1960s.

Conditions have slowly gotten better for African Americans, but you only have to look at the questionable shootings of Trayvon Martin in 2012, Michael Brown in 2014, Philando Castile in 2016, and countless others to realize that life today is still very dangerous for a person of color. But I do believe, if we work together, we can make the world a safe place for all people, no matter their ethnicity, gender, sexual orientation, ability, or religion.

We have a long way to go, but I believe we'll get there.

THE EVOLUTION OF THE FIRST CHAPTER OF
THE PARKER INHERITANCE

I've found that when I'm writing a book, the first chapter doesn't often reveal itself to me until *after* I've written a full first draft. I have to know how the story ends before I know how it begins. I have to learn who my characters are—what's important to them, what makes them tick. I have to care for my characters—I need to be able to root for them with my mind and my heart. And finally, I have to know what I'm trying to say with a novel—what I hope a reader will get from it. This isn't the most efficient writing process, but it works for me, so I've come to (begrudgingly) accept it.

That being said, this scenario was taken to the extreme for *The Parker Inheritance*. The opening of the book changed more than any other work I've published (though to be fair, the entire novel changed more than any other book I've published).

I first began toying with the idea of a puzzle book while in graduate school. I had been rereading Ellen Raskin's *The Westing Game*; studying her use of omniscient narration with multiple characters. I was working on my own mystery book at the time—or rather, my own *heist* book—and I needed a way to hide various pieces of information from the characters and the reader. (That manuscript would eventually become *The Great*

Greene Heist, my first middle grade novel.) But the more and more I reread *The Westing Game* for its narrative structure, the more I found myself falling in love with the puzzle. Eventually, the idea sank in that maybe I could write a puzzle mystery as well.

I finalized the "bones" of the puzzle in 2012, but it would be three more years before I had the story, and main character, to go along with it. The story was initially set in the late 1980s; Candice had just moved to Lambert, South Carolina, for the summer.

Chapter 1
Bobby Brown
(First Draft: 3/25/2015)

The worst part about having a new bedroom was that Mom wouldn't let me tape my New Edition posters to the wall.

Actually, the *worst* part of having a new bedroom was that it wasn't really mine. My real bedroom was in my real house in Atlanta, a whole four hours away. This house was a rental. According to Mom, the owner had just repainted the walls the week before we moved in. So for the time being, poor Ralph, Ronnie, Ricky, Michael, and Johnny had to stay all curled up in a blue milk crate, along with pictures of Janet Jackson from

Control and Michael in his all-black *Bad* outfit. I also had a poster of Bobby Brown, but since he and the rest of New Edition didn't get along so well anymore, I kept him in the closet on the other side of the room.

Mom said that she'd take me to the store to get some poster frames, but it had been two weeks and we still hadn't gone. Dad promised to take me when he came to visit next weekend, though I was scared he would change his mind once he saw what I wanted to hang on the wall.

He didn't trust that Bobby Brown. Not even in poster form.

———————————

I sent the first few chapters, along with an outline of the rest of the book, to my agent, Sara Crowe, and editor, Cheryl Klein. They were curious . . . but not sold. I had envisioned the book being set in the past—I wanted to avoid the benefits of technology to solve the puzzle. Sara and Cheryl felt strongly that I should set the novel in contemporary times, and "figure out" a way to avoid the benefits of technology. (Easy for them to say!) They also questioned my overemphasis on music. I revised accordingly and sent in new pages after a couple of revisions.

———————————

Chapter 1
The New-To-Me Bedroom
(Third Draft: 6/5/2015)

The worst part about having a new bedroom was that Mom wouldn't let me tape any of my stuff to the wall.

Actually, the *worst* part of having a new bedroom was that it wasn't really mine. My real bedroom was in my real house in Atlanta. A house that would probably be sold by the time we returned in August, if everything went according to Mom's plan.

Mom had been trying to sell the house for months, but lucky for me, no one seemed interested in our "cozy" bedrooms and "classic" kitchen. So Mom moved us out, with the idea that it would be faster for the contractor to finish the remodel without us underfoot. But instead of renting a nearby apartment, she moved us four hours and a million miles away to a summer rental in Podunk, USA, otherwise known as Lambert, South Carolina.

When we first got here, Mom said that she'd take me to the store to get frames and hooks so I could hang my giant picture of me and my best friends DeeDee and Courtney from this year's Memorial Day party at the community pool. But when she burst into my room on Saturday morning—almost a full week later—my walls were still bare.

"How about we grab some lunch and make a library run?" she asked.

I turned off my music, pulled out my earphones, and sat up from the bed. The family desktop had died on us a month ago, so the only music I had was all the old-school songs on Dad's abandoned MP3 player.

Gone were all the references to New Edition and Janet Jackson. I even threw in an "abandoned" MP3 player to show how "contemporary" my characters were. Perfect, right?

Well, not quite. The setting was better, but there was no hint of a mystery. For a novel that was meant to be a puzzle book, there was very little for Candice to actually puzzle over in that first chapter. But at least I'd improved those sample chapters enough to convince my editor that I could turn this into a book.

I jumped into writing a full draft of *The Parker Inheritance*. I learned many things about the book along the way. I realized that the novel would require multiple timelines, with multiple point-of-view characters, so I switched the book from first-person point of view to omniscient (third-person) point of view. I also realized that my initial plan for how the kids would discover all the puzzle clues (a newspaper article) would not work; I instead incorporated the puzzle into a letter sent to Candice's deceased great aunt. And of course, as I neared the end of the draft, I acknowledged all the problems with that opening chapter and revised it again.

Chapter 1
The Letter
(Sixth Draft: 6/1/2016)

Candice Miller stared at the letter.

The letter stared back.

The paper was stiff. Stale. Brittle. Like peanut butter cookies that had been left out for too long. The letter, with its black, typed, single-spaced words and yellow edges, was a mystery.

A seventeen-year-old mystery, though Candice didn't know this yet.

She hadn't even been looking for the letter. She was searching through the attic for something new to read. Searching through the attic of a house that did not belong to her; a house in a city she had no desire to be living in. The house had belonged to her Great Aunt Abigail—a woman she had never met.

She found the letter in a box of books. Candice had initially been excited about the box, until she realized that it was full of textbooks, dictionaries, and old encyclopedias. Boring.

Candice picked up a thick book about Greek mythology. She cracked it open, and the letter fell out and floated to the ground.

She didn't know it was a letter at first. She thought it was just a random sheet of paper that had been used as a bookmark long ago.

She unfolded it, and immediately realized that it was a personal letter, addressed to someone she didn't know.

She almost placed it back between the pages of the book.

Almost.

But she was a reader. Readers read.

And so, she read the letter.

It took over a year, but I had a full draft! I was on the right track . . . or so I thought. After Cheryl read the manuscript, we met and discussed the book in-depth. She followed up a few weeks later with a short editorial letter. The book had real promise, but as Cheryl told me, if I was going to write a book like this, I had to be prepared to "go big." That meant more emphasis on the past. More emphasis on the present. More. More. More. The manuscript at that time was about 60,000 words. It would balloon to over 87,000 words in the next draft.

Cheryl also wanted to care more about the characters. Candice's primary motivation was money in those earlier drafts. By finding Parker's fortune, she could stop her mother from selling their house. It was a good motivation, but Cheryl challenged me to make it better. Stronger.

I got back to work. Great Aunt Abigail—a woman who Candice had never met—was replaced by Abigail Caldwell, Candice's beloved grandmother, a former city employee who was forced to resign after a scandal about the letter. Now Candice wasn't just looking for the money for herself; she was hoping to clear her grandmother's name and legacy.

Chapter 1

The Letter

(Seventh Draft: 11/08/2016)

Candice Miller stared at the letter.

The letter stared back.

The paper was stiff. Stale. Brittle. Like peanut butter cookies that had been left out for too long. The letter, with its small, black, single-spaced words and yellow edges, spoke of a mystery.

A fifty-year-old mystery, though Candice didn't know this yet.

She hadn't even been looking for the letter. She was searching through the attic for something new to read—or if she was lucky, one of the puzzle books that her grandmother used to buy her. The attic, small and cramped, sat at the top of a house unfamiliar to Candice; a house in a city she had no desire to be living in. The house had belonged to her grandmother, Abigail Caldwell. Her grandmother had been dead for two years, but being surrounded by all of her things had brought a dull ache back to Candice's heart.

Okay! So I'd succeeded in making a more personal connection between Candice and her grandmother—and Candice and the puzzle—but it was all "telling" and in retrospect. In addition, both Cheryl and I wanted to give the readers the opportunity—the space—to really care about Candice and her family. I was jumping too quickly into the mystery elements of the plot, without first exploring who Abigail Caldwell was, and *her* reasons for trying to solve the puzzle.

At this point, Cheryl left Scholastic to take a new position with another publishing house, and I was paired with Nick Thomas—my current editor. Nick agreed with the idea of further exploring Candice's relationship with her grandmother.

I went back and spent time studying the end of the novel, and eventually, that led to a revelation on how to begin the book. The novel's final chapter was told from Abigail's point of view. What if the book began in her point of view as well? That way, I could introduce Abigail and the mystery, then slow down and allow the story to build, giving the reader more room to care about Candice before thrusting her into the heart of the puzzle.

Chapter 1
Abigail Caldwell
(Tenth Draft: 3/13/2017)

October 17, 2007

Abigail Caldwell stared at the letter.

The letter stared back.

The paper was bright. Crisp. Smooth. Like the pages of a new book that had yet to be cracked open. The letter, with its small, black, single-spaced words and sharp edges, spoke of a great injustice. It was written by a man who did not exist. And it promised almost $40 million to the city—if its puzzle could be solved.

She refolded the letter, then placed it in her purse. Dusk was just beginning to set in Lambert, South Carolina. Except for the handful of teens playing basketball, Vickers Park was empty. She sat on a bench outside of the Enoch Washington Memorial Tennis Courts. A small crew had already removed the rusted fence surrounding the courts, and was now carrying jackhammers to the worksite. A large, yellow backhoe loomed in the distance.

By starting with Abigail, readers would see firsthand how she'd dug up those tennis courts, the large backhoe working through the night. Of course, Abigail was incorrect about the puzzle—she was looking in the wrong place—and she would lose her job and tarnish her reputation as a result.

But now that I'd introduced the letter—and Abigail's failure—I could take my time in developing Candice's relationship with her grandmother without needing to dive right back into the mystery. I could show how Abigail loved her granddaughter; how she believed that Candice was smart enough to tackle *any* problem.

Eventually Candice would find the letter—along with a note encouraging her to take on the puzzle herself.

Laughing, Candice walked to the far corner of the room. Then she smiled. "Over here," she said to Brandon. There, against the wall, was a box labeled *FOR CANDICE*.

She had slid the box top off by the time Brandon reached her. At first, all they found inside were textbooks, dictionaries, and old encyclopedias.

"Not quite the new reading I was hoping for," Brandon said.

They continued pulling book after book out of the box, but nothing seemed remotely interesting to Candice. Brandon had stopped looking through the box to flip through a book on Greek Mythology. "This isn't that bad," he said, as he paged through the book. "Can I borrow it?"

"Fine by me," Candice said, as she removed the last textbook. So much for puzzle books, she thought.

And that's when she saw the envelope.

Candice picked it up, thinking it was an old piece of mail that had been dropped in the box by accident. She flipped it over, looking for an address. Instead, she found a small note.

Find the path. Solve the puzzle.

It was her grandmother's handwriting—swirling loops in dark blue ink. The words reminded Candice of what her grandmother used to always say to her when her mother brought up something about Lambert: *Just because you don't see the path doesn't mean it's not there.*

Candice wiped her hands. They were sweaty. And shaking. The note felt like a message from beyond the grave.

Clearly, there's a strong connection between Candice, her grandmother, and the letter. And the better Candice's motivation for solving the puzzle, the more satisfying it becomes for the reader when she's ultimately successful.

I would go on to revise the novel *three* more times with Nick before the book was sent off to be printed—though if I'm being honest, I'm sure I would have kept revising if I'd had the time. That's the thing about novels. They're never perfect. There are always parts—words, phrases, characters—that we'd go back and tweak if we could. But here's another truth: *The Parker Inheritance* greatly improved between the first and thirteenth drafts. I can look back at that book and tell myself that every draft was worth it.

Though now that it's coming out in paperback, maybe I can revise it one more time. . . .

ACKNOWLEDGMENTS

The Parker Inheritance is a labor of love, and would not be published without the support of so many fine people: my friend and agent, Sara Crowe; my editors Cheryl Klein and Nick Thomas, who encouraged me to "go big"—both literally and figuratively; and Arthur Levine, for always being a voice of reason, support, and love. Additional thanks goes to my entire Scholastic family, including: Kait Feldmann, Weslie Turner, William Franke, Nina Goffi, Rachel Gluckstern, Lizette Serrano, Emily Heddleson, Michelle Campbell, Tracy van Straaten, Lauren Donovan, Brooke Shearouse, Rachel Feld, Vaishali Nayak, Jennifer Abbots, Robin Hoffman, Lori Benton, and Ellie Berger.

Thank you to my critique group: Brian Yansky, Frances Yansky, April Lurie, Julie Lake, and Sean Petrie, and my beloved VCFA Beverly Shores retreat crew. This book would not exist without you all. I would also like to thank Ebony Wilkins, Mark O'Brien, and Bill Konigsberg for your expert guidance and feedback on the novel, and Rachel Hylton for your review of the puzzles, support during copyediting, and overall encouragement.

Special thanks goes to Ruth Carson and Marilyn McClain for your oral history of Florence, South Carolina, and Wilson High School in the 1950s. Thank you for opening my eyes to what life was truly like back then.

I would like to thank my family. I love you all very, very much.

While there are many works that inspired this book, I would be remiss if I didn't specifically highlight *The Westing Game* by Ellen Raskin. Thank you, Ms. Raskin—your novel captivated me as a child, then again as an adult. I will forever be in awe of your skills as both puzzlemaster and novelist.

Finally, I would like to thank Dr. Bruce W. Russell, P.E., for telling me two stories: one about a former student with two passions and how he chose to follow both, and another about an unusually named intramural flag football team at Rice University. See—I was listening in class after all!

ABOUT THE AUTHOR

Varian Johnson is the author of several novels for children and young adults, including *The Great Greene Heist*, which was an ALA Notable Children's Book, a *Kirkus Reviews* Best Book, and a Texas Library Association Lone Star List selection, and *To Catch a Cheat*, another Jackson Greene adventure, which was a Kids' Indie Next List pick. He lives with his family near Austin, Texas. You can find him on the web at varianjohnson.com and @varianjohnson.